I0599885

THE LEAGUE OF HEROES

THE LEAGUE OF HEROES

BOOK 2 OF THE SUPER SAGA

TAYLOR A. JENKINS

BLUE MAGNOLIA
STORY HOUSE

Copyright © 2025 by Taylor A. Jenkins

All rights reserved.

No part of this book may be reproduced in any form or by any electronic or mechanical means, including information storage and retrieval systems, without written permission from the author, except for the use of brief quotations in a book review.

Published by Blue Magnolia Story House

www.authortaylorajenkins.com

To Mom, the most powerful person I know. Thank you for helping me through the darkness.

CONTENTS

"The events that transpired at the Academy for Young Super-heroes and Supervillains were a travesty. The violent attacks and deadly explosions performed by students could've killed innocent civilians. Thankfully, the only victims were a few unnamed supers who hadn't managed to escape the building. If humans have learned anything from this experience, it's that we need to seriously reconsider our place in humanity's food chain.

If we have become prey, then we must learn to protect ourselves from the predators."

-Press release from current U.S. President Knox

1

THE BEGINNING OF THE END

T heodore Palmer sat at the edge of a cliff, with an emerald-green forest and black asphalt road below him. The summer breeze brushed through his hair, tickling his nose with the scent of fresh pollen. He lowered a pair of binoculars from his face and said, "This isn't going to work."

The walkie-talkie on his hip crackled. Dion's voice carried through with, "You always say that, and it always works."

"Well, one of these times, it won't."

"How about a little optimism? We've faced worse."

Theo nodded, allowing himself a spare moment to indulge in his memories. The Academy for Young Supervillains and Heroes had been destroyed, now an eyesore to anyone passing by in New York. In fact, it had been almost four months since Theo and his team escaped and vowed to save the rest of their supernatural friends.

He almost frowned as he remembered the time. The news had a field day with the sudden downfall of the school. Reporters from all over the world wondered how such a fine establishment could've crumbled to the dust, but not a single story was accurate. In the rare instances where staff were found, they used the power of attorney to protect themselves. NDAs were signed, orders were put in place, and Theo guessed a few had been put into the Witness Protection Program.

Most of the students returned to their families…as long as they had a family to return to. One hero student had been daring enough to tell the truth of what happened, albeit with a few alterations. She claimed she had been peer-pressured into fighting and fleeing, and insisted there was nothing wrong with the academy.

She had garnered a substantial social media audience before her arrest. The news report stated that, although she wasn't a willing participant in the destruction, she still played a role in it.

After that, every student kept silent.

Dozens of new laws had been introduced, including a curfew for supers, which only allowed them in certain places at certain times, and restrictions on their power use in public. Such rules weren't official yet, but Theo could guess it was only a matter of time.

By Peter's approximations, there were at least three hundred thousand people in the world with known supernatural powers. Of course, more than two thousand had attended the academy in years past, so the number of supers was quickly declining.

Without any witnesses to speak out against Principal Jones's abuse, he was free to continue his bad habits. Although he wasn't forthright with his strategies, Theo had deduced that bounty hunters were hired in secret to kidnap supers and deliver them to Jones.

That was why, at Theo's suggestion, he and his team tracked and stopped every bus, van, or car loaded with these supers and brought them to a safer location. Some rescue missions were chance encounters. Others took hours of research, monitoring the news, and even sneaking into local police stations to listen to the radio. Most detectives were too busy to investigate kidnapping claims, but Theo wasn't.

On multiple occasions, he'd heard from rescued victims that their homes were broken into, and they were drugged, gagged, and taken. None of them were older than Theo. And no one cared.

Theo worked his mouth from side to side. It wasn't that people didn't care; it's that they didn't argue. From his research, he learned that there *were* investigations into the disappearing super children. However, they had been placed on the back burner. With more and more supers using their powers in public—and thereby frightening humans—those arrests took priority, leaving the kids to fend for themselves.

It seemed the entire world agreed: Humans were more important.

For the life of him, Theo couldn't find Jones's hiding place. Each transport with supers headed to a different location. But Theo refused to give up. He couldn't leave any super behind.

Theo huffed. Years ago, when he attended therapy, he was told he had "survivor's guilt." Meaning, he wasn't at fault for his father's death, but because Theo lived and Dad didn't, Theo blamed himself. For a long time, Theo believed the therapist was wrong; he *was* the perpetrator of his dad's demise. As Theo pondered it, the more he realized its truth. He couldn't prevent Dad's murder, nor could he prevent the aftermath of the academies' destruction. Both had left Theo alive, and others who loved him had died.

So here he was again, suffering from survivor's guilt.

But this time would be different. Unlike the school and Dad's death, Theo wouldn't be afraid to act.

He forced himself to focus on the road. A bright yellow school bus exited the tunnel a few miles away. He stood. No matter how many times he did this, his heart still raced. He flipped the walkie-talkie into his hand and said, "Coming your way. Hope you're ready."

Dion responded, "Copy that, Sergeant. Let's blow this popsicle stand."

Theo started down the rock. "You always say that. Why don't you come up with something else?"

The radio beeped as Yasmine joined in. "I like it. It's his catchphrase."

"Exactly," Dion agreed. "Just like yours is—"

"We don't have time for this!" Theo reached the bottom and wound through the trees to get a better view of the oncoming bus. "Do your job, okay?"

Dion and Yasmine laughed to themselves before the walkie-talkies clicked off completely.

Breathless, Theo trotted to a stop behind an aspen tree and waited for the plan to unfold. Dion and Yasmine were supposed to drive alongside the bus and shoot out the back tire so it couldn't escape. Thanks to the winding road, the bus could only rumble along at thirty miles an hour, limiting the possibility of a spinout. Then, once the bus rolled to a stop (and Theo didn't want to think about what would happen if it didn't), they would rescue the super-powered passengers and go home. Simple.

"Hey," Penny suddenly greeted behind him.

Upon noticing her, he smiled. The morning sun made her blond locks appear golden. In the few months that they had been living on their own, Penny had cut her hair so that it barely skimmed her shoulders. During one of their earlier rescue attempts, she'd nearly been killed because the driver pulled on her hair. As much as Theo missed her longer hair, he enjoyed the change.

"Rest my beating heart," he said, swooning. "An angel has blessed my path."

Teasingly, she rolled her eyes. "Can't you be serious for one second?"

Being serious meant focusing on his thoughts, and that was a dangerous path. "Just trying to keep the situation light," he remarked. "We always need comic relief."

"Yes, and that's Peter's job." Penny touched Theo's cheek, healing his fear and filling him with warmth. "Don't worry. It'll be fine."

Here, in the shade, the dark voices in Theo's head were louder. They were incomprehensible, but he could feel their demands urging him to use his power. He wrapped Penny in a hug, ceasing the darkness. "What would I do without you?" he asked.

Leaning in, she kissed him on the cheek. "I think the same."

She pulled away and returned to her position, allowing Theo to study the empty road in peace. Like always, his peace was short-lived.

"Psst," Peter whispered.

Theo nearly jumped out of his skin. "What is it?"

As Peter flickered into view, he scratched his neck. "We have a bit of a problem."

"Problem? What kind?"

Peter reverted to wringing his hands. "Uh, well, Dion's van isn't starting, so…"

Unable to listen to the excuses, Theo dug his walkie-talkie from his pocket and hissed, "Dion, what are you doing over there?"

Dion's timid voice answered with, "I think the battery is dead. I can jumpstart it, but it'll take a few minutes."

That would be too late. The team had to act *now* if they wanted to prevent the bus from leaving.

"Get away from the van," Theo ordered, stressed by both the approaching bus and crumbling plan. "Rendezvous with Peter. Be ready for my signal."

"What are you going to do?" Peter and Dion said in unison.

Theo pushed the radio into Peter's hands. "Get hit by a bus."

Once, when Theo was very young, he was hit by a taxi, courtesy of the wonderful drivers in New York City. It wasn't serious, and the man who hit him apologized profusely and offered to give them a ride to the hospital.

Obviously, Theo's parents refused.

He only remembered bits and pieces of the incident, but as he walked toward the road, those terrifying pieces flashed before him.

The hot noon sun glared down his back, reducing his powers further. Pushing through the fear, he stepped out directly in front of the oncoming bus. If this didn't go according to plan, he could very well die. And this time, there was no polite taxi driver to take him to the hospital.

The bus blared a loud, prolonged honk to warn Theo that it was, "Move or I'll flatten you like a pancake."

Theo's chest rose and fell quickly; his heart pounded louder than the bus's engine. In the corner of his eye, he could see his team's black van pull into the designated spot and heard Penny scream from the window.

The bus was a hundred yards away. Seventy-five. Fifty. When Theo could see the eyes of the driver—a man whose eyes were narrow and unforgiving—he moved.

Well, not out of the way.

Using every drop of strength he could summon, he wrapped a shadow-like chain around the bus, looping it in and around the wheels. A squeal filled the air, the noise so high it nearly deafened Theo. The stench of burning rubber followed.

The front of the bus lingered a foot from Theo's face. The force of the sudden stop slammed the driver into the window and launched the children from their seats.

With screaming, aching muscles, Theo turned to his friends and exclaimed, "Aren't you going to help?"

They all stood at the side of the road, watching in awe at his display of power. Upon his orders, they scurried into action. Peter shot at one of the back tires, flattening it almost instantly. Yasmine made a motion for the children to cover their ears, then shattered the windows with her voice.

It must've knocked out the driver—either that or his head injury did—because he slumped in his chair. As Theo dropped to his knees, Penny rushed to his side and helped him stand.

"Never do that again," she demanded. "You could've gotten yourself killed."

Exhaustion plagued every inch of Theo's body, from his muscles down to his bones. Even if he could answer, he wouldn't have.

While Penny dragged Theo to the grass, he studied the bus. Since the driver couldn't open the doors, Dion and Yasmine carefully removed the kids from the windows.

"We got the van to start," Penny said. "I'll load up. Don't do anything stupid."

"No promises," Theo responded, eyeing the bus.

Normally, each mission went relatively similarly. They'd stop a car, take the cell phone and cash from the driver, and drive off. Phones would be dismantled and abandoned a few miles down the road before continuing to the base, and the money was kept for necessities. This mission, however, was the bumpiest yet.

Replacing Penny's company, a little girl with dark brown hair tapped Theo on the hand, shocking him out of his thoughts. By the looks of her, she couldn't have been more than eight years old. "What are you doing?" she wondered aloud.

"Keeping lookout." He nudged her toward the van. "Run along. The closer you are to me, the more dangerous it gets."

The girl raised a brow yet obeyed anyway. Just then, the driver staggered from the broken doors, his nose flowing with blood and a huge lump growing on the side of his head. "Get back," he ordered, pointing a shaky finger at Theo. "If you don't stop this, I'll—"

"I don't have time to hear the classic bad guy speech," Theo cut in. "Surrender your cell phone and any money you've got. The closest town is about ten miles north of here. I think you can manage getting there on your own."

The threat made the driver swallow. He crept for the bus, seemingly to give in or flee, but jumped to grab the little girl instead. As the man pressed her in a headlock, Theo felt his heart stop. The man shouted over her cries. "Stand down, or I'll kill her!"

Amidst the panicked children, Theo noticed his team remained calm. They had prepared for such a situation, promising each other that if the mission went south, there was nothing wrong with killing an evil man. It was an unspoken bet to see who would be brave enough to commit the act first.

A few tense moments passed in the otherwise quiet field. Penny herded the kids to their own van, but a dozen children remained inside the bus. Dion worked as quickly as he could without drawing attention.

Suddenly, a resounding crack echoed, similar to the sound of wood colliding with bone. The man cried out and released the girl, his hands flying to his head. While he dropped to his knees, an invisible Peter appeared behind him, wielding a thick log. "Picking on kids isn't cool, dude," Peter spat. "Get a life."

The young girl scrambled to conceal herself by Theo's leg. Dion called out for Peter's help, leaving the driver in Theo's company.

Without hesitation, Theo shackled the driver with his own shadow against the bus. "You're making this very difficult for us," Theo said. "People usually do what we say."

The driver gritted his teeth. "Jones's rewards are too good to pass on. He warned me I might run into you."

Theo's stomach flipped. Not a single driver from past missions had ratted Jones out. Perhaps they didn't understand the extent of their work, or perhaps they were better at lying. Regardless, this was Theo's opportunity to find out more.

"What else has he said to you?" Theo inquired.

The driver, despite being in obvious pain, smirked. "If I tell you, I'll die. Jones doesn't take kindly to snitches."

I have to keep prying, Theo thought. *This is the closest I've ever gotten to one of Jones's men.*

Ready to constrict the shadows tighter over the man, Theo raised his hand. Then, he felt a tiny tug on his shirt. The little girl lingered beside him, watching. Attacking this man in front of her would scare her, and Theo needed to win her trust.

With a long, slow exhale, Theo forced the darkness to free the man. "Just leave," Theo ordered.

The man rubbed his wrists. "Thanks, kid. Y'know what, I have a bit of information from Jones. He wanted me to tell you, 'Say hi to your father for me.'" In a flash, the driver reached into his pocket and pulled out a small, silver pen.

Theo's feet moved without him realizing, and he dove to reach the little girl. He covered her with his body right as the bus exploded. Heat pounded against him. Metallic shrapnel rained from the sky. It littered the ground around them, smashing onto the street and slicing the forest into shreds.

Then, the only sound was the crackling of the fire left behind. Heavy smoke clung to the air, but Theo found his voice to ask, "Are you okay?"

The little girl nodded and gripped his shirt tighter. "C-can we go?"

"Yes." He bundled her in his arms and went to stand, but the strength in his left leg gave out.

The girl yelped in fear, alerting Dion. "Is anyone hurt?" he asked.

Theo grimaced and touched his ripped pants. The fabric around his calf was oddly wet, almost like...

"You're bleeding!" the girl exclaimed.

At first, he didn't believe it. Then, his vision flickered, and he collapsed to the grass. Pain, an old friend, pulsed from his leg.

Thankfully, Dion whisked the girl to the van, preventing her from witnessing Theo's full injury.

"Ouch," Peter remarked, kneeling beside Theo. Peter's hair and clothes were singed, and he had small scratches on his arms, but other than that, he seemed fine. He withdrew a roll of bandages from his pocket. "Why so close to the explosion?" he teased. "Trying to be a hero?"

Theo rolled his pants to expose his wound. Judging by the long slash in his calf, he must've been hit by a piece of metal. It was a miracle it hadn't lodged in his leg. As Peter strapped the gauze around the bloody cut, Theo bit his tongue. "I had to save her," he muttered.

"Well, your sacrifice paid off," Peter said. "Good news is, more than half of the kids survived the blast with minor injuries."

Theo analyzed the red spot growing on his white bandages. "How many are dead?"

"We saved a lot—"

"How many?"

Peter turned invisible as he quietly admitted, "Five."

A pit formed in Theo's stomach, swallowing any emotion whatsoever. His gaze wandered to the burning fire, accompanied by melting metal and other unspeakable things. Kids were screaming, crying, and hiding in bushes or behind trees. The sight they had witnessed was horrific. It shouldn't have happened.

"Okay," Theo began, "we need to regroup at the base. Give anyone who's injured medical attention."

"And you?"

Theo forced himself to stand. "I can wait."

He didn't see Peter leave, but he heard small sniffs and leaves crunching as he did. Limping as he walked, Theo dismissed anyone who tried to assist him. *Don't panic,* he told himself. *We'll get to the base safe and sound, and the kids will forget what they saw.*

He stopped to give one last look at the smoking, mangled mess of the bus. *I wish I could forget too.*

2

ALL GROWN UP

Theo and Dion sat in the back of the van—the section of the car without seats or safety restraints. The younger kids were allowed to take the seats, but Theo settled for the hard floor. They had rescued about ten, the biggest rescue mission to date. During previous attempts, they'd only saved one or two children at a time.

When police eventually discovered the burning mass, they'd likely assume that the bus had crashed. Or, maybe, they'd suspect foul play, thanks to the bullet buried in the tire. Ultimately, since the majority of the victims were supers, it wouldn't make national news. Heavens, it'd be lucky to make local news.

"How badly does it hurt?" Dion motioned to Theo's bright red bandage.

As the van rumbled over a bump in the road, Theo bit the inside of his cheek. "I can handle it."

"You shouldn't have to. I could get Penny."

"Don't!"

Dion's eyes widened, so Theo backtracked and insisted, "I'd rather help the kids first."

Whether Dion believed it or not didn't matter. He removed his phone from his pocket and said, "I'll let base know we're on our way."

It was a basic burner phone, only capable of making calls and sending text messages. He, Theo, and Penny each had one when they split up for missions, but this time, she'd left hers at the base. It felt strange to have it; they weren't doing anything illegal, and yet, they had to act like criminals.

In turn, Theo studied each of his friends, noting they shared the same tired look. They were mere teenagers when they escaped the academies, and now, they had taken on the responsibility of the world. In fact, Peter was so exhausted that he couldn't maintain his invisibility.

As he called them, the League of Heroes had to become much more than they ever expected. Penny couldn't be everywhere at once, so they all learned how to play nurse. Since their enemies were skilled with guns, so were the teens. Even with the powers they wielded, it was wise to be trained in other forms of protection.

Sighing, Theo rested his head against the wall of the van. He wished he could travel back in time and tweak a few of his decisions. Perhaps then, he wouldn't be living his life like he was older than seventeen.

The little girl he had saved from the explosion suddenly scooted beside him, her gaze trained on his face. He couldn't force a smile for her, so he said, "Hi."

Her eyes flickered to his bloody leg, and her cheeks paled. To distract them both, he continued, "I'm Theo. What's your name?"

"Rebecca Weiss," she quietly answered. "My mom calls me Becca."

The van lurched violently, making Rebecca grab onto Theo's hand.

He nearly pulled away, but sensing the girl's fear, he didn't. His friends might've seen him as a hero, and maybe Rebecca did too.

It didn't mean he did.

The road became gravelly and rough, signifying they were approaching their destination. When the car finally rolled to a stop, Rebecca startled, eyes wide and panicked. "You're safe here," Theo assured her. "I'm with you."

Like Dion had promised, his old family cabin was their refuge. Since he visited the woods frequently as a kid, he knew which plants were safe to eat, and he built rain catchers to collect extra water. Theo always worried about what would happen if Dion's family discovered they were stowing away here. But Dion claimed he had it taken care of, so Theo didn't question him.

In the driveway, a girl helped the kids hop down from the van, giving each of them a tight hug and a compliment. To some, she said, "Wow, you're so pretty!" Or, "You look like a superhero!" She waved them to another teen, then once the van was empty, she lingered to speak with the weary team. "How'd it go?" she asked, her peppy voice dropping to a whisper.

Peter nearly tumbled out of the van. "Terrible. Thanks for asking, Giselle."

She twisted her dirty-blond braids. "Were there any major setbacks? You recovered a decent number of kids."

Theo hobbled to stand, his ears tuned into their conversation. Giselle had been with the team for a month. When they intercepted her on her way to Jones's new hideout, she explained that she had been living in France with her sister, but after she used her telekinetic powers to attack someone, she was shipped to the U.S. to be "taken care of."

Theo wanted to trust her. Although she didn't divulge every detail of her past, he suspected that was due to its traumatic nature. She seemed committed to the team, but ever since they met, she acted strangely around him.

Looking past the others, she locked eyes with Theo. Immediately, she shoved everyone aside. "Oh my! What—?"

"I tried to help," he explained. "It was the dumbest decision I've ever made."

Peter gave a small chuckle. "We could debate about that."

Giselle whirled on Penny, who was collecting items the children had left behind: jackets, hats, and a few pairs of shoes. "Why didn't you heal him? I bet he's two seconds away from passing out!"

Penny caught sight of him, and her items dropped to the floor. "I'm fine," he said. "It's just a small scratch!" Right after the words left his mouth, he lost his balance and fell sideways into a seat. Yelling erupted between the two girls, so Dion led Theo out of the van.

The mahogany and mossy trees surrounding the cabin swirled together in Theo's vision. It wasn't the most ideal hideout, but it was all they had. A few of the more technical teens had rigged the forest with traps and snares, not for animals, but for humans. The team had a basic escape plan, only to be executed in the worst-case scenario.

Inside the large, rustic home, Dion assisted Theo in sitting on the stairs near the front door. "Are you *sure* you can wait for Penny?" Dion asked. "No offense, but you look awful."

Theo wheezed quietly, trying to steady his breath from the short walk. "Just get me water."

Dion moved to obey. Thanks to the new arrival of kids, their pounding footsteps could be heard throughout the cabin, creaking the wood. Later, they'd have to be organized into rooms, and, if willing, explain how they came to be trapped on that bus. Theo closed his eyes, yet his pulse continued to pound.

He sensed someone's presence, and when he peeked open, he spotted a girl sitting on the stairs below him. "You feel stressed," she said.

If Theo had the strength, he would've pushed her. "Leave me alone. I think I know what I'm feeling."

The girl, Lily, was once a citizen of China. According to her, she was hoping for more freedoms in America. But upon arrival, she was captured and almost sent to Jones. Although Theo hadn't been there when his team rescued her a few weeks ago, he heard it had been quite an eventful mission.

Lily's black hair fell from behind her ear as she leaned forward. "You're scared, too."

"Yeah? Of what?"

"Of taking a life."

Theo fought his reaction. Speaking to Lily was always unnerving, considering she was the one person who could read him perfectly. In front of her, he was transparent. Vulnerable. Which was an emotion he couldn't bear to feel.

Fortunately, Dion returned, stopping Lily from prying into Theo's aura any longer. She was like Penny in the sense that they could manipulate pain, but Lily could only alter the emotion, not remove it.

Dion handed a glass of water to Theo, who accepted it with cold hands. "Lily," Dion said, "maybe you should comfort the new kids. They need more help than Theo does."

Her stare darted between the two boys. "I see he's convinced you of that, too." She started off, then paused to add, "You should get your leg checked out. You're in a great deal of pain."

Dion shot Theo a look, who kept his gaze locked on the water in his cup. The front door opened for Penny and Giselle.

"He's your boyfriend!" Giselle was saying. "Don't you care about him?"

Without answering, Penny sat next to him on the stairs. He opened his mouth to tell her to leave, but she pulled his leg into her lap, the sharp movement making him cry out. Hardly a second later, the pain faded, filling him with bliss. He rested his head on the banister behind him and muttered, "I said I was fine."

Sheepishly, Giselle scurried away. Theo wanted to tell Penny to stop, yet she cut in with, "Don't."

"There are people who need you more."

"You're first because I care about you most." With her healing finished, she kissed him on the forehead, and honestly, it felt better than being healed.

A boy with curly blond hair entered the room next. Immediately, Theo's nose wrinkled. Unbeknownst to everyone else, Carter had also been at the academy and was working alongside Principal Jones to wipe the memories of expelled or graduating students. When Carter found them the day they escaped the school, he begged for mercy, claiming he was protecting himself. Theo let him stay, but with every passing day, he regretted that decision more and more.

"Great, we got another batch of crying children." Carter rolled his eyes. "I swear, you guys are trying to make this place worse."

"By improving the lives of other people?" Dion said. "Yeah, we suck."

Shrugging, Carter suggested, "I can wipe them. Then, they won't have the trauma."

"That's thievery," Penny fired back. "You don't get to decide what memories they keep."

Carter threw his hands in the air. "It was just a suggestion. If I do it, it'll stop them from crying themselves to sleep for the next eternity. We won't have to deal with their whining."

The shadows underneath Theo twitched, responding to his short bout of frustration. Then, Penny held his free hand, doing both to calm him and urge him to leave. He placed his glass of untouched water on the floor, and together, they walked up the stairs.

Carter called after them with, "It'll be quick and painless! Er, I think!"

Penny's grip tightened on Theo as she moved faster.

"What about after a week?" Carter continued to say. "Can I do it then?"

When they were out of earshot in the upstairs hallway, Penny muttered, "I hate that guy."

"Little Miss Sunshine hates someone?" Theo joked. "That's a first."

"Hey, I hate a lot of people! But they're all for good reasons."

Theo let himself chuckle. Penny had stopped in front of their makeshift infirmary room and lowered her voice to say, "By the way, what you did today was—"

Predicting where the conversation was heading, he interrupted, "It wasn't a big deal."

"Yes, it was. You saved that little girl, even if it meant killing yourself in the process. And while I think it's a risky decision, it's one I'm proud you made." With that, Penny entered the infirmary, leaving Theo alone in the hall.

Part of him wanted to follow her, mainly because being in her presence soothed some of the aching sorrow in his mind. But the other part, the part that controlled him, insisted she didn't need him.

He wandered to the nearest bedroom. Now that the cabin was gaining more inhabitants, five or six kids would have to fit in a room.

Rebecca sat on the rug, away from the other little girls. Her brown hair had been braided with a pink ribbon tied to the end of it. Despite the horrors she witnessed, she brightened when she saw Theo.

"Hi, Theo," she greeted.

He knelt beside her. "Hello, Rebecca. How are you?"

"Good. Yasmine did my hair and gave me this." Rebecca placed a teddy bear into Theo's lap.

Early on, Penny decided it would be best to have toys and other stuffed animals in the cabin to comfort anyone who had endured particularly traumatic events. The decision seemed small, but it made all the difference.

"That's very nice," Theo said, hoping he sounded encouraging.

"Guess what else? I'm not scared like the others. I like it here."

Hardly a day ago, this girl had possibly been kidnapped from her home and placed on a bus with strangers. The least Theo could do was warm up to her. "That's amazing! It's my job to keep you safe."

Suddenly somber, Rebecca played with the zipper on her jacket. "Do you think my mom is safe?"

"Why wouldn't she be?"

"Bad men broke into our house. I can't remember what happened to her."

Mentally, Theo cursed. Such vulgarity would offend Rebecca, or worse, prompt her to repeat it. This wasn't the first he'd heard of this happening. Multiple children had divulged that their homes were being raided in the middle of the night by bounty hunters. Few stories had been released about these attacks, and when they were, the public majority wrote them off as, "If supers weren't dangerous, they wouldn't be arrested."

"I'm sure your mom is fine," Theo said. "And I promise I'll return you to her." Giving empty promises filled him with shame, but it was his last resort to comfort people.

Beaming, Rebecca gushed, "Really?"

"Of course. What kind of hero do you take me for?"

Giggling, she threw her arms around his neck. He hugged her, yet his stomach twisted in knots. He hated lying. However, it seemed lying was the last good thing in their upside-down world.

With Rebecca taken care of, Theo entered the next room. Accompanied by a trio of girls, Yasmine sat on the floor, braiding their hair in turn. Upon noticing him, the girls fell quiet, but Yasmine stiffened.

"Hi," he said, waving. As long as she saw his hands, she'd know he wouldn't attack her. Ever since he scared her half to death at the academy, she feared him. "Can we talk?"

"I'd rather not," Yasmine said, crossing her arms.

"It's about this morning."

Immediately, the trio of girls fled the room. Judging by their tear-stained cheeks, they'd lost friends in the explosion.

In their absence, Theo sat across from Yasmine. Making himself smaller seemed to diminish her fear. "How are they?" he asked.

"How do you think?" she snapped. "We had an airtight plan, and it failed. Kids died because of us." She brushed her knuckles over her eye. "Whatever."

More survivor's guilt. Yasmine and Dion couldn't be blamed for the van sputtering out. Just like none of them could be blamed for the explosion that followed. But Theo could almost read Yasmine's mind. If she'd been quicker to remove the kids from the bus—if she hadn't run away—perhaps she could've saved them.

"Remember that trip to West Virginia last month?" Theo said, tracing the wood paneling.

"You shouldn't call it a trip," Yasmine answered, packing her hair bands, combs, and pins. "We almost died." She paused. "But yes, I remember."

Most of the team's rescue missions blended in Theo's mind, but this one stood out. It was much like the events of this morning, where they stopped a van carrying two kids. Except that had gone according to plan. Yasmine shot out the back tire, which slowly released air and forced the van to a screeching stop. Then, Theo and his team safely escorted the captured supers to their own vehicle.

The driver was a confused older woman who claimed she had no idea where she was taking them. Theo wanted to take her money, just as they had done to the others, but Yasmine advocated for her release. "If we treat them like they're human," she had said, "maybe they'll treat us the same." Her sudden kindness was astounding yet refreshing. The school mean girl had a heart after all.

"You're a good person," Theo said. "Well, what I'm trying to say is I appreciate you."

Yasmine raised a brow.

"Your work," Theo corrected. "You didn't have to stay, but you have, and I'm glad."

He scooted back, then stood, knowing she'd cower if he towered above her. When he reached for the doorknob, she said, "I almost didn't. After we escaped the school, I was tempted to go home. Although doing so might've put my family in danger, I wanted to see them. Being around these kids reminds me of my brother. I've stayed to protect them, just like I'd protect him." She smiled. "I'm glad I'm here."

That made one of them.

The evening dragged by in a flurry of endless emotions. Everywhere he went, there would be a child begging for attention. Out of the thirty-five-ish people living in the cabin, the youngest inhabitant was about six. The vast majority were in their teen years. The oldest were only eighteen, the title held by Felix and Giselle.

As Theo cooked dinner, two girls approached him. Apparently, they had known each other previously and claimed they would absolutely "die" if they had to sleep in the same room. He was able to settle the debate by saying, "You can always sleep outside."

That convinced the girls to cease their complaining.

As Theo finished dinner, he debated bringing some to Penny. After rescue missions, the victims were usually shaken, more so today than ever. Likely, she was spending her time healing. A process like that shouldn't be interrupted.

Once everyone in the cabin had eaten, the kids settled down for the night. Theo secured the locks, assigned patrol shifts, and returned to his room. Every step sent pain shooting through his legs, a result of his aching feet. He eased his door open and saw his bed, already unmade for the night. *Finally*, he thought, flopping into the covers. *I can't wait for this day to end.*

But his worries never ceased.

Within the first week of their stay, a real estate agent visited to assess the home. Attacking her wouldn't have been an option, so at Peter's suggestion, the team hid in the forest until she left. Since then, there hadn't been any incidents, but Theo couldn't shake the fear of being found. To provide them with extra security, they instituted a rule that no one was allowed to contact their families. They could be easily tracked that way.

Theo turned in bed, feeling a pit form in his gut. He knew this feeling well; he'd had it once before. Except it wasn't really a feeling, more an empty void of apathy and silent misery. He couldn't pinpoint exactly what had brought it on, but it could've been any number of things. Was it watching Professor Beckham and Camilla die? Was it being apart from his family?

Or perhaps it was something much darker. During past nights, his dreams weren't tormented by his father's death. Instead, they'd been replaced by a new horror. His friends, terrified and bleeding, crouched at the mercy of a horrific, shadowy beast. *Theo* hurt them. *He* hurt all of them.

One fact was certain. The worse the depression became, the more the shadows controlled him.

Unlike everyone else, he *had* to keep in contact with his family. They mailed him money to keep the cabin afloat, enabling him to purchase essentials. Although most of their supplies were already stocked in the cabin—lightbulbs, blankets, guns, and mattresses—there was a constant need for food. As far as the team was concerned, Theo obtained the food with cash stolen from drivers or by accepting expired, free products at the grocery store. No one else had ever made a shopping trip, so they believed whatever he told them. Besides, it didn't matter how he got the stuff, as long as they had it.

Plus, Mom had sent the burner phones. When Theo showed them to Penny, she asked, "Where did you get these?"

So, he lied, claiming he got them from a store in town. Luckily, Penny didn't question him further.

His mom also mailed him antidepressants, a valuable resource to both calm the dark influence and his negative thoughts. It was a win-win scenario.

Well, it would've been, if it weren't for his powers being less potent. It was a miracle they worked on the bus today.

The bedroom door opened again, letting Dion and Peter inside. They exchanged a few quiet words before going off to their own corners.

The cabin had three bathrooms and six bedrooms. Theo had to share a room with Dion, Peter, and Felix. Now that they'd shed their school labels, they'd grown close. Considering they were Theo's friends, he should've enjoyed their company, but he never realized how annoying some people's habits were. Even now, Peter rapped his pencil on his notebook as Dion popped his gum. Hoping to muffle the sounds, Theo stuffed a pillow over his head.

Felix arrived not long after, the loudest of the four. Dion had been playing solitaire in the corner until Felix asked, "Wanna play Rummy instead?"

"Only if you can handle losing," Dion teased.

"Deal me in!" Peter called, hurrying to their circle.

With no other choice, Theo stomped out of the room, off to find someone who would let him sleep in peace.

Penny shared a room with Yasmine, Lily, and Giselle, but they usually left Penny alone until the late hours. Theo couldn't have been more grateful for that until tonight.

He cracked open her door, finding the lights off and the room encased in silence. Through the darkness, he could see Penny snuggled on her bed. He took a step to leave her alone, but she stopped him with, "Wait. Don't go." Her voice was soft with exhaustion.

Reluctantly, Theo approached her. "How was your day?" he asked.

Groaning, Penny stuck her face in her pillow. "I feel like I'm dying."

"Please don't," Theo joked, sitting down on the edge of her bed.

She managed to sit up and heaved a sigh. "I know what I'm doing is good, but it makes me feel so…ugh."

"Yeah, I get that."

She scooted closer to him, her green eyes illuminating the dark room. "How are you feeling?"

An equal amount of panic and shock battled for dominance in Theo's chest. "I'm normal," he tried to say.

Snickering, she moved her hand to the back of his neck, softly stroking his hair. "What does 'normal' mean?"

Theo's shock melted into ease, so he leaned over to rest his head on her shoulder. Wrapping an arm around him, she let the remainder of her healing power seep into his body. "You don't have to—" he began, until she interrupted, "I know."

The pain escaped his mind. If he could, he would fall asleep right here in her arms. But she was too tired to heal him all night. "There's so much to do," he whispered. "Every time we save a group, it makes life harder in the house."

"But it makes life better for them." She ran her fingernails down his back. "Have you thought about making a to-do list? Put the most important tasks at the top and the ones that aren't as important at the bottom. Then, it'll be easier to focus."

He nodded. "Okay, I'll try it."

They sat together, simply enjoying each other's company after a long, draining day. The walls in the cabin were thick, but not thick enough to mask the sounds of crying. After leaving the school, Theo wanted to abandon the responsibility of taking care of supers. Yet his past clung to him like the shadows on the wall.

Theo lifted his head to look at Penny. "Do you remember the day we escaped the academy?"

"It's hard to forget," she answered, her expression impossible to read.

His next question came quietly, almost silently. "Do you regret staying with me?"

Penny's lashes fluttered as she met his gaze. "Not one bit."

Theo's heart stumbled to beat. The need to tell her how he felt—how stressed he was, how much he liked her—ate at him. Over the edge of her shoulder, he caught a glimpse of the shadows on the wall, contorting their shapes and slinking onto the bed.

"I should go," Theo said as he pulled away.

Without his company, Penny faltered. "I hope you're leaving so you can sleep, not so you can work."

Wanting to avoid another argument, Theo kissed her on the head. "I won't. Good night."

She grabbed the front of his shirt and pulled him in for a real kiss, one that nearly swept him off his feet. When she ended it, she said, "Good night."

She nudged him to the door, so he exited, making sure to be extra quiet. By this time, many of the inhabitants, including the teens, were in their rooms to sleep. He inched the door open to his own room, finding his friends passed out as well.

Theo rested his head on his pillow and stared up at the boards of the bunk bed, almost wishing his friends were awake to be noisy. Now that they weren't, he had to listen to his thoughts.

You promised Penny you would sleep. You told her you'd rest. He pressed his palms against his face, hoping it would block out his terrible memories. *You should be stronger than this. Everyone else is. Why can't you move on? Why can't you forget?*

Why are you so weak?

It wasn't long before Theo was out of bed and checking the cabin, ensuring the doors were locked and the windows secured shut. He promised Penny he'd sleep, but he'd made a lot of promises, mostly to himself, that he couldn't keep.

3

BROKEN PROMISES

Penny knew what Theo had done. From the second she awoke and saw him, she knew. Happily, he greeted her at her bedroom door, saying, "Hi, Penny! How did you sleep?" His tone might've been chipper, but his lids drooped.

"Fine," she replied, "how about you?"

"Meh, alright. I had a weird dream and woke up at five, so I've been preparing for initiation!" Before she could answer, he kissed her on the cheek and said, "I'm off to check the perimeter. Can you help Dion make breakfast?"

Penny managed a smile. "Sure. See you in a bit."

Instead of watching Theo leave, she quickly returned to her room, dressed for the day, and hurried downstairs. The kitchen was connected to the dining room, glowing with bright lights, wooden cabinets, and pristine black appliances. Through the window above the sink, she could see the forest beyond. Judging by the vastness of the cabin and its surrounding land, she suspected Dion's family was successful. She never asked where his parents got their money; doing so would be rude.

The boy in question stood at the counter, dressed in his pajamas. As he poured blueberries into a bowl of pancake batter, he swiped a few. "Hey, Penny!" Dion said, muffled. "What's with the frown?"

She switched the stovetop on. "Theo didn't sleep last night."

"How do you know?"

"I can just tell. He's off."

Dion placed a pan on the warming stove and retrieved a measuring cup for the batter. "So, he's got a sleeping problem. Trust me, when he needs to rest, his body will make him."

The pancakes bubbled and browned, filling the room with their sweet scent. "There's something else," Penny confessed. "I feel like he's hiding a secret from me. I can't tell what it is."

Dion fell into a solemn silence. He even stopped chewing. After the first pancakes were golden, he said, "I bet I know what's going on."

Penny's breath caught in her throat. "You do? What is it?"

Ignoring her request, Dion stated, "You don't need to help everyone."

Hot, angry tears burned in her eyes. "But I *want* to help him."

Dion's expression hardened. "Give him time to tell you himself. The more you pressure him for answers, the more stress you'll put him under. If he's keeping a secret, then he's doing it to protect you. Don't go poking around."

Penny didn't answer or give Dion any indication that she heard him. He carried the plate piled with pancakes and walked away, off to serve the children breakfast.

Her fist tightened on the spatula. Her main job in the house was to heal people. She wasn't talented at anything else, regardless of how much she tried. Every time she touched Theo, she could tell he needed her power the most. But why?

"Hey," Theo suddenly said from behind her.

She whirled around, hoping he would want to talk, but his attention was directed elsewhere. "You need any help?" he continued, reaching out to take the spatula.

"No," she insisted, drawing away from him. "I can do it."

A corner of his mouth quirked into a half-grin. "I know you can. But if you need me, ask."

"Nope! How are you?"

As his gaze traveled to the dining room, he exhaled. "I'm worried how everyone will take initiation."

Since Penny was distracted, she switched the stove off. Every time new members joined the cabin, Theo would have to tell them the rules. And every time, without fail, there were arguments, issues, and disobedience. Mentally, Penny crossed her fingers, hoping today would be different.

"You're going to do great," she offered as she grazed his arm.

He leaned into her touch. "Could you be there with me? You don't have to talk, but I could use your support."

Penny's heart fluttered. "I'd love to."

Very briefly and almost hesitantly, he hugged her, yet it was a hug all the same. "You're the best. It'll start in thirty minutes in the living room."

He walked to the dining room yet didn't get very far before Rebecca stepped in his path. The pair engaged in a hushed conversation, one in which Rebecca pointed to Penny. Hiding her blush, Penny turned to the stove and finished the pancakes. It felt like forever since Theo told her he needed her. Not her healing, but *her* as a person.

Once she completed her cooking, she sat with Yasmine and a few other kids. Aside from the dining room table, which seated eight, Dion had set up scuffed, white card tables from the garage to provide additional seating.

Yasmine elbowed Penny in the ribs and whispered, "You see that kid at the end of the table?"

Penny glanced there, finding a boy with a long, tangled brown mullet. She recognized him as one of the teens they had rescued yesterday, and one she had to care for. Although his injuries had been shallow, he refused to leave her presence. She wanted to give him the benefit of the doubt, but the way he studied her made her skin crawl.

"Max?" she asked. "What about him?"

"I heard him talking about you to the other boys," Yasmine explained. "Seems like he's going to make a move."

Penny felt her whole body burn. "What? Why would he—I don't—"

Yasmine cut her pancakes into smaller pieces. "I'm just warning you. He also asked Giselle if she was a good kisser, since she's French."

A sour taste filled Penny's mouth. Personal feelings for Giselle aside, it made Penny nauseous to hear how the girl had been treated. "Maybe I should tell Theo," Penny suggested.

"You don't have to." Yasmine lifted her plastic knife. "If you want me to gut the kid like a fish, I'll do it."

Penny fought her laugh. Twisted as it sounded, Yasmine's offer of protection assured Penny. It was enjoyable to know she had people on her side.

Interrupting their conversation, Felix dropped into the chair across from her. With a charming grin, he asked, "How is our lovely Angel today?"

Penny gritted her teeth. Truthfully, she hadn't been too overjoyed when he decided to stay with the group after fleeing the school, but he *was* working hard to be less of a jerk.

Or so he claimed.

"What do you want, Felix?" Yasmine interjected, coming to Penny's rescue. "We don't need you wasting our time."

"Why do you assume I want something?" Clearing his throat, he corrected, "Okay, so I want one teeny tiny favor." He pointed down the table at Giselle. "She's single, right?"

Yasmine burst into laughter. "Are you asking for yourself or for a friend?"

Not embarrassed by his question, Felix scoffed. "Myself, obviously. I figured if we're eventually going to die a horrible death, I'd like to have a girlfriend at least. So, is that a yes or a no?"

Snickering, Penny focused on her food. "I'll look into it," she promised, despite having zero intention of keeping it.

As it turned out, Penny broke promises just like Theo did.

4

BUCKET LISTS

T hirty minutes passed. In that time, Penny cleaned the kitchen from breakfast, then ushered the new kids into the living room. It was one of the larger rooms in the cabin, big enough to fit two leather couches, a recliner, a television set, and a tall brick fireplace. Above the fireplace, a deer head mounted on the wall, marking the first—and last—time Dion's dad killed a buck. That was all Dion had said, and no one asked for more.

While everyone settled on the couches or the floor, Theo approached Penny along the wall and stated, "You look nervous."

She opened her mouth to tell him what Yasmine had heard, but doing so would either make him extremely upset or extremely vengeful. Neither sounded like a viable option to her, so she insisted, "I'm great."

He eyed her for a second longer, then swiveled to address the children. "Good morning, and welcome to your new home. You probably already know who I am, but feel free to call me Theo. This is Penny, our healer. I hope each one of you thanked her for her service yesterday."

A combined, half-happy, half-muttered "Thank you" chorused throughout the room. Their appreciation today didn't quite make up for their dismissal yesterday, but she forced a grateful smile.

As Theo repeated the cabin's list of rules, he paced the floor. "Your schedule will be as follows. Everyone must be awake by eight unless you have special permission. Breakfast will be served at eight thirty. Lunch will be at noon, sharp, and dinner will be served between 5:30 and 6:00. Quiet time is at 9:00. This is to accommodate some of our younger inhabitants." He flashed a wink to Rebecca, who was sitting cross-legged on the ground.

Max raised his hand from his place on the recliner. "Are we allowed to do stuff after nine, Dad?"

To prevent her gasp from escaping, Penny pursed her lips. Mentions of parents, especially fathers, were sensitive around Theo. The team had made it a point to never, under any circumstances, mention his dad.

Like she expected, his eyes narrowed the tiniest bit. "Yes. But make too much noise and you're grounded."

A few laughs trickled amongst the kids, mostly from Rebecca and a hesitant one from Penny.

Theo straightened his shoulders. "Chores will be assigned at the beginning of every week. Some of you will have more or less, depending on your age and whether you need extra consequences." Though he didn't explicitly say it, Penny knew he was referring to Max.

"What kind of chores do we have to do?" the boy chimed in once more.

"Normal stuff. Dishes, cooking, cleaning. Other than that, I will take care of—"

"Whatever, how do I request new clothes? The ones you gave me are too big."

Theo concealed his clenched fists behind his back. "Sorry to hear that," he bit out. "But this is the best we can do. If you don't like it, talk to Yasmine."

Max nodded knowingly. "Ah, yeah, the mouthy girl! I can do that."

This time, it was Penny's turn to bristle.

Theo ignored the comments and continued. "You get one hot shower a week. You're free to take another, but you can only use the warm water once for under five minutes. This ensures we each have a chance to use it."

A unified groan went up. Penny gave them a sympathetic nod, but she couldn't relate to their annoyance. Ever since the team instituted the rule, Theo gave her his hot shower, allowing her to use the warm water twice a week. Regardless of how much she argued, he refused to reconsider. It might've been a small gesture, but every selfless act made a big statement.

This time, Max didn't bother raising his hand. "Can we use our powers?"

Theo winced as he spoke. "I'm sorry, but we can't risk anyone exposing our whereabouts. Your powers will have to be limited."

Protests rifled through the children. In dire circumstances, they'd be brought to the basement to release any suppressed energy, but Penny had to agree with Theo. It was the safest option.

"Who died and made you king of the cabin?" Max demanded.

"Technically, no one died," Theo said uncomfortably.

Scoffing, Max drooped his legs over the armrest. "This is dumb! I'm not taking orders from an outlaw."

"I'm not an outlaw," Theo defended.

"Why'd you kidnap us anyway? I was told we were going to a—"

"I'm sure you were told you were going to a safe place," Theo interrupted sharply. "A place where you can be yourselves and don't have to worry about hurting others. A place where supers are welcome. But every bit of that is a lie. *This* is the safe place, and you should be —" Suddenly, Theo paused and pinched the bridge of his nose. "Do you have any *real* questions?"

Max smirked, unfazed by Theo's near eruption. "Just one. What will happen if I hit on your girlfriend?"

Penny felt everyone's attention divert to her. She covered her cheeks, but it did nothing to slow her rising blush.

Theo didn't react. "I'm confused by your question," he responded coolly. "Are you asking what she will do? Or are you asking what *I* will do to *you*?"

Max stared Theo down. "Both."

Theo motioned to Penny to answer first, but honestly, she didn't know what to say. This boy was hardly fourteen, the exact opposite of her type, and certainly *not* her boyfriend. Since she couldn't utter a single word, Max snickered and said, "Come on, baby. I'm not making you nervous, am I?"

No one laughed. But Theo did smile. It was the kind of sneaky, mischievous grin she'd seen very rarely on him, yet every time it emerged, she knew he was planning something fun. Now, more than ever, she couldn't wait to see what it was.

"Alright," he said, "my turn. If you make any degrading, inappropriate remarks to Penny or any other girl in this cabin, I will mount your head next to Bambi's on the wall." He pointed to the deer head nailed above the fireplace, the one with glassy marble eyes and a lone pensive stare.

Max glanced at it, and his complexion dyed a lighter shade. "You're bluffing!"

Theo's smile widened. "In case you haven't noticed, we're pretty deep in the forest. All kinds of bears and wild creatures are out there. You won't ever be found. Do I make myself clear?"

Nodding, Max shrank into the cushions, his cocky demeanor breaking away to his true, terrified self.

"Good." Theo addressed the crowd. "We respect each other here. There is no arguing, no enemies, and most importantly, no thinking you're better than anyone else. We get along, we protect each other, and we stick together. Understand?"

Some of the kids flashed him a thumbs-up, while others confirmed verbally. As soon as they agreed, he waved them off. Max shot out of the room like a bullet leaving a gun.

In their absence, Penny hugged Theo and gushed, "That was amazing!"

"I wasn't too mean, was I?"

"Don't feel bad. He needed to hear it."

Theo's embrace softened around her waist. "I hope you weren't uncomfortable. If he says anything to you, I'll—"

Penny stuck her finger to Theo's lips, cutting his threat short. "As charming as it is to see you fight for me," she teased, "I'd rather you didn't. Stay out of trouble."

He kissed her finger. "I'll try."

Butterflies took flight in her stomach. During the first month at the cabin, he didn't touch her at all. They didn't so much as hold hands. Then, around the same time he began acting strangely happy, he started touching her more. Small moments of hugging at first, and he quickly moved on to kissing her. He had yet to explain his sudden personality change, but at least Penny had her Theo back.

Well, almost Theo.

With her heart pounding in her throat, she said, "Would you like to go on a date tonight?"

His brows bunched. "What kind of date?"

"Maybe some stargazing? A little talk outside?" Sensing her own desperation, she shook her head and hurriedly added, "We don't have to."

Luckily, she was spared of any humiliation as Theo beamed. "Sounds fun! I'll meet you outside at seven."

Relief flooded her mind, allowing her shoulders to relax. "Perfect. I can't wait."

With that, he waved her farewell, off to do another thousand tasks.

Feeling lighter than air, Penny made her own way toward her bedroom. Just inside the door, Yasmine stood at their shared white vanity, combing a young girl's hair. Both of them brightened at the sight of Penny in the mirror.

"Hey," Yasmine greeted, "what's going on downstairs?"

Dreamily, Penny sighed and lay on her bed. "You should've seen it, Yasmine. Max made a few too many snarky comments, so Theo threatened him. I think he's going to stay away from all the girls in the house."

Yasmine chuckled. "I bet he will. Theo's terrifying."

Penny laughed along. It was true that Theo could take his intimidation a bit too far sometimes, but when it came to protecting her, he didn't hesitate. And it made her like him more.

As Peter struggled to fit a ladder through the garage doorway, Theo waited nearby with a checklist. He couldn't complete the tasks on his own, so he enlisted the help of Peter and Dion.

"I hate this place," Peter muttered. "Who designed it?"

"My mom," Dion answered. He removed a box of lightbulbs from a grocery bag and studied them carefully. "She didn't really take my dad's opinions into account. I can't blame her. He's not 'all there' in the head."

Finally, Peter managed to escape the garage with the ladder. He spotted Theo and Dion's smug grins and growled, "Shut up."

Snickering, Theo led them into the nearest bedroom. The lights on the ceiling had burned out completely, encasing the room in shadows. There was only a single bed, since the team couldn't afford any more than that. As a result, sleeping bags and air mattresses littered the floor, serving as beds instead.

A pang of guilt poisoned Theo's heart, but before he could ponder too long on it, Peter snapped the ladder into place. Dion handed new bulbs to Theo, so he climbed on top of the steps.

"So," Peter started, dragging the word out, "tell me, Dion, have you told Yasmine how much you like her yet?"

Dion huffed. "I'm trying to become her friend first."

"I thought confessing was on your bucket list."

Dion punched Peter, wiggling the stability of the ladder. "You snoop!"

Theo caught his balance and shot a glare at his friends. Peter stabilized his position and accepted the dead lightbulb. "Bucket list, huh?" He made a humming sound. "What else is on it?"

"You didn't read the rest?"

"Nonsense! That would be an invasion of privacy."

Dion rolled his eyes, yet underneath his obvious annoyance, a sliver of amusement remained. "When I was a kid, I wanted to be a doctor. But if I had the choice, I'd—"

"Work in a morgue," Peter finished.

"Actually," Dion said over Theo's laugh, "I'd go into architecture."

Laughter subsiding, Theo twisted a second lightbulb into place. "Interesting," he said. "I always figured you'd be a teacher or something with numbers."

Dion smiled sadly. "Yeah, I had a pretty awesome teacher. But being an architect would be more fun."

"That's cool." Peter rested his elbows on one of the ladder steps. "I want to be an engineer."

"Not an actor?" Theo teased. "Or a stand-up comedian? What about a talk show host?"

"The spotlight loves me, but it's a love I cannot return." Peter looked at Theo. "What's in your future?"

Theo pondered that. Growing up, he wanted to be a superhero. With every passing day, that dream felt more and more ridiculous. It was the idea of a child who had hope for a world that didn't exist. As a super, there wasn't much that Theo could do. Except one thing.

"I want to have a family," he declared.

His friends nodded in satisfaction. With task one completed, Theo made a motion to turn on the light switch. In an instant, the bulbs shone bright and illuminated the entire room. Theo always felt uneasy after the light bulbs were replaced. He never realized how dark it had been without them.

He climbed down and said, "Ready for the next room?"

Peter's brows furrowed. "So, none of us are going to continue being superheroes?"

"Superheroes aren't legal," Theo reminded them. "I'm sure life will be harder for us in the future."

"I know," Peter said. "But do we really want to live in a world that doesn't allow us to *exist*? Just because we get rid of Principal Jones doesn't mean our problems will disappear."

"I hear some countries are considering scientific testing," Dion said. "Any super that uses their powers in public, even to help someone, can basically be killed."

"That's not our problem to fix," Theo tried to say.

"It *is* our problem," Peter insisted. "It would've happened to Giselle and Lily if we hadn't intervened. We don't get treated like normal people because we aren't normal. Are we supposed to let it stay like that forever?"

"All I'm saying is we don't have to do everything. I thought you wanted to start your life."

"I do," Peter explained. "It just feels weird to abandon everyone like us."

The mood in the room grew gloomier. For once, Theo was the upbeat one, forced to drag his friends from the brink of the void. "Guys, let's take this one step at a time. Maybe we'll defeat Jones in a month, or maybe we'll have to wait another year."

"Then what?" Peter interrupted. His panicked complaints grew faster. "What if when we kill Jones, we get in trouble for it? It's not like we're model citizens."

"I promise I'll look into it," Theo assured them.

Their apprehension hung in the air, thick and tense. It was practically tangible—a dark energy fueled by fear. Unable to take part in their anxiety-ridden debate, Theo said, "I've gotta run! You guys can finish this, right?"

Before either of them could protest, Theo darted out of the room. In a way, Peter's frenzied worries prompted Theo to think. Killing Principal Jones wouldn't solve their problems. In fact, it'd cause more. Theo needed evidence to prove that what they were doing was right. And the only person he knew who might have evidence was Dad.

Theo reached his—thankfully empty—bedroom, tore a sheet out of his notebook, and wrote,

> Dear M,
> I know we haven't talked in a week. Thank you for sending us money; I appreciate it. It's difficult making sure everyone gets enough to eat, but you've been keeping us stable. The responsibility of caring for all these supers is intense. Luckily, the medication helps me manage my stress. So, thanks.
> Also, I need to know what Dad was doing when he was a hero student. I know he didn't tell you everything, but see

what you can find. I need more information if I'm supposed to pick up where he left off.

Love, T-Bear

P.S. Can you send me a new prescription? I'm out again.

Then, knowing how annoyed Tara would be without a letter of her own, Theo ripped out another piece of paper.

Dear T,

I'm sorry for taking so long to respond to you. It's been busy; I haven't had time to think. Now I know what you meant about jobs being the worst. But you don't need to worry about me. How are you?

Also, I think it's been established that I'm not sheltered anymore. Maybe it's time for you to move out, too. The world is much larger than I realized. It makes me wonder why I wanted to grow up so badly.

I wish I could see you and M. I love you both.

Once he completed his letter, he folded it, placed it in the envelope with the note to his mom, and headed into town to mail it. No one saw him leave.

5

A WORLD LIKE THIS

Once noon hit, Penny's internal clock struck too. Every day was the same routine. After retrieving her notepad from under her bed, she headed to the back patio. Fresh forest air rushed into her, chilling her nerves.

Lily had been standing at the far end of the patio, staring off into the woods, yet she heard Penny's steps and turned around. Oftentimes, she'd be found dissociating alone, but Penny chalked it up to her powers overwhelming her.

"Why do you take notes?" Lily pointed out, eyeing the pad of paper in Penny's hands. "We're here to ease their pain, not talk them through it."

Every time the cabin retrieved more kids, a session of therapy would be performed. Well, not so much therapy but toying with their emotions to make them forget any pain.

Penny's shoulders sagged. Lily couldn't understand Penny's hesitance; after all, her power was a distraction. Penny, on the other hand, had to use her own energy to heal people, and the effects of her power lasted longer than Lily's emotional manipulation. Penny was already exhausted from healing everyone's physical injuries from yesterday, and now she had to work even more to heal their minds.

As terrible as it was, the cabin reminded her of the school. During her first few weeks at the academy, she didn't attend class. Principal Jones would excuse her so she could be in the nurse's office, helping whoever came to her.

She shivered as she thought of the hundreds of hours spent in that cramped room, healing to the point of her own physical sickness. At the end of those weeks, she fainted in front of Yasmine, yet she'd managed to lie it off. Still, the consequences of her overworking took their toll. Until recently, Penny didn't realize that Jones was using her. He didn't care if she was hurting; he didn't care if he was abusing her ability. So long as he got what he wanted.

But today, nothing had changed. She was expected to heal everyone constantly, regardless of her own health. And yet, no matter how much she hated it, how much she loathed being selfless, there was a part of her that knew if she didn't heal, then every single person in this cabin would be dead or injured. Only she could cure them.

And that was a heavy burden to bear.

At the academy, she learned how to fight to create a new role for herself and ensure she was a threat. These days, she couldn't spend as much time training. After all, a nurse was more important than a soldier.

It made her wonder: How many of the residents saw her as a real person? As more than a nurse? Did her friends see her as Penny or as Angel?

"I don't enjoy manipulating like that," Penny finally explained, her fingernail picking at her torn notebook cover. "Solving their problems is better than having a biweekly emotional checkup."

Lily shook her head. "You and I can't fix their problems. Their problem is being a super."

She waved to one of the waiting children, beckoning him to the hammocks strung in the trees. Plastering a smile on her face, Penny motioned to the next boy in line. He stood with his arms crossed and his brows bunched, which resembled every single kid Penny had dealt with thus far.

"Hi," she greeted as she led him to a quiet corner of the patio. They each sat down in a white plastic lawn chair, one across from the other. "I'm Penny. What's your name?"

His glare didn't budge. "Hudson."

"It's nice to meet you, Hudson. How old are you?"

"Twelve."

"What's your superpower? You know, besides being charming." She laughed after she said it, yet he didn't find her compliment amusing.

"I have heat vision."

"That's super cool! I haven't heard of that one yet."

He grunted in response.

So much for being open to conversation. Penny cleared her throat. "Well, these meetings are to get to know you and to give you a chance to talk about your thoughts and emotions. But if you don't want to speak, you don't have to."

Hudson exhaled through his nose. "I guess I've got stuff to say."

Penny bolted upright in her chair. Finally! Someone wanted to talk! "What should we talk about?"

"My family."

Penny began to write that down. She'd seen Theo make notes of the supers; why couldn't she? "You must miss them," she said sadly.

Hudson scratched his nose. "Yeah, I mean, I have a mom and a dad at home, but I've always thought of my family as my brother. He was awesome."

"What made him so awesome?"

For a long minute, Hudson's mouth opened and closed repeatedly, mustering the nerve to speak. "He used to be a super too," the boy admitted.

Penny's voice lowered. "Used to be?"

"He, um, he gave up."

That was it. Penny didn't need any additional explanation to know what Hudson was insinuating. Living was difficult for many people, but it was especially hard for supers. She laid a hand on his knee, healing his grief. "I'm sorry to hear that," she mourned.

Shrugging, Hudson toyed with a string on his shirt, yet Penny suspected he was hiding his tears. "When it happened, I thought he was dumber than me for quitting. Nowadays, I think I'm dumber than him."

"Why do you say that?"

Hudson glimpsed up. "What kind of super wants to live in a world like this?"

"I miss the days when superheroes were nothing but characters in comic books. Back then, supers knew their place and the world was normal."

"Are you serious? Unless you grew up under a rock, the world has never been normal."

"Well, it should be."

"Obviously, it's impossible to win an argument with an idiot, so let's agree to disagree."

-Twitter Debate

6

THE DATE

An hour before Theo had to meet Penny outside, he locked himself in his bathroom. With the night setting in, the shadows were even louder. Their deprecating voices swarmed Theo's mind in cold demands. Silently, but quickly, he removed his pills from behind the counter and swallowed one.

Within minutes, the medication took hold, and his panicked, dizzying worry ceased. The dark whispers stopped, leaving him feeling empty, yet calm. His reflection smiled. It was getting increasingly easier these days, but each one was faker than the last. Every day for the past four months, he had to gather the courage to take his disgusting pills and be the boy Penny needed, the one she wanted.

The one she liked.

This is for her, he reminded himself. *She loves it when you're happy, and it takes the pressure off of her to heal you. How hard can it be to pretend?*

Once Theo re-entered the bedroom and found his roommates

playing cards, he ordered, "Don't bother me. Penny wants tonight to be just us, like a normal date."

Dion nodded, but Felix jumped in with, "What makes a date normal?"

"As if Theo would know about that," Peter said, flicking a card at Theo's head.

"It's uninterrupted by nosy friends or needy children," Theo explained in exasperation. Whilst looking at Dion, Theo added, "Keep them in line. By any means necessary."

A smirk spread on Dion's face. As the three engaged in yet another smack-talk session, Theo snuck out to the backyard. One of his favorite parts of the cabin was the outdoors. The patio had enough space for a few chairs and a table, along with a swinging chair and grill. The grill had only been used once. After Felix started a fire, it hadn't been lit again.

A dozen feet away from the patio, Penny had draped a blanket on the grass. The stars and moon above glimmered, providing light. Theo never considered himself a romantic, despite his upbringing with a steady diet of romantic comedies. But he felt differently around Penny. Her excitement made it easier to enjoy the experience. It made him think those silly ideas of true love and soulmates could be real.

Penny had clearly dedicated a portion of her day to getting ready, because her hair hung in flawless waves and she wore her nicest white shirt.

She bolted to her feet. "Hi," she said.

Theo stepped down the stairs. "Hello. You look pretty."

The mention made Penny blush. "Oh, thanks, I did my best."

Together, they sat on the blanket, keeping close to retain warmth. Penny rested her head on his shoulder and said, "I miss this."

Theo wrapped his arm around her. In the future, life would be different. Entire days would be dedicated to doing nothing but sitting with her. He would give her whatever she asked for. Penny should've had more than this dusty old cabin.

But to get to that point, he had to confess his feelings, overcome the darkness, and, of course, defeat Principal Jones. It would take so much time. Theo wished they could pick up and move now.

Go ahead, the dark voice inside him hissed, breaking through a crack in his walls. *Ask her. Admit how you feel. See how that works out.*

Theo squeezed Penny tighter. "How was your day?" he asked, ignoring his thoughts.

"Just like every other day. You?"

"Same."

Maybe she sensed the hesitation in his voice, or maybe she didn't. Either way, she suddenly straightened and said, "Can I ask you a question?"

"Sure, but don't make it too complicated. My brain has done enough work for today."

"When we first got here, you were really distant. Recently, you've changed. Why is that?"

Theo felt his heart sink into the ground. While straining to keep his expression blank, he said, "I feel fine."

"Then, what happened? Why are you so happy?" She frowned. "You're not faking it, are you?"

The combination of her healing and the clouding effects of the anti-depressants kept him calm. Gently, he squeezed her hand and threaded the other through her hair. "I'm happy because I'm with you. That's all that matters to me."

Her lips parted with hope. "Really?"

Instead of answering, he bridged the gap between them and kissed her. "You know," he murmured, "if we were normal teenagers, I'd be taking you on a real date tonight. In fact, we'd go to the skating rink in town."

"I'm terrible at skating."

48

"So am I. It'd give me an excuse to hold your hand."

Penny giggled. "You don't need an excuse."

"Maybe not now, but if we were human, I'd need one. You're way out of my league."

She rolled her eyes as if she was saying, "Yeah, right!" Aloud, she said, "What else would we do?"

"I'd use my allowance to buy us ice cream. Then, we'd go to a park and eat it while sitting on the swings. We'd stay out until midnight, just talking."

"My dad would kill you," Penny pointed out. "Curfew is at ten."

"I'd risk my life to spend a second longer with you." Theo intended the conversation to be light, fun, and comedic. However, the more he thought about it, the sadder he became. He would never have those dates with Penny; he would never have that *future* with her. He swallowed the lump in his throat. "If we were human—"

"I wouldn't have met you," Penny said. Her fingertips trailed up and down his arm, leaving a path of sparks in their wake. Faintly, he recalled his mother doing this to comfort him after nightmares. "I like the life we have. I like having super problems, because it means I have you."

Theo closed his eyes, partly in relaxation and partly to slow the rising tears. "I want more with you."

"And we can have it. I promise."

The two of them lay on the blanket, facing each other. Softly, Theo traced her freckles, following the pattern across her nose and cheeks. As if she were shy or embarrassed, she exhaled a small laugh. "Why are you looking at me like that?" she asked.

"Like what?"

She shook her head, refusing to answer, but Theo could infer what it was. "I'm staring because you're beautiful," he explained. "Every time I look at you, it's like seeing you for the first time."

"You grew up around supermodels."

He scoffed. "You think I'm that shallow?" He paused, then added, "But you *are* pretty."

Through Penny's giggles, she managed to say, "Who taught you how to talk to girls?"

"I grew up with a mom and sister who made me watch romantic movies every weekend. I think I learned a few tricks."

"It shows." Penny kissed him. "I love when you're like this."

She didn't have to explain herself for him to know what she meant. She loved him when he was happy. When he wasn't depressed, anxious, or stressed. Ignoring that, he chose to focus on the feeling of her arms around him, easing every bad emotion.

Moments like these made him happy to be alive, even if they were few and far between.

7

FINDING THEO

Theo awoke to someone shaking him. Expecting the worst, he shot upright, pulse racing, but Dion hovered above him with a bright smile. "Hey," he teased, "about time."

While scrubbing the sleep out of his eyes, Theo managed a, "What are you talking about?"

"We know what you did last night," Dion explained as Peter made a bunch of kissing noises.

Theo felt his face burn. "How?"

"You two came in after ten and tripped the alarms."

Theo blushed underneath his friends' teasing. He and Penny had enjoyed the quiet night to themselves. When the cold breeze chilled them to the bone, they returned inside, only to have the alarms at the doors go off. Within seconds, he fixed it, but apparently, the entire cabin knew who had done it.

"We were just hanging out! That's all that happened!"

Felix pushed Dion aside so he could yank Theo out of bed. "What's your secret, dude? How do you pick up girls so easily?"

Somehow, Theo squirmed out of Felix's grasp and started for the bathroom. "I don't have time for this."

"Yeah," Peter chimed in. "That time is reserved for Penny."

The three of them burst into manic laughter, while Theo rolled his eyes and locked the bathroom door. Their behavior was becoming increasingly childish. When would they start acting their ages?

After popping one of his pills—his *last* pill—Theo hurried to the kitchen to make breakfast. Thankfully, Yasmine had already finished cooking a mound of toast and eggs.

"I thought it was my turn today," he said.

"Yes, it was." Summoning a grin, she patted him on the shoulder. "Consider this my appreciation for protecting Penny."

At the mention, Theo faced the dining room, catching a glimpse of the young boy, Max. They made eye contact before Max scurried away. "I didn't want to scare him," Theo lied.

"Yes, you did," Yasmine corrected. "Don't worry. He had it coming."

As she walked to the tables, Felix snatched Theo into a bear hug. "I don't know what you did to that kid," Felix said, "but he's intimidated! Teach me your ways, Boogeyman!"

Theo tried to shove Felix off, but he was too strong. "Don't call me that! All I did was help Penny!"

"Hey, bro, calm down. I meant it as a good thing. It's nice having my friend be the most feared guy in the cabin."

Theo ceased his struggle. The idea that he was the most feared in the cabin was laced with dramatization. But there was a significant chance that it was the truth.

"Hi, boys!" Giselle said behind them. "What's going on?"

In a flash, Felix released Theo and swept a hand through his hair. "Hey, Giselle," he greeted. "We were just having a little guy's chat, you know how it is."

Brows raised, she retorted, "Not really, no."

Although Felix might've been the epitome of charm, Giselle's gaze stuck to Theo. He could practically see her light up. "I had a wonderful idea!" she said. "I found an old projector in the garage, so we should have a movie night! Wouldn't that be fun?"

"That's an awesome idea!" Felix offered her a high five.

Ignoring him, Giselle asked, "Do you think so, Theo?"

The way she was treating Felix, even if he deserved it, made Theo's stomach churn. However, he couldn't focus on that. "Sure," he said. "I'll ask Dion if we have any movies."

Without warning, Giselle kissed Theo on the cheek. He was certain his shock mirrored Felix's as she said, "Thanks! Let me know how I can help!"

The instant she disappeared, Felix's fists curled so tightly his knuckles cracked. Anticipating a fight, Theo raised his own hands in front of him. Except Felix's expression didn't contain malice. He almost appeared sad. "I can't believe she kissed you," he whispered.

"It's a custom in France," Theo explained, unsure if it would fool Felix. "It's meant to be polite."

"Right, customs."

"I've been once or twice with my mom for fashion week. They did it a lot."

"Huh." The excuses did nothing to smooth Felix's creased forehead. "Hey," he said, "can I take the lead on this with her instead of Dion?"

Theo wasn't quite sure how to answer. He and Felix hadn't fought since attending the academy, but Felix was unpredictable. His temper made him dangerous.

"If you want to," Theo said. "I'm sure there are movies in the basement if you need ideas."

Felix brightened. "Thanks. I'll take care of tonight. Then, you'll get to spend more time with your precious angel."

As Theo stifled his groan, he escaped the kitchen. He wasn't about to give Felix the benefit of a reaction. Unfortunately, the teasing did make Theo think. His feelings for Penny might have been too obvious. A weakness like that could be used against him.

Hopefully, it never would be.

At seven thirty, Felix and Giselle gathered the kids and escorted them outside. As they settled in, Theo waited on the back porch. Throughout the day, the couple had hung a projector screen on one of the cabin's exterior walls. Blankets and chairs littered the grass, a few already inhabited by some of the supers.

Peter passed, his arms full of steaming popcorn bags. As Dion approached, Theo mused, "Looks good."

"I'm surprised," Dion responded. "Who knew Felix had more than one brain cell?"

"He only did this so he'd have an excuse to hang out with Giselle."

"Really?" Dion clicked his tongue. "Man, I should've thought of that. Maybe Yasmine and I will come up with another activity for tomorrow."

Theo swallowed his laugh yet couldn't stop his smile from escaping. There weren't very many activities to do in the middle of the woods, but he wasn't about to discourage Dion from trying. "Great idea," Theo said. "What movie are we watching?"

"*Finding Nemo*." Dion nudged Theo to the door. "Speaking of finding things, your girlfriend is missing."

No longer amused, Theo tossed Dion a weak glare. "Will the jokes ever end?"

"Does it matter?" Dion took Theo's arms and physically moved him into the cabin. "I'll save you both a seat!"

Despite Theo appreciating the sentiment, he made certain he didn't react. He liked Penny more than anything—maybe even loved her—but it was embarrassing to discuss that with his friends.

As he made his way upstairs, he brainstormed topics to discuss. They hadn't spoken much since their date last night, and if she was like the girls in his movies, she probably wanted to talk about their relationship.

At the top of the stairs, a small window seat overlooked the driveway and forest beyond. It was a favorite spot for many of the children, but Penny spent the most time there. According to her, it was the best place to watch the sunset.

Which was where Theo found her. She wrote in her journal; her pen eagerly scribbled across the page. The faded red New York sweatshirt she wore was familiar. After all, it belonged to Theo. Due to their height difference, the shirt looked baggy on her small frame. Theo had seen Tara come home with her boyfriend's sweatshirts before; did that make Theo and Penny a real couple?

Once she realized he was staring, she set her journal on the floor and said, "Hey! Care to watch the sunset with me?"

The urge to say, "Yes," gripped Theo's throat. He would watch a million sunsets with her; he'd do whatever she asked. "I would," he said, "but we've got a group activity going on. People are expecting us to make an appearance."

The light in Penny's eyes dimmed. "Of course they are," she muttered, turning to the window. "Why can't they leave us alone?" Suddenly, she grimaced and corrected, "I don't mean that. I meant…I don't know, it's frustrating to be depended on."

As much as he enjoyed their honest conversation, he said, "Maybe we should head outside anyway. In case you haven't noticed, they've been talking about us."

"So? I want them to know how I feel about you."

His pulse staggered. "And *how* do you feel about me?"

Penny grabbed his wrists, her grin sparkling with mischief. "You need to ask?"

"I just like hearing you say it."

"I have a better idea." She tugged him forward until he was sitting on the window seat. As the setting sun cast its orange glow over them, they kissed, covered in the color.

"You always have to distract me," he remarked.

She giggled. "I try."

Being with Penny was a lot easier when Theo had the antidepressants limiting the effects of his powers. His mind was no longer filled with darkness, and he was free to enjoy her company.

Their light, playful kisses melted into lingering, meaningful ones. Theo had been too afraid to admit his feelings—too scared to ask how she felt about him—but right now, he felt loved. He hoped she did, too.

Her body was warm to the touch, filling him with fire everywhere she touched him. She was the sun, the golden morning, the promise of hope in the early dawn.

In contrast, Theo tucked his cold fingers against her back. He was the moon, the inky night, the dread of doom in the misty twilight. In rare moments like this, they'd cross each other's paths and finally have a chance to eclipse.

But in those moments, one always overshadowed the other. As opposites, it was inevitable.

The more Theo's thoughts spiraled, the more he hesitated. Penny deserved the world because she meant the world to him. But how could the moon give the sun anything of value when she was already bright on her own?

Penny stopped and moved to study Theo. "What's with the look?" she asked, squishing his frown. "You're not thinking about the school, are you?"

Dread pitted in Theo's stomach. He wasn't then, but he definitely was now. In unison, his memories unburied themselves and sprang to the surface.

On that last day, Jones had Penny by the throat. He wouldn't release her, not unless he thought he had a reason to. So, Theo feigned hatred for her and acted like he would leave her for dead.

To this moment, Theo remembered Penny's terror. That day, she believed he would hurt her. Not that Theo blamed her. He scared himself.

The best option was to ensure she'd *never* have to be afraid of him. By limiting his powers, he'd remove her reason to fear. The less she saw of the shadows, the better. Then, it'd be easier to accept him. To love him.

Theo shook his head once. The pills were supposed to prevent these dark thoughts from surfacing! They were supposed to stop—

The shadows loomed on the wall.

Penny traced the lines in Theo's forehead, peaking the indentation of his brows. "Did I do something wrong?"

He gulped. "I-I got lost in thought. Not about the school."

"Thinking about the others, hmm?" Penny continued to sketch the details of his face, soothing his sadness with a touch. "I wish you wouldn't. I wish I wouldn't. I wish," her gaze flickered to meet his, "I wish we could be alone forever."

Forever, the dark voice echoed. *How silly. You can't have her forever.* The shadows on the wall slithered onto the seat, almost touching her. Theo tugged her away from them. He tried to ignore the whispers by focusing on Penny, but they grew louder.

Do it, they urged him. *Tell her you want to be with her. Then, it'll only be a matter of time before you snap and hurt her, or she realizes how terrified she is of you.*

Penny brushed her thumbs over his cheeks, making him realize he was crying. Similar tears pooled on her lashes. "You're in pain," she whispered.

At the academy, Theo was forced to ignore Penny to keep her safe. Since the threats of expulsion and Jones were gone, Theo had to worry about himself—the monster she truly feared.

He didn't deserve to be with her. Not here, not like this, not until he learned how to control his powers. Otherwise, his nightmare would become reality.

Penny wasn't the only one in danger, either. Every single person in the cabin was at risk because of Theo's lack of control.

It was best never to get to that point. They could hate him; it didn't matter. Their safety was more important.

Theo's arms tightened around her waist. He pushed his face into her neck, breathing in the perfume of her fruity shampoo. The smell—so familiar, so simple—comforted him. Yet he no longer felt the effect of her healing. She was still touching him, so it should've worked, but there was something within him, rejecting it.

"Penny?" His voice was muffled against her hair. "I'm sorry."

"For what?"

"Everything."

She squeezed him close, enough that he could feel her heart racing against his chest. "You have nothing to apologize for," she said.

He didn't want to close his eyes, because every time he did, he saw darkness. He almost jumped up and turned the light on to diminish the shadows' influence.

Then, she spoke again. "Did I upset you?"

Theo shook his head. "I'm just tired."

"Oh." Her shoulders rose and fell with her deep breaths. "Can I help?"

What was she referring to? His stress? The nightmares? Either way, it was evident she knew how terribly he slept. Being with Penny would undoubtedly help, but after the thoughts he just had, he couldn't stay.

"No," he forced out. "It's my fault."

"Don't say that," she insisted. "I'm not angry."

Blinking away his tears, he clutched the sleeve of her sweatshirt. "I'm so sorry, Penny. Please forgive me."

8

GAME NIGHT

The feeling of loss wasn't an emotion that Penny was accustomed to. Up until last year, her life had been relatively easy. Recently, however, an aching emptiness had attached to her heart, a pain that even her own power could not heal.

When she awoke in the morning, that feeling intensified. Not only had Theo escaped from her last night, but he was keeping a secret from her. About exactly what, Penny couldn't be sure. All she knew was that it was hurting him, and that, in turn, hurt her.

After brushing her teeth, combing her hair, and throwing on a new outfit, she left her room in the direction of Theo's. His door was shut, but she could hear his and Dion's voices trailing out from the crack at the bottom.

"...impossible to ignore," Theo whispered. "They keep bugging me."

Penny pressed her ear into the wall. Was he talking about the kids? Or worse, what if he was talking about her?

Dion huffed something between a sigh and a laugh. "I know what that's like. It'll get better."

"Sometimes I don't believe that."

Penny's stomach churned, not only at the conversation but also from her guilt of eavesdropping. She rapped her knuckles on the door, silencing both boys. Cautiously, Dion opened the door.

"Hey," she greeted. "Can I talk to Theo?"

Behind Dion, Theo's entire body went rigid. "Can't we talk right here?"

"It's kinda personal."

Dion took a step back. "No worries, I can take a hint. I'll be right outside if you guys need me!" The last sentence was clearly directed to Theo, as Dion pointedly looked at him.

The bedroom door shut with a click. "What do you need?" Theo asked.

"I think we should have a discussion." Penny reached out to take his hands, but he recoiled sharply from her touch. The skin around his fingers and nail beds was red, raw, and picked apart.

"Discussion?" he repeated. "About what?"

"About us."

Like he'd seen a ghost, Theo paled. "Not now," he said, slipping past her. "I'm busy."

Penny's frown was impossible to stop. "When will you not be busy?"

"When I'm dead, I guess!" Theo spoke with a chuckle, yet it was far from funny.

"This is serious!" While blinking the tears out of her eyes, Penny said, "I'm worried about you."

Some of Theo's panic faded. A bit of color flushed back into his complexion. "You don't need to worry. I swear."

Penny swallowed. It felt like her throat was burning. "Okay."

"So, are we good?"

Questioning him further would upset him. Penny had to accept that he was lying for a reason. She forced a nod. "As long as you are."

Theo hugged her. However, it was too quick, too distant. "Yep! See you later!"

And with that, he took off out of the room, far away from her. He was lying, about what, remained a mystery. But Penny knew that something was seriously wrong.

Penny didn't see Theo for the rest of the day. Hours passed with endless healing, cooking, and cleaning. After most of the children had gone to bed, or at least retired to their rooms, she was finally able to relax. She entered the living room, finding Theo sitting there with her friends. He had taken one of the recliners, so she took a seat on the couch closest to him.

"We should play a game," Giselle said from her place on the floor. "We could use some fun."

Peter stretched on the cushion beside Penny and snorted loudly. "Let me guess, you're going to suggest Clue? I know there's not a lot of games here, but I'd rather watch paint dry than play with you again."

Before an argument could break out, Yasmine suggested, "One of the kids we saved the other day can read the future. Maybe we should have her read ours."

Everyone froze. Penny was the only one who found her voice. "How do you know that?"

Yasmine fluffed her hair. "She told me. It'd be fun, wouldn't it?"

"No," Theo cut in, "we're not using their powers for entertainment. They're not circus animals."

"We can ask her," Giselle said. "And if she's not comfortable with it, then we'll play Clue!"

As Giselle and Yasmine hustled out of the room, Penny noticed Theo shake his head. On his lap, he held a spiral notebook, where he'd been documenting the people in the cabin, from name to superpower. He flipped to the section with the girl and angled it in Penny's direction.

"Her name is Jade," he said. "She's thirteen years old and has five other siblings."

Penny's eyes widened. "That's a big family."

"Definitely." Theo flipped his notebook closed and must've caught sight of Penny's frown, because he asked, "What's wrong?"

Many things were wrong. This was just the tip of the iceberg. "It makes me think of my own parents," Penny admitted. "None of us has seen our families for such a long time. I...I miss them."

Theo patted her hand, yet his touch was hardly there. "Me too."

Suddenly, Yasmine and Giselle returned, this time with Jade in tow. Her black hair draped down her back in a sheet of midnight, almost reaching her waist. Much to Penny's surprise, the girl's hypnotic green eyes were alight with excitement, nearly matching that of Yasmine's.

"Hi, guys!" Jade waved. "I'm Jade Myers, and I heard you want to have your futures read!"

"You're okay with this?" Theo asked. "It doesn't feel like we're using you?"

Jade's black brows drew together. "Should it?"

"Absolutely not!" Yasmine positioned herself between Jade and Theo. "How does this work?"

Jade tapped her chin. "Well, I think we should conduct these readings in private. Sometimes, futures are really specific, and I'd hate to expose anybody."

Penny glanced at Theo, but he didn't look at her.

"Any particular room?" Peter inquired.

"One with limited lighting and a comfortable place to sit. That'll help me concentrate."

"I know just the place." Peter stood to escort Jade out of the room, yet she paused to add, "You guys shouldn't expect your future to be exactly like I say. It depends on the choices you make."

Yasmine swatted the air in a dismissive motion. "Blah, blah, warnings and all that jazz. I'm first!"

As the trio left the room, Penny fiddled with her hands. Growing up, she always believed in fate. But having her future exposed was like cheating destiny. It might lead to heartbreak.

Something weighed on her shoulder. Thinking it was Theo, she swiveled to the side, yet he remained engrossed in his notes. Penny scratched her shoulder and faced the front. No one else was sitting near her; what had touched her?

Again, the same sensation tickled her neck. As she turned, she spotted the shadows behind the couch shifting. Although their brushes weren't harsh, she shivered. She had never seen them move without Theo's direct manipulation. Was this his subconscious trying to reach out to her?

Yasmine re-entered the room, and a cacophony of questions exploded. "How'd it go?" Felix inquired.

"What did you hear?" Giselle asked.

"Who are you getting married to?" Dion chimed in.

While Yasmine crossed her arms, the slightest smirk teased her lips. "I want to keep my results a secret. I'd hate to lose out on my wonderful future." She beckoned to Penny, saying, "Jade wants to see you next."

Everyone's attention zeroed in on Penny, making her blush. "Me? Why?"

"I don't know. She just said she felt your 'aura.'" Yasmine crooked her fingers in air quotes.

When Penny moved to stand, Theo said, "You really believe in this stuff?"

"It's her *superpower*. Clearly, there has to be some truth to what she says."

"Futures can change in the blink of an eye," he pointed out. "You'll be setting yourself up for disappointment."

His dreary, melancholy ideals almost convinced Penny to sit down, but her curiosity won, and she declared, "What you call disappointment, I call hope."

Penny followed Yasmine through the halls and into the front room. The curtains were drawn, and the lights were dimmed, casting an eerie yet comforting yellow haze in the room. On the floor, Jade sat cross-legged, surrounded by pillows and blankets. Without opening her eyes, she waved Penny closer. Slightly unnerved by the silence, she sat across from Jade on a pillow.

Jade took Penny's hand, and a cold feeling consumed her. Time practically froze, leaving them in the space between. "Penelope Nicole Bradshaw," Jade began, her voice echoing and wistful, "there are many futures in your path. Your capabilities make you valuable, both to the world and to your friends."

Penny's posture straightened, pleased to hear such kind words.

"However," Jade continued, "there are two most likely directions. There's someone in your life who you desperately want to heal. But it won't work."

Instantly, Penny's smile fell. "What do you mean?"

"Your healing won't affect them. If you continue to push it on them, your future will end in broken relationships, sadness, and loss."

No names were mentioned. Regardless, Penny knew they were talking about Theo. She cleared her throat. "Am I supposed to quit, then?"

"Your love for them will be tested, as will theirs for you. If you decide to stay together, your future will end in happiness. But be warned. This path is long and difficult. Achieving this will take time. You must decide how much you're willing to fight to get what you want."

Jade released Penny, and the icy feeling disappeared. Now, a different chill had taken hold of her. Slowly, she climbed to her feet and exited the room.

As soon as she entered the hall, she spotted Theo against the wall. He noticed her too, and asked, "How'd it go?"

Almost annoyed at the question, Penny pursed her lips. Her healing was the one skill she had in the cabin, and yet, it wasn't working on him. Was he resisting it somehow? And if so, why?

"It was nice," she answered. "Pretty basic stuff."

"Cool," he said, nervously shifting his weight. "So, um, listen, I was thinking about what you said—about having hope." His blue eyes drifted to meet hers. "Will you go in with me?"

Unable to contain her surprise, Penny's jaw dropped. "You don't want to do it alone?"

"Honestly, I'm a bit nervous. I don't want to go in there, but I also can't live without knowing what the future has in store for me." Carefully, he reached for her arm, a whisper of a touch. "It'd be easier if you were there with me."

And just like that, his raw transparency melted Penny's frigid heart. Jade's prophecy was wrong; nothing would break Theo and Penny apart. "I'd love to," she said.

Together, they walked into the fortress of pillows and sat side by side in front of Jade. At the displacement of weight, her forehead wrinkled a little. Still, she grabbed Theo's free hand.

Penny scooted closer to him, her bones thrumming with anticipation. Would he defeat Principal Jones and bring peace? Or would he be with Penny forever?

Jade's lips moved. She fidgeted in her seat—the picture of unease. Suddenly, her eyes flew open, shocking Theo into falling backward. Her voice echoed throughout the room as she said, "Theodore Alexander Palmer, you will be consumed by darkness."

9

THE SHADOW

Theo stormed out of the front room, slamming the doors open and startling Jade from her prophetic concentration. Instead of assisting her, Penny followed Theo.

"I knew I shouldn't have done this!" he exclaimed, stomping outside. The night air slammed into him, eliciting goosebumps across his arms. "Knowing that my future gets worse is so inspiring!"

On the porch steps, Penny pulled him to a stop. "You don't know that! Maybe there was a mistake!"

"A mistake? How could there be a mistake? She's reading the *future*, Penny. The only mistake I made was sitting down to hear this junk!"

"You said it yourself—futures can change! We can fix this!"

She's lying. I can't change who I am.

The shadows on the grass twisted up Theo's legs, immobilizing him. Another slunk to the front door, easing it shut. Penny moved, seeing the darkness dissipate. Her face lifted, catching the moonlight. "I'm not afraid of you," she said.

So she claimed, but the tiniest hint of hesitation caught her, making her pause for half a second.

"I want to be alone," Theo answered, nodding to the closed door. "Please, give me a minute to myself."

Carefully, he backed away from her. The shadows pushed against him, limiting his speed, yet he ventured into the forest. Once he couldn't see the cabin, he sat against a tree trunk, watching the wind blow through the sycamore leaves. Unlike Long Island, where people and cars were everywhere, here, the only noise came from chirping, howling animals, singing together in harmony. He almost liked it more than home. The quiet simplicity, the beauty of nature. It'd be perfect were it not for the weight on his shoulders.

What did Jade mean by "consumed by darkness?" Was it because of his powers? Or was it something much, *much* worse?

He buried his head in his knees. Though he hated thinking about it, he considered the possibility of turning evil. Jade could've meant it to be metaphorical. They often referred to Principal Jones as being a dark person. If that was to be Theo's future, then he had to ensure he wouldn't hurt anyone close to him. Perhaps if he fled the cabin, he could protect his friends. Then again, that might've been what led him to darkness.

Theo's eyes burned. He wished he could worry about things that didn't matter; things that normal teenagers worried about. Life shouldn't have been this complicated.

A sound from behind Theo pricked his senses, but he didn't turn around. It wasn't until the unknown sound slipped and swore, its voice identical to…

"Dion?" Theo shifted to see his friend standing in the mud.

"Oh, hey!" Dion sat next to Theo, suddenly forgetting about his dirty shoes. "Mind scooting over?" He swept the shadows surrounding Theo, and a few of them faded, but the others remained.

"You shouldn't be out here with me," Theo said.

"Who else am I going to play with?" Dion reached into his pocket and displayed a deck of cartoonish Go Fish cards, similar to the deck he owned at the academy.

Without thinking, Theo burst into laughter. As he accepted his cards, he said, "Thanks, Dion. I'm glad you have the hobbies of a child."

"Don't be jealous that I'm better at this game than you." Dion organized his stack. "Do you want to talk?"

The abrupt shift in tone muted Theo's mood. He shook his head.

"Then, I'll talk. Jade might've said you'll be consumed by darkness, but I refuse to let it happen."

Let it happen? The shadows laughed. *No one can stop the inevitability of the future.*

Darkness perched on Theo's shoulder, forcing him to shake it off. But their claws were already deep, squeezing his throat. The trees rustled above him, restless with the shadows. Not even the stars could be spotted through their thick leaves, removing Theo's last possible failsafe.

He released his cards to hold his head. They fluttered to the dirt like fallen butterflies, dejected and broken.

Dion's afraid of you, too, those horrible voices insisted.

No, Theo told himself. Dion had never shown the slightest hint of terror toward Theo. On every mission, during every training, Dion was the only person who never shied away from Theo's powers. Plus, he came out here *alone*. He had been trusted with every secret, including the ones that made Theo look like a monster.

Everyone, except Dion, feared Theo.

Theo caught his breath. Gradually, his pulse slowed. The darkness shrank into their original places, with a few to linger around his feet. To test his theory, he flicked a finger in Dion's direction, allowing a shadow to slink over the cards. Hardly blinking, Dion said, "Quit trying to cheat."

"You're braver than me," Theo answered.

"Not really. I could never save a bus full of children."

"No, but you could face the Boogeyman."

Dion's expression steeled. Finally, he lowered his cards and stated, "I'm not afraid because that's not who you are."

"The darkness doesn't scare you?"

"You use your powers to help people. That's how I know you're good. You will *never* be lost, Theo, not while I'm here."

The shadows conceded. The dark thoughts abandoned Theo's mind, allowing him a rare moment of clarity. With Penny, he felt healed. Comfortable. She could take his pain and transform it into joy, into love, into light.

With Dion, Theo felt content. Understood. There were some afflictions that Dion could fix because he knew what it was like to feel dark, to feel like a monster, to feel like one didn't deserve to be alive.

Maybe there is good in my powers, Theo realized. *Maybe there doesn't have to be sadness all the time.*

"Since when did you start spouting such sage advice?" he teased, retrieving his cards.

"Since forever! Have you not been listening?"

They laughed. The future Theo dreaded had floated away, and for this small, yet precious glimpse of time, he enjoyed being in the shadows.

10

ALONE BUT TOGETHER

Despite only sleeping a few hours, Theo awoke before anyone else. He squished the dark circles under his eyelids, wishing he had concealer to cover them. Although his friends would probably tease him for owning makeup, he couldn't stand to see himself like this—so messy and tired.

Once the sun rose, everyone else gradually awakened. The morning dragged by as it always did, with him having to console a crying child or restrain Dion from eating more than his fair share.

Theo cleared the table from breakfast, stacking the bowls to make them easier to carry. An abrupt, searing bolt of pain shot through his head, throbbing at the temples. His knuckles whitened on the dishes. He wouldn't let a migraine stop him from doing his job.

Jade tiptoed toward him, her black hair hiding her face. "I'm sorry about what I said yesterday," she squeaked.

"Don't sweat it," Theo said. "Futures can change. I'm sure there were a thousand different options for me."

Jade forced her stiff neck into a nod. His curiosity lingered, so to satisfy it, he said, "Was I in Penny's future?"

"I'm not allowed to say."

"Right, duh." Hoping to escape the conversation, Theo carried the bowls to the sink.

"If you need help," she said, "let me know!"

He waved goodbye to her, then rolled his sleeves to wash the dishes. *Why do you care so much about Penny's future?* He asked himself. *You know you're not going to be a part of it, not at this rate. You're on the path to be consumed by darkness, and you really want to keep dragging her down with you? It would be better if you—*

Trying to silence himself, Theo deliberately turned the water to a scalding temperature. He grimaced, both from the hot water and from his worsening headache.

Abruptly, someone's arms entwined around his waist, and a familiar healing flooded his body. His tense muscles relaxed. But only momentarily.

He ripped out of Penny's grasp, the force of his strength sending him stumbling into the sink. Penny shrank, out of embarrassment or disappointment, he didn't know. "What's wrong?" she inquired, as gently as ever.

"I've got a headache," he snapped. Part of his frustration stemmed from the pain, but the other part, the part he wished would disappear, sprouted from the need to be far away from her.

Her determination didn't change. In fact, she brightened upon hearing he needed help. "Want me to make it better?"

"No thanks." He nudged her aside to wash the dishes, feeling his heart banging against his ribs. *Please go,* he mentally begged her. *I hate this feeling; I hate what I'm doing, but I don't want to hurt you.*

Penny pressed a playful kiss to his jaw, then another on his temple. When he didn't react, she tilted his face to the side and kissed him on the lips.

He jerked away. "What do you need, Penny?"

She giggled. "I need you to smile!"

"Okay, well, can we do this later? I'm trying to work, and you're being very disruptive."

"Come on, we haven't had time together. Can't you—?"

"*Enough*, Penny! Leave me alone!"

Almost immediately, her eyes filled to the brim with tears. As she drew her arms around herself, she faced the wall.

Regret flushed the anger out, consuming Theo in its toxic wave. "I'm sorry," he offered, much softer. "I didn't mean to yell."

Reluctantly, she turned to him. "I shouldn't have bothered you."

Without thinking, he grabbed her wrist. He must've moved too roughly, because she winced. "You weren't bothering me, honestly! I'm glad you're here! I love being around you!"

Penny held her wrist. Her gaze never left the ground. "I was just trying to heal you."

"And you can! I-I mean, if you want to, it will certainly help me feel better."

She hesitated, then touched his head with her hand. Within seconds, the pain dissipated, taking his migraine and negative thoughts with it. "Thank you," he whispered.

"Is that better?"

"Very much. Can I hug you?"

Penny's sadness melted into softness. "Of course you can."

He wrapped her into his chest, shut his eyes, and imagined he wasn't in the cabin. Instead, he and Penny were somewhere far away, preferably in the city. There were no super-powered kids to worry about, no plans to make, or world to save. He imagined he was happy, safe, and thriving, with or without powers.

It was just him and Penny. Alone but together.

She exhaled deeply, her breath ruffling his shirt. "You know, there's a lot of good that's come from escaping the school."

"But?"

Penny drew back so he could see her sad grin. "Sometimes I wish I'd accepted your offer to leave at the beach. Maybe then I'd see my parents again."

Theo's stomach rocked. This was the perfect moment to reveal his secrets to her—to admit he'd kept in touch with his family.

Until a small hand tugged on the hem of his shirt, startling him into releasing Penny. One of the younger boys stood behind him, sniffling. "Excuse me, sir," he said, "but my finger hurts really bad."

Penny knelt in front of him. "What happened?"

"I was climbing the trees with the older kids and got a splinter!" Tearfully, the boy extended his finger, showing off a sliver barely bigger than a millimeter.

Regardless, Penny took the boy into her arms and retrieved a pair of tweezers from one of the drawers. With the splinter removed, the boy returned outside, good as new. Being so eager to help was a quality Theo loved about Penny, but he didn't like it very much at the moment.

He stepped back and stumbled directly into someone else. "Nice going," Carter growled, brushing off his shirt. "Do you even know how to walk?"

Theo conjured a dozen comebacks, yet before he could use a single one, Carter nodded at the hall and added, "We've got a big problem. Dion's in the surveillance room and—"

Theo shoved past Carter; Penny followed close behind. A big problem could mean anything, especially when it involved the cameras. After Dion's cousin died years ago, the cabin had been outfitted with surveillance both inside and outside, with a few hiding in the trees.

The room was located on the ground floor and should have been considered more of a closet than a room. Theo slammed the door open, spooking Dion and Peter, who waited inside.

"What's going on?" Theo blurted, glancing between the double monitors on the desk.

"Aiden's gone missing," Dion said.

When confusion contorted Theo's brows rather than recognition, Dion added, "The super-speed kid from school. We just saw it on the news. His aunt said she last saw him going to the store."

"In New York," Peter finished.

Feeling as though he might topple over, Theo grabbed onto Penny. "How were they able to find him?" he asked. "If they caught Aiden, then we don't stand a chance."

"We have something he didn't," Dion pointed out. "We've got a team. We're not going solo on this."

Everyone glanced at Theo at that part, but he pretended he didn't notice. Jones was able to catch the fastest person on the planet. The cabin no longer felt like a haven. It was a ticking time bomb.

The darkness on the floor pooled around Theo's feet. *Killing Jones will protect them. You're capable of murder.*

Theo clenched his fists. The letter to his mother had been sent days ago. Surely, she would've answered by now, sending Theo all the available information on Dad. "I'm going into town to look for supplies," Theo announced. "We're low on food."

"Can I go with you?" Penny asked.

"No," he answered, perhaps too quickly. "I'll be back before you know it."

"That's not a good idea," Peter tried to say. "Being alone is—"

"I said I'll handle it!" The lightbulbs on the ceiling shorted out, and his friends recoiled. Without wasting time on a goodbye, Theo left the room. Chances were that his new medication was in Mom's package. As soon as he had those, he would be back to normal.

He just had to hurry.

11

OUT OF SIGHT

While waiting for the mail to be delivered, Theo visited the grocery store. It was barely stocked with produce, frozen dinners, chips, and other preservative foods. Rather than look for snacks, he crouched in front of the gray toy machines at the front. For fifty cents, he could purchase a bouncy ball or a piece of jewelry. The prospect of the ball was enticing, certainly to entertain him while he was here today, but his eyes kept catching on the jewelry.

He dug into his pocket, hoping for spare change, yet he was only fooling himself. He'd left every scrap of money at the cabin. Returning without supplies would spark suspicion, and an interrogation would inevitably follow.

A young mother entered the store, simultaneously carrying a baby and holding her toddler's hand. Instantly, Theo averted his face. If any of the workers had ever recognized him, then they'd never snitched. That assurance didn't extend to strangers.

As the family walked behind Theo, the toddler dug her heels into the floor. "Mommy, wait! Can I get a prize?"

In unison, the infant began to cry. "Oh, okay," the mom said, sighing, "make it quick." She dropped her purse into the toddler's grasp, then left to wander the store.

The little girl dumped the contents of her mom's purse onto the floor, then touched a few random coins. Before she could call for help, Theo knelt and whispered, "Here." He selected two quarters and handed them to her, adding, "You put these in the slot."

Giddy with excitement, the girl skipped to the bouncy ball machine and turned the dial. It clacked and clanked, moving slowly from its old age. Finally, her reward spilled forth. A shiny blue ball dropped from the machine, eliciting a shriek of delight from the girl.

"Thanks," she said, showing it off to Theo. "You want one?"

"Yes, I would."

She handed him the remaining quarters from the ground, packed the rest of her mother's money, and waved goodbye. Then, she chased her ball around the store.

Theo stared at the silver in his palm. Logically, it was a better idea to save the money, regardless of how little it was. But he was already inserting the coins into the jewelry machine and twisting the knob until he received what he desired.

The door dinged again, and on instinct, he glanced over. A bearded man in camouflage entered. Many of the people in town were hunters, so his appearance wasn't off-putting, but the shadows stirred beneath Theo's feet.

Immediately, his head dropped. He fiddled with the knob on the machine, feigning distraction. It put him facing away from the man, forcing Theo to tune into his hearing.

The man hardly made a sound, except for his boots scuffing the floor. He walked with purpose; clearly, he was here for one reason only. In the corner of Theo's left eye, he spotted the man approach the cashier. He pulled a wrinkled paper from his pocket and slapped it onto the counter, saying, "Have you seen this boy?"

Theo's stomach dropped, almost bringing him to a seated position. *Maybe it's not me,* he tried to convince himself.

"Isn't that Theodore Palmer?" the female cashier asked.

"My people call him 'Nightwave.'"

Theo staggered to catch his balance. *Okay, they're definitely talking about me.* The darkness teased his shoelaces, urging him to disappear, but he couldn't risk it. Too many people had seen him enter the store; if he randomly faded away, there'd be questions. Slowly, he crept behind a shelf.

"Is he dangerous?"

"Very. That's why I'm here." Theo could hear the man lean onto the counter, based on its squeak of protest. "My boss is looking to turn this world into a safer place. He'd be extremely pleased if you assisted him in that journey."

Theo clutched onto the shelf to keep standing. His brain swirled with panicked ideas, all dependent on the woman's answer. Would the supers have to pack and leave tonight? Where would they go? What if Jones was already on his way?

"Can't say I've seen him," the cashier finally said, her voice light with naivety. "It's a small town—folks come and go so quickly."

The man grunted. "Are you sure?"

"I haven't seen him either," the mother interjected. "And my family has lived here for decades. We know everyone."

"Yep!" the little girl chimed in, bouncing her ball.

The man crumpled his paper and muttered a reluctant, "Thank you," before trudging out of the store. Theo pressed himself amongst the chips, concealing his body the best he could. Once the man could no longer be seen through the windows, Theo allowed himself to exhale. To think, Jones was *this* close to finding them. Thanks to this woman's help, he'd look right over this little forest town.

Securing the ring in his pocket, he abandoned his hiding place and walked right in the line of sight of the cashier. She hardly blinked at him, just gave him a wave and a, "Have a nice day!"

He raised his hand in a weak wave. Fortunately, some humans still supported him. However, the same couldn't be said for everyone, so he faded into the shadows and lingered outside the post office.

Hours dragged by. He could've returned to the cabin, yet every time he prepared to make the trip back, his anxiety insisted, *The second you leave, the mail will get delivered. You can't go home without your medicine.*

So, he watched as tourists and distant neighbors shopped. According to Dion, the town spanned a few dozen miles, but every other cabin was too far from theirs.

The pink toy capsule rested heavily in his pocket. He figured that if he gave it to Penny, it'd relieve some of the guilt plaguing him.

At the last shimmering beams of sunlight, the mail truck arrived. While the delivery driver lugged boxes inside the shop, Theo separated from the darkness and hurried to the back of the van. To avoid suspicion, he and his family used a fake name for him: Thomas Partridge, which was the name plastered across a box along the wall. Mission accomplished.

Now, he had to complete a much more difficult task: Sneak into the cabin without being seen.

Theo crept around the tripwires and traps scattered around the forest. The team had purposely left the forest floor undisturbed. Every walking trail had to be different to prevent creating a path. Leaves and sticks were scattered everywhere, so that any attempt to catch them by surprise would be foiled. Theo resorted to walking very carefully, which also meant very slowly. His pulse thrummed with excitement as he wondered what awaited him in the box. Secret plans from his father? Tips on how to use their powers? The possibilities were endless!

His impatience got the better of him, and he quickened his pace. The tip of his foot caught on a string, but he managed to leap out of the way before the trap pinned him to the ground. He stumbled through the leaves, cracking and snapping twigs underneath every step. Finally, he caught himself and froze, his eyes squeezed shut as if it would make him invisible.

A few moments passed, the only sounds coming from Theo's pounding heart. Suddenly, a bright white flashlight cut through the trees. He almost ran or disappeared into the shadows, but he couldn't move.

"Stop right there!" Felix shouted. "Don't take another step, or I'll shoot!" He stalked closer, holding his gun exactly like they practiced. In another situation, Theo would've been proud.

Felix barked, "Drop what you're holding and put your hands up!" Then, the glare of the flashlight shifted downward, and his face came into view. "Whoa, wait. Theo? What are you doing out here?" His gaze lowered, and his tone changed. "What's in the box?"

At the mention, Theo held the package closer. "Supplies."

"Really? Let me see."

When Felix reached forth, Theo yanked away. Even if Theo managed to slip past this conversation, Felix would pester him about it for days. Theo looked at the dirt and whispered, "It's from my mom."

A quiet curse huffed from Felix's mouth. "You're talking to her? I thought we weren't allowed to do that."

"We're not. I just—I needed her."

"Oh." Felix toyed with his gun, flipping the safety on. "Does Penny know?"

In a similar anxious habit, Theo picked at the tape on the side of the box. If she knew he lied, she would be so disappointed. So upset. So betrayed. Theo wouldn't be able to handle that, not for an instant.

"It's complicated," he said aloud.

Felix whistled a low tune. "Never in a million years would I guess that you'd go behind everyone's back. You always act like you've got it under control. Apparently, you don't."

Darkness tangled in Theo's shoelaces, tugging them loose. *He can't talk to you like that. He's going to use this as blackmail; once a bully, always a bully. Attack him; teach him a lesson!*

"I know a bit about pretending, too," Felix continued, much quieter. "My mom sent me to the Academy for Young Supervillains to straighten me out—teach me how to be a good kid. It killed me to know that my own mother saw me as a bad person. So, I embraced it. Being tough is better than being hurt." He kicked a stick with his boot. "I don't say this nearly as often as I should, but I'm sorry for how I treated you. You deserved better."

For Theo's whole life, he felt like he was split into two sides: human and super. His human side was marked by gushy emotions, such as empathy and foolishness. His super side was reserved for his instincts, his knowledge, and his practicality. At that moment, the two sides connected.

"I know I'm wrong," Theo said. "I need my own time to be honest."

Felix nodded. "Well, then, okay."

"Okay, what?"

"I'll tell you one of my secrets, then you know I won't tell yours."

"Please, Felix, that isn't necessary."

"You saved my life at the academy even when I was a jerk to you, so this is how I'll pay the favor forward." Felix cleared his throat. His balance rocked. Finally, he admitted, "I'm not really a super."

The box dropped from Theo's grasp.

Felix thrust his hands out, hurriedly explaining, "Not like that! I mean, I *am* a super but not like you and the others. According to my mom, I inherited my powers from my great-grandfather, making my genes very weak. I've only been able to use my powers once in my whole life, and she still sent me to the academy. I didn't fit in there, and I don't fit in here, so I'm glad you've accepted me." Felix smiled. "It's my turn to do the same for you."

Theo's mind reeled. The explanation made perfect sense—why Felix had never used his power at the school. He simply couldn't. According to Lily, powers were a recessive gene, much like blue eyes or red hair. The farther back the inherited DNA, the weaker the powers would be. Unlike Theo, who gained his powers from his father, Felix had a great-grandfather to thank for his powers.

"What happened the first time you used them?" Theo asked.

"All I can remember is it was a moment of life and death." Felix blew out a long stream of air. "And I did it for my sister."

Theo retrieved his package and squeezed it to his chest, recalling his own sister. Intense emotions made him more powerful, too, so that might be the only way Felix could use his. Hopefully, someday, it'd work with him.

"Thank you," Theo said. "Let's keep each other's secrets."

"Sure. You should probably get inside before anyone else notices you."

Theo started off, until Felix called out, "Why didn't you use your powers? I never would've seen you coming!"

Theo echoed back a shaky laugh. If Felix knew the truth, or anyone, for that matter, Theo would no longer be the one to depend on.

When Theo reentered his room, Dion and Peter were sound asleep. The curtains had been drawn over the windows, and if it hadn't been for Theo's ability to see through the dark, he would've tripped.

Upon opening the box, he found his new bottle of antidepressants resting on top of the other items. The name on the side read, "Tara Palmer." Although she loathed the idea of having to retrieve medicine in her name—especially considering the pitied looks she received—it was the safest bet to ensure Theo couldn't be tracked.

Within seconds, he shook a pill into his palm, swallowed it, and calmed his mind. He couldn't understand why he'd been so hesitant to take these when he was younger. They made him feel normal. Wasn't that what everyone wanted?

He rummaged through the other items, finding two envelopes of cash. The large withdrawals might have looked suspicious on Mom's part, but they were necessary to prevent creating a credit card trail. Beneath the money, he retrieved his mother's newest magazine. The last time he checked the news, he discovered his mother was suing the school for "reckless endangerment," as well as a few other dozen claims. Principal Jones must not have liked that, but he hadn't spoken out against them. Yet. For now, it seemed, Theo's family would remain safe.

Theo flipped a page in the magazine and grinned. Royal blue gowns and intricately designed silver tiaras decorated the paper. Camilla created each one.

A few weeks after the school was abandoned, Theo had returned to sift through the remains. By some miracle, he'd found Camilla's stash of notebooks, each one filled to the brim with fashion designs. Although some of the books were charred and black, he sent the salvageable ones to his mother.

Camilla may have been lost to the academy, but she'd be remembered forever in her work.

Setting aside the magazine, he found a crisp, white letter. Based on the purple text and doodles in the corners, it was from Tara.

T-Bear,

First of all, I'm supposed to worry about you. You're not safe out there. This would be easier if you came home. The police don't have to know.

In other news, I have had no luck in finding a boyfriend. M has kept me busy. Plus, it's next to impossible to find a guy who's comfortable dating the sister of a suspected outlaw.

Speaking of romance, how is your girlfriend? M and I found a picture of her on the internet. How did you manage to get someone that cute? Maybe she doesn't know how dorky you are yet.

Theo rolled his eyes yet felt a blush burning his cheeks. He regretted telling his family about Penny. It was all they wanted to talk about anymore.

I'll move out as soon as you return. I can't leave M alone, especially now. She'd fall apart. Her letter is short this time because she's working on the magazine and digging up dirt on the school. She misses you a lot. I do too, though definitely not as much as she does. She spends so much time in your room.

By the way, there's nothing wrong with growing up. No matter how old you get, you'll always be my little brother.

Talk to you soon. Love, T

In that same envelope, a cream-colored letter from his mother read,

T-Bear-

This is all I could find of your father. I'm sorry to say, but I don't know what you'll discover in here. I've never been able to muster the courage to read his private journals. They remind me too much of him. Regardless, I hope this helps.

Love, M

Theo hugged the letter, imagining he was embracing her instead.

He regretted ever dodging one of her hugs or kisses—regretted that he ever thought it was embarrassing.

Inside the box were several notebooks and other loose-leaf transcripts. Theo lifted the first one out, situated to get more comfortable, and cracked the journal open. A folded slip of paper drifted from the cover of the spine before fluttering to the floor.

He dove to catch it, creaking the bed in his sharp movement. Dion stirred. His breathing sounded shallow, more gasping than actual breaths. Whispering incoherently, he tossed in his bed, his voice croaking.

Slowly, Theo crawled into his own corner yet couldn't stop listening to Dion's nightmare. Whatever he was dreaming about must've been intense. Once Dion stopped mumbling, Theo opened the note from the journal.

TEDDY—
IF YOU'RE READING THIS, IT MUST MEAN I'M DEAD. I'M GOING TO ASSUME YOUR MOTHER TOLD YOU ABOUT OUR SHARED POWERS. TARA AND I WISH YOU KNEW SOONER, BUT MOM WANTED TO WAIT UNTIL YOU WERE OLDER. FOR WHAT IT'S WORTH, I'M SURE YOU'LL GROW UP TO BE SPECTACULAR.

Theo stopped. Months ago at the school, Mom admitted that Dad had been a super, sharing his powers with Theo. Not only had his parents hidden the secret, but Tara did, too. At least she *wanted* Theo to know. Perhaps that was why she was constantly at odds with Mom; the two disagreed on how Theo should've been raised.

He continued reading.

THIS LIFE OF OURS IS DIFFICULT. OUR POWER IS DANGEROUS. MUCH LIKE ANY OTHER POWER, IT CAN CORRUPT. YOU

MUST REMEMBER TO CONTROL IT; OTHERWISE, IT WILL
CONTROL YOU.

I WISH I COULD'VE TAUGHT YOU SOME OF MY TRICKS. MANY
OF THEM ARE DIFFICULT TO EXPLAIN IN WRITING ALTHOUGH I
HAVE ATTEMPTED TO DO SO IN THIS JOURNAL. I HOPE YOU USE
THIS ABILITY TO HELP PEOPLE.

ALWAYS LEAD WITH YOUR HEART. IT'S YOUR GREATEST
SUPERPOWER.

TAKE CARE OF MOM AND TARA FOR ME. I LOVE YOU.
—DAD

Theo folded the letter and set it in the box. He expected to be crying after reading his dad's words or maybe feel a little frustrated, but he didn't feel anything. That might have been a result of using medication. Regardless, Theo shifted his attention to the journal. It had been dated all the way back to when his dad attended the Academy for Young Superheroes. Theo poured over every word.

AUGUST 24:
TODAY IS MY FIRST DAY AT THE ACADEMY FOR YOUNG
SUPERHEROES. PART OF ME CAN'T BELIEVE I JUST SAID
THAT. AFTER ALL MY HARD WORK, IT'S FINALLY PAYING OFF.
TO THINK—SOMEDAY SOON, I'LL BE FAMOUS!

Theo had to smile at that. Clearly, he was more alike to his father than he realized.

For almost three pages, Dad talked about Mom: How sad he was to leave her, how scared he was of her finding someone else, and how much he loved her.

A few pages later, the vibe altered from sweet—slightly corny— hopeless romanticism to apprehensive anxiety.

AUGUST 30:

TODAY, I SAT ALONE AGAIN AT LUNCH. THERE ARE ABOUT A COUPLE DOZEN STUDENTS HERE, WHICH MAKES SENSE. EVEN IN THE FOUNDERS' TIME, THIS ACADEMY WASN'T VERY POPULAR. HEROES ARE HARD TO COME BY THESE DAYS, BUT THAT WON'T STOP ME FROM TRYING.

I WAS FEELING LIKE A LOSER UNTIL SOMEONE SAT NEXT TO ME. IT WAS THE NEW PRINCIPAL, JASON JONES. ODD FOR HIM TO MINGLE AMONGST HIS STUDENTS, BUT I APPRECIATED HIS COMPANY. HE'S LIKE THE BROTHER I NEVER HAD. WELL, HE ALREADY HAS A BROTHER, BUT JASON EXPLAINED THAT THEIR RELATIONSHIP IS...COMPLICATED.

I CONFESSED HOW NERVOUS I WAS, AND HE SHARED HIS OWN SECRET. HE'S HUMAN. HIS FATHER CONCEALED THAT FACT, SUPPOSEDLY TO PROTECT JASON FROM SCRUTINY. DESPITE THAT, HE RUNS THE SCHOOL WITH REMARKABLE EASE. JASON WISHES HE WERE INVINCIBLE LIKE HIS BROTHER AND LATE FATHER, AND SAID, "MAYBE THEN, PEOPLE WILL LISTEN TO ME." I HOPE WE'LL CONTINUE TO BE FRIENDS.

SEPTEMBER 15:

JASON IS USUALLY VERY QUIET, BUT TODAY, HE TOLD ME MORE ABOUT HIMSELF. HIS PARENTS ARE DECEASED; HE HAS AN OLDER BROTHER; AND HE IS MARRIED TO A WOMAN NAMED SAMANTHA. IN RETURN, I TOLD HIM ABOUT TERESA. HE MADE ME PROMISE TO WRITE HER, SO I DID. I HOPE SHE RECEIVES MY LETTERS AND KNOWS HOW MUCH I CARE ABOUT HER.

Theo readjusted his seating as he felt the toy capsule dig into his thigh. Dad spoke of Mom so tenderly; it was apparent they were in love.

SEPTEMBER 29:

TERESA WROTE TO ME TODAY. AS I WAS COMPOSING A

MESSAGE BACK TO HER, A STUDENT SPOTTED ME AND ACCUSED ME OF BREAKING THE RULES. I EXPLAINED I WAS WRITING A LETTER, WHICH WE COULD ALL DO, BUT SHE CLAIMED SHE HADN'T BEEN ALLOWED TO WRITE TO HER FAMILY SINCE SHE HAD INSULTED JASON. I COULDN'T FATHOM IT. I WANTED TO ASK HER MORE ABOUT IT, BUT THE NEXT DAY, SHE WAS GONE. A CLASSMATE SAID TO ME, "SHE OFFENDED THE PRINCIPAL. HE DOESN'T TAKE THAT STUFF LYING DOWN." SOME STUDENTS SAY THAT JASON WAS THE CULPRIT OF HIS FATHER'S DEATH, ALLOWING JASON THE OPPORTUNITY TO TAKE CONTROL OF THE SCHOOL. OTHERS CLAIM THAT HIS MURDERS HAVEN'T ENDED. I DON'T BELIEVE A WORD OF IT. THE STUDENTS WHO TELL SUCH TERRIBLE STORIES ARE NEGLIGENT, BRASH, AND RUDE. I'M SURE THEY'RE MAKING UP LIES FOR ATTENTION.

NOVEMBER 20:
JASON'S BROTHER, AARON, INTERRUPTED OUR TRAINING CLASS TO ARGUE. THEY WERE TALKING ABOUT THEIR FATHER, ABOUT SUPERS, AND ABOUT WHO DESERVED WHAT. I DIDN'T HEAR MUCH OF WHAT THEY SAID, BUT I COULD FEEL THEIR HATRED FOR EACH OTHER. IT'S ONLY A MATTER OF TIME BEFORE ONE OF THEM DOES SOMETHING THAT THEY'LL REGRET.

NOVEMBER 30:
AARON VISITS THE SCHOOL FREQUENTLY. I BET HE BELIEVES THAT HE SHOULD'VE INHERITED IT INSTEAD OF JASON.

DECEMBER 17:
TODAY AT LUNCH, AARON WALKED RIGHT THROUGH THE FRONT DOOR AND SLAPPED A STACK OF PAPERS INTO JASON'S FACE. HE INQUIRED ABOUT THE WHEREABOUTS OF ONE OF MY PAST CLASSMATES, CLAIMING THAT THERE WAS NO INFORMATION ON HER. JASON IGNORED EVERY QUESTION.

When he didn't answer, Aaron said, "You always were jealous of us."

No one else knows about Jason's human heritage. They probably didn't think twice about Aaron's confrontation. But I can't stop recalling it. Humans have had a habit of hating supers, going so far as to want us dead. A few of my classmates have graduated recently; is that what Aaron is referring to? It certainly matches the suspicions of some of my...difficult colleagues. If students have truly been disappearing, what kind of support does Jason have? And what's stopping him from getting rid of me, too?

January 8:

My curiosity got the better of me. I had to know the truth about the school. I cornered Jason in his office today and begged for honesty. Friends don't lie to each other. He admitted that he's been under stress because his wife is having a difficult pregnancy. He denied that his school or his plans were nefarious, and he was hurt that I'd dare to accuse him. His admission, while tragic, isn't entirely believable. I know he's lying to me. I can sense it. If Jason won't tell me what's going on, I'll find out myself.

February 13:

It's been a month since I've written, but what a crazy month it has been. It appears that my constant questions have annoyed Jason, as I have been forced to cease contact with anyone from the outside world, including Teresa. When I ask Jason why, he says, "Friends are supposed to trust each other." I understand his frustration with me, but he's taking this too far. It kills me to ignore Teresa. I can only pray she doesn't take offense.

AARON HAS STOPPED HARASSING JASON. LAST I HEARD, HE FOUND A GIRLFRIEND AND WANTS TO KEEP HER FAR AWAY FROM JASON'S INFLUENCE. AS ODD AS IT SOUNDS, I MISS AARON'S BRAVERY. HE SAID WHATEVER HE WANTED TO WITHOUT FEAR OF CONSEQUENCE, THOUGH I SUPPOSE THAT COMES FROM BEING INDESTRUCTIBLE. IT'S THE KIND OF COURAGE I WISH I HAD, ESPECIALLY TODAY. I'M GOING TO DO SOMETHING RECKLESS, STUPID, AND SELFISH. IF I DIE TRYING, AT LEAST I DIE WITH MY CURIOSITY SATISFIED.

Theo paused to catch his breath. The idea that his dad and Principal Jones were friends was impossible! Could Dad not see the evil hiding behind the mask of goodness? Was he so disillusioned by his optimism that he trusted a man who didn't deserve it?

FEBRUARY 16:
I'M SHAKING SO BADLY I CAN BARELY WRITE. BUT I NEED TO EXPLAIN WHAT HAPPENED. LATE LAST NIGHT, I SHIFTED INTO MY SHADOW FORM AND WAS ON MY WAY TO SPEAK WITH JASON AND, ADMITTEDLY, BEG FOR FORGIVENESS. WHEN I GOT TO HIS OFFICE, HE WAS ALONE WITH A CLASSMATE. THE DETAILS BLUR IN MY MIND, BUT I'M SURE ABOUT WHAT I SAW. JASON KILLED A SUPER.

To Theo's knowledge, he'd only seen Principal Jones strip students of their power and wipe their memories. He hadn't killed any students. But that didn't mean he *never* had.

WITHOUT DRAWING ATTENTION TO MYSELF, I RETURNED TO MY ROOM, PACKED MY BAGS, AND ESCAPED. I'M A COWARD FOR NOT SAVING MY CLASSMATES, BUT I COULDN'T RUN THE RISK OF STAYING.

I CAN'T STOP THINKING OF JASON'S LIES. I BELIEVE HE STUDIED US IN CLASSES TO PINPOINT OUR WEAKNESSES AND THEN KILL US OFF ONE BY ONE. HE HAS, HOWEVER, RELEASED SOME CLASSMATES TO RETURN HOME. THEY WERE ALWAYS THE OVERPERFORMING ONES, THE ONES WHO NEVER SPOKE OUT OF TURN, THE ONES WHO NEVER QUESTIONED HIM. THEY WERE THE ONES THAT WERE TOO POWERFUL FOR A SIMPLE HUMAN TO GET RID OF.

I WANT TO THINK HE'D NEVER HURT ME, HIS FRIEND, BUT THE MORE I LEARN ABOUT HIM, THE MORE I REALIZE THAT A MONSTER DOESN'T NEED FRIENDS. HE NEEDS VICTIMS. I'M CURRENTLY ON A FLIGHT TO MEET TERESA, AND WRITING TAKES MY MIND OFF WHAT I'M POSSIBLY SUPPOSED TO SAY TO HER. HOW DO I EXPLAIN WHAT I'VE ENDURED? I DON'T EXPECT HER, OR ANYONE, TO BELIEVE ME. IN THE PUBLIC, JASON JONES IS A SAINT. HEAVENS, HE HAD ME CONVINCED OF THAT!

I DON'T KNOW WHAT TO SAY ANYMORE. I'M JUST TIRED.

The following entry occurred many months after the previous one, leaving Theo to wonder: How did Mom react? What did Dad say to her? He must have told her a *very* tame and basic version of his experience; otherwise, she would have outright refused to let Theo attend the same school. If Dad had told the truth, Theo never would've been stuck at the academy. Then again, he never would've met his friends either.

AUGUST 4:
THE STRANGEST THING HAPPENED YESTERDAY. I HAD A VISITOR. WHICH DOESN'T SOUND ODD, BUT THE PERSON ON THE DOORSTEP WAS CERTAINLY A SURPRISE. IT WAS AARON! I ALMOST ATTACKED HIM, THINKING HE WAS HERE TO KILL ME, BUT HE QUICKLY ASSURED ME THAT HE WAS ON MY SIDE. HE'S SKEPTICAL OF HOW HIS BROTHER RUNS THE SCHOOL AND

HEARD I ESCAPED. HE ASKED WHAT I KNEW. I TALKED ABOUT IT ALL—FROM HAVING MY COMMUNICATION CLOSED OFF TO WITNESSING A MURDER.

AARON AND I PLANNED TO EXPOSE JASON'S CRIMES TO THE WORLD. TO DO THAT, WE NEEDED EVIDENCE. AARON TOLD ME ABOUT HOW HE'D VISIT FAMILIES WITH MISSING CHILDREN, YET THE CASES NEVER WENT VERY FAR. RUMORS ARE REMOVED ALMOST IMMEDIATELY FROM THE NEWS CIRCUIT. PLUS, WITHOUT A BODY, POLICE CAN'T MAKE A CONVICTION. EVEN THE SUPERS WE HAVE FOUND WHO WERE ALLOWED TO LEAVE THE ACADEMY WERE SERVED WITH LEGAL DOCUMENTS, PREVENTING THEM FROM SPEAKING ABOUT THEIR EXPERIENCE. MOST FAMILIES OUTRIGHT REFUSED TO MEET WITH AARON, GIVEN HIS CONNECTIONS TO THE SCHOOL.

I HAVE NOT DARED TO SHARE ANY OF MY FINDINGS WITH TERESA. EVERY TIME SHE ASKS ABOUT MY EXPERIENCE AT THE ACADEMY OR MY MEETING WITH AARON, I LIE. I CAN'T ALLOW HER TO GET INVOLVED WITH MY PROBLEMS. I HOPE I'LL HAVE MORE NEWS TOMORROW.

Dion stirred in bed again, whispering a name Theo didn't recognize. As Theo chewed on his nails, he crept farther into the corner.

Jones's hatred for Dad had to come from a real, deep, dark place. Men as accomplished and smart as them wouldn't be after each other for petty qualms. So, what had Dad done to warrant such anger? Theo flipped the next page, and his breath caught in his throat.

MAY 6:
I KILLED SOMEONE TODAY.

"Amidst the chaos and confusion of the past few months, I am here to set the record straight.

No, I did not harm any student or staff at my academy.

No, I do not hate supers. I hate their lack of responsibility.

No, I will not give up. An esteemed building crumbled to pieces hardly four months ago, thanks to the reckless acts of a group of supers. Now, they are loose, causing trouble and hurting others. I failed to contain them in my school, but I will not fail a second time.

I appreciate all those who continue to support me. Someday, hopefully soon, goodness will triumph."

-Social media post from (formerly) Principal Jones

12

ALREADY GONE

Theo couldn't breathe. It felt like he was being squeezed to death by an anaconda. Dad would never kill anyone; he'd never harm a fly! But on that last day in the academy, Principal Jones accused Dad of killing his wife. Could it have been true?

The May 6th entry was dated years after the previous time Dad wrote. During that gap, he and Aaron must've been doing whatever it took to dig up dirt on Principal Jones. Even if that meant using extreme measures.

Theo gulped. How extreme had his father gone?

Regardless of what it was, Theo had to know the truth. He'd come too far to give in now. He read as quickly as he could, quick enough to skip words.

MAY 6:
I KILLED SOMEONE TODAY.
AFTER COUNTLESS FAILURES, I'D BECOME DESPERATE FOR
ANSWERS. SO, EARLIER THIS EVENING I SNUCK INTO JASON'S

APARTMENT TO SEARCH FOR ANY INCRIMINATING INFOR-
MATION. HIS WIFE, SAMANTHA, AND THEIR YOUNG SON,
DRAKE, WERE HOME, ASLEEP, SAFE AND SOUND. I DIDN'T THINK
OF HURTING THEM OR USING THEM AS LEVERAGE FOR MY
MISSION, THOUGH AARON HAS VOICED THAT IDEA ON
NUMEROUS OCCASIONS.

I HAD JUST FOUND JASON'S COMPUTER WHEN I HEARD THE
FRONT DOOR CREAK OPEN. OUT OF FEAR THAT IT WAS
JASON, I FADED INTO THE SHADOWS AND HURRIEDLY
CONTINUED MY SEARCH.

UNTIL I HEARD SAMANTHA SCREAM.

I RUSHED OUT OF THE OFFICE TO FIND A RANDOM MAN
PINNING HER TO THE WALL. HE SAID HE WANTED REVENGE ON
JASON. BUT I'D SEEN ENOUGH. I RUSHED AT THE MAN AND
TOOK US BOTH TO THE FLOOR. THE SECOND WE HIT THE
GROUND, HE PHASED DIRECTLY OUT OF MY GRASP. HE REAP-
PEARED BY SAMANTHA'S SIDE, AND I REALIZED I WAS DEALING
WITH A SUPER. ONE THAT WAS MUCH BIGGER, STRONGER,
AND MADDER THAN ME.

USING THE SHADOWS IN THE ROOM, I RESTRAINED HIM AND
YELLED AT SAMANTHA TO GRAB DRAKE AND RUN. I
REMEMBER THE LOOK OF BLOODLUST IN THE SUPER'S EYES.
WITH A SNEER, HE SAID, "JASON HAS A SON, TOO?"

THAT'S WHEN I KNEW: TO SAVE THIS FAMILY, I'D HAVE TO KILL
THIS SUPER.

THE ENSUING FIGHT REMAINS A BLUR TO ME. SINCE THE
ONLY ESCAPE WAS THROUGH THE FRONT DOOR, WHICH WAS
DIRECTLY IN THE SUPER'S PATH, SAMANTHA HAD BARRI-
CADED HERSELF AND DRAKE INTO HER BEDROOM. EVERY
TIME I WOULD GET CLOSE TO THE SUPER, HE'D PHASE AWAY
FROM ME. IT WAS A MIRACLE HE WAS DISTRACTED BY MY
COMPANY. AT ANY GIVEN MOMENT, HE COULD'VE BECOME
BORED AND KILLED SAMANTHA IN THE BEDROOM.

DURING OUR CHAOS, WE CRASHED FROM THE BALCONY
AND FELL TWO STORIES TO THE GROUND. I THINK MY RIBS

ARE CRACKED FROM THE FALL. BUT I HAD HIM RIGHT WHERE I WANTED HIM. HE WAS EXHAUSTED, AND HIS ARM WAS BROKEN.

I THOUGHT IT WAS OVER. THEN, I WHIFFED THE FAINTEST SMELL OF SMOKE. WITH A BIG SMILE, THE SUPER SAID, "ALWAYS HAVE A BACKUP PLAN."

I TURNED TO THE APARTMENT. RED-HOT FLAMES CRAWLED OUT OF THE BUILDING, BURNING FROM THE INSIDE OUT. SAMANTHA AND DRAKE WERE TRAPPED.

I HAVE NO IDEA WHEN THE SUPER MANAGED TO START THE FIRE, BUT ONE THING WAS CERTAIN. THE FIGHT WAS ALSO MEANT TO DISTRACT ME.

"IT'S HIS TURN," I REMEMBER THE SUPER HISSED. "JONES HAS TO PAY FOR WHAT HE'S DONE TO MY FAMILY."

I'M REALIZING NOW, SITTING IN MY ROOM, WHAT HE MEANT. I DIDN'T KNOW ALL THE STUDENTS AT THE SCHOOL, YET I WOULDN'T BE SURPRISED IF A STUDENT WHO DISAPPEARED WAS THIS MAN'S CHILD. HE DIDN'T HAVE PROOF TO CONVICT JASON, BUT A FATHER'S INTUITION NEVER LIES.

I DIDN'T WANT TO KILL HIM. I COULD UNDERSTAND HIS RAGE FROM BEING MANIPULATED. HOWEVER, TAKING HIS ANGER OUT ON INNOCENT PEOPLE WASN'T THE WAY TO GET REVENGE. I COULDN'T TAKE THE CHANCE OF LETTING HIM GO.

I GATHERED A SHADOW IN MY HAND, MORPHED IT INTO A BLADE, AND STABBED THE SUPER ONCE IN THE CHEST. HE PUSHED ME OFF ALMOST IMMEDIATELY AND CLUMSILY PHASED OUT OF SIGHT, YET I KNEW HE WOULDN'T SURVIVE MY ATTACK. WHEREVER HE'D DISAPPEARED TO, HE WOULD DIE A QUICK, CLEAN DEATH, ONE THAT WOULDN'T BE DELIVERED TO SAMANTHA AND DRAKE. ONE THAT LIKELY WASN'T GIVEN TO THE MAN'S CHILD EITHER.

PEOPLE WERE FLEEING THE BUILDING AND RUSHING ONTO THE STREET, COUGHING AND CALLING FOR HELP. AN AMBULANCE WOULDN'T ARRIVE IN TIME.

I CLIMBED THE STAIRS OF THE FIRE ESCAPE AND JUMPED

Back onto Samantha's apartment balcony. Smoke billowed out in blinding heaps. Thanks to my mask, I was able to limit some of the smog, but I'm wheezing as I write. Teresa wants to take me to the hospital. I promised I'd be fine.

I couldn't transform into my shadow form in the building either; it was too dangerous with the fire. I found Samantha and Drake huddled together on the bedroom floor. Both were coated in ash and burns.

I can't recall the details of our escape. My clothes are singed, telling stories of brushes with death, but all I know is that, by some miraculous burst of strength, I carried them down the fire escape steps to the sidewalk. Samantha was unresponsive, and Drake was barely breathing. I would've stayed to help them, but then Jason broke through the crowd. I've never seen someone harbor so much hatred at one time.

I couldn't find the words to explain the truth. Would he believe me? Did I want him to?

I couldn't face him, not after what he'd done. So, I disappeared and fled the scene.

It's been a few hours. From what I heard, Samantha was declared dead from smoke inhalation and burn complications. Drake isn't doing too well either. I'm sure he'll pass soon.

Teresa has been a constant support. She doesn't blame me for my actions and insists I shouldn't feel guilty. But I do. I hate what I had to do to that super. However, it taught me a valuable lesson. Some supers are horrible, evil beings. They abuse their power and use it to scare others. Supers like that don't deserve their power. Although my experience with humans

HASN'T BEEN ENTIRELY ENJOYABLE, I WON'T HESITATE TO HELP THEM AGAIN.

A lone teardrop hit the page, alerting Theo to wipe his eyes. In one night, Jones had lost his entire family and pinned the blame on Dad because of a misunderstanding. Theo rested his head on his pillow, hoping to slow his incessant tears.

Growing up, he envisioned his father as the pinnacle of goodness and perfection. He always spoke highly of supers and constantly advocated for them. However, he had *killed* one of them. One of his own.

Theo thought of Mom. If she were here, she'd tell him that Dad had to do this; he had to be this person to protect their family. His motives were pure, despite his actions being wrong.

If anyone knew about doing the wrong things for the right reasons, it was Theo.

He breathed a heavy sigh. Dad kept a lot of secrets, but they were all for Theo's benefit. He opened the journal again, finding a crude letter with crossed-out words and shaky handwriting.

DEAR JASON, I KNOW WE'VE HURT EACH OTHER AND RUINED OUR FRIENDSHIP. I DON'T WANT TO BELIEVE YOU ARE THE MONSTER YOU'VE BECOME. I WANT TO THINK THERE'S GOOD INSIDE OF YOU, BURIED BENEATH YOUR SORROW. BUT EVEN I CAN'T BE THAT OPTIMISTIC. FOR WHAT IT'S WORTH, I DIDN'T KILL YOUR WIFE AND SON. THERE WAS ANOTHER SUPER THERE, AND I KILLED HIM HE WAS TRYING TO HURT YOUR FAMILY. I DID MY BEST TO SAVE THEM. MY SINCEREST APOLO-GIES. I HOPE YOU'LL LEARN TO EMBRACE A FUTURE OF HOPE AND SUPERS. WE'RE HERE WHETHER YOU LIKE IT OR NOT.

Theo wondered what would've happened if Dad had sent the letter. Would Jones have a change of heart? Would his vengeance fully consume him? There was no way of knowing, and honestly, Theo preferred it like that.

He flipped the page. The last journal entry was dated almost ten years after the fire.

> July 17:
>
> I haven't written in a long time. This past week has been a bit hectic, and it started with Aaron's death.
>
> Aaron told me he would be speaking with his brother today. He was going to confront him with our suspicions and tell Jason to leave the school. I knew it wasn't a good idea, but Aaron wouldn't listen.
>
> He promised he'd let me know what happened before five o'clock. After five came and went, and after a few days passed, I had a feeling he'd not survived the altercation. Somehow, Jones got rid of his invincible brother. Maybe he used the same strategy to kill his father, too.
>
> Jason has also acquired a new project: renovating his school. He will be expanding to housing young super criminals.
>
> As painful as it is to admit, I can't stop him. I don't have any evidence to prove his guilt.
>
> For the sake of my family, my investigation and vigilantism must cease. I can no longer pursue exposing Jason for the monster he is. Instead, I have to believe his own ego will bring his destruction. I can only hope he never finds me.

The journal entries ended there. Theo flipped through the other notebooks in the box, yet they were all filled with stories from Dad's everyday life, marking the success of teaching Tara to ride a bike or Theo losing his first tooth.

Theo returned to the journal and found a list of tips from his dad, tucked between the last page and the book jacket. Euphoria rushed into him, drowning him in its consuming tide. He never received the training he deserved from his dad, but this was a start.

Without bothering to look the list over, he tucked it into his pocket, placed the items back in the box, and shoved it under his bed, concealing it amongst a pile of extra blankets. He couldn't risk being caught by his friends, so although it made his stomach ache, he shifted into his shadow form and disappeared into the forest.

Theo cast a glance at the shrinking cabin, ensuring he was deep enough in the woods not to be spotted by anyone. The trees swayed and whistled above him in the wind. He sat with his back against one of the tall sycamores and unfolded his father's letter, hardly able to contain his excitement.

List of Known Abilities:

1. Shadow form: renders you almost invisible to the outside world. Remaining in the light exposes you. Stick to the darkness.

2. Manipulation: allows you to make anything you want, but constructing it into solid form requires high levels of concentration. Creating people and animals is much more challenging than crafting weapons or shields.

(If you dare to try and make shadow clones, keep constant control over them. They will develop a mind of their own based on your emotions.)

UNDER NO CIRCUMSTANCES DO YOU ALLOW THE SHADOWS TO TAKE OVER. REMAINING IN SHADOW FORM FOR TOO LONG OR OVERUSING YOUR POWER CAN HAVE DRASTIC CONSEQUENCES, ONES YOU MAY NEVER BE ABLE TO RETURN FROM. BE CAREFUL

Scoffing, Theo flipped the page. But it was blank. A toxic mixture of anger and confusion bubbled in his gut. *Why didn't Dad give me a better list? Does he not want me to improve?*

Or was it possible that he didn't fully understand their capabilities? There were skills not listed that Theo discovered he could do, such as overwhelming the light in a room and concealing others in the darkness. He straightened proudly against the trunk. *I know more than Dad does!*

Then, he deflated as he realized, *I know more than Dad does.*

Theo had to develop his power on his own. Though sad to say, he'd already had to go through most of his life without his dad's help. This was no different.

He tucked the note into his jeans pocket and rubbed his hands together. Due to the antidepressants limiting his powers, they'd be weak. At least, that's what he was counting on. The shadows woke inside of him, filling his veins with ice.

An owl hooted from somewhere above him, so he morphed a bird first. He'd never considered creating animals before, so at least he had Dad to thank for this. Theo twisted and manipulated the darkness around him to form a rough, clunky crow. It was nowhere near perfect, but when he made it flap its wings and fly, he didn't care how it looked. His face split into a smile. Like Dad said, maybe this power did more than destroy. Perhaps it could create, too.

Once when Theo was eight, his mother had grounded him for breaking her most prized vase. To deal with his boredom, he conjured a shadowy friend to accompany him. They weren't solid, weren't really human. Instead, it was more of a shapeless blob that Theo pretended could talk. It horrified Mom and made Dad laugh. Now, Theo knew why.

But what if he took it one step further? He had cloned himself by accident at the academy. He'd escaped for a night to prevent a robbery, and the shadow he created actually talked. Although Theo had been afraid to try anything like that again, he didn't have another choice.

Besides, as long as he followed his dad's warnings, what could go wrong?

Theo squeezed his eyes shut as he concentrated. Thankfully, with it being dark outside, he didn't have to think too hard. He copied himself, thinking it would be best to create an object he was familiar with.

He felt a presence forming in front of him, so he peeked open to check the process. Much like all that time ago, a shadowy figure materialized from the darkness and stood across from Theo. It almost resembled him; they were the same height and build. Theo's smile widened as the shadow glanced around. It was like it was alive.

Its gaze landed on Theo. Although it didn't have a face, he assumed it was smiling. But he couldn't have been more wrong.

It grabbed his arm, as solid as any human. The grip felt like a shackle, preventing Theo from withdrawing. That didn't stop him from trying. He ripped his arm against the shadow's hand, to no avail.

"Don't be scared," it said, the voice sounding eerily close to Theo's. "You're me."

"I'll never be you!"

"You already are."

Filled with pure adrenaline, Theo tugged one last time, and the shadow vanished into the forest. He hit a tree, his chest heaving with quick gasps of breath. Feeling numb, he looked down at his arm.

Except his arm wasn't solid anymore. Instead, it was made of darkness.

Panicked, he willed the shadows to leave, yet they didn't obey. He cursed under his breath, wishing he'd never tried such risky tricks. What if he stayed this way forever? What if he couldn't hold Penny again?

Stay calm, he told himself. *Concentrate.*

Theo released a long, calming exhale and squinted at his arm.

Slowly, it returned to flesh and bone, the shadows lingering at his fingertips. His antidepressants were supposed to stop the darkness from controlling him. Clearly, they weren't doing the trick anymore.

With the dawn rising against his back, Theo returned to the cabin. His arms shook, and his legs felt like jelly. He slipped through the front door and couldn't have arrived a moment too soon. The kids were waking and running downstairs, accompanied by their yawning friends.

Theo checked every room in the house for Penny, needing her light to combat the darkness creeping in on him. Except she was nowhere to be found.

He stumbled upon Yasmine in the kitchen and asked, "Where's Penny? It's urgent."

Felix chimed in with, "Yeah, we've gotta start training soon."

Yasmine eyed them both. "The last I saw, she was in our room. Then, she left because Giselle was being rude."

Felix scoffed and started to bicker, but Theo was already leaving. With every step, his heart beat harder.

Where was Penny?

13

RISKY DETERMINATIONS

As Penny stomped away from the cabin, she crossed her arms to conserve body heat. The morning had brought on lower temperatures, yet she couldn't have been more grateful for it than she was right now.

Hardly ten minutes ago, she had been writing in her journal when Giselle suggested playing a game of Truth or Dare while they got ready for the day. All the girls had been up early on account of Yasmine's snoring.

Penny refused to play, so the rest of her roommates went on without her. Giselle had asked the first truth question to Yasmine, saying, "If Dion was the last person in the world, would you kiss him?"

Yasmine had laughed. "Come on, guys! He's cute but kissing him would be like kissing a zombie." After much goading, she admitted, "Fine, yes. If he was the last person in the world, I'd kiss him."

Penny grinned to herself. The questions continued, with a few of them being tiny dares, such as wearing pigtails or sleeping in the basement for a night. Giselle revealed she could speak French fluently, to which Yasmine dared her to talk like that for an entire day. "I'm sure Felix would love it," she joked.

Then, Giselle had shifted the conversation. She asked a question about Theo—exactly what, Penny couldn't be sure—but Lily and Yasmine quieted. Penny looked up from her notebook to see everyone staring at her.

"What?" she asked.

"Do you think you could beat Theo in a fight?" Giselle repeated.

Penny's brows bunched together. "Why would I have to beat him in a fight?"

"It's just a 'truth.' If you're too offended to answer—"

"Why would you ask that?" Penny snapped her journal closed. "What makes you think we'd have to fight him?"

Yasmine shifted on the floor. "Pen, it's just part of the game."

"No, it's not." Penny rested her glare on Giselle, who didn't budge. "Theo would never turn on us. I know you're new here, but you need to understand that."

Giselle glared in return. During the month she'd been here, tensions had always been high between them. Giselle stood to be at Penny's eye level and being a few inches taller, basically sneered down on Penny. "Unlike you, I *know* what I'm talking about. You've got rose-colored glasses on. If the worst happens—and heaven forbid it does—you won't be able to stand a chance against him."

Penny had never felt anger like that before. As she wandered through the forest, it burned in her stomach, filling her blood with fire. "He cares about me," she had said. "I'm sure you wouldn't know what that's like."

Giselle had recoiled. She obviously hadn't expected Penny to be so determined to win an argument. But she fired right back with an insult of her own. "Face it, Angel, your relationship with him is heading out the door. If he really cared for you, he'd—"

It was at that moment that Penny had to leave. Staying would mean getting into a fight or bursting into tears.

Here she was, fleeing from yet another confrontation. Eventually, she stopped in a clearing of trees and sat on the wet grass. She was far from the cabin, at least far enough away that if anything happened to her, she doubted they would hear it.

The leaves in the branches broke apart and brushed against each other again, setting the periwinkle sky behind them. If Penny squinted, the fragments of sky almost resembled diamonds, flickering and sparkling.

The weather was perfect—blue-purple skies, a slight breeze, and the promise of a rainstorm in the coming hours. She exhaled, but her breath caught short when a twig snapped behind her.

"What are you doing out here?" Theo asked.

At the sound of his voice, she relaxed. "Enjoying the peace of nature," she said. "What are you doing?"

He sat next to her. "Looking for you. After you weren't in your room, I got worried."

Pleased he was concerned, she snickered. "I can take care of myself."

He threw her a teasing look. Behind that was something different, something darker. "Can't you let me have this? I walked a long way to find you."

"Yes, thank you. I don't know what I would've done if you hadn't come to my rescue."

"That's better." He reached out for her hand. She pulled him in, letting his body heat chase away the chill. Almost like he was trying to distract himself, he looked at the trees, the dirt, their entwined fingers. "Do you ever think about healing people?" he wondered. "Like, do you have to think about it, or does it just happen?"

"It just happens," Penny explained. "If I touch someone and feel them hurting, my power takes over. Why?"

He shrugged. "I started feeling it when you touched me. I wondered how you knew."

She scooted closer to him so that they were squished together, side by side. She couldn't help but recall Giselle's words—that Theo wouldn't care about her anymore. If that were to happen, she'd enjoy every second while she could.

"Why'd you need to talk to me?" she asked quietly.

Theo cleared his throat. "Well, a couple of reasons. A few days ago, Peter, Dion, and I were discussing what we'd do in the future. It got me thinking. What will you do?"

Penny paused to think. "I don't know. I could be a nurse."

"You'd want to heal for a living?"

Her hesitance was answer enough. Theo waved that off and added, "It doesn't matter. Keep going."

"I want to return home to my family. And," she blushed, "I'd bring you."

She peeked up at him, but his focus was distant. Realizing she was staring, he blinked hard and stammered, "Sorry, I-I'm a little distract-ed." He dug into his pocket, saying, "It's because of this."

He displayed one of the colored balls from the toy machines at the town store. With furrowed brows, Penny popped the pink lid off, finding a silver ring with a green gem inside.

Theo scratched the back of his neck. "It's silly, but I wanted you to have this to remember how much I care about you."

Happiness rushed into her. At long last, he'd said it. Sure, it was obvious that they liked each other, but having a physical object repre-sent his feelings was thrilling.

"This doesn't mean you have to stay with me," he continued, casting a pall over her elation. "I just thought you should have it."

Previously, at the school, he had asked her to leave with him, and she'd refused. She wasn't going to make the same mistake again. "I'll always stay with you," she said. "No matter what."

"No matter what?" he repeated. "Peter is starting to think we should keep fighting after Jones is defeated. I don't think I can. If I quit, would you come with me?"

"Where?"

"Somewhere we don't have to be superheroes. A place where we can be selfish and be whoever we want. No powers, no threats, just you and me."

The offer sounded *very* tempting. "And our families?" she clarified. "We'll see them, right?"

Lines creased Theo's forehead. "If that's what you want."

A few questions remained in Penny's mind. Among them were: "Why would we need to hide?" and "What about the rest of the team?" On the other hand, asking would dishearten Theo, so she smiled. "I can't wait."

Immediately, he leaned forward and hugged her. The proposition wasn't a guarantee; in fact, it was the farthest thing from it. But seeing his immense excitement reassured Penny in ways she couldn't describe.

Once he pulled away, he added, "Um, I also came to get you because Felix wants to train. He needs you there in case he gets his butt kicked."

Penny wanted to laugh. Clearly, Theo was trying to joke with her. However, pain lingered within him, deep and unmoving. "Okay," she said. "Let's go."

He stood with her. "Let's take our time. I prefer to arrive and see him black and blue."

Penny slid the ring onto her right ring finger and watched it sparkle in the light. Such a small gift, and yet, she knew it had come from Theo's heart. She spotted him hiding his pleased, bashful grin, so she looped her arm in his. "When we leave for good," she said, "are we going to a big city?"

"I'm not sure. I do love the peace here, but I wish there were more places to get pizza. Where would you like to go?"

"Maybe we should go to a small town. I bet you'd like the country."

He wrinkled his nose. "Whatever you say."

As Penny giggled, she kissed him on the cheek. Despite enjoying imagining their futures together, she couldn't help but feel apprehensive. There was a significant chance they wouldn't live to see next week.

The basement was the most spacious place in the cabin. As Dion explained, the main room was going to be a theater, but at the last second, his mother decided a television would've enticed him to stay inside. She never decided what to put there instead, so it was just an expansive, empty room. Naturally, the team repurposed it into their training area.

When Theo and Penny arrived, Felix and Dion were wearing headphones and had guns dangling from their grips. Theo moved behind Penny.

"About time!" Felix swept the headphones off his head and fixed his hair. "I was getting ready to beat Peter."

From Peter's place against the wall, he scoffed. "You won't see me coming."

"That's not fair! You shouldn't be allowed to turn invisible."

"Why not?"

"Because my powers are impossible to use."

"Yeah," Dion chimed in. "Why is that?"

"Um…" Felix looked to Theo desperately, begging him to speak.

"Stopping time is complicated," Theo explained. "I bet it's hard to control."

"Exactly," Felix continued, gaining traction with the fabricated excuse. "It's *so* easy for you guys. Like, Theo can turn shadows into solid objects, and I can't even stop time."

Theo forced a laugh. If only they knew what he could *really* do.

"It's not impossible," Lily countered. She switched the safety on her gun and returned it to its box, continuing, "It just takes a great deal of concentration, focus, and control."

"All things I lack in."

"It also takes patience and humility."

"Now you're trying to make me feel bad."

Peter burst into laughter while Lily tried to talk over him. "I have studied human emotion for years. A great deal of our power relies on it. So, if we endure trauma, our bodies and minds will shut down. Our powers either react to that trauma or act upon it. They either disappear or take control of our subconscious."

"Like a fight or flight instinct?" Dion inquired, tapping his chin.

"Yes. Penny's healing power prompts her to avoid confrontation. It entices her to remedy problems by any means necessary."

"Being pushed into healing isn't bad," Theo defended, laying a hand on Penny's shoulder. Admittedly, he was a bit jealous of her. Unlike her comforting abilities, his powers only brought dark thoughts.

"I'm not saying it is," Lily said. "I think we should be careful that our powers don't force us to act. We can't let them control us."

Penny faltered underneath Theo's touch. "I'm sorry," he said. "They don't understand."

"It's not just them." She left him to stand near Felix and Peter, analyzing their fight with her arms crossed.

Not wanting to feel abandoned, Theo sought out Dion, who was busy retrieving the spent shell casings from the floor. The gold metal clinked together in his cupped palms. "Hi," Dion said, "what were you and Penny up to outside?"

"Stuff." Theo saw her heal a cut on Felix's jaw while Peter apologized profusely. "I feel like she's mad at me."

"For what?"

"I was hoping you knew."

"I have no clue."

There was a slight waver in Dion's voice, but Theo didn't dwell on it. If he was lying, so be it. Theo had told tons of lies. And why *wouldn't* she be mad at him? He was a rollercoaster of emotions; he must've been exhausting to be around.

But he tried; he tried so hard to pretend for Penny. He acted like he was happy and content. He joked to see her smile, since any other attitude would have upset her. But he was getting tired of pretending. He couldn't do it for much longer.

"Hello!" Felix shouted, snapping Theo out of his daze. A snakelike shadow had wrapped itself around Felix's legs and was creeping toward his neck. He braced himself on the wall so as not to fall over, and seemed more confused than scared.

Quickly, Theo forced the shadow back into the corner. "Oops," he stammered. "My bad."

Felix nodded to Peter. "I bet Theo did it to save you. I was *this* close to destroying you."

"You're delusional. The dust in the air must be getting to your head."

"Well, I bet I can shoot better than you!"

Peter retrieved two small handguns and replaced the paper targets on the wall. "Let's see what you've got!"

The gunshots started. With every single bullet that pierced the target, Theo's breathing quickened. Embarrassingly, he still hadn't overcome his fear. Why wasn't he strong enough?

"Theodore," Lily suddenly said. "I think you should practice with a weapon."

"What?" Dion and Penny said in unison.

"He's uncomfortable. He needs to be adjusted to them." She placed a black revolver into his hands. It scorched him at the touch.

Simultaneously, Dion and Penny tried to vouch for him, spouting off excuses why he shouldn't, or rather, couldn't shoot. Lily ignored them and pulled him to stand across from the target, physically pushing Peter and Felix aside.

The target was the shape of a person's head and torso.

"Face your fears," Lily told him. "It's the only way you will get past this."

This is okay, he said to himself. *You're not doing anything bad; this is just practice! It's a piece of paper; it's not a real person.* He raised the gun to level with the target, shaking violently with the effort.

Shadows swirled in his heart; they danced in his mind, encouraging him—no, *ordering* him to shoot.

He dropped the gun onto the floor. "I'm not shooting anyone!"

Everyone froze at his exclamation. He hadn't intended to be so loud, but his panic outweighed his embarrassment. Penny ran to reach him, holding his arms and saying, "If you don't want to practice with a gun—"

"I'm not," he repeated, yanking away from her. "I'm not touching one of those things."

Peter rolled his eyes, and although Theo spotted it, he didn't speak. He was supposed to be their fearless leader, and here he was, terrified of a three-pound piece of metal.

Thankfully, Dion came to the rescue with, "Don't you have research to do? That's a whole lot more important than this."

Theo nodded, slow at first. "Oh yeah, I did. Thanks for reminding me. You guys have fun."

"Good luck," Penny joined in, waving to Theo.

He hurried to the stairs yet stopped once the wall concealed him. He listened to Peter reload his gun and mutter, "We're letting him skip out on training? How typical."

"Shut up," Dion snapped. "Wars are won from the technical side as much as they are from fighting. We can't have mindless soldiers." He paused, then added, "Felix doesn't count."

The team laughed, except for Felix, who exclaimed, "Hey! Uncalled for!" Still, his tone was light with amusement.

Penny led Dion to the other side of Theo's wall to whisper, "Thank you."

"For what? Roasting Felix or—?"

"For getting Theo out of here. It's good he listens to one of us."

Theo inched up the remaining stairs, going on his tiptoes so they wouldn't creak.

"I know Dark Week is a sensitive subject, but why don't we ever face the facts of the tragedy? People claim the supers were 'unprovoked' terrorists. But they attacked SPECIFIC places. These places were facilities owned by the SPP. For those who don't know, it's an old company called the Super Protection Program."

"Records of this place were seriously buried."

"Exactly. We've been told that the SPP was founded to help super babies develop and grow, but if that is the truth, then why were the facilities attacked? Why do we as a society not ask the serious questions? Why do we accept a rose-colored fantasy?"

"Maybe because it's easier than facing the dark reality."

"What do you think that reality is?"

"That humans are not blameless in the mess we're in."

-excerpt from the "Super Crimes, Super Times" podcast

14

ELEMENTARY, MY DEAR REBECCA

Theo sat in front of the computer in his bedroom, never before so thankful to be alone. Researching Principal Jones's plans was by no means fun; in fact, the endeavor was like finding a needle in a haystack. But it was easier than wielding a gun.

Although Principal Jones rarely did live interviews, he posted on social media constantly. *"I tried to help young supers become better members of society,"* one of these posts read. *"Sadly, I realize that superhumans, especially those under the age of 21, are too dangerous to be an equal part of society. We need supers that are both mentally and physically capable of harnessing the effects of their powers. Unfortunately, the world is on short, if not empty, supply of supers like those."*

Underneath the post, he'd attached news articles and videos of supers attacking people. If he planned to turn humanity against them, then it was working.

Toward the beginning of the principal's weekly superhuman hate, he posted a lengthy explanation detailing why he loathed supers so much. Theo wasn't sure he should read it, but his eyes betrayed him and skimmed the screen.

"I've received countless questions about my distaste for superhumans. I assure you—it comes from a very real and personal place. I do not know how my father and older brother died, nor am I sad that they're gone. They were manipulative, vile people. They treated my mother like dirt, simply because she wasn't a super. I have lost many people in my life due to those who misuse their power. I will not stand for the abuse any longer."

The claims of having an emotionally distant father and a harsh older brother were like reality TV show gold. By making himself appear sympathetic, he won more people to his side.

Theo frowned. With all the talk of Jones's family, there was no mention of his wife and son anywhere. The tragedy of a double death would have been popular news during its time, and it would make for an even more tragic story now. But regardless of how much Theo searched, it couldn't be found. In fact, the only story remotely close to it was a report of an accidental apartment fire that didn't claim any victims.

Before Theo attended the academy, he had never heard Jones mention that he was married. In every interview, he wasn't forthcoming with details of his private life, instead speaking solely about the school and his accomplishments. Perhaps the pain of losing his wife and child was too much to bear, so he erased them from the internet, using the story to stagger Theo and manipulate his employees at the school. After all, the witnesses to the truth were dead.

Theo clicked off and reverted to the news, but Jones was everywhere there, too. He'd begun a petition for the U.S. government to pass a law stating supers couldn't have children. It already had 3,000 signatures.

Like he'd eaten something he was allergic to, Theo's throat closed. This law was inhumane; surely, everyone saw that!

His clicking searches grew faster. One article from the New York Times stated, "The bill has been proposed, but a decision hasn't been made thus far. Senate members say they're waiting for Jones to produce real evidence that passing it would be good for the nation."

A sliver of consolation filled Theo. But he wasn't finished yet.

Next, he searched for his mother. Thankfully, she was doing more than her fair share to protect supers from Jones's relentless attacks. Every chance she could, she bashed Principal Jones and the school. Theo watched a few interviews with her, almost melting from embarrassment when he saw her cursing out the reporters for their stupidity. On one last video, Theo pushed play and crossed his fingers, praying she wasn't putting too big a target on their family.

The host, Don Summers, a celebrity Theo recognized immediately, wore a sleek black suit with a red tie. He sat at his desk while Mom sat on a couch, adorned in a glittering blue gown. Theo beamed. It was Camilla's dress. In an instant, he was teleported back to the art club, watching in admiration as she sketched a gown the color of the night sky. Her memory made his heart ache, but it was a soft pain.

Don waved to the crowd, saying, "Welcome, welcome! Today, we're honored to speak with Mrs. Beckett-Palmer."

She waved humbly. "Please, call me Teresa."

"Teresa, let's get right to it. Is it true your son is a super?"

"Yes." Her tone dripped with sarcasm. "That isn't exactly groundbreaking news. The world has known for some time."

The two of them laughed good-naturedly, but it was apparent Mom faked it. She hated interviews; she told Theo herself. She used to make him help her get ready, approving outfits and practicing questions with her.

As the crowd's exaggerated laughter faded, Don continued,

"Teresa, you're a very opinionated woman. One of your opinions is that Jason Jones, the owner and principal of the Academy for Young Superheroes, is a bad person."

Her nose wrinkled. "Like I've said in other interviews, Principal Jones has ulterior motives, and people refuse to acknowledge that fact. He has poisoned the public to believe that supers are the harmful ones. Well, every super except for himself."

"And is it your understanding that Principal Jones caused students to go missing?"

"Students disappeared constantly without another peep. Every time parents and families questioned the safety of their children, they, too, were silenced. My son was lucky to escape with his life."

Don spun a coffee cup on his desk. "Where is your son, Teresa?"

She stiffened. "Even if I knew, that's none of your business."

Meaning no offense, Don raised his hands. "My deepest apologies. But have you considered the problem wasn't with the school, but with your son?"

Knowing exactly where this was going, Theo almost shut the computer off. Mom's eyes narrowed into thin slits; her nostrils flared. "Excuse me?" she growled.

The screen behind them displayed a sheet of paper bearing the academy's seal. At the bottom, it had been signed by Principal Jones, his black flourishes swirling nearly a mile long.

"This is an official letter from Principal Jones," Don said, motioning to it. "In it, you can clearly read, 'Theodore is an unstable boy who cannot manage his powers or impulses. This has likely stemmed from a lack of parenting—'"

Mom shot to her feet. "How *dare* you? Neither you nor that idiot Jason has any idea what kind of parenting I've done! My son is *not* unstable. He is completely in control of his abilities. Believing this bully makes you just as foolish!"

"Teresa," Don pleaded, "let's calm down."

Except Mom gained traction. "If anyone should be on trial for neglecting their child, it should be Mr. Jones! He was so concerned with managing his school that he abandoned his son and let him die!"

The crowd murmured. Theo grimaced to himself, wishing his mom would stop talking.

"What do you mean?" Don asked, his voice shaking slightly.

Mom folded her arms. "Unbeknownst to you, and probably to many people, Jason Jones used to be married and have a child. After the pair died in a fire, he expunged the information and stories from the internet, effectively erasing them from history. But *I* remember."

"That's not true," an audience member called out. The camera panned to him, allowing him to more clearly say, "The fire you're referring to didn't claim any lives! You're remembering wrong!"

Mom fixed her steely gaze on the man. "Am I? Or have you been led to believe a false narrative?"

Awkwardly, the man sat again.

The cameras swiveled to Don, who said, "Teresa, it sounds like you're suggesting a conspiracy. Do you believe Jason Jones has that much influence to sway what journalists are writing? To manipulate the news?"

"Absolutely," she said. "He's been controlling the media for years to keep with his story that supers are the enemy. I know a lot of people who would fear an invincible man."

She swept off stage, ignoring Don and the other producers begging her to stay. Some people in the audience applauded her, and while Theo was proud of his mother, he couldn't help but feel a sense of dread. He told her to be careful, *not* to go after the school. Didn't she understand how much danger she was in?

The door suddenly creaked open, interrupting Theo's worry. As he paused the video, Rebecca pattered into the room. "Hi," she said, using her teddy bear's paw to greet him.

"Hey, Becca," he said, doing his best to sound casual. "What's up?"

"Nothing." She glanced at the computer and crept closer. "What are you doing?"

"Research."

"About what?"

"Sort of about my mom."

Gasping, Rebecca pointed her finger at the paused video. "Is that her? She's pretty!"

"Oh, thanks." He closed out of the interview. "Anyway, now I'm thinking about the founders of the academy. I figured if they're out there, they might help us."

Rebecca's head tilted. "Why do we need them? Aren't you powerful?"

Theo directed her attention to a dog on the screen and successfully avoided the question. Recruiting older supers would lift the weight off Theo's shoulders, a weight that Rebecca wouldn't understand.

After watching a few too many puppy clips, Theo searched for the names of the academy founders. In the school library, he'd read a book about them, detailing their odd disappearances and deaths. To truly understand them, he'd have to dig deeper.

A specific article with the title, "Founders Keepers: The Aftermath of the Academy," caught his attention. Together, he and Rebecca scanned the screen.

She stole the mouse to wave the cursor around wildly. "Does this say they're dead?"

Given Rebecca's young age, Theo wondered if she'd ever been told about the tragedy of death. Carefully, he explained, "Actually, it says that Annabelle Maryweather and Malcolm Jones died. Maya Anderson and William Stirling went *missing*. There's a difference."

As Rebecca pondered that, she clicked her tongue. Theo selected another adjoining article, which provided detailed information about each founder. He scrolled to William's page.

Becca tapped Theo's knee. "Wait, hold on!" she exclaimed. "There's a picture of a plane crash! That means he has to be dead!"

"Thanks, Watson. But Mr. Stirling had the power of flight. Even if his plane had crashed, he could've flown out. Plus, they never found his body."

"Maybe he faked it."

The theory made Theo pause. After Malcolm Jones died and Jason obtained the rights to the school, William Stirling might have known the truth of his old friend's demise. Perhaps Stirling faked his death to prevent being targeted next. Theo couldn't be sure, but he wondered.

"Good point," he finally said to Rebecca. "This is serious stuff, so why don't you go see what Penny's doing? I'm sure she'd love company."

Rebecca stomped her foot. "That's what she said about you! I can't be running all over the place!"

Theo grinned. "Okay, fine. I guess I could use help cracking these mysteries."

The young girl brightened and dragged a chair to sit beside Theo, pumping the seat so she could put her elbows on the desk. "Let's do this!"

For the rest of the day, Theo and Rebecca scoured the internet for any clues. Dion brought them lunch and then dinner, yet she never chose to leave. When she became bored, Theo handed her a piece of paper and markers. While she colored, she pondered aloud. "How come Miss Maya disappeared?"

"I'm not sure," Theo admitted. He scanned through Maya's information, from her date of birth to the date of her disappearance. "Controlling the weather is arguably one of the strongest superpowers out there. If she was kidnapped, she obviously didn't put up much of a fight."

"Maybe she was eaten by a lion." Rebecca showed off her paper, which depicted a big yellow lion. "She was in Africa, right?"

"I suppose that is true."

The conversation seemed silly, but it gave Theo another idea. His fingers flew across the keyboard as he searched for every major storm in the last decade. No superhuman could last a whole year without using their powers. It wasn't possible. Theo had tried it once to make his mother happy, but after a few months, he lost control and blacked out the lights in the home for an entire week.

The storms listed were mostly tsunamis, hurricanes, and rainstorms —nothing too out of the ordinary. Fortunately, Theo recalled reading that Maya's favorite storms to summon were water-based. The weather reports even stated that the disasters seemed to come out of nowhere.

So, if Maya was alive, then she was in hiding and only coming out to release her pent-up power.

Malcolm Jones and Annabelle Maryweather, on the other hand, were deceased. Theo found their tombstones and obituaries, proving that fact. The causes of their deaths remained private because, apparently, "Leaking the method in which supers die is a privacy violation, since the information can be used against any descendants."

This left Theo with Stirling, the flying freak, and Anderson, a walking storm.

"Becca?" Theo asked as he tapped his pen against his chin. "I need advice."

She glanced up from her drawing. The lion was now jumping over a rainbow. "I'm really good at advice. My mom says so all the time."

"Do you think I should try to find these heroes? Do you think they'd help us?"

The question sobered the little girl. "I think they wanna be alone," she said.

"Why do you say that?"

"I think they ran away 'cause they were tired of being heroes."

Theo considered her perspective. There were days when he felt like running away. However, no matter how much the world hated heroes, Theo couldn't fathom two of the world's greatest supers leaving their team and academy behind without waiting to see the end of it.

Unless there was an immediate threat to their lives.

The door squeaked open, and Giselle's head poked through. "How's it going?" she said. "You've been in here for hours."

"We're solving a mystery!" Rebecca announced, standing with her fists on her hips. "And you're interrupting!"

Giselle looked to Theo, and he could only chuckle. "She's right," he said. "If you really need me—"

"We found someone."

Theo nearly toppled out of his chair. "You what?"

Giselle beckoned for him. "Scouts were checking the perimeter and said one of the traps got tripped."

Before she could continue, Theo bolted into the hall. Rebecca stood behind them, exclaiming, "But what about the mystery?"

The surveillance room was packed with teens, Carter amongst them. A blond-haired kid named Liam sat in the chair, talking. All conversation ceased when Theo walked in; everyone's pale faces turned to him.

Another boy pushed to the front. "We caught something on the edge of the base."

Theo's eyes narrowed as he neared the camera feed. The image was too dark to tell, but a faint white outline lay on the forest floor. "Is it dead?"

"I'm not sure," Liam said. "I saw it move a couple of minutes ago, but that was it."

"It's probably a rabbit," Carter pointed out. "Let's not be overdramatic about an animal."

Ignoring that, Theo nodded to Liam. "Take some backup. See what's going on. If it's anything that talks, shoot it."

"But what if—?"

Theo's stern glare cut Liam off. "Get Millie."

15

THE TRAPPER

While waiting for Millie to arrive, Theo paced. There wasn't another super he trusted more to perform this patrol. Her superpower allowed her to use any weapon like she'd mastered it for centuries. She never missed her shots, she never failed her mission, and she never left anyone behind. A girl like her ought to serve in the military. Unfortunately, due to her super DNA, she was rejected.

Bringing her to the cabin was a haze. Theo vaguely remembered having a chance encounter with her at a random gas station, whereupon she admitted her stepmother had abandoned her. She joined him on the condition that he would utilize her skills.

Within minutes, Millie sauntered into the surveillance room. Like usual, her curly brown hair was tamed into a ponytail, and a smug grin teased her lips. "What's the situation, boss?"

"We have a possible intruder," Theo explained, bristling at the title. "You and your team need to scout the area."

The news would have unnerved any other super, but it made Millie beam. "Well, then what are we waiting for? Let's go, boys!"

Liam and the others accompanied her out of the room, off to retrieve their supplies and weapons. Theo took the seat in front of the monitors and turned on his walkie-talkie. "Can you hear me?"

"Yes, sir," Millie responded. "Getting ready now."

Theo rubbed his face. He'd asked her not to call him 'sir' dozens of times. Clearly, it was a habit she was sticking to.

At the very least, her stubbornness could be appreciated. Whoever infiltrated their base might have to die. She was capable of fulfilling that.

The radio crackled. "Hey, Mils!" one of the boys, Adam, called out. "You seem anxious."

"Not anxious," she responded coolly. "But I am in the mood to fight."

As Theo listened to their conversation, he chewed the inside of his cheek. Millie and her boys were some of the most loyal supers here. Whatever Theo said, they would do. It was a lot of power to wield— almost too *much* power.

"Let's do this," she ordered.

From the camera showing the front door, Theo watched the boys follow her out, all of them dressed in black and clutching a weapon. When they entered the forest, it was nearly midnight. Darkness surrounded the group; the stars weren't even visible through the thick treetops. Rain dumped from the sky in curtains, glowing green on the screen.

As they neared the target, Millie's teammates split off to surround the trap. She was left to confront it on her own. The rain softly pitter-pattered around her, echoing through the walkie-talkie. Her flashlight scanned the area, illuminating the drops as flashes of silver. The storm concealed the sound of her footsteps, yet Theo suspected it made it harder to move. Her shoes sank so deeply in the mud that she had to yank her leg to walk.

Upon reaching the trap, she sprang behind a tree and switched her light off. "I thought you were wrong," she whispered into the radio. "I expected an animal, but it's not a rabbit, a bear, or a fox. It's a person."

Theo's posture slouched in the chair. His greatest fear had been realized. "Can you see what they look like? Do they have any weapons?"

Very cautiously, Millie crept to take a closer look. "Not that I can tell. He's bleeding, though. And his ankle is swollen."

Undoubtedly a result of trying to drag himself out of the trap. Theo squinted at the figure lying on the ground, wondering who it was.

Millie accidentally stepped on a stick, the sound making him stir. His eyelids cracked open, so she drew her gun. The skinny muzzle hovered near the boy's nose. "State your business or die," she demanded.

"Don't hurt him," Theo insisted. "Not yet." This boy was entitled to the right to speech. If he wanted to explain himself before Millie shot him, then by all means, he was allowed to talk.

The boy strained to free himself one last time, but after she fired a warning shot in the tree beside him, he froze. "I'm sorry," he cried, his voice hardly audible. "Please, I need to speak with Nightwave."

"Why?" Millie inquired.

"I have information. About Jones."

Theo inhaled so sharply he choked himself on the air. As he fought to slow his coughing, he saw Millie withdraw her gun. "What information?" she asked.

Rather than answer, the boy lay on the ground and repeated, "I need to talk to Nightwave."

"What's your call?" Millie said into the radio.

Theo's instincts urged him to stick to the plan. Getting rid of the boy would effectively eliminate their problem. But sympathy took hold of Theo's mind, alerting him to shake his head at himself. *I can't turn someone away when I know nothing about them. Maybe he can help us.*

"Bring him in," Theo said. "I'll hear him out."

Millie didn't question him. "Get him out of the trap," she commanded.

Her teammates converged on her spot, obeying immediately. Once the snare was cut, Millie bent down to help the boy to his feet. He couldn't stand on his own, so she wrapped an arm around his waist to drag him along. Seeing as he was skin and bones, she likely could've carried him.

Millie snapped to Adam, ordering, "Get him some food. We can't have him passing out on us."

"Aren't you going to blindfold him?" Adam inquired. "What if he remembers the path?"

"You're just trying to protect your precious snacks."

Groaning, Adam dug through his bag to grab an apple. The boy accepted it but didn't bite into it. When they approached the cabin, Theo switched cameras, anxiously analyzing every second.

"Calm down," Millie said to her captive, stern yet gentle. "We're not going to hurt you."

"You're not?" the boy answered. "Thank you."

"I'm just following orders."

As she dragged the mystery boy into the cabin, Theo spun out of his chair and hurried to the foyer. Millie sat the boy on the floor, who wrapped his shivering arms around himself.

"I hope you made the right call," she muttered. "If you change your mind, I'll take him outside."

"I don't think that will be..." Theo stopped talking. The skeleton on the floor seemed familiar. His appearance was unknown, but his dimmed vitality and fearful movements gave Theo pause. "Take him to the bunker," he said. "I'll be down in a bit."

Millie clapped to get the boy's attention. This time, she wasn't going to help him walk. She had her dignity. On the way to the basement, their voices gradually faded, but Theo heard one last bit.

"Is Nightwave always like that?" the boy said.

"Like what?"

"Scary."

Millie faked a laugh. "It's just the persona he uses. Trust me, Nightwave is probably the nicest guy you'll ever meet."

"So, what if he doesn't like what I have to say?"

"I guess I'll see you outside."

16

SEEING RED

Theo stood in front of the basement entrance, gnawing on his fingernails. Having an intruder so close to the cabin, and now inside, set him on edge. The lights flickered weakly above him, hardly able to stay on.

The boy downstairs claimed to have information about Jones. But he addressed Theo by his school name, Nightwave. He must've been a student or otherwise connected to Jones.

Footsteps neared him, accompanied by Dion's, "What's going on?"

"We have an intruder," Theo said, keeping his voice hushed from the children nearby.

Dion wasn't as careful and gasped. "What? Who is it?"

"I'm not sure," Theo admitted. "But Millie found him in the forest, and we have to question him. Let's go."

The two walked down the stairs. "Question him?" Dion asked. "We're not detectives. What are we going to say?"

"I don't know, but it's dangerous to go alone. I need you."

131

The heavy dilemma bore no weight on Dion. Playfully, he elbowed Theo in the ribs and remarked, "You know I love being a sacrifice."

At the bottom of the basement stairs, Millie stood guard at the bunker door. "Just so you're aware," she said, "the kid and I tracked in mud, so you might have to clean that."

Theo cocked his head to the side. "Go away."

Millie saluted. "Yes, sir."

While she bounded up the stairs, Theo continued, "We'll ask him what he's doing here, how he got here. We need to know everything so we can prevent this from ever happening again."

Dion stared at the bunker door. It wasn't really a bunker, just a room without windows. "Are we doing 'good cop, bad cop'? Because if so, can I be the bad cop?"

Hoping to restrain his grin, Theo pressed his mouth into a line. "We're not doing that. It's stupid."

"Stupid enough to work. Watch this!" Dion cracked the door, then kicked it open with a slam. "Listen, punk," he said to the shaking boy at the table. "You made a grave mistake coming here. And if you want any chance of leaving alive, you'll do exactly what we say. Understand?"

Quickly, the boy nodded. Dion flashed Theo a smug look, yet Theo rolled his eyes.

Dion loomed over the desk. "How'd you get here? Huh?"

"I-I took the bus for a little bit and then I walked when I realized…"

Dion raised a fist, which enticed the boy to finish, "I realized I could be tracked! I didn't want anyone to know I came here."

"Were you followed?" Dion inquired.

"No," the boy insisted. "Risking your safety was my last intention."

"How did you know about this place?" Theo interrupted from his spot near the door.

"It was a guess."

Dion scoffed. "A guess, he says! Then, you must be the luckiest person in the world!"

The boy almost smiled at that part. "I knew you guys had escaped the academy, and I figured you'd stick together, so I did a little research and came across this cabin."

Dion and Theo looked at each other, sharing the same uneasy glance. Were they being watched that day they left the school?

"So, you're a super?" Dion asked, much more reserved.

"Yes," the boy forced out.

"What can you do?"

"I-I'd like to tell Nightwave in private. Please."

"Why?" Theo demanded. He felt the shadows behind him sharpen and prickle, feeding off his fear. "Whatever you need to say can be said to both of us."

The boy wrung his hands, no longer finding amusement in the interrogation. "I'm sorry, I-I don't think I'm comfortable with that."

Comfortable? The darkness spat. *You spared his life; you offered him mercy, and this is how he repays you?*

Theo slammed his palms on the tabletop, nearly startling the boy out of his chair. "I'm risking the safety of my team to hear you out!" Theo yelled. "You should be thankful I'm not leaving you alone with me. Trust me, you *don't* want that!"

The threats made the boy clam up. Literally. He wrapped his arms around his knees and curled into a tight ball. With the interrogation halted, Dion dragged Theo out of the bunker and said, "Bad cop was a bad idea. We need him to cooperate."

Theo buried his hands in his hair. "Then, what do you suggest we do?"

The door at the top of the basement stairs creaked open, and Lily popped through. "I overheard about our little predicament," she said. "Let me try cracking the prisoner."

Her offer, while generous, heightened Theo's stress. "Lily, *please* leave. I don't want anyone else involved."

Lily's expression remained blank. "I can read and alter emotions. Even if our prisoner tries to lie to me, I will be able to tell. I can coerce him into telling the truth."

Dion gave a one-shoulder shrug. "She's right."

Theo directed his glare between the two of them, eventually settling on Lily. "Do you need any backup?"

Just before entering the bunker, she stated, "You will just get in my way."

Minutes dragged like hours. As Theo waited on the staircase, he tapped his foot in the rhythm of Für Elise. It was the first song he ever mastered. Playing it always brought him an ounce of comfort, knowing he'd perfected at least one thing.

"This guy must've known us," Dion mused aloud. He sprawled on the floor, squinting at the ceiling. "Could he have been a previous student?"

Theo's music paused. "He wasn't a villain. We would've recognized him."

"A hero, then?"

"Possibly. I'm more worried about the fact that he found us." Theo's musical tapping resumed, but in a tempo that was too fast to fit the melody. Unable to stop, Theo's pulse quickened with every beat.

Behind him, the door squeaked, and quiet footsteps crept down the stairs. Penny draped her arms around Theo's neck and touched a gentle kiss to his temple. "Are you okay?" she asked, innocent as ever.

Für Elise was restored. Calmed once more, Theo leaned his head against her legs. "Always."

"What are you doing down here?"

"Millie caught a guy sneaking into the cabin," Dion explained. "Lily's questioning him."

Penny gasped and released Theo. A rush of cold air slammed into him. "Is he dangerous?" she asked.

"I can't tell," Theo answered, turning to her. "But I promise I won't let him hurt us."

Penny's concerned frown relaxed. "You mean me?"

"I'll especially be sure with you."

She laughed. The sound erased any anxiety plaguing Theo; he couldn't remember the last time she laughed like this. He would have continued, yet Lily, unscathed and safe, emerged from the bunker. "His name is Daniel Turner," she informed them. "He's twenty-one."

Dion shot into a sitting position. "Are you serious? That dude looks like he's sixteen! Poor guy must've been through a lot."

"He has. Recently, he was the victim of trauma, both physically and emotionally." Lily motioned to Penny. "I believe the only person to talk to him should be Penelope."

Theo's heart stopped. At the same time, he moved in front of her, his head shaking as he said, "Not a chance. We can't trust this guy."

"We can't," Lily agreed. "But he's telling the truth. He wasn't followed and discovered the cabin on his own." She cleared her throat. "There is a small problem. His superpower is the ability to take other powers. He could render any of us vulnerable in a matter of minutes."

Theo stiffened. Not only was this boy dangerous, but he was the one working with Principal Jones to take the students' powers.

He was *Red*.

The boy who'd made students suffer, who nearly caught Dion, who hurt so many other supers. If he found them, then Jones must be on his way.

"Not happening," Theo said, feeling like he had marbles in his mouth. "We need to get rid of this guy. We need to—"

"He has information about Jones," Lily argued. "We can't afford to lose that."

"This isn't your decision!" Theo exclaimed. "I am not sacrificing the safety of my supers for him!"

"He needs our help! Are you going to deny him?"

Lily's sudden fire made Theo hesitate. Allowing Red to stay, even for the night, might prove to be deadly. A killing machine could be camouflaged underneath his shaky persona.

However, Theo had welcomed Carter into the cabin, regardless of his past with Principal Jones. Theo had promised to help every super, including those that he didn't like. One thing was certain: This decision would affect the entire cabin.

Penny took Theo's hand. At her touch, he knelt in front of her. "I'm going in there," she whispered.

His grip tightened. "You can't. What if he takes your powers?"

"I don't rely on my power to fight."

Still, Theo resisted. "I won't let you be alone with him."

"I'll call for you at the first sign of trouble. Just stay right here, and it'll be fine."

Theo knew he was fighting a losing battle. Upon first hearing that Red needed help, Penny was interested. The danger didn't matter to her, not when there was someone to heal. She couldn't help it; Theo knew that. Yet it made the situation so much harder to swallow.

He released her and stood against the wall, allowing Penny access to the bunker. As she tiptoed through the door, Theo swore that if any harm befell her, he'd paint the room red.

17

THE NEW MEMBER

Right as Penny entered, the boy in the chair tensed. "It's okay," she assured. "My name is Penny. Lily thought you could use my company."

Daniel remained stiff, allowing Penny an opportunity to study him closer. Cracked mud and dried blood covered every inch of his skin. Undoubtedly, it fed his discomfort. Keeping one eye on him, she snuck into the corner with a small shelf. Out of the few supplies there, she grabbed a towel.

Approaching the boy once more, she asked, "Can I help you?"

He didn't dare look at her. "I guess."

Up close, she could see his dozens of injuries. Bruises from every shade imaginable peppered his face and neck. Minor scratches sliced his arms and legs, but that would be consistent if he tumbled through the forest.

Being cautious around his wounds, she tried to be as gentle as possible as she scrubbed off the dirt. He looked like he hadn't eaten for days; his cheeks were sunken, and his clothes hung on his small frame.

Suffering hovered around him like a cloud. She had to fight the urge to embrace him right then and there.

Daniel's brown eyes flitted from one corner of the room to the next, anywhere to avoid Penny's gaze. He had relaxed somewhat since she arrived, but there was a tightness in his jaw.

"I know you," he said, his voice hoarse. "Your name is Penelope Bradshaw. Your birthday is April 21st. You were born in Youngstown, Ohio."

"I'm not very interesting." Penny gave a light laugh to ease the tension.

"That's not what Jones thought. He wasn't too happy when you connected with Nightwave."

Satisfied with her work, Penny rested the towel on the table. "You kept tabs on me."

"I had to. I needed to ensure you were safe from him."

Penny reached out again, and this time, Daniel let her take his wrist. Gradually, his bruises faded. The scratches sealed. Unfortunately, no matter how much pain was erased, he remained uneasy. "I know you don't trust me," he said. "I know Nightwave absolutely doesn't. I can't blame him. I'm a terrible person."

"We all make mistakes," Penny said.

Daniel yanked away. "Angel, you don't understand. I-I did something awful."

The door clicked open, cutting off whatever explanation Daniel was about to give. As Theo entered the room, he said, "Penny? You good?"

With a nod, she met him at the doorway. Almost immediately, he hugged her. His concern seeped into her.

She pressed her palms flat against him, urging her healing to prepare him for her following words. "I think Daniel should stay," she said.

Theo recoiled sharply. "*Stay?*" he repeated. "What, like, here? Are you insane?"

"He doesn't want to go back to wherever he came from," Penny insisted. "Clearly, he found us because he wants to be one of us."

"He took your friends' powers at the school," Theo accused. "He let Jones do whatever he pleased, and the whole time, he could've taken Jones's invincibility!" Theo pointed at Daniel. "Why didn't you fight?"

As difficult as it was to stomach, Theo's claims were valid. Daniel had hurt many of Penny's school friends and didn't stop Jones when he clearly had the capability. Unfortunately, Daniel needed healing. His pain couldn't be ignored.

Penny cupped Theo's cheek to make him look at her. "I know it's complicated," she said, "but please trust me."

At least if nothing else, Penny knew that Theo would listen to her. Even though he sighed, he relented, "We don't have any open rooms yet, so I'll figure it out. For tonight, he can sleep in here, and I'll have some volunteers guard the door."

"No need. I'm staying with him."

"Penny—"

"Daniel needs me. It's how he'll trust us to tell the full truth. I can get him to talk, but I need time." She spoke the next part in a much quieter voice. "And I need to be alone."

Like she expected, Theo blurted, "I'm not leaving you overnight!"

"Look at him," Penny pleaded. "He can't hurt me, regardless of whether he takes my power. Can you *please* trust me?"

Theo's jaw clenched. Behind him, the shadows on the wall contorted. Despite his exterior reactions, he didn't seem angry. His distress was palpable in his tender grip. "It's impossible to convince you otherwise," he said. "Stay safe. I'll have my phone on all night if you need me, and I'll return at sunrise." He moved past Penny to deliver a final message to Daniel. "Just so you know, you're only here because she sees good in you. You'd better prove her right."

Daniel swallowed. "I'll do my best."

Theo paused to give Penny one last tight embrace before hurrying out.

From the closet, she retrieved spare blankets and pillows for Daniel. She patted it, coaxing him to abandon his chair. Reluctantly, he moved to his makeshift mattress.

"Please don't stay," he begged. "I shouldn't be treated kindly."

Penny brushed the shaggy hair from his forehead. "Why do you say that?"

"I've killed people." The words came out far easier than she would've expected, as if he had been practicing them in his head. "Maybe I wasn't the 'trigger man,' but I helped commit the crime."

"You were forced to," she pointed out, hoping it was true.

"Whether I was or wasn't doesn't change the fact that it happened. There are no excuses." Daniel shuffled his position. "We always have a choice. I didn't make good ones."

Penny wanted to tell him to think positively, to forgive himself, but she couldn't find her voice to speak. "Go to sleep, Daniel," she said instead. "I'll be here for you."

Sensing his hesitation, she squeezed his wrist. Her power cleared the stress from his mind, and his eyelids drooped with exhaustion. He curled up in his blankets and whispered, "You're amazing."

She couldn't resist her smile. "Good night, Daniel."

It only took thirty seconds for him to fall asleep. She suspected he hadn't slept for days prior, but because of her power, he was calm enough to shut his brain off.

When she grew tired, she lay on the floor and turned to face him. Willing herself to stay awake, she pinched her arm repeatedly. Regardless of how much she wanted to trust Daniel, she wasn't sure if she could. He seemed remorseful for his mistakes; to what extent, she wasn't sure.

Inside her pocket, her phone buzzed, alerting her to dig it out. Admittedly, she'd been a bit unsure of using burner phones, but they'd become a valuable tool to communicate in secret. There, on the screen, Theo's message read,

Hope you're okay.

Penny shifted her position so that she could answer while holding onto Daniel.

I am. Stop worrying about me and go to bed.

I'll stay awake for as long as you do. :)

Butterflies took flight in Penny's stomach.

We might be here for a long time.

Sounds good to me. Let's talk.

The door slammed open, waking both Penny and Daniel. The sound startled Daniel into recoiling against the wall, his eyes wide and panicked.

"Whoops," Dion said, "I just came to see if you guys needed breakfast."

Not having the strength to reach for Daniel, Penny nodded. Healing him continuously throughout the night made his injuries disappear, but now, she was more tired than she could describe.

"Did you stay up all night?" Daniel asked, his breathing short.

She couldn't answer. However, the truth was more than evident in her sluggish movements. She could barely keep her head upright.

"Penny needs to leave," Daniel announced, his voice surprisingly defiant. "She can't listen to me if she's exhausted. I'll talk to someone else."

That definitely woke Penny. Her power stuttered back to life, almost like it was saying, *"I'm never tired! I can heal forever and ever!"*

Dion didn't seem as offended as she was and shrugged. "Alright, I'll tell Theo."

"I'm fine!" Penny claimed. "I can—"

"If you stay," Daniel interrupted, "I won't say another word. I saw you work yourself to the bone at the academy. I won't let you do it again."

An odd combination of comfort and frustration battled in Penny's chest. At long last, she found someone who saw past her healing. Of all people, *Daniel* prioritized her health over his own.

After a few tense seconds, she stood. Her power prompted her to stop. Daniel was still injured and sad! How could she turn her back on those who needed her?

Each step up the stairs felt like lifting a thousand pounds. Penny hoped she'd be able to make it to her room.

18

HONEST LIES

As Theo folded his laundry, he hummed a song he remembered Tara sung frequently at home. Despite the circumstances, he almost felt at ease. Minutes prior, Penny had stumbled into his room and spouted an incoherent greeting. He had to carry her to her room and tuck her into bed. She was tired, but she was safe. That was all that mattered.

The shadows disrupted behind him, accompanied by the physical presence of a person. Without looking, Theo said, "Is Red gone yet?"

"Nope," Dion responded, "and he wants to talk to you."

"I'm not talking to him," Theo spat. "It's bad enough that he's in our house!"

Dion crossed his arms. "He's been nothing but civil to us. What's your problem?"

Theo's fists clenched, wrinkling the shirt he was holding. "My *problem* is that we can't trust him. What if Jones knows he's here?"

"Daniel said he wasn't followed. Plus, he definitely seems like the kind of guy who makes his moves very carefully, so I doubt he's lying."

"He was stealing powers from the students," Theo hissed. "This 'nice boy' act might fool you and Penny, but he can't pull the wool over my eyes. Anyone associated with Jones can't be near us."

A crease formed between Dion's brows. "Carter was working with Jones, not by choice, but by necessity. I think that's what happened to Daniel, too. Can't we give him a second chance?"

Second chance? Theo thought with a scoff. *I let him stay last night. There's his second chance.*

Dion removed the shirt from Theo's grasp and folded it neatly. "I vote we let him stay," Dion said. "At least for a while. We can't let him go back to wherever he was. He needs us."

"Whatever," Theo grumbled, tossing the remainder of his clothes onto the bed. "But you're on the hook for this kid."

Dion grinned. "Good thing I'm your favorite."

Theo retrieved his journal and marched into the hallway yet paused at Penny's bedroom door. He peeked inside, confirming she was still peacefully snoozing.

Equipped with a notebook full of questions, Theo hurried downstairs and entered the living room. Daniel sat in the corner recliner, cautiously watching a few of the kids play Monopoly on the floor.

Theo stepped over them and approached Daniel, ignoring the way he stiffened. "I heard you were ready to talk to me," Theo said. "I've got some questions for you, too."

Daniel nodded. "I'm ready to cooperate."

Theo sat on the couch beside him and opened his notes. "Where is Jones's hideout?"

"He has a couple," Daniel answered. "The only one I've ever been to is New York. Exactly where in the city, I can't be sure."

"Does he ever leave the country?" Theo went on.

"Never. He's terrified of flying."

The statement piqued Theo's interest. It wasn't uncommon for people to have a phobia of flying, but it seemed too specific in Jones's case. Did he fear flying because of a particular super he was avoiding?

As Theo scribbled his notes, Daniel stated, "Dion really likes to eat."

Theo glanced over his shoulder, catching Dion stuffing his face with a mound of pancakes. "Yeah," Theo agreed, a lilt of laughter gracing his voice. "No matter how much he eats, he'll never gain weight."

"It must make him feel bad," Daniel continued mournfully. "Unlike the other guys in the cabin, he can't retain muscle. It's like he's... dead." Daniel's gaze drifted down to his own arm, a skinny, pale layer of flesh against bone.

Theo cleared his throat. "Listen, I regret how I treated you yesterday."

Daniel folded like a lawn chair. "I can't be trusted. Your reactions were logical."

"That doesn't defend my behavior. My mom taught me better."

A ghost of a smile hinted at Daniel's mouth. "You're close to her?"

At the thought of his mother, Theo almost grinned. Almost. "Yeah. Are you close with your mother?"

A lull fell in the room while Daniel worked himself up to say, "My mom died giving birth to me. I never knew her."

Theo's almost-grin disappeared. Something in Daniel's admission, whether it be his story or his tone, disturbed Theo. He almost didn't want to continue talking. "And your dad?" Theo asked, forcing the question.

"I don't know where to start."

"Too much to talk about?"

"Too little. I don't really remember him."

Theo clicked his pen once, twice, three times. To this point, Daniel had been genuine. There was no reason for Theo not to do the same.

"Growing up," he said, "I thought I knew my dad pretty well. But recently, I've discovered that I don't."

"I'm sorry," Daniel whispered. "That must be difficult."

Silence stretched and ebbed between the two of them. Like molasses, it dripped from the walls, encasing them in a quiet bubble. Theo scanned his list of questions, each one underlined with harsh black ink. *"How many people have you killed? What happened to the expelled supers? Why didn't you stop Jones?"* None of it felt appropriate anymore.

"In case you're wondering," Daniel said, "I can take any power, but I can't use it as my own." He chuckled to himself. "I'm not good at stealing either. Anything that blocks the connection stops me. A distraction, for instance, or even my own feelings."

"It must have been hard to hurt other supers," Theo said. "I used to think it was a fate worse than death to have your powers removed. I thought the loss of oneself was more tragic. Now, I'm thinking the opposite."

"You shouldn't. Our powers make us who we are."

"Sometimes, I don't want mine."

"You don't have a choice," Daniel spoke gently, despite his statement being a bit harsh.

Theo flipped his notebook closed. "I guess you didn't have a choice either, being picked as Jones's sidekick. How did you arrive at the school? Were you supposed to be a student like Carter?"

Color drained from Daniel's complexion. He fidgeted in his seat; his gaze roamed. "I-I don't remember."

Lies. Theo felt the shadows tickling his ear. *He's lying.*

Ignoring them, Theo tried again. "Come on, you must remember. How long were you at the school? Longer than Peter?"

"It's hard to say." Proving himself right, Daniel gulped repeatedly, as if hoping to swallow his own words.

Theo pivoted out of his chair. "I really hope you're telling the truth,

Daniel. By allowing you to stay, I'm putting the safety of my friends at risk. But they see good in you, so don't prove them wrong."

Then, Theo trudged upstairs. The answers he received were informative but not entirely satisfying. He had to know every detail about Daniel; he had to know precisely who they welcomed into their home.

He carried his notebook under one arm as he approached his bedroom. The internet might have more information on Daniel's checkered past, especially if he was connected to Jones. But the second Theo eased his door open, he froze. A box rested on his bed. The contents spilled out across Penny's lap—journals, letters, and magazines.

His heart lurched in his throat. "What are you doing?"

She didn't look at him. "What is this stuff? Why is it here?"

"What are you doing?" he repeated, harder this time.

"I came to find extra blankets for Daniel. But then I found this." She gently flipped Tara's letter over. "You've been talking to your family and didn't tell me?"

"Wait. Don't be upset."

"I'm allowed to be upset!" Penny was yelling, but it wasn't angry yelling. It was the kind of fury plagued by sadness, wet and treacherous. "How could you lie to me? To all of us? You knew how much we missed our own families and you—" Suddenly, she stopped. With her focus glued to the box, she retrieved an item that made Theo wince. The pills in the bottle rattled, accompanied by her accusatory, "What are these?"

The walls felt like they were closing in on Theo. The oxygen sucked out of the room, leaving him to gasp for air. He wished he'd taken Felix's advice to tell Penny, and also wished he'd hidden his secret better.

"Dion must've put those there as a joke," Theo explained. He tried to take the bottle, but Penny held onto it.

"Antidepressants." Her volume dropped to a whisper. "Why didn't you tell me?"

"Because."

She frowned. "Because?"

"Because I was…"

Embarrassed. Upset. *Terrified.*

"I just couldn't," he finally answered. "It's hard to talk about."

"So, that's why you've been acting differently," she muttered. "Yet you lied and said you were happier because of me."

"That's the truth!"

She slammed the box onto the ground. The green in her eyes flared like fire, burning past the tears. "No more lies, Theo! What is going on?"

Beneath the bed, the shadows curled around Theo's ankles, rooting him. He couldn't run. Not anymore.

He swiped the medication from her. "Fine, you want the truth? I took these for you! I know you're afraid of me, and I hoped these would fix me, so you didn't have to!"

"I never said I was afraid!"

"You didn't have to!" His tone softened. "I thought this would make me normal. You've been trying to heal me since the school. I did it for you."

"This isn't healing! This is—" Penny bit her lip, turning the pink into a pale.

Theo sat next to her on the bed. There were hundreds of words he wanted to say to her. Doing this made him feel *safe*. He felt like himself again; he felt like he was accepted again. No one wanted to deal with him when he was depressed, but when he was happy, everyone loved him! Was it really so wrong to pursue that feeling?

"Hey," he murmured as he lifted her chin. "Nothing I say will fix this. I know that. But I guess I was…"

Penny leaned forward, hung on his every syllable. "Tell me how you feel, Theo. Don't pretend or cover it up."

His brain screamed at him to speak, to tell the truth, to explain how agonizing every moment was.

His mouth didn't move.

A few minutes passed in heartbreaking silence. Finally, Penny stood. "Whatever," she growled, "don't tell me. I'll add that to the list of secrets you're keeping from me."

When she reached the door, he blurted, "I'm sorry."

"If you were really sorry, you'd change."

In a blink, she was gone. With her absence, Theo had every opportunity to reflect on what he'd done: the lies, the manipulation, the pain he'd caused her. In an act of defiance, mostly against himself, he snatched his pill bottle and stomped to the bathroom.

Without a second thought, he dumped the pills into the toilet and flushed them away. He thought antidepressants would've been a blessing. A chance for him to return to the boy he used to be, the boy everyone liked.

The boy Penny wanted.

For her, he vowed to fix himself on his own—no prescriptions or pretending.

Yet as he left the bathroom, his pulse raced. *Turn around*, his mind insisted. *You need those to be normal! Your friends won't care about you if you're not normal! Are you really going to discard your happiness for her?*

But much like his act, his happiness wasn't real.

19

A DARK REQUIEM

Theo and Penny didn't talk all afternoon. They didn't even look at each other. Never before had Theo felt this low. Not when his dad died, not when he was at the school, never. She deserved more than this. More than him.

Eventually, he sat across from her at dinner, but only because Daniel had stolen the seat beside her. The meal wasn't anything extravagant. In fact, it was just leftover breakfast from earlier, but Theo focused on his food like it was the best he'd ever eaten. It was his sole distraction from Penny and Daniel.

"I'm not hungry," Daniel claimed.

"Peter made it," Penny urged. "If you don't at least try it, he'll be so upset."

With that, Daniel nibbled on a pancake. Penny squeezed his hand with her own, exposing her ring-free fingers.

A toxic mixture of disappointment and jealousy boiled in Theo's gut. He'd always liked Penny, but this feeling was deeper. Thoughts of her plagued his mind, constantly replaying the memory of her kisses. It physically pained him to be apart from her. Was love supposed to be this overwhelming?

Every time Penny laughed at Peter's jokes or stared too long at Daniel, Theo's gut twisted. *He* wanted her attention; *he* wanted to make her laugh. He wanted her to be *his*.

Theo returned his gaze to his plate. This was selfish thinking. No wonder she was frustrated with him.

Once Daniel finished his food, he rested his head on Penny's shoulder, his eyes half-lidded in bliss. Undeterred, she continued talking with Yasmine yet stumbled over her words.

Her constant healing is hurting her. Theo couldn't be sure where the realization was coming from—his personal thoughts or the shadows. The two were starting to sound eerily similar. *See how Daniel doesn't care? He's taking her power.*

Theo bent his fork in half. Above the table, the lights flickered. A few kids whispered about ghosts. But Penny looked right at Theo.

"Can I talk to you?" he asked, unable to camouflage the tightness in his voice.

Penny hesitated, then tapped Daniel's head and said, "I'll be right back."

He nodded sheepishly and pulled away. By some miracle, Theo didn't react. Instead, he led her from the room and shut the door behind them.

Penny breathed a deep sigh. "Theo, I don't want to fight."

Predicting her escape, he snatched her wrist. "We have a few things to discuss."

"If this is about your communication with your family, I was mad for a while, but I understand. We needed the money they sent. I just wish you didn't lie about it."

"It's not about that. It's about…" Theo tilted his head toward the dining room.

Recognition dawned on Penny's expression. "*Daniel*? You made me leave because you're jealous?"

"I made you leave because you're *exhausted*," Theo corrected. "You don't have to heal him twenty-four hours a day."

Penny planted her fists on her hips. "Actually, I do. You don't know what he's been through."

"You're going to sacrifice your strength for some dude you met a day ago? Why?"

She shook her head. "I don't want to talk about this."

The shadows crossed in an X, blocking the door. "Why does he mean so much to you?" Theo asked. "After what he's done, why are you going to help him?"

Penny flung her arms out wide. "Because this is all I have, Theo! I'm a *healer*!"

"You're more than that!"

Her lips parted in soft surprise, almost like she didn't believe him. But Theo understood how much she'd sacrificed to become their 24/7 nurse. She used to love sparring and physical training—activities she hadn't been able to partake in very much since being at the cabin. Deep down, she *was* more than a healer. Sadly, she didn't get the chance to show that.

"I wish that were true," she mourned. "Except I have to spend every waking moment knowing that if I don't heal, then someone will suffer for it. I have no other choice but to use my power."

Their argument, though loud and disruptive, was the most honest conversation they'd had in weeks. It was oddly refreshing. "You can be selfish sometimes," he suggested.

Penny pinched the bridge of her nose, trying to quell her rising tears. "I can't. I know you think it's easy, but it's not. My power compels me to sacrifice everything I have."

Like Lily explained, their powers had a strong influence over their emotions. Theo used to believe Penny healed out of kindness, but that couldn't be farther from the truth. She could only care so much. And when she couldn't, her powers forced her to.

"Maybe you can fight your instincts," he said.

Her eyes narrowed into thin slits. "Like you have?"

In a sudden rush, Theo felt the blood drain from his face. Penny's aggravation was justified yet knowing that made the regret worse. Being gutted with a knife would've felt better than this.

She must have sensed his pain, because she blurted, "I'm sorry, I-I didn't mean it like that. Our powers must have more of an effect on us than we thought. It's hard to disobey."

Theo bit the inside of his cheek. It felt like his tongue was swollen, practically preventing him from speaking. "I'm trying to protect you," he mumbled. "You're neglecting yourself and your own needs."

"That's what you've been doing for months," she answered softly. "Now, you know how I feel." She turned for the door, and the darkness covering it faded. "For the record," she added, "I'm helping him because I can't help you. At least he lets me try."

Theo didn't stop her exit. The door shut behind her, and her praise for Daniel filtered through the crack at the bottom. "I'm so proud of you!"

Theo bit his tongue until blood filled his mouth. In the corners of the room, the shadows slithered. Their demands grew louder. *Life was perfect before Daniel showed up. He has to go. You have to—*

Theo switched the lights on, muffling the cold voices in his mind. They weren't gone, but they had quieted. Thinking about Penny would make him unhinged, yet it seemed it was all he could do.

A knock echoed on the wooden door, and Dion slipped through. "Why aren't you at dinner?" he inquired.

"Because."

"Great. Now, I know what it was like when my mom tried to talk to me."

"Are you upset with me?" Theo asked.

Dion's smirk exuded more confusion than amusement. "About what? Unless you ate my cupcakes, I don't think there's anything that'd make me very mad at you."

"Do you think I…ignore myself?"

The look of *Penny told you* dawned on Dion. His grin disappeared. "Well, to start, I think it's good you care for the kids."

"But?"

"But sometimes you forget you're human and need all the things you're giving them. You put their desires above your own. Sometimes it can go a little too far."

Based on Dion's hesitance, Theo assumed he was nervous. Except Theo wasn't angry; at least, not with Dion. Theo rubbed his palms together, generating warmth in his otherwise freezing body. "I hate Daniel," he proclaimed.

"Why?"

"I feel like he's keeping a secret. But no one believes me because I'm…"

Dion glanced up. "Different?"

"Difficult," Theo corrected. "I'm not the same guy I used to be."

"As far as I'm concerned, you're still my best friend. That will never change."

The sentiment may have touched Theo, but he didn't bother to thank Dion. "I wish I could fix myself," Theo admitted. "Maybe then Penny wouldn't be so upset."

"Who says you need to fix yourself? Just because you're in a bit of a rough patch doesn't mean you're any less awesome." When that didn't strike either, Dion added, "I know it's hard, but maybe Penny isn't the one for you. I can think of a ton of girls who would love it if you were single."

What girl in their right mind would be interested in Theo? And why?

"It doesn't matter," Theo said. "No one else would compare."

A smile ghosted Dion's mouth. "Sounds like you love her."

"I don't." Theo paused, then corrected, "I do." But that didn't feel right either. "How would I know?"

"I guess you just know."

And what would happen after Theo told her? Even if she did feel the same, it wouldn't make a difference. She would be used as another liability, a weakness. Admitting his feelings for her would make her feel tied down to him, as if he were one more person to heal. He didn't need anyone to take care of him.

"I'm going downstairs," he said. "I think I need a minute alone."

"You sure?"

The shadows twisted across the floor, directing Theo to the basement. He nodded and answered, "I'm sure."

Dion didn't follow, allowing Theo to creep downstairs and around the corner of the training room. Upon finding it empty, a wave of relief enveloped him. His emotions were sky high; he had to subdue his powers before he exploded.

He debated asking Lily to manipulate him, but she would've refused and told him to deal with it on his own. He could ask Penny to heal him but couldn't run the risk of hurting her. He could tell Daniel to remove his power, but Theo didn't trust him with anything, let alone his own safety.

Rather than do any of that, Theo turned every light on, smothering the influence of his power. As he released a breath, he sat against the wall. Strangely, the silence helped calm his mind, when so often before it plagued him. His pulse slowed; his muscles eased. A morsel of the darkness broke apart, allowing him to catch a rare glimpse of clarity and content.

The door to the basement creaked open, and a flurry of footsteps pattered on the stairs. Theo inched farther into the corner to make himself smaller.

Unfortunately, Daniel spotted Theo and immediately beelined for him. "I was looking for you!"

"Funny, I was avoiding you."

Ignoring the sarcasm, Daniel said, "Nightwave, I—"

"That's not my name."

Awkwardly, Daniel shifted his weight. "Right, Theo. Apologies."

Hearing Daniel speak Theo's name, the one primarily reserved for friends and family, made a bad taste linger in Theo's mouth.

"I know you don't like me," Daniel continued, "but I wanted to say that I'm really grateful for the kindness you've shown me."

Theo shut his eyes. "I'm just doing my job."

A shuffling sounded from Daniel's proximity. Theo peeked, finding Daniel sitting on the floor. He kept his distance yet was close enough so that Theo could hear him speak. "Your determination is admirable," Daniel said. "Jones tried to break that in you."

"Like he did with you?" In the back of Theo's mind, he knew what he said was cruel, but he didn't care. It was a true statement; what was so wrong with saying it?

"I guess exactly like that," Daniel forced out. "I thought family was supposed to love each other, but he didn't."

Theo's stomach dropped to his feet. Despite desperately wanting to run away, he couldn't move a centimeter. "Family?" he repeated.

"I swear he doesn't know I'm here," Daniel assured. "I couldn't stand being around him anymore, and I saw how you and your friends defended each other at the academy, so I figured you might welcome me too."

Theo shook his head. "Go back. How are you related to him?"

As if he were ashamed, Daniel hid his face. "Principal Jones is my uncle. After my dad died, I went to live with him. I didn't want you to know, so I used my mom's maiden name instead—Turner."

"Your dad was invincible," Theo pointed out. Daniel could transfer powers from one person to another. The only way his dad would've been killed was if…

That's impossible, Theo said to himself. *Daniel wouldn't help kill his own father by transferring his invincibility to Principal Jones. Right?*

"He was," Daniel said, not noticing Theo's growing discomfort. "I don't remember how he died, but I'm sure Jones did it. He'd talk about your family constantly. He obsessed over your father because he wanted revenge for his wife and son's deaths."

"My dad didn't kill them," Theo defended, a snap to his tone.

"Jones doesn't believe that. For years, he tracked every move your father made in the hopes he'd catch him off guard. Which is why he finally snapped and…" Daniel's voice died.

The house squeaked as children ran around upstairs, their heavy stomping just feet from Theo's head. Daniel kept his gaze locked on the floor as he said, "Not every super hurt Jones, but he's become addicted to hurting them. He told me once how enjoyable it is to take their power, to reduce them to weak humans like he used to be."

"So, why does he want to be a super?" Theo accused. "For the power?"

"It's not just about power for him. If he's the last super standing, then maybe the world will be as safe as he imagines. After all, he'll be the sole danger remaining." Daniel pinched his arm, as if he was rooting himself in the present moment. "Your father was a good man. He shouldn't have been portrayed as the villain."

"Quit talking about him," Theo ordered, feeling his composure crack. "You didn't know him."

"I heard—"

"Stop it!" Theo didn't want to be so rude, but the emotional discussion stoked a fire in his gut. "I can't listen to you try to relate to me! My father was killed right in front of me! I was there—*I* knew him!"

"I was there, too!" Daniel exclaimed, almost as loudly. "I know what happened!"

Both boys froze. They were equally horrified at Daniel's proclamation; the blood drained from their complexions. Somehow, the words, "What did you say?" were uttered from Theo's mouth.

A wince contorted Daniel's features. Through gritted teeth, he explained, "A long time ago, Jones was preparing me for something big. He took me and a few of his bodyguards into the city." Daniel picked at the wooden paneling on the ground. "I didn't understand what we were doing, really. One of my uncle's friends split off while we waited a few blocks away. That's when I noticed we were following someone. Jones told me that it was a super who abused his powers. He needed me to take your father's powers so he wouldn't fight back."

Theo turned cold. Shadows swirled at his fingertips.

"I was ready to obey. But then I saw how terrified you were. How *young* you were. I couldn't bring myself to take another kid's father when I had lost mine. So, I didn't." Daniel's tone shifted; he was almost happy. "Your dad nearly killed Jones. I had no idea your power could injure an invincible man. I was actually excited, thinking his abuse would come to an end."

"It didn't make a difference. My dad was murdered."

"I know. I have to live with the regret of knowing I could've saved your dad, and I didn't. I'm sorry."

Theo stood. Simple apologies would not win his forgiveness; he wouldn't allow it. Instinctively, he wanted to attack Daniel. If Daniel had resisted just once, then Dad would be alive. The students would be safe.

That was the darkness talking. Instead of listening, Theo spat, "Congratulations. You're exactly like your uncle."

"Please, I'm trying to make up for it."

"Nothing will ever make up for it! I had to watch my father bleed to death in front of me! I had to listen to him take his last breath! I had to sit there alone after he slowly, painfully died." Theo bit his lip. "You don't know what it's like to be powerless."

"Yes, I do," Daniel whispered, his eyes misting. "I feel it every day."

Theo's own tears dried. Anger shriveled his sadness. *He ruined my life, and all he can do is say sorry.*

Theo took a step toward Daniel, making him flinch. "My dad trusted your family," Theo growled. "That's a mistake I won't be repeating. I expect you to be gone by the morning."

Daniel bowed his head, granting Theo permission to the stairs. Darkness pushed against his legs, slowing him. Without his medication and Penny's continuous healing, his powers didn't have a barrier anymore. The wall was destroyed. And their demands were louder than ever.

He took Penny from you, they hissed. *He took Dad from you. You should kill Daniel.*

Theo's pace quickened. He had to get away from *everyone.*

He spun around the corner to the stairs and slammed right into Penny and Dion. They were clearly talking about him, since they stopped upon seeing him. Her expression softened as she took his hands and said, "What's going on? You look flushed."

"Go away," he ordered, ripping out of her grasp.

He sounded harsh instead of pleading, which was probably why Penny soured. "I'm trying to help you," she said.

"I don't want it! I want you to leave!" The only oxygen Theo was able to receive was in broken increments. The stairs were blocked off. The basement felt darker.

Penny stepped closer. Theo pressed himself against the wall. "Penny," Dion warned, "let's go."

Ignoring Dion, Penny entwined her fingers in Theo's. "I know you're in pain," she said. "And I'm not going to leave you."

Please leave, he begged. *I don't want to hurt you. This will be easier if you LEAVE ME ALONE!*

The shadows from the wall enveloped Theo, wrapping him in their cold presence. When he opened his eyes, he found himself in utter darkness. His limbs moved, but the feeling was disjointed. It was like he was in the backseat of his own brain, allowing the shadows to dictate what he did. The lightbulbs popped. He heard Daniel struggling to breathe, like he was choking.

Theo thrashed against the darkness. *Let me go! This isn't who I am!*

They reformed into a copy of Theo, the exact figure he'd seen in the forest. *No, it's **who we are.***

A hand touched Theo's elbow. Golden light erupted, separating him and the shadows just an inch. But he took that chance and forced them into the confines of their walled prisons.

Gasping, Theo sank to his knees. The hand was still holding him. Knowing it was Penny, he glanced over, ready to thank her for her assistance.

But her eyes were wide with fear.

Theo's heart plummeted. ***She's afraid of you. She lied.***

Cautiously, she released him and inched backward, putting space between them. Her gaze darted to Daniel in the corner. Dion was at his side, instructing him to take slow, deep breaths. "Are you okay?" she asked.

The question was directed to Theo, but he felt how empty it was. A hot lump grew in his throat. He almost killed Daniel; he almost hurt his friends. "No, I'm not okay, is that what you want to hear? Now do you see why I lied to you? I'm a monster!"

"Theo, that's not what I—"

"You don't need to apologize," Dion cut in, nudging Penny aside. "You're not a monster."

"Don't lie to me!" Theo exclaimed. "I know you hate what I've become! Well, guess what? I hate it too! I've tried to fix myself, but I can't. I'm just-just—"

Not knowing what else to do, Theo covered his face and sobbed. This was the first time he'd let himself feel any emotion in months. The flurry of grief overwhelmed him; he almost felt like he was dying.

And as terrible as it was, he wished he would. At least then, he'd guarantee he couldn't hurt anyone else.

The basement door opened, and someone tumbled down the steps. Rebecca embraced him as tightly as humanly possible. "Don't cry, Theo," she instructed. "I'm here for you."

That was the problem. But little Rebecca would never understand.

"Do you want to hold my bear?" she added. "It always helps me when I'm sad."

A younger Theo believed the same. Until he grew up.

Regardless, he accepted the toy, feeling a new wave of sorrow burn through him. Slowly, Dion crept out of the basement, taking Penny and Daniel with him.

Penny stumbled in her path up the stairs. Countless emotions raged within her, overwhelming and nameless. She'd never seen Theo, or anyone, break down like that.

Once the door shut behind her, Dion reprimanded, "You should've left him alone."

Dion spoke like he was spitting venom. And he might as well have been; it hurt Penny the same. "I just wanted to help," she pleaded.

"Doesn't matter. He saw how scared you were. There's no going back from that." Dion started off, but turned back to deliver one last harsh order. "And don't try to apologize to him either. In fact, you should stay away from him."

Every word out of Dion's mouth made Penny's guilt grow. "You've been feeling the same."

"Yes, but I don't pressure him! I understood that he was suffering, and he needed space to ask for help himself! Now, he's going to feel ten times worse because of you!"

Because of you, echoed in her head. It was *her* fault. She broke Theo instead of fixing him, the one thing she had promised to do. Jade's prophecy was coming true.

Letting her exasperation spill forth, Penny whirled on Daniel. "What happened down there?"

"It was my fault." Daniel failed multiple times to make eye contact. "Don't be upset with Theo."

"I'm not upset!" Except that was a lie. Truthfully, she was heartbroken—absolutely gutted that he had been hiding so much suffering from her. And for what, because he thought she was afraid of him?

"You need to know how he feels," Daniel said. "I'm not saying what he did was right, but it is understandable. He's always dealt with grief on his own. Except this time, it's too much for him to handle. I bet he thinks he's weak because he *can't* deal with it."

Penny's jaw clenched. "Then, why won't he tell me that himself?"

"He's also scared."

"Of what?"

"Of being a burden."

20

FAIRYTALE

The next few days passed in an uncomfortable haze. Since Theo spent all his time in his room, Penny didn't see him. Dion convinced Lily to manipulate Theo into sleeping so he could finally, truly rest.

Rebecca stayed with Theo constantly. She was his bodyguard, tasked with keeping everyone, especially Penny, at a distance. She had tried to visit him, but Rebecca always cut her off with, "You can after he wakes up."

It was twisted, really, how relieved Penny was that he was finally taking care of himself. Unfortunately, it spawned from a total mental breakdown.

For those days of being alone, Penny pondered her part in this. She couldn't deny the truth: She *was* afraid of Theo, but that fear couldn't be so easily defined. Deep down, she knew he'd never hurt her, yet every time she saw the shadows move, she felt the irresistible urge to run. It wasn't him she feared. It was the darkness.

When they'd first met at the school, Theo used his powers for mischief. Sure, they were intimidating but not horrifying. After enduring Jones's abuse, Theo changed. His powers changed. Penny believed that if she healed him enough, then the shadows wouldn't be a threat.

Then again, how could she heal someone who wanted nothing from her?

Though she'd never admit it, she'd endured more than one nightmare replaying the last day at the school. Except in her dreams, Theo killed her. Enticed by the darkness, he took her life, just like he almost did with Daniel. And every morning, she told herself she had no reason to worry.

Yet she did.

On the third day, Theo emerged from his room. His hair was brushed, his clothes were clean, and he was well-rested. But he didn't smile. He didn't even fake it anymore. He avoided the children whenever he could. It was the darkest Penny had ever seen him.

As she hovered over the pan of sizzling eggs, she twisted the ring on her finger. Days ago, she'd been angry with him, so she removed it, but wearing it was the last piece of Theo she had left.

Peter rested his elbows on the counter. "What's going on with Theo? He seems more depressed than usual."

"I don't know," Penny lied. "I think he's having an off day."

Peter exhaled through his nose. "That's great. We were supposed to discuss possible rescue missions today."

"I can do it."

"No offense, but being a leader isn't exactly your forte."

Penny blushed. "I can try. I don't think we should bother Theo today."

Peter remained unconvinced, but without Theo here to refuse, Peter didn't have another option. Groaning, he motioned to her, so she ordered a nearby girl to watch the eggs. As Penny followed Peter to the surveillance room, she crossed her fingers, hoping this would be the start of a new role.

Except that Theo was already in the room, clicking around on the computer. He hunched over the keyboard; his typing was too fast. Despite resting for the past two days, Penny could feel the pain emanating from him like a storm cloud.

"What's going on?" Peter said.

Theo cursed under his breath. "Jones is trying to arrest my family."

"What?" Peter and Penny exclaimed in unison.

Theo pushed the chair back so that they could see the computer screen. He made a gesture, as if to say, "See for yourself." Sure enough, Principal Jones was plastered all over the page. Reports of him making repeated 911 calls, interviews where he bashed the Palmer family, and social media posts illustrating his distaste were everywhere.

"He's saying they're working with a criminal," Theo spat. "But there's no evidence that they've been in contact with me!"

"He's just trying to shake your nerves," Peter explained. "I bet he's bluffing."

Theo stood up so fast his chair slammed into the wall. "*Bluffing*? This man doesn't bluff! If he had the chance, he'd kill them! I know he would!"

Peter didn't run, but his body did flicker like he wanted to turn invisible. Penny cut between them and reached for Theo, only to have him recoil. "Theo, please calm down. We'll work through this together."

His blue eyes were colder than she'd ever seen them. "I'm leaving."

Penny shook her head. Partly because she couldn't believe—didn't *want* to believe—what he was saying. "You can't go alone. It's what Jones wants."

"I'd rather die than let him have my family."

Anticipating Theo's exit, she blocked the door. "He'll kill you!"

"That doesn't matter. He's trying to end supers, and I have a chance to stop him. I need to stop living in a fairytale. We both do."

As Penny's heart broke, she searched for an ally. Always a sucker for awkward situations, Peter turned invisible. On her own again, she begged, "Theo, please, we can have more time."

Theo sighed. "Time for what? Late-night talks because I can't fall asleep? You repeating over and over that I can get through this, that I'm stronger than what Principal Jones did to me? I'll save you a lot of time right now. I'm *not* better. This is how I'll be for the rest of my life, which, if I lose to him, won't be very long."

He moved to leave, but Penny caught him by the wrist, ignoring how he instantly stiffened. "Don't think like that! What about us?"

Theo ripped his arm out of her grasp. "What about us, Penny? We don't belong together! I'm hurting you!"

"You're not! I wasn't scared of you—I was scared of the shadows!"

"They're a part of *me*, Penny! You can't have me without them!"

"I can try!"

Theo's eyes widened for a fluttering second. Then, his brows furrowed. "Stop trying," he said. "Please, Penny. For your sake, give up. I have."

This time, she didn't stop him from leaving. The dull sounds of the wooden door closing reverberated in her body. She felt like screaming, crying, and vomiting all at once. Instead, she could only stand there, letting the cold numbness overtake her.

When Theo exited the surveillance room, a group of kids scrambled to appear busy so it wouldn't be obvious they were eavesdropping. He

continued past them. It was time he used his dangerous power for something useful.

He grabbed a backpack from under his bed. Clothes and notebooks were shoved inside without organization. At the sight of his father's journal, stuffed into the bottom of the bag, Theo's vision blurred. Maybe if he had more training, none of this would've happened.

Suddenly, Dion cleared his throat, making Theo jump. He whirled around, finding Dion leaning against the wall with crossed arms. "I hear you're leaving," Dion stated.

"Who told you?"

"I actually *heard* you say it. Your argument with Penny was so loud that the whole cabin knows."

Theo continued to fill his backpack, ensuring to grab one of the two envelopes of cash from his mother. "I need to kill Jones. If I don't, he'll make more people suffer."

Wearing a confident smile, Dion walked closer. "Say no more. I'm coming with you."

"You're not. This is my—"

"Stop talking. My best friend isn't going to face the end of the world alone. Period."

Theo blinked. "It's dangerous."

"What in our lives hasn't been?"

Someone knocked on the door, then entered without being given permission. "I'm coming too," Peter announced. "You stand a better chance at a stealth mission."

"We should bring Yasmine!" Dion added as he bounced on his feet.

"This isn't a vacation," Theo snapped. "What does she bring to the table that we don't already have?"

"Intimidation?" Dion suggested, as Peter said, "She's tough."

"This is a secret mission," Theo pointed out, shouldering his backpack. "We don't need anyone to distract us. If you want to come along, then hurry up."

Although he said it wasn't a vacation, Dion and Peter beamed at each other and hurried to pack. While they chattered, Theo slipped out of the room. He entered the kitchen, where Daniel sat at the bar, nibbling on an apple. Before Daniel could flee, Theo said, "I want to apologize for the other day. I wasn't in my right mind."

"It was my fault," Daniel assured through a muffled mouth.

"It wasn't," Theo insisted. "None of it was, including my dad's death. It was wrong of me to blame it on you."

Slowly, Daniel lowered his apple to the table. "Thank you."

"Don't mention it." Theo glanced to both sides, checking that they were alone. "While I'm gone, I need you to take care of Penny."

Daniel's jaw dropped so fast, Theo thought it would snap off. "What?"

"You have a connection with her that I don't." Theo had to force the words out; he didn't take pleasure in saying them. "I know you care about her, maybe as much as I do. I don't trust you, but I think I'll have to for her sake."

"Why not ask your friends?"

"I don't think anyone else respects her or values her the way I do." Theo shook his head and corrected himself. "The way *we* do. If I asked them to protect her, I'm afraid they might prioritize their own safety above hers. I know you won't."

Daniel bowed his head low. "I swear I'll keep her safe."

"I know." With that resolved, Theo turned to leave the kitchen for the last time.

Rebecca cut him off, thrusting her tiny arms to both sides. "Don't go," she begged.

Theo crouched to her level. "Penny will protect you," he assured.

"Who will protect *you*?"

Theo's heart urged him to hug or comfort her. Children didn't understand the cost of sacrifice, and he wasn't about to explain it to her. Rather than respond, he patted her on the head and reached the foyer, where Dion and Peter were talking to Yasmine.

She stuck her fists on her hips. "You're leaving?"

Theo threw a weak glare at Dion, who acted very interested in a lamp. "I can't sit around and wait for Jones to find us. Not when I have a chance to stop him."

"And what's your plan? Did you forget how badly he kicked your butt at the school?"

She dares to question you? Doesn't she know her opinion is meaningless?

"I don't need to waste time sharing my plan," Theo stated. "I'm leaving, and Dion and Peter are joining me."

Yasmine pursed her lips. "What about Penny? The kids?"

"They'll be safer without me."

Yasmine's beady gaze flickered to his bags, then shifted behind her to the door. "Okay," she grumbled, "I'll come."

"We don't need a huge group," Theo explained.

"I doubt three teenage boys will be able to pull this off without help. Besides," she crossed her arms, "someone has to be the voice of reason."

Disobedience should be punished, the shadows grumbled. *She doesn't respect your authority*.

"Whatever," Theo muttered. "You have two minutes to pack."

"I'll help!" Dion announced, following Yasmine to her room.

As more unwanted company approached, the darkness disrupted. "I can come too," Penny said softly.

I should bring her.

She's afraid of you. You can't.

She means too much.

Theo's knuckles turned white on the handles of his bag. "Penny, don't start with me."

"I can help! Please, Theo, I want—"

"You're not coming, okay? *I* don't want *you*!" Avoiding her reach, he muttered, "Peter, meet me outside. I need to grab a jacket."

Although Peter obeyed, Penny didn't. Relentlessly, she trailed him up the stairs and toward his room. "I can be an asset!" she pleaded. "I won't distract you or ruin the plans, I promise! Just let me go with you!"

Theo retrieved his jacket from the closet, but Penny blocked the doorway. "Theo, *please* wait. I need to tell you something."

He faded into the shadows, passing right through her. "Stay safe," he said, returning to solid form at the top of the stairs. "We'll talk after I get back."

Tears rose in Penny's eyes. "Fine! Go, then! I don't care!"

Theo didn't pause. He didn't even blink. The bedroom door slammed shut, the sound echoing off the wooden walls.

Penny's fists clenched, but only a second passed before they were loose. She pressed her hands to her face as she cried, wishing Theo would hear and stay. Wishing he cared about her. Wishing she could take back everything she had said to him, because none of it was true; she was hurting, betrayed, and terrified.

He didn't return.

She lay on his bed and curled up in the covers. The sheets smelled like him, mingled with rich pine. She tried to imagine he was here, holding her in his arms like he used to. He was always so careful when he hugged her, as if he expected her to break. And yet, he hugged her tightly, like he would never have the chance again.

Penny grabbed his pillow, but her fingers caught on the edge of a metal spiral. Underneath the pillow, Theo's notebook rested, practically begging to be read. Despite knowing it was an invasion of his privacy, she cracked it open and scanned the pages.

She found his list of the kids and their superpowers, ages, and backgrounds. Some he had highlighted and written in the margins: "Needs additional attention. Dealt with trauma."

She flipped the page, continuing to read his notes. She'd never realized how closely he watched the residents in the cabin, ensuring each of them was happy and healthy. Kids she knew nothing about; Theo knew every detail, from diet restrictions to allergies to foods they didn't like.

On another page, scribbled and crossed-out notes were visible. Penny caught Principal Jones's name a few times; Theo must've been trying to make plans. But there were also names she barely recognized. They were written in bold, so they had to have been important, yet Penny doubted she'd ever heard of William Stirling and Maya Anderson. Were they relatives of Theo? Relatives of Principal Jones? Penny skipped around, stopping on a marked page.

It was a to-do list.

Penny had given him the advice to write one long ago. She thought he'd forgotten about it or ignored her. But here it was.

Many of the tasks were mundane and straightforward, such as replacing the lightbulbs in the basement. The second objective, one that Theo deemed the second most important task, was to save their team.

And at the very top, adorned with a star, was:

#1- Tell Penny how I feel.

21

BOUNTIES

The bus rumbled away from the cabin and its safety. Theo and his team sat in the very back, avoiding the driver's wandering attention. Through a smudged window, Theo watched the forest flash by him in blurs of brown and green. His throat burned, yet he refused to cry. He was leaving everyone behind on the fragile hope he could save them. Failure wasn't an option, but lately it seemed it was all he'd done.

Dion settled beside Theo. "I'm sorry about Penny."

Theo drew the hood on his jacket and physically turned to the window.

"You can't escape me that easily," Dion teased. "I brought my burner, just in case you wanted to talk to her."

Theo wasn't in the mood to talk, not about his feelings and definitely not about Penny. She was scared, and rightfully so, but he was too. His greatest fear had been realized. She wanted him—*not* the darkness—not the thing that utterly consumed him.

Shadows swirled in his thoughts; it pumped cold in his blood. He no longer found the comfort in it he once had. Lily's conversation flashed back to him, the one where their powers already gave them a predisposition to certain emotions or actions.

So truly, no one could fix him. No one could remove the darkness in his soul or make him feel better. He couldn't ignore it anymore. This was who he was. It was time for him and his friends to accept that.

The old Theo was gone. For good.

Hours crawled by. As soon as more people climbed onto the bus, Theo and his team made their way off. They'd been dropped on the sidewalk of a city, not as big as New York, but much more populated than the town near the cabin. The sun fought to peek through the clouds, stamping the sky with pale blues and whites, promising an oncoming storm.

"I know where we are," Dion said happily. "This is Clearfield! My aunt and uncle used to live here. I'd visit my cousin every..." he drowned off.

Peter and Yasmine didn't know Dion's backstory. Their questioning glances almost erupted into vocalizing, but Theo cut them off by saying, "Let's get lunch. I'm sure you guys are starving."

After passing a few more blocks, the team entered what Dion called the "best place on Earth." While the bakery had the appearance of an eccentric, monochromatic coffee house, it also had the feeling of home. The warm, savory smell of baking bread enveloped them like a hug. They released a collective sigh; their stomachs rumbling louder than the indie music.

"I usually stick with a basic meal," Dion was saying as he waltzed to the counter. He proceeded to order five crepes filled with chocolate and topped with whipped cream.

The menu had been written on chalkboards in differing colors of chalk, the blues and pinks blending for Theo. He blinked to focus.

"I'll have a water," Yasmine stated.

Dion gaped. "That's it?"

"I'm not very hungry." To be fair, she'd appeared ill all day; she must've been too stressed to eat.

When it came to Theo's turn, he said, "I'll have pancakes."

Peter gagged. "Aren't you sick of having those?"

"They taste better when you don't make them." Theo hadn't meant to snap, but he couldn't stop himself.

Thankfully, Peter snickered. "You got me there, Teddy."

Using the money from Theo's bag, Dion paid the cashier and selected a table for them, one in a corner. The walls consisted of wide windows, so there wasn't any place to hide, but this was good enough. Once seated, he remarked, "Just be glad it's not Thursday. That's poetry night, and this place is stocked with weirdos."

"I bet you wrote poetry," Yasmine teased, swirling her straw in her water.

"Maybe every now and then. But only to pick up girls."

Whilst shaking her head, she smiled like she was saying, *You're so weird.* But Theo knew it was an endearing kind of weird. Penny often gave him that look.

Well, she used to.

A waitress delivered their food, staring a bit too long in Theo's direction. Dion offered Yasmine a little of his meal. As soon as she tasted it, she was hooked. She ate more of his crepes than he did. But Dion never looked happier.

Theo picked at his pancakes, his mind elsewhere. He'd left the cabin without a solid plan, with little more than the clothes on his back. They had no weapons, no vehicle, and the small remainder of Mom's money. He guessed there were two hundred dollars left, which could buy them a taxi, but for how long? They didn't even know where Jones was.

Theo glanced around the café. By now, more teenagers were entering, ordering fancy coffees and talking loudly. A tall, lanky man hovered near the back of the line, staring at Theo with cold, unblinking eyes.

Immediately, Theo shifted to face the other direction. Catching a stranger's attention was already awkward, but being outlaws meant avoiding any attention. When Theo glanced back again, the man was already gone.

"You look like you've seen a ghost," Peter suddenly remarked, kicking Theo's shin from under the table. "What's got you so rattled?"

Theo shook his head, hoping the movement would clear his goosebumps. "Nothing."

"Well, whenever you're ready, I think we should head out. I'll let you wrangle the lovebirds." Peter pointed to another corner. This one was designed as a sort of stage, complete with a microphone and speakers. Yasmine's singing filled the café, putting the customers in a trance.

Theo shot a glare at Peter, who said, "You try telling her no!"

Theo hurried to the stage, but before he could pull Yasmine off, Dion stopped him. "Let her finish the song," he pleaded.

"You want to risk our lives just because you have a crush?"

"I want her to be *happy*," Dion corrected. "This has nothing to do with a crush."

Despite Theo's better judgment, he waited on pins and needles for Yasmine to stop singing. As soon as she was, the café erupted into applause. She must've seen Theo's annoyance, because she suddenly switched from bashful to serious.

"That was a waste of time," she said.

"It wasn't," Dion tried to say.

"Yes, it was," she snapped. "Let's leave."

She joined Peter on his path to the exit, ducking past congratulating customers and requests for an encore. "I'm sorry," Theo said, walking with Dion. "I didn't mean to offend her."

Dion attempted to shrug, but his shoulders were too heavy. "It was my fault."

Seeing a saddened Dion filled Theo to the brim with guilt. "If it was anyone's fault, it was mine. I promise if there's an opportunity for you to have a moment with Yasmine, I won't interfere."

Dion managed a grin. "So, you're my wingman?"

"You need all the help you can get."

Dion punched Theo in the arm. "Hey! You jerk!"

Theo laughed, and his stress began to dissipate. Nothing bad would happen so long as they remained a team.

For the next hour, Dion showed them around town, allowing Theo to brainstorm ideas. The constant movement charged his creativity, and it helped that Peter bounced inspiration off of him.

"Maybe he's in New York," Peter suggested, kicking a pebble like a soccer ball.

"That's what I was hoping," Theo responded. "But it doesn't make sense for Jones to stay in the same spot. It lends itself to being found."

Peter's forehead creased in thought. "I know that the best way to stay invisible is to do something unexpected. I guess we have to think about what would be unexpected for him."

The two fell silent as they debated that. In front of them, Yasmine giggled and playfully pushed Dion, who seemed like he would burst into pieces. Meanwhile, Theo fixed his backpack and—

His backpack! How could he have forgotten? He ripped it off his shoulders and knelt on the sidewalk. While he tore through the contents, the rest of the team stopped. "I kept notes from my research at the cabin," Theo explained. "It might give us a lead."

"Nice thinking!" Dion praised.

Until Theo retrieved his notebook. It had a green cover. The notebook he needed was red. Heaving a sigh, he sat on the ground, holding the empty green notebook in his lap. Dion noticed and sucked in a sharp breath. "It'll be okay!" he insisted. "Was it really that important?"

Theo shook his head, partly to express his response and partly out of sheer disbelief. The notebook didn't contain vital information, but it was a setback nonetheless. Not to mention embarrassing. Theo had made it a goal to tell Penny his true feelings. What if she found his list and read it?

Yasmine tapped her foot on the ground. "Maybe if we didn't leave in such a rush," she said, "you wouldn't have forgotten it. But you were too eager to ditch Penny."

Pitiful excuses and explanations threatened to burst out of Theo's mouth, so he pressed it shut. Arguing wouldn't do any good. Like Penny, Yasmine had a right to be angry.

"I don't know why you think it's easier to lie to her," Yasmine continued, gaining traction. "I shouldn't tell you this, but Penny cared about you so much that it literally killed her to see you struggle. She cried herself to *sleep* because of it. When we're done, I think the two of you need to sit down and have a heart-to-heart. There's a lot of secrets you're keeping from each other."

With Yasmine's lecture complete, Theo burned with humiliation. He never realized how much Penny paid attention to him—how much he hurt her. That was the last thing he ever wanted for her. If what Yasmine was saying was true, then he had a lot of apologizing to do.

He moved to a bench and opened his notebook, this one blank and fresh. Since he was unable to verbalize the truth, he decided to take pen to paper and confess.

Dear Penny, you mean so much to me. That's why I pushed you away.

Theo cringed. That didn't sound right. He crossed the sentence out and tried again.

Penny- you've been one of my closest friends for such a long time.

Did girls like being referred to as friends? Should he call her his girlfriend? Theo started over.

Penny- I love you! Please don't ask me how I know because I actually have no idea. Maybe this isn't love, and I'm an idiot. Maybe I just really, really like you. How should I know?

"That's not very romantic," Peter mused behind Theo's shoulder.

Theo snapped his notebook shut. "Back off!"

Defensively, Peter raised his hands. "I know women, Teddy. Women like romance. You've gotta crank this up a couple of notches if you want to get the effect you're looking for."

"I'm not looking for any effect! I'm just trying to sort out my emotions."

"Carry on, then."

Even though Peter left, Theo didn't continue writing. He had endured one too many uncomfortable moments today. As he stuffed the notebook into his bag, he promised himself he'd finish his letter later... once he was alone.

Slinging his bag over his shoulders, he found Peter and Yasmine walking on, practically abandoning him. But Dion lingered. Grinning, he only moved when Theo did. Dion's continual kindness and undying loyalty usually cured Theo's bad moods. Not now.

If he knew how much you lied, he wouldn't be treating you this well. You should be ashamed.

Theo downcast his gaze. "Dion, I-I have to tell you something."

"About what?"

Theo wrung the straps on his backpack. "I wrote my family," he blurted. "I convinced myself I was doing it to get money and supplies, but the truth is, I contacted them because I needed them. It's not fair that I talked to them and no one else was allowed to." The following confession struggled to stay secret, consuming Theo with unbearable shame. Summoning every morsel of strength, he said, "And I was taking antidepressants to muffle some of the darkness in my head. I should've come clean and admitted how I was feeling, but I...I don't know. I couldn't say it aloud. I understand if you feel betrayed."

Dion scratched his neck. "Huh."

"What?"

"Nothing, I'm glad you told me. I always suspected something was going on, and you hinted at it multiple times, but I wanted to give you space until you felt comfortable to confess it all." Dion shrugged. "I guess I wasn't expecting it to be this serious."

"Are you mad?"

"I'm bothered you kept this away for so long, but I'm more disappointed with myself for letting you suffer."

"It isn't your fault," Theo insisted. "Even if you had asked, I would've lied."

Dion stared at Theo, unamused. "You can't keep lying to me. We're best friends—we're supposed to trust each other."

"I know that—really, I do. Sometimes, the darkness makes it hard to accept that."

Dion leaned closer as he said, "Your powers must really be affecting you."

"It didn't use to be like this," Theo said. "It was bad after my dad died, but I improved thanks to my mom and sister. Recently, for whatever reason, I feel like I've lost control. Taking the medicine made me feel normal, which I know is what people want. I'm sorry I didn't tell you."

"You did what you thought was best for you and everyone else. How can I be mad?"

Theo adjusted his bag. His voice stayed quiet. "Because I'm a liar."

Dion patted Theo on the back. "Don't beat yourself up about the past. To be honest, I struggle too. I've got nightmares keeping me awake at night. There have been times when I have had to take meds, too. It doesn't make us any less super, it just means we have quirks."

"That's a fun way to say problems."

Dion chuckled. "I'm serious. I don't care what you do as long as you're safe. Superpowers are a lot to put on a person, so deal with it however you want."

Theo shut his eyes. He could hardly say, "Thank you," without choking up. Penny's reaction to his secrets was immensely different from Dion's reaction. Dion understood; he knew the reasons behind keeping them. Penny only saw the lies.

But Theo couldn't blame her for being mad.

"Maybe you've been struggling with your powers because you haven't taken the time to heal," Dion wondered aloud. "And not Penny's short-term healing, but real, internal healing."

Theo considered that. For his entire life, he constantly reminded himself about his losses, as if keeping the guilt alive would've kept the people he loved alive. Replacing his sorrow wouldn't be easy, especially now. "I can't afford to stop and heal," Theo insisted. "Not yet."

"I know, just keep it in mind." Dion tugged at his shirt, then his sleeves, and finally, his hair. "Um, listen, while we're confessing, I may have also kept a secret." He stopped, allowing Yasmine and Peter to continue further ahead. "Do you remember the first week at the cabin, and that lady came to assess the place?"

Theo nodded. It was a moment he recalled frequently.

"After she left, I reached out to my mom." Dion grimaced. "I was surprised she even answered the phone. Then again, she didn't know it was me until I told her. She was intending to sell the cabin and split the profit with my dad, so I told her I was there. I said I was alone—that I needed to get my head on straight after the academy was destroyed. As long as I didn't wreck the cabin or drag her into any drama, she let me stay. Er, let us stay. That's why the agent never returned—that's why our electricity and water always stayed on. She was paying for it. I knew it was risky, but I couldn't think of another option." Seemingly finished, Dion held his breath.

Theo gaped. *This* was what Dion meant by "taking care of the cabin." A lie of this magnitude would've infuriated Theo...if he hadn't been lying for months, too. Instead, he mustered a smile. By trusting Dion, the team had been allowed to live in a hidden home, paid for by his mother. She might not have loved Dion wholeheartedly, but she stepped in when he needed help.

"Have you talked since then?" Theo asked.

"No, but I'd like to. During our call, she actually sounded happy." Dion tried to shrug off his excitement yet failed miserably. "After this is over, I might be able to go home."

Home. Such a wonderful word—such a foreign word. To think, Theo could be home within the month. The mere idea sent a thrill down his spine.

Together, he and Dion reached Peter and Yasmine. "There should be a bus stop ahead," Dion said.

Except with every minute that passed, the town grew progressively smaller. Dion's head swiveled from side to side. Brows furrowed, he stopped at a crosswalk and glanced between the right and the left.

"Do you know where we're going?" Yasmine asked.

"Totally," he answered. "We're supposed to go, uh, left."

His fake confidence passed on the others, but Theo hesitated. The shadows prickled beneath his feet. *Someone is here.*

The street was empty. Whoever was spying on them was hiding in the shadows, lurking, waiting for the perfect moment to strike. The rest of the team was a few feet ahead of him, so Theo called, "Guys, I think we should—"

A sharp shrieking fired through the street, making every teen cover their ears, including Yasmine, the girl comfortable with high pitches.

Through the pain, Theo forced his eyes open. A small black ball rolled onto the sidewalk, coming to a stop in the midst of them. Before anyone could move, a strange smoke drifted from a hole at the top of it, filling the air. Upon inhaling it, Dion swayed.

Theo's head throbbed from the ache of the noise, and now from holding his breath. The ringing had stopped, but the smoke grew thicker. It stung Theo's eyeballs, scorching them like fire. He searched for his friends, but his fingers found the brick wall of a building. His lungs screamed for air. So, with no other choice, he sucked in a deep breath.

The effect was instantaneous. His muscles slackened, and his knees gave out. His brain melted into mush.

And his power was gone.

He worked up the strength to stagger to his feet yet stumbled into someone. They were taller than him; a realization that, in a situation where Theo wasn't drugged, would've sent cold fear coursing through his veins. He was taller than the rest of his team. This newcomer was a stranger.

"I got him!" the stranger announced, followed by a cacophony of cheers. "Let's get out of here!"

Theo could feel his backpack being ripped from his shoulders. Then, he felt himself getting dragged away. He tried to blink, yet all he saw was a blurry and unfocused town. With the last strains of his coherent mind, he wondered where his friends were. He wondered if they were safe.

But those were problems to deal with later. Right now, he let himself drift into peaceful slumber.

REWARD FOR CAPTURE

"Any super who was incriminated in the explosion of the academies can be caught and rewarded with cash.

WARNING: Supers are unpredictable and may inflict bodily harm. It's recommended to use sedatives or other deterrents to avoid this. Anyone who kills supers in the process of capture will be prosecuted appropriately.

Jones wants his supers unscathed when he sees them."

-Black Market Ad

22

PAIN AND PREJUDICE

Theo awoke with a start. Rusty, metal cuffs had been clamped tightly at his wrists, so tightly in fact that his skin burned with blisters. The chain was connected to the wall behind him, leaving only a few feet of space. Ignoring the pain plaguing his body, he struggled to sit.

"Dion?" he whispered into the veil of darkness. Usually, he'd be able to see, but his powers were still gone. "Peter? Are you guys there?"

Metal clanked. "Theo?" Dion answered. "What's going on?"

"We've been kidnapped," Peter said, as if it were obvious. "And whatever was in that smoke drugged our powers."

"Don't worry," Theo assured. "We'll escape."

While he studied the chains, Dion shifted again. "Yasmine? Are you here?"

Everyone stopped. The boys held their breath.

Dion's volume rose. "Yasmine, where are you? This isn't funny!"

"Cut it out," Peter hissed. "You're going to draw attention to us!"

Dion's fear was like a contagious virus. It claimed hold of Theo's body, pumping his blood with electrifying terror. He jerked against his handcuffs, pathetically hoping he could rip them free from the wall. Fresh, warm blood trickled down his aching wrists, so he forced himself to focus on Dion.

"We need to find her!" he was saying. "She could be in trouble!"

"Shut up!" Peter snapped. "We'll get in trouble if you keep screaming!"

Dion could hardly contain himself. The mere thought of Yasmine being hurt sent him into a wild frenzy to escape.

Theo hesitated to catch his breath. So softly he could hardly hear it, a snore swirled beside him. He froze, yet over the sound of Dion's yelling, he couldn't catch it.

"Wait," Theo demanded, "hush."

In the silence, he heard it again—a deep, quiet exhale. Trying to reach the source, he stretched across the floor. The tip of his shoe brushed against someone's leg, and a soft groan murmured from Yasmine's mouth.

"She's here," he told Dion. "She's safe."

Dion yanked at his restraints. "Is she awake?"

"Not that I can tell. She must've had a bigger dose of whatever drug we got."

"I'm gonna kill them," Dion growled. "They have no idea who they're messing with."

"On the contrary," a gravelly voice suddenly said. "We know exactly who you are."

A bright light shot on in the room, causing Theo to wince. The stranger must've gotten close to Yasmine, because Dion cursed and spat, "If you lay a hand on her, I'll rip your arms off!"

The stranger laughed. By this time, Theo was able to squint at his surroundings. The stranger was the same man who had been stalking them in the café. A hat concealed his greasy black hair. Purple and blue veins bruised prominently underneath his transparent skin. He noticed Theo staring and said, "You look like you're in pain. Why don't you have your girlfriend heal you?"

Theo wanted to prove the man wrong by claiming Penny wasn't here, but he stopped. Should he lie and say they had backup coming? Would the lie even sound believable?

"She's not my girlfriend," he decided to say.

The stranger tilted his head in a fake show of sympathy. "Aw, she doesn't like monsters? Shocker."

Theo's jaw clenched, willing himself not to take offense. Now that his powers had been drugged into submission, his mind was clear. Behaving was the best course of action, at least until the team figured out a plan.

However, Theo couldn't stop himself from growling, "You wanna see a monster? Look in the mirror."

From the corner, Dion burst into laughter, but it was exaggerated and likely fueled by his disgust. Peter let a chuckle slip, which felt much more genuine.

A sneer contorted the man's already ugly features. He bent down, sharing his stench with Theo. A sharp snap shot through the room, alerting the man to standing straight as a board.

"I told you to get them out of here," another man said as he entered. "*Not* make small talk." He towered so tall his head skimmed the ceiling. He vaguely resembled an army general, with his camouflaged clothing, dog tags around his neck, and a gun at his hip. But there was a coldness in his gaze that made Theo shiver. No doubt about it. This was the leader.

"Sorry, sir," the greasy man said. Quickly, he unwound the chains from the wall, starting with Yasmine. The drugs remained in her system, so she didn't fight when he pulled her from the room. He went to Dion next, but the second he was close, Dion kicked him hard in the shin.

The man swore, cradled his leg, and hopped on one foot. Dion's laugh became a bit more real.

The leader pinched the bridge of his nose. "Jack," he muttered, "you're useless." The leader pulled a syringe from his pocket and jabbed it into Dion's arm.

Dion winced at the prick of the needle, yet he couldn't resist. His limbs weakened. "You think this'll stop me?" he challenged as Jack dragged him away. "It won't!"

The leader angled the needle toward Peter, who blurted, "You don't have to use that! I'll go peacefully."

The leader raised a brow. "You will?"

Peter nodded. "Promise."

"Make any sudden moves, and I'll fill you with lead."

Jack, limping, returned to escort Peter out of the room. Just before vanishing behind the door, Peter cast a glance at Theo and mouthed, "Be good."

Theo wasn't sure what Peter meant by it, but it didn't matter. The leader squatted to meet Theo's eye line, and a smile crossed the man's face. "I've been waiting a long time for this," he said. "The money I get from your bounty will set me up for life."

Bounty? Who would want Theo alive? His mother, probably.

"Why did we find you in Pennsylvania?" the hunter asked. "Is that where you've made your base?"

Theo willed himself to remain poker-faced. Any slip, and there would be a horde of hunters storming the cabin. He had to conjure a lie, a believable one at that.

"Close," Theo said, "but no. We're passing through."

"So, you came from where? West Virginia? Washington D.C.? Ohio?"

Theo averted his gaze at the last one. He'd intended to let the leader flounder, but Theo couldn't help his reaction. Distantly, he recalled Penny's family living in Ohio. Instead of his team, he might have condemned her parents to death.

"Ohio, then," the leader stated. "Thanks for your cooperation."

He stood and snapped again, beckoning two more hunters into the room. They freed Theo from the wall, yet much like his friends, kept the cuffs around his wrists. He didn't struggle, mostly because he didn't want to deal with the consequences of whatever drug had been placed in those needles.

They led him into the back lot. A row of cars parked in front of a chain-link fence, ranging from big black vans to small sleek cars. Yasmine sat on the asphalt, slumped against Dion's shoulder. He was fighting sleep, but judging by his drooping eyelids, it was a fight he was about to lose.

One of the hunters behind Theo shoved him roughly, making him stumble to catch his footing. "Keep walking," the man ordered.

Theo bit back his snarky reply and searched for Peter. He wasn't near Yasmine and Dion, but instead, waiting inside a van, talking with another bounty hunter. Did Peter not understand the severity of the situation? They were about to be shipped off to who knew where, and Peter was acting like these guys were some of his oldest friends!

As Theo neared the van, he noticed Peter's buddy holding some familiar items. "Hey," Theo shouted, "those are our bags!"

The hunter scoffed. "Yeah, so? Not like you need 'em."

"Not like anyone needs them," Peter muttered. "He packed useless stuff."

With a chortle, the backpack thief climbed out of the van, allowing the other two hunters to sit Theo across from Peter and chain him to the wall. In contrast, Peter was allowed to sit freely.

Once the men walked away to do the same to Dion and Yasmine, Theo whispered, "This is your plan? Butter them up and make a grand escape? It's not going to work."

"I plan to cause as little trouble as possible," Peter corrected. "The harder we struggle, the harder they'll be on us. We're lucky they're only using tranquilizers."

"We need to get out of here."

"And we will. Eventually."

Theo wanted to argue further, but the leader grabbed the back doors of their van and mocked, "Get comfortable. We have a long drive."

Then, he slammed the doors shut, enveloping Theo in a world of darkness.

Except this time, he could see.

He didn't have all of his power back, a realization which disappointed him more than he expected. But at least it was a start. As difficult as it was, he'd have to take Peter's advice and wait for the perfect moment to strike.

The vans rumbled along for hours. Every jostle made Theo's wrists ache. Though he wasn't presently bleeding, his injuries were still tender.

Not that his captors cared. A large, bearded man sat next to Theo and smoked a pack of cigarettes, filling the car with their wretched odor.

He must've seen Theo's disgust, because he leaned in and blew the smoke directly into Theo's nose. Weakly, the shadows underneath him prickled. *He has no idea who he's messing with.*

The man laughed obnoxiously loud. He offered a cigarette to Theo, and when he didn't accept it, the man said, "Too much of a wimp, huh? Gotta ask Mommy's permission first, don't ya?"

"Leave the kids alone, Roger," the leader demanded. He sat in the passenger seat but spun around to give Roger a stern glare. "If not, I'll let them show you what they can really do."

Grunting, Roger turned away, not finding joy in his smoking anymore.

Theo snickered quietly, yet apparently, not quietly enough. The leader's attention zeroed in on Theo as he ordered, "Wipe that look off your face, freak, or I'll do it for you."

Due to the lingering effects of the drugs in Theo's body, the darkness wasn't overbearing. Instead, it spoke in jerking movements, prodding Theo to act.

Peter nudged Theo's foot and looked pointedly at his hands, which were slowly disappearing. They nodded to each other, agreeing that at the first possible second, they'd attack.

"Stop here," the leader commanded. "We'll get some lunch and finish the trip after."

Roger lumbered past Theo to the back doors, whisking them open and letting the sunshine in. They'd parked inside the lot of a fast-food restaurant—the smell of grease hanging in thick, heavy blankets.

"Mind if we stretch our legs?" Peter asked innocently.

With a wave of approval from the leader, Roger escorted Peter outside, then returned for Theo. Roger tugged on Theo's arms, but because he remained handcuffed to the wall, the metal scraped against his wounded wrists.

"Stop!" Theo exclaimed, hearing his voice break. "I'm stuck, you idiot!"

"'Idiot' is an understatement," the leader grumbled. He climbed into the back, retrieved a key from his pocket, and freed Theo from the wall. Rather than lecturing his subordinate, the leader pointed at Theo and added, "Don't pull any tricks."

Theo stood on shaking legs and followed Roger out of the van, glancing behind to see the leader return the key to his front pants pocket.

Two of the hunters' cars had been parked on either side of the van, sandwiching them in. There was only about three feet of space to move around, limiting Theo's options in a fight.

Roger collected orders and went inside the restaurant, leaving the leader and a few other hunters on the curb. Theo suspected Dion and Yasmine remained asleep in their van, seeing as theirs was parked across the lot by itself. At least, Theo hoped they were sleeping.

Peter bounced on his feet, his carefree demeanor unnerving Theo. It even seemed to disturb the leader, who watched the pair cautiously.

"It sure is a hot one today," Peter lamented, dramatically fanning himself with his cuffed hands. "Don't you think so, Simon?"

Although the name meant nothing to Theo, it certainly meant something to the men. In unison, they stiffened, and the leader's eyes sank into a glare. "Leave us," he said to his comrades. "I can handle this on my own."

Hesitantly, his teammates wandered inside the restaurant, leaving Simon, the leader, alone. He stalked over to Peter, who said, "You can't be upset with me for knowing your name. It's literally on your tag."

Immediately, Simon stuffed his dog tags into his shirt, concealing them from view. "You filthy supers aren't allowed to call me by name," he spat. He was so tall that he blocked out the entire sun.

Darkness twitched in between Theo's fingers. This was the perfect moment to attack. Why wasn't Peter moving?

"I didn't mean to offend you," Peter said. "But at least now, you can have a reason to hate me."

"I have a reason! I have *lots* of reasons!"

Peter tapped his chin, the picture of tranquility. "Let me guess. You're still wearing your tags because your troop was killed, and you think you'll be able to rid yourself of the guilt you feel by also dying in a fight. Because you didn't die, you were spared, and you spend every day waiting for your heroic moment. Oh, and you hate supers because they were somehow responsible." Finished with his monologue, Peter grinned. "How did I do?"

"You're pretty observant," Simon said, remaining oddly emotion-less. "A smart kid like yourself should know *why* the super attacked us."

"Self-defense," Peter answered dismissively. "Supers don't attack for no reason."

"But supers do," Simon countered. "It happened in the middle of the night. The press might've tried to cover it up, saying it was a random hurricane, but I knew what it was. I *saw* the super that caused it. It was a purposeful act of violence."

Theo gasped. He hadn't meant to, but his surprise preceded him. There was a single known person in the world who could control storms, and she supposedly disappeared years ago.

Before Theo could ask when the tragedy occurred, Peter continued. "I'm sorry that happened to you. Not all of us are bad, you know."

Simon had mellowed somewhat, whether from remorse over his past or exhaustion from yelling. "There's a reason we have the laws we do. People can't be trusted with power, regardless of how good they seem. You may think it's unfair. The rest of us know it isn't."

"You're generalizing us based on one bad experience."

"I've had plenty. This conversation is too close for comfort." Simon leaned against the van and removed his gun from its holster in a silent threat.

Peter spoke once more. "Just because we're not exactly like you doesn't mean we're not human. We have feelings."

"I don't care."

"I think you do. I think you're scared, like we are. Deep down, you know this isn't right, but you do it because—"

Simon slammed Peter into the side of the van, nearly rocking it off the ground. Theo flinched as Peter did, almost feeling the impact for himself. Rather than refuting Peter's claims, Simon stated, "Get in the van."

The teens obeyed, but Peter moved with a bit more difficulty. Once they were sitting in their designated spots, Simon slammed the doors shut.

"Sorry about that," Peter whispered. "I thought I could talk him into letting us go. I'm not strong enough for full invisibility yet."

Admittedly, Theo's powers weren't fully prepared either. He couldn't let his eagerness to escape impair his ability to strategize. "There'll be another chance," he assured. "Just give it time."

The end of their conversation couldn't have come a moment too soon. The front doors suddenly opened, allowing Roger to plant himself in the driver's seat. Simon settled in beside him, and the two burrowed into their brown paper bags.

Whilst chewing on his French fries, Roger asked, "Did they give ya any trouble, sir?"

Simon glanced at Theo and Peter, who were huddled in the back. "Nothing I couldn't handle. Let's get going before we're late."

23

WISHES

S ometime during their arduous journey, Theo must've drifted
off because the abrupt jarring of the van jolted him awake.
Before he could regain awareness, the back doors clanked
open, and Roger yanked him onto the street.

They'd stopped along the road in a city. Night had set in, cloaking
the criminals in further darkness. A dingy motel sat on Theo's right,
likely their place to rest. The air reeked of fish and lake water, making
Theo wrinkle his nose. He was starting to miss the cabin more and more.

Jack complained, "Why do we keep staying in crappy places? If
these kids are worth what you say—"

"We can't spend money we don't have," Simon said. "Once we
turn in these wannabe heroes, we'll be able to stay wherever we want.
Go check us in."

Jack trudged off. The slamming of a car door pulled Theo's focus,
and he spotted Dion and Yasmine being dragged out of their own van.
Based on her swollen cheeks, she'd been crying. Theo raised his hand

in a wave, believing the greeting would comfort her, when an unknown fist grabbed him by the shirt.

The man holding Theo was also a stranger. A long, puckered red scar traced across his nose. His eyes were so light blue they seemed white. And if that wasn't terrifying enough, he had a utility belt full of knives, each one sharper than the last.

"This is a surprise," he said, his voice hissing like a snake. "I know I sent you to find the most valuable catch, but I didn't think you'd actually succeed."

Simon pushed Peter out of the van. "We found some more, too. I'm guessing you could get twenty thousand each."

The man released Theo. "Nonsense. We only need *him*." His gaze lowered, and he motioned to Theo's red-stained arms. "Why is he bloodied and bruised?"

"He did it to himself, sir," Simon answered. "He was trying to escape."

"You think we'll get paid for damaged goods?" The scarred man grunted. "What else did you find?"

"They said they came from Ohio."

Theo glanced at his friends, silently urging them not to react. Luckily, they took the hint and didn't utter a sound.

The scarred man scratched his chin. "Ah, so that's why you wanted to meet here. Where exactly did they come from?"

"Not sure yet. But Jones offered us double if we managed to find the healer. I don't think we should return until we have both of them. Plus, if she's with the other supers, that'll be more money in our pockets."

Theo's nonchalant mask dropped as he realized, *Jones hired these men to find us. To find me.*

"Quit bringing up other supers," the scarred man hissed. "They're a waste of energy. She and Nightwave will be more than enough to allow us to live comfortably. Now, prep the car. We'll start searching in the morning."

Theo never thought he'd see Simon, the man he assumed was a leader, cower from confrontation. However, he shrank upon being yelled at. Without hesitation, Simon hurried toward a nicer black vehicle, this one unable to seat all the supers. Theo gulped down his fear, refusing to let his friends see him scared.

The scarred man paced around Theo, studying him carefully. "Black hair, blue eyes, cocky attitude. You must be the elusive Nightwave. I've been looking for you for some time."

Theo's eyes narrowed. "And you are? I don't feel bad for not knowing your name, since we've clearly never met before."

"Maybe you have," Dion chimed in. "He knows you, so you must've had some kind of altercation."

Theo shook his head. "No way. I've never seen someone this ugly."

"Enough!" The scarred man snatched the collar of Theo's shirt again. "Stop blabbering! You're going to drive me insane."

Theo smirked. "If that's all it takes."

The man shoved Theo into another hunter. "My *name* is Axel. Your old friend Jones hired me to locate you and your friends. His only instructions were to keep *you* alive. As for the others," Axel chuckled, "I could do whatever I wanted."

"You're a crappy bad guy," Dion growled to hide the waver in his voice. "I would know. I used to be one."

"You failed to be a villain." Axel sneered at each of the teens in turn, eventually resting on Theo. "And now you're failing at being heroes. You couldn't even save those children on the bus."

Prepared to fight, Theo stepped forward, but Roger restrained him.

Axel clapped. "This is going to be so much fun! Roger, escort them inside."

He obeyed, pinching Theo and Peter's arms to drag them along. Theo dug his heels in the ground and broke away for an instant, but at the first sign of defiance, Axel flipped a knife directly underneath Yasmine's chin. "Let's not make this difficult," he warned, resting the tip of the blade against her throat. "I'd hate for blood to be spilled on our first impressions."

"Alright, stop!" Theo exclaimed. "I won't run, I promise."

Axel nodded in approval and withdrew his weapon, allowing Yasmine to exhale shakily and fall into Dion.

Don't give in, the darkness urged. ***The night is here; you can kill everyone on this street.***

As liberating as that would be, Theo couldn't ensure his friends' survival. "Touch them," he growled, "and I'll give you a new scar to remember me by."

Even if Axel was going to answer, Theo didn't hear it. He was forced into the motel room and tossed like a doll into the corner with Peter. "Quit talking back," Roger said, whipping out his own dagger. "Or I'll cut your tongue out."

Theo glared. "You don't scare me. You're human."

Calling Roger a human was a compliment. The man was a beast. A rabid dog that only knew violence. As if surprised to hear the words, he recoiled. Or maybe he thought Theo was actually going to attack him. Either way, he waved in two more guards, who accompanied Yasmine and Dion. Upon sitting, she immediately squeezed Theo's hand.

There were two king-sized beds in the room, along with two couches. The beds combined should've fit six or seven, but Axel was allowed his own bed. Theo suspected they had rented a second room, since he hadn't seen Simon.

A large platter was brought to the room, courtesy of room service. The men gorged themselves on hamburgers and fried chicken. They stained their shirts with grease and got drunk on soda. Watching them eat made Theo lose his appetite.

Axel was the only one who didn't eat like a wild animal. As he chewed with his mouth closed, he sat on his bed and watched the news.

"I hope the drugs weren't too intense," he said without looking at Theo. "It's my own concoction—a mixture of barbiturates and tranq. They turn off the parts of the brain that control powers. I hope they wear off in time for Jones."

Theo sat up straighter. "Why?"

"He wants a fight."

The horror didn't fully set in for Theo, since Peter joked, "Speaking of fight, what's wrong with your face?"

The heavy sarcasm made Theo's muscles tense, but Axel burst into laughter. "*That's* a good story! My team and I were scoping out one of the freaks like you. We thought it'd be easy to take down a girl your age. Then, bam!" Axel shouted so loud it made the blinds shudder. "There was a flurry of silver and ice. She cut me wide open and nearly killed three of my men."

Dion sucked in a sharp breath. "Did she escape?"

"Unfortunately, yes. But you needn't worry. I'll find her again."

Peter shifted to get more comfortable, yet it was nearly impossible in the tight corner and metal cuffs. "Follow-up question. What was the deal with the high-pitched ringing?"

"Jones informed us that supers have finely tuned senses. Noise like that disorients you." Axel snorted. "You're like dogs!"

"And what happens to your packages after you deliver them?" Peter pressed.

"When you put it like that, I sound like a mailman." Axel chewed thoughtfully, then answered, "I have it on great authority that the 'packages' get…thrown away." He spotted Peter's saddening expression and added, "Don't look so upset! You didn't have a future anyway."

Axel increased the volume on the TV, but Theo wasn't done talking. "Wait until our friends arrive," he said. "Then, you'll—"

"Then, I'll kill every last one of them." Axel grinned. His mouth was too broad; his teeth too sharp. "And the world will thank me for it. No one wants you supers alive, Nightwave. Everyone *hates* you."

If there was anything to say to crush Theo's spirit, that was it. He held his sore wrists in his lap and sagged against the wall.

"What's going to happen to us?" Yasmine whispered.

"Nothing," Peter answered. "Jones doesn't have Daniel or Carter anymore. He can't take our powers, and he can't wipe our memories."

"He can still *kill* us," Dion pointed out quietly.

During their conversation, Theo remained silent. Principal Jones didn't need supers to be normal; he needed them dead. His twisted morals had decayed; his odd mercy had dissipated.

Yasmine sniffed. "I wish I never left the cabin. We rushed out without a plan, and now, we're going to die."

"I wish I could eat," Peter chimed in, a weak attempt at a joke. "Might as well die on a full stomach."

"I wish we'd never turned into that stupid street," Dion said. "None of this would've happened."

Softly, Theo said, "I wish I didn't have superpowers."

His friends didn't respond. Not that they needed to. The door groaned open, and Simon's body filled the frame.

"Ah, Simon!" Axel cheered, throwing his arms in the air. "I know I promised you your own room, but the supers should be split up. They're more powerful together. So, take Nightwave."

Somehow, Simon's shock eclipsed Theo's. "Take him?" Simon repeated. He sounded numb, almost afraid.

"Think of this as a test," Axel said. "I can't have any more panicky breakdowns from you in the field, so I'm putting you in charge of the scariest super alive. Then, you can overcome your fear."

The other hunters laughed. Simon's jaw clenched.

"Besides," Axel chortled, "Nightwave's been pumped with so many drugs, he's basically useless. They're not threats."

Dion and Yasmine each grabbed one of Theo's arms. Meanwhile,

Peter scoffed. "How dare you! I'm a threat—an intimidating threat, too!"

Undeterred, Simon hoisted Theo to his feet.

"Please stop!" Dion begged, clinging to Theo's arm. "Don't take him!"

Simon's hand curled into a fist, and fearing he'd hit Dion, Theo interjected, "It's okay! I'll go!" Then to his friends, he said, "I'll see you in the morning."

Axel snorted, likely thinking the exact opposite, but Peter met Theo's gaze and nodded once.

Simon quite literally dragged Theo into the next room. It was much smaller than Axel's, containing a bed, a couch, and a TV set.

"Why aren't you partying with your buddies in the other room?" Theo asked.

With an unwavering expression, Simon threw Theo to the couch. "They're not my friends. If I could do this job alone, I would."

"Bad idea. I could kill you right now, and no one would know."

Simon returned to his bed and played his show. "I expect nothing less from a super."

Theo huddled on the couch cushion, drawing his arms in close to his body. The shadows engulfed him in a blanket, yet they couldn't fight the cold. His mind wandered to the cabin. Sure, his bed had never been comfortable, and he hardly slept, but it had been more than enough because he was with his friends. Because he knew Penny was safe, a few rooms away from his.

Wretched tears trickled onto the couch, staining the hideous brown cushions. Once more, his impulsivity had ruined his life. Jumping the gun and leaving the cabin without sufficient supplies or planning would kill his best friends. It would deliver him right into the clutches of his greatest enemy. And it would leave Penny alone.

"Enough of the weeping," Simon suddenly said. "I can't hear my show."

Theo bolted into an upright position, though the movement strained his wrists. "I've had the worst week of my life! I think I'm entitled to cry about it!"

"That's the problem with you supers! You're entitled and—"

"Stop it," Theo demanded weakly. His previous fire extinguished; he couldn't summon the spirit to be angry. Slowly, he settled onto the couch and said, "I can't hear this anymore. Everyone hates supers. I get it."

The mumblings from the TV replaced conversation. The actor's heavy Southern accents and the static behind their voices told Theo it was an old Western movie, the kind Dad watched after Mom was asleep.

"I don't *hate* supers," Simon started slowly. "It's…complicated."

Theo sniffed and turned his back to the bed. "Whatever."

"My granddaughter is a super," Simon explained. "She's got hyper perception, so she's able to sense danger before it happens. She saved my life once. I was driving, and she told me to pull over. Right as I did, an out-of-control semi blared past us and smashed into another car."

"I don't care," Theo said.

"I always had a problem with my daughter marrying a super," Simon continued plainly. "She knew why, but she still betrayed me. Ever since I accepted this job, I haven't been allowed to visit her or my granddaughter."

"Good. You're facing the consequences of your own actions."

"What would you suggest I do?" Simon replied with the same amount of venom. "Neglect my personal beliefs for her?"

"As someone who had their dad ripped out of their life, I would give anything to spend one more day with him. *You* took *yourself* out of her life. If you cared about your family, you'd return home."

Simon punched the headboard. "You act like I have another choice! Supers killed my friends!"

"So, killing supers will make you feel better?"

The darkness twitched on Theo's shoulder. It slithered to his ear, whispering, **He's stunned. This is your chance to attack.**

Theo shook them off. Literally. He wiggled until they dissipated, granting him an extra five minutes of peace.

"I can't stop this," Simon said, hushed. "Supers are dangerous."

"Is your granddaughter dangerous?"

"She's a kid."

Theo traced light, soothing circles over the sores on his wrists. "So was I."

24

RETRIBUTION

A rush of cold water splashed into Theo's face, shocking him into bolting upright. As he sputtered and coughed, Simon shook him by the shoulders. "Get up," the man ordered.

Theo wiped the water from his nose. Through squinted vision, he could see the murky twilight outside. He guessed it was fairly early in the morning, just before dawn. "What?" he croaked. "We're leaving already?"

"Loading the car now," Simon said gruffly. "Stay here and out of trouble. I'd hate to hurt your friends."

"They're going to die anyway," Theo responded.

Simon paused, then said, "I won't let them suffer."

As he lumbered into the hall, Theo felt the darkness jump beneath the couch. Although they didn't speak, he knew exactly what they were instructing him to do.

Escape.

Theo debated his options. Fleeing wasn't possible until he removed the cuffs from his wrists. The key was in Simon's front pocket. He was a tough guy; to swipe the key, Theo would have to take Simon out first.

Heart pounding, Theo dropped his feet to the floor and glanced at the door. At any given moment, Simon might return. Theo had to act fast.

A shadow tickled Theo's chin, shifting his gaze to the bedside table. A silver briefcase rested there, half concealed by Simon's jacket. Theo rushed to the briefcase, repeatedly wishing, *Please don't be locked.*

The two latches popped easily, changing his panicked thoughts into excitement. Inside the briefcase, an array of syringes and green vials stuck in their designated spots, waiting for their chance to be injected into a bloodstream.

Theo picked up one of the syringes. Today, it was either him or Simon.

Beside the door leading to the hallway, Theo faded into the shadows, ignoring their reaching grips. ***Let us take over,*** they whispered. ***We've protected you so many times; don't you trust us?***

The doorknob twisted. The voices silenced.

Simon reentered the room, immediately noticing Theo's missing body from the couch. His mouth dropped open, but before he could scream for help, Theo appeared and plunged the syringe into Simon's neck.

Whilst clutching his throat and wheezing, Simon said, "You're making this harder than it has to be."

Theo tossed the empty syringe to the carpet. "Yeah, well, you threatened my friends."

With a final curse, Simon crumpled to the carpet, fast asleep. The drugs must've worked a lot faster on humans. Shadows slithered across his unconscious form and retrieved a key from his pocket. They dangled it in front of Theo's nose, almost like they were saying, "Found it!"

The celebration couldn't be enjoyed. At any given moment, another hunter could've burst in. Simon was a large man; his collapsing body made a loud noise. Theo scrambled to unlock his cuffs, biting his tongue when he dropped the key.

Finally, he was free. In a rush of elation, he kissed the key, then buried it safely in his pocket. He'd defeated one enemy, but there was an entire room of them next door.

Theo melted into the darkness and slipped through the wall. His friends were crammed in the corner, and Roger had Dion by the throat. "We don't need you anymore," Roger hissed through gritted teeth. "By the time I'm finished with you, the police won't be able to identify your body."

"Stop it!" Yasmine begged. "Don't hurt him!"

Roger was the only hunter in the hotel room. Theo could hear Axel, but his voice was far, so he must've been in the parking lot. There were more men outside, but they wouldn't dare to shoot Theo. However, his friends could've been used for target practice. This wasn't just about escaping; it was about escaping *alive*.

Roger had unsheathed his notched blade and was raising it to Dion's head when a shadow yanked the two of them apart, sending Dion onto the bed and Roger crashing into the TV. Before he could recover, Theo flicked a hand, and the darkness launched Roger through the window. The glass shattered. An alarm blared in the room.

"About time!" Peter exclaimed. He jumped to his feet, a little shaky from weakness, and marched to Theo's solidifying form. After Theo unlocked Peter's cuffs, he immediately went invisible.

Two confused hunters entered the room. One of them wore Theo's backpack. Theo meshed his hands together, forcing the shadows to wrap around the men, trapping their limbs to their sides. As they squirmed and screamed, Peter cuffed them together and reappeared.

"This was fun," he said breathlessly, yanking the backpack from the hunter's shoulders. "We should get kidnapped more often."

"What was that?" Yasmine shrieked. "Did you—?"

"Do you have a plan?" Dion interrupted. "If not, you made them *super* mad."

Theo didn't waste time answering them. He threw his backpack on, relieved to find it weighed the same, and led his friends to the sidewalk. Roger lay unconscious on the concrete, surrounded by shattered glass. A few feet away, a humming van parked.

Suddenly, Axel ran from the side of the building. His hunters followed him, guns drawn.

Theo pushed his friends into the van. "Time to bail!"

Dion and Yasmine climbed into the back as Peter and Theo leapt into the front of the car. Gunshots echoed, pelting the metal side of the van.

"Nice of them to leave the keys!" Peter said, admiring the keychain hanging from the ignition.

More shots rattled the car. One broke Theo's window. "Step on it!"

Peter obeyed and thrust the van out of park. The abrupt speed sent everyone flying backward. The tires squealed, accompanied by the sound of yelling men. As the motel faded behind them, Peter laughed in delight. "We did it! I can't believe we actually did it!" He paused, then added, "Get buckled."

Theo smiled, but as he glanced in the side mirror, his celebration was cut short. A set of headlights trailed the van: Axel.

"We're not out of the woods yet," Theo said, fixing the rearview for Peter.

Peter cursed under his breath. "I guess we'll have to lose them."

"This is crazy!" Yasmine was nearing hysteria, going so far as to hold Dion to attain some comfort. "Can't we let the police handle this?"

"The police hate us," Dion explained. "Everyone kinda does. Considering the fact that Theo destroyed a window and assaulted a guy, I don't think they're going to treat us very kindly."

Theo glanced behind him, able to see everything now that he had his powers back. Along the floor of the van, there were multiple brief-cases filled with needles. There were also maps, weapons, and, oddly enough, snacks.

The two small windows on each door in the back of the van allowed Theo to catch a glimpse of Axel's black car. Theo whirled to face Peter. "Can't you drive any faster?"

Peter appeared offended. "I'm already going ten over the speed limit! Any higher and I'll get a ticket." He spotted Theo unstrapped in his seat. "I told you to get buckled! Did anyone listen to me?"

"Yasmine and I don't have seats!" Dion frantically pointed out.

"Well, then we're going to die in a fiery car crash instead of a hail of gunfire."

Ahead, the light burned red, so Peter began to slow down.

"Peter!" Everyone screamed in unison.

"I'm not running a red light!" he defended. "Especially when no one is buckled!"

Since Peter refused to break the rules of the road, Axel's car quickly approached. Theo spotted the passenger aiming a gun at the van.

The bullet pierced a hole in the back window and grazed Dion's arm until it buried itself in the upholstery of Theo's seat. Dion grabbed his bicep and bit his tongue to keep from screaming, but it didn't stop the tears from flowing down his cheeks. Yasmine hugged him and sat them close to the wall.

Amongst the glares, Peter turned invisible.

Before they could get showered in bullets, Theo took a shadow and made it slam on the gas pedal, sending them flying through the inter-section. Cars honked and swerved to miss the fleeing van, but Axel wasn't so lucky. A semi-truck caught the tail end of his car, spinning them into a telephone pole. Within a minute, they disappeared from view. Despite the victory, no one was pleased.

"Thanks a lot, Peter," Yasmine muttered as she analyzed Dion's wound. "Without Theo, we would've died."

Peter reclaimed control of the car. "Okay, you're right. I took road safety a bit too far. We'll get them next time, guys!"

The words were obviously meant as a joke, but they sobered the team. *Next time.* This wouldn't be the last they'd see of Axel, or of anyone who wanted them dead.

Peter drove until the car ran out of gas. It was only a quarter filled when they'd gotten it, but any distance was enough. Peter pulled into a cheap motel's parking lot, swiped the money from the glovebox, and purchased a room. They could barely afford one bed and a pull-out couch, meaning someone would have to sleep on the floor. Theo guessed it would be him.

As the team settled in, Theo freed Yasmine and Dion from their cuffs with Simon's key. Rather than focus on herself, she brought Dion to the bed and said, "I saw an emergency kit underneath your seat in the car, Theo. Go get it."

Without hesitation, Theo returned outside. Their ground-level room was a few feet from the parking lot, making his trip infinitely easier. In his opinion, they were located in the middle of nowhere, surrounded by dilapidated buildings and dead trees. With any luck, the anonymity would ensure their safety.

Like Yasmine claimed, a medical kit filled with bandages and antiseptic rested underneath the passenger seat. Theo retrieved it, locked the doors, and then sat on the ground. In all the chaos, he'd forgotten about the backpack strapped to him. Inside, he found his clothes, notebook, and money envelope, but fifty dollars was missing, leaving him with about one hundred dollars. From now on, they had to make every cent count.

It was a shame his friends' supplies couldn't be salvaged. Axel likely discarded them, given his intention to kill them. Without Dion's burner phone, they couldn't keep in contact with Penny. Hopefully, she'd be safe at the cabin.

With both his backpack and the med kit, he hurried into the room. He passed the kit to Yasmine and asked, "Do you know what you're doing?"

"Of course," she retorted. "Penny taught me."

Penny doesn't need to wrap wounds, Theo almost teased. *She's a healer.*

Given the emotionally charged morning, any teasing might worsen Yasmine's mood, so Theo occupied himself with securing the bedroom locks and drawing the curtains closed.

"All done," Yasmine announced, patting Dion's newly bandaged arm. "Your turn, Theo."

Theo stiffened. He'd hoped—prayed, actually—that his injuries would fly under the radar. Without Penny here to remove the pain, he wasn't sure he could handle Yasmine's rough care. "No thanks," he said.

Suddenly, Yasmine grabbed him by the shoulders and forcibly directed him to the bed. "You smell like blood," she fired back. "Let me take a look."

Despite not wanting to obey, he displayed his wrists. Gently, Yasmine trailed her finger over his purple and red skin, checking if any spots were actively bleeding. "You can't go one day without hurting yourself," she mumbled. "This is why Penny had to stay close to you."

"I didn't do it on purpose," he insisted. "I was trying to escape."

"Any idiot with half a brain wouldn't have gotten into a tug of war with metal." Sitting them both on the bed, she called, "Get me a towel, Peter."

He rushed to and from the bathroom, delivering Yasmine a wet rag. She dabbed the cold fabric onto Theo's skin, brushing against his wounds.

"Ow!" Theo yelled, recoiling. "Take it easy!"

"I am," she said. "Come here and let me clean you up."

When she reached out, he withdrew so fast he nearly tumbled off the bed.

"If you don't listen," Yasmine warned, "we'll restrain you."

Theo glanced at Peter and Dion, who, though hesitant, nodded along with her claim. Begrudgingly, Theo allowed her to scrub the dried blood, biting his lip whenever the pain became too intense.

Once his wrists were blood-free and raw, she wrapped him like a mummy, securing the gauze tightly on his wounds. "You're welcome," she remarked.

He held himself carefully. Although the cleaning made his wrists throb with pain, he felt much safer. "Thank you. Really, I mean it."

A flicker of sympathy crossed Yasmine's gaze. "Thanks for saving us today. Penny would be proud." She tilted her head to Dion in a silent order, so he followed her to the bathroom to wash the blood off the towels.

In their absence, Peter plopped beside Theo on the bed and retrieved the TV remote. "Don't look so sad," Peter advised. "Girls love scars."

Theo ran his fingertips across the gauze. There wasn't a guarantee that he *would* scar, but the idea disturbed him. Penny hated scars. For her, it served as a reminder of every time she failed to help someone.

After a few moments of static and random voices, Peter said, "You know what? We had a long morning, and I'm starving. I'm getting room service."

Logic kicked in for Theo. Saving the remainder of their money would've been the better choice, but this wasn't the time to be judgmental.

Besides, Theo's stomach was growling louder than a car engine. He'd forgotten how little they'd eaten in the past day. Once Peter made their order through the phone, the team gathered in front of the door, excited for their meal to arrive.

Needless to say, they forgot all about manners when the food cart was pushed into their room. They ate until they couldn't eat anymore. Until the mere thought of food made them want to hurl. They lay on the bed and stared at the ceiling, almost woozy from the sugar rush.

"That was the best meal I've ever had," Dion said with an exhale.

Theo didn't have the heart to tell them that their grand feast was toast, bacon, and eggs. Instead, he said, "Do you guys think we should return to the cabin?"

Without hesitation, Yasmine declared, "We're not quitting because we faced a little setback."

"You wanted to go back," Theo pointed out.

"That's when I thought I was about to die." Yasmine's expression softened. "I don't like leaving Penny vulnerable, but she's the best protector for those kids."

"I'm still worried about them," Theo admitted.

"I'm sure they're fine," Peter said with a yawn. "What's the worst that could happen?"

Theo could think of a few things.

Dion rolled to sit and stretched. "I don't know about you guys, but I didn't sleep a wink last night. We should get some rest."

Theo shot up so fast his head spun. "I'll take first watch."

"We're safe here," Dion countered. "We don't need to do shifts."

"I will."

Peter worked a toothpick in between his teeth. "No offense, Teddy, but you look terrible. If anyone needs to nap, it's you."

Theo jumped into a corner of the room, half tempted to cloak himself in darkness. Now that he was off his medication, he wasn't sure how violently his nightmares would return. "I'm not going to sleep," he said.

Dion's head tilted. "C'mon. A little rest will be good for you."

Theo hid his wrists in his armpits. "I don't want to."

Dion looked to Yasmine, and the two exchanged a short nod.

Cautiously, Theo watched them, waiting for the moment either of them would pounce. Dion was supposed to be on *Theo's* side, considering how many of Theo's secrets he knew.

"We'll make you," she proclaimed.

Theo had to scoff. "Make me? And how would you do that?"

A sudden, sharp, stinging pain similar to that of a mosquito bite stabbed into Theo's upper arm. He cried out and rubbed the new tiny pinprick in his skin. A familiar feeling flowed into him, loosening his muscles and turning his bones to liquid.

It was the drugs Axel had used on him.

Swaying, Theo caught himself on the desk. Refusing to waste a second, Yasmine forced him onto the mattress. She wrapped her arms and legs around him, pinning his own limbs to his sides and preventing him from moving.

Peter appeared from thin air, gripping the empty needle canister. He must have swiped one from the van when Theo wasn't looking. "Sincerest apologies, Teddy," he mourned, "but you've gotta rest."

Theo thrashed to escape Yasmine's vice-like grip. Unfortunately, his movements resembled those of wet spaghetti noodles. "I can't sleep! Don't make me go back there!"

They didn't ask "where" he was referencing. Maybe they already knew. Maybe they didn't want to know.

The second he exhausted his strength, Yasmine moved his head onto her lap and pushed the hair from his forehead. As she brushed away his tears, her thumbs tickled his skin, treating him with the gentle care that Penny would. "You're safe here," Yasmine said. "You're with us."

Theo's attention shifted to Dion, but that focus quickly clouded. "How could you do this to me? I trusted you!"

"It's not his fault," Yasmine defended. "We're doing this for your own good."

Theo blinked hard to clear his vision. "Please let me stay. I'll behave, I promise."

His pleading must've worked, because Peter cut Dion off and whispered a few words, holding him back by the shoulders.

The drugs finally kicked in. Theo's body numbed over. The dark, creeping influence of his power fled his mind. He looked up at Yasmine. "Just don't let me..." Before he could finish, his eyes closed, and his brain finally let him rest.

25

WRONG THINGS

Penny sat at Daniel's bedside, holding his arm to ease him into slumber. With her free hand, she scrolled on her phone, reading her old texts with Theo. The sweet words the couple exchanged over text were far preferable to the ones they screamed before he left. He hadn't taken his phone with him when he left, and Dion hadn't been responding to her, so even though she wanted to communicate with them, she couldn't.

Sighing, Penny tucked her phone into her pocket. During Theo's absence, the cabin had been uncharacteristically quiet. Without a leader, no one knew who to turn to. Especially her.

Training took her mind off her sorrow. Every hour that she wasn't healing, she was in the basement exercising, lifting weights, and sparring with Felix. Like Theo believed, Penny was more than a healer. But it was difficult to prove.

Crickets chirped outside; there had to be at least a hundred of them. The moonlight shone through the window, dancing off the crystals on the lamp. The sight made her look to the gem on her finger, the ring that symbolized Theo's feelings for her.

Her throat closed. Penny dreamt of growing old with Theo. It didn't matter where they lived, so long as they were together. She would even settle for living in this dusty, cramped cabin. Now, it seemed her future wouldn't pan out how she imagined.

"How's your boyfriend?"

Penny whipped around to see Carter leaning against the wall, his arms crossed smugly. She hadn't heard the door open; she must've been too lost in her thoughts. Yanking away from Daniel, she said, "He's not my boyfriend."

"Sure." Carter waltzed to her. "In any case, I need you to leave. I'm going to read Dan's memories."

"Why would you do that?"

"Daniel could be hiding secrets from us, whether he realizes it or not. If I pry into his memories, we'll be able to find them."

"It's an invasion of privacy," Penny protested.

"We don't know his past or how he got here. How long will it take for him to tell us?" Carter noticed Penny's hesitation and finished, "Sometimes you have to do the wrong things for the right reasons."

Without waiting for permission, Carter laid a hand on Daniel's head and fell into a trance. Penny stood there in silence, fighting herself over what she should do. Personally, she didn't think she could forgive anyone for searching her memories. She couldn't stand the thought of Daniel not trusting her.

But she didn't trust Carter either.

She grabbed onto his arm, not expecting anything to happen. But after a violent rocking sensation, she opened her eyes to find herself in a completely different room. The walls were painted a dark navy blue, and a yellow lamp stood alight on a dresser. A small twin-sized bed squished into a corner, and a familiar boy sat on top, reading from a picture book.

Penny opened her mouth to greet Daniel, but Carter hissed, "What are you doing? You're not supposed to be here!"

She shoved him. "Neither are you!" Their argument didn't alert young Daniel, so Penny could've been as loud as she wanted. "You're abusing his trust!"

"Cry me a river, Angel. I'm not leaving, so if you're going to stay, I guess I should bring you up to speed." Carter gestured to the young boy. "That's Daniel. I'm guessing he's about four. His dad and uncle are arguing downstairs. The memory was a little fuzzy at first—he probably barely remembers it."

Yelling rattled the lamp. Daniel cast a fearful glance at the door, then vainly attempted to distract himself with his book. Penny's maternal instincts kicked in, and she went to embrace him, but her arms passed right through him.

"We're not real to him," Carter said. "Duh."

She crossed her arms. "So, we just sit here, then?"

"Actually, we can do this." Carter proceeded to fade out of the room. Penny followed him, right into the heart of the fight.

A much younger Principal Jones and his brother, Aaron, argued in the living room. Plates and glasses had already been smashed to smithereens. Aaron angled in front of Daniel's room, as if he were protecting him. Penny took Carter's hand, not because she wanted to, but because she had never been more scared in her life.

"You're a monster," Aaron was saying as he pointed at his brother. "You might be able to fool everyone else, but you'll never fool me."

"I haven't done anything inhumane in my life!" Principal Jones retorted. "It's freaks like you that cause the most damage!"

"Freaks like me? Then, why don't you give me the school if you're so disgusted? Dad never wanted you to have it anyway!"

"It's my school now! I'd rather burn with it than let you take something from me again!"

The edges of the room grew distorted; the brothers' words faded into oblivion. Carter held tight to Penny. "Here we go!"

Moving from memory to memory was a bit like being on an elevator. Except instead of the soft, up-and-down movements, it was sharp and abrupt. Penny braced her stomach, willing herself not to vomit.

This time, they sat in a blue minivan, all the way in the backseats. Aaron wound through traffic as an older Daniel, still only a child, stared out the window blankly.

"I have to, Tim," Aaron whispered. "He's taking this too far. I'll let you know how it goes."

Aaron snapped his flip phone shut with a click and tossed it into the seat next to him. His eyes flickered in the rearview mirror at Daniel. "Almost there, bud. Remember, when we go in, you sit outside the office, okay?"

"Okay," came the timid response.

Aaron parked on the side of the road, just in front of the hero academy. The building seemed dark. Empty. Almost abandoned. But Penny knew there was at least one person inside. Although she didn't have a body right now, she almost felt her heart beating out of her chest. "Looks different than I remember," she said to Carter as they followed Aaron and Daniel to the doors.

"This is how Daniel recalls it. It's not gonna be identical to how you see it."

"Oh. Are you scared?"

Carter buried his shaking hands in his pockets. "Nope, shut up."

Ahead, Aaron pulled Daniel along by holding his wrist yet released him to open the double doors. Aaron approached the office behind the front desk, ordering Daniel to "Sit and stay put."

Suddenly, the office door opened. And Principal Jones stepped out.

"Aaron, back so soon?" Jones's voice dripped with sarcastic venom. "I might have to get a restraining order against you."

"Don't play with me," Aaron growled, stabbing his finger into

Jason's chest. "I've been talking with a previous student of yours, and he says he saw you kill a super. What kind of school are you running here?"

"Do you have a warrant? Or evidence? Legally, I don't have to speak to you." His attention drifted to the side, catching Daniel sitting obediently in a chair. "Why don't you enroll your son in my school? He's a super—he'll learn a lot." Jones signaled to Daniel. "Come here, kid."

Daniel stood, but Aaron extended an arm to cut him off. "Daniel, sit down."

Jones's expression melted with compassion. His act was so good that Penny believed him. "You don't have to fear me, Danny. I just want to talk to you."

Daniel inched closer. His dad pushed him back.

"I know you're scared about your powers," Jones continued. "I'm sure you're feeling lonely. You could make friends here. Friends that are like you."

Finally, Daniel spoke. "Friends?"

"Of course, kiddo. They're freaks too."

Within the span of a second—or maybe it felt that way because of Daniel's memory—Principal Jones snatched Daniel's arm and yanked him close, drilling the muzzle of a silver pistol into the young boy's skull. Big, rolling tears fell down Daniel's cheeks.

"Stop it!" Penny screamed. "Let him go!"

"Let him go!" Aaron ordered, mimicking Penny's desperate pleas. "I swear, if you harm a hair on his head, I'll—"

"Kill me? Oh, I know you will. But not before I kill him." The pistol dug in deeper. Daniel winced.

"Alright!" Aaron threw his arms up. "Make your demands!"

Jones stared him down. "I want your power."

"You're psychotic! That's not possible!"

"It is, actually." Jones mockingly caressed Daniel's hair with his free hand. "Your sweet, darling son can steal powers and transfer them to new hosts. Make him do it."

"Jason, please, he's only a kid."

"Give me your power and I'll never bother you again. You'll be free to live this domestic dream you've made. How would you like that?"

Aaron seemed to consider the proposition. Penny wanted to shout at him to refuse the deal, but it was impossible.

"You can't be trusted with power," Aaron said, gaining an edge. "It won't make you happy."

Jones clenched his jaw. "Careful, Aaron. I'd hate to upset the child." The gun clicked.

"Fine!" Aaron exclaimed. "You can have my power. But Daniel stays alive."

"I won't kill him," Jones promised.

Penny could see the gears spinning in Aaron's head. Any move he made might've resulted in the demise of his son. Despite facing inevitability, Aaron knelt to be at Daniel's eye level and said, "Hey, it's going to be fine, buddy. Just take my power and give it to Uncle Jason. You can do it."

The young, sniveling Daniel reached for his father. Like a bad internet connection, the memory flickered and skipped. One minute, Aaron was comforting his son, and the next, he was on his hands and knees, exhausted. In contrast, Jones stood a little taller. Penny spotted Daniel hiding behind the front desk chair, shivering.

"There," Aaron gasped, "you have everything you ever wanted."

Jones raised the gun. "Almost."

The memory flickered again, and in the next instant, Aaron had disappeared. In his absence, Jones roughly tousled Daniel's hair and said, "Now, we're both freaks."

The next set of memories dumped Penny and Carter into the principal's office. Dozens of events of Daniel taking students' powers; some

Penny recognized. Their screams of pain sent chills down her arms. A few tried to flee the office, but would collapse on the floor, writhing in agony. Others tried to attack Daniel or Principal Jones. They failed too. Then, once the deed was done, a past version of Carter would step in and wipe their memories clean.

"I was so selfish," the real Carter whispered.

Penny glanced at him, managing to tear her gaze from the newest suffering teen.

"Jones told me if I wanted to stay alive," Carter said, "then I had to erase their memories. Don't get me wrong—it was *so* easy to do it. Until I saw how scared they were—heard how they begged me for help. And I ignored them." Carter averted his stare to the floor. "Jones would send letters to curious families, claiming their children were doing well and were busy with assignments. Some families asked too many questions. So, Jones brought them in for a meeting and I...I had to make them forget their children. Principal Jones always told me that if I didn't, then he'd kill them. I guess I thought I was doing a good thing."

It was both tragic and honorable of the parents to fight so hard for their children. But Penny knew not every student was blessed with a decent family. The villains, for example, didn't have anyone to watch out for them outside of the academy. She wondered where Carter's relationships stood.

"What happened to the students after that?" Penny found herself asking.

"All I know is that they were transported to different places. Some stayed in New York. Others were taken farther away. Jones saw it as a chance for them to create new lives. I wouldn't be surprised if most of them are—" Carter changed his own subject. "It's hard to pay attention to missing kids if not a lot of people know they're missing."

"Did you and Daniel ever try to stop it?"

"I hardly ever saw Daniel. We were kept separate from each other. I don't know about him, but I tried to erase Jones's memory. Maybe I was too nervous, or maybe he's invincible to my power, because it didn't work. After I was caught, he," Carter cleared his throat, "I didn't try again."

The memory shifted once more. This new house was spacious and bright, but it had a feeling of darkness. A grown-up Daniel hid behind a couch. He had a computer on his lap and clacked on the keys, trying to hack into it.

When he finally figured out the passcode, he delved into each former student's personal file. It was almost as if he were searching for information.

He paused on Penny's file and studied her picture at the top. Carter gazed at her slightly, yet she was preoccupied with her photo, too. She looked like a child, no more than twelve. Had she matured that much in the last year?

In a flash, Daniel switched to Theo's file, scanned it, and moved on. He ended on Dion's and read every word.

"Dion Decker: Ghost Boy. Cousin had a heart attack in the Penn-sylvania woods when Decker was eleven. Parents separated at age twelve. Lived with his mom; never visited his dad. Single child."

As if he had solved a great riddle, Daniel beamed and added another tab to his screen. He researched cabins deep in the Pennsyl-vania forests, and after a grueling process of trial and error, he found it.

Penny sucked in a sharp breath. A picture of *their* cabin appeared on screen. Although it wasn't currently for sale, the description on the site instructed users to contact Janice Decker for more information. *"Great getaway!"* She'd written under the pictures. *"It's ideally for a family; tons of room and land around the cabin! This cabin is perfect for those who want to disappear from the outside world!"*

Daniel couldn't have looked more excited. Penny could see the plan brewing in his mind. He'd find this cabin and ask to join the team, finally exacting revenge on his awful uncle. Quickly, Daniel closed the tabs and returned the laptop to its place on the table.

But Penny couldn't take her eyes off the computer. Just because Daniel had closed the tabs didn't mean he had erased his tracks.

A loud boom fired into the memory, yet it didn't seem to alert anyone other than Penny and Carter. His concentration broke, and they appeared back in the cabin. Gasping, he collapsed to the floor. Penny rushed to help him as he said, "Daniel was followed."

Another explosion rocked the cabin, knocking them both off their feet. Daniel woke with a jump and asked, "What's going on?"

As the chaos of running and screaming thundered down the hall, Penny swallowed. "We're under attack."

26

MASTER OF ESCAPE

"What?" Daniel blurted.

"Under attack!" Carter repeated, yelling into Daniel's face. "You might as well have drawn a map right to our hideout!"

Daniel blinked. "I-I—"

"You didn't clear your browser history! Principal Jones knew you came here!"

Daniel looked to Penny for help, but she couldn't meet his gaze. There was no defense to give him. This truly was his fault.

Carter paced the floor. "Theo isn't here to protect us. What are we supposed to do?"

"Calm down," Penny said shakily. "We've planned for this."

"Those plans consisted of Theo helping us!" Tears welled on Carter's bottom lashes. "We're going to die."

Truthfully, Penny was just as terrified as Carter, if not more. She wasn't like Theo; she couldn't lead with confidence and strategy. All she knew how to do was heal people's pain. And even *that,* she wasn't perfect at.

But right now, people were relying on her to make a plan and get them out safely. "We're going to be fine," she said, somehow controlling her tone. "Carter, I need you to gather everyone in the living room. We don't have much time."

Carter sprinted to obey while Daniel stood. "What can I do?"

Ignoring him, Penny knelt on the window seat and squinted to see their attackers. The explosions they'd felt weren't real bombs, simply concussion grenades. She couldn't see the army yet, but knew they were close.

"Stay here," she ordered. "I can handle this."

Before she could rush out, he grabbed her hand. "Penny, please believe me. I didn't mean for any of this to happen!"

"I know. But this is happening because of you."

As if she'd slapped him, he flinched. "I-I can help," he begged. "I can fix this!"

"If you really want to help, tell Millie and her troop to get ready. She'll need to hold the enemies off until we make a solid plan."

Daniel nodded. "I swear I won't let you down."

She smiled for him as he left, but the second he was gone, it faded. She didn't believe him. Not one bit.

Penny hurried out of the room and down the stairs, milling through the swarms of screaming children to make it to the living room. Giselle, Felix, Lily, and Carter were already there, deep in conversation.

"Theo didn't tell me anything!" Felix protested. "Why would he?" Felix spotted Penny and immediately pointed her out. "Penny's got a plan! I can see it in her eyes!"

"Do you?" Giselle asked, sounding equally hopeful and doubtful.

"Um, totally." Penny turned to Lily, who, for once, wasn't stoic. "I need you to calm the crowd. They won't listen to me if they're scared."

"Fear is one of the biggest motivators," Lily countered. "But since we don't have time to argue, I will do it."

Almost like she was giving everyone a big hug, she spread her arms wide. The room relaxed with a collective sigh; their minds manipulated into feeling relieved. The screams stopped, encompassing the cabin in an eerie silence.

Penny stood on the coffee table to address the crowd. "There's no need to panic!" she announced. "Defending the cabin is one of the situations we trained for."

"But they already know we're here," Carter pointed out. "Even if we beat them, they'll come back."

She stuck her tongue out at him. "My friends and I have a plan," she said to the children. "I promise all of you will live to see tomorrow."

Penny jumped off the table and dragged Felix, Giselle, Lily, and Carter into the far corner of the room. Just before she could begin formulating an attack plan, a fully equipped Millie shoved into their circle. Breathless, she leaned in and whispered the two words Penny didn't want to hear. "They're here."

Penny bit her bottom lip so hard it bled. The metallic taste dripped into her mouth, mingling with her adrenaline.

"Thirty yards from the cabin perimeter," Millie added. "What do you need me to do?"

Penny looked out over the sea of hopeful faces and thought, *If Theo were here, he'd stay and fight. But I'm not Theo.*

"New plan," she said, "we're going to run."

A muffled chorus of "what" traveled through her friends. Knowing their time was valuable and limited, Penny continued, "Our main priority is getting the kids to safety. We have two functioning vans in the garage. Pack them as full as you can. Lily, you and Natalie are our designated drivers. I need you to take the kids to..." The team didn't have another safe house. That left one other option. "Take them to the Palmer's house in Long Island," Penny declared.

Lily's jaw dropped. "Did Nightwave approve this?"

"No, but his mom will." *Hopefully,* Penny thought to herself. "Theo should have left us some money upstairs. You should split it between you two for gas and food."

"It'll be in the box under Theo's bed," Felix added. "The one on the right side of the room."

The two girls hurried to obey. Another explosion rocked the cabin. The lights swung precariously above Penny's head. Her remaining friends stared at her with wide eyes.

"Millie, her boys, and I will distract the soldiers for as long as we can," she said, kneeling and grabbing a gun from its hiding spot under the couch. "Get the kids in the vans."

"What about the rest of us?" Giselle steepled her shaking hands to her chest. "I-I don't want to die."

Penny gave a tight-lipped smile. Dying wasn't on her bucket list either, yet it seemed there wasn't an alternative.

Without warning, Felix draped an arm around her shoulders and proclaimed, "There's no better way to die than to die bravely. I'd be honored to go down fighting for these kids."

Penny's jaw dropped. There wasn't an ounce of cockiness in his tone. Truly, he was doing this because it was the right thing to do. "Thank you, Felix," she said.

"'Course, Pen." He embraced her as hard as he could without hurting her. "Please stay alive."

"I'll try."

Carter nodded shortly, his face stony with determination. "Enough of the flowery talk. Let's get this over with."

As everyone rushed to complete their tasks, Millie escorted Penny to the front door. "I can't find Daniel," Millie explained, hushed. "After he told us the situation, he ran into the trees."

Penny's heart lurched into her throat. Leaving Daniel behind wasn't an option, but she couldn't risk anyone else to save him. This was a battle that he'd have to fight himself.

"Don't worry about him," Penny said. "Our job is to minimize the threat to those kids. I trust you to do that."

Millie tapped her fist against her chest. "Good luck, Angel. I hope to see you at the end."

While Millie leapt through an open window, Penny cracked the front door. Every limb trembled, practically immobilizing her. Was this how Theo felt every night, prepping the cabin for a possible attack? Did he fear for his life when he checked the perimeter, compiled research, and made sacrifices so the children could eat? If he had, then he'd never let it slip.

She couldn't either.

Penny's quivering steps stopped on the gravel driveway. Her breath fogged out in front of her like a cloud. She resisted the urge to shiver, both from the cold and from the impending doom. At least she could finally utilize her fighting skills.

The echoing marches of the army approached in the forest, not just toward the front of the cabin, but from all sides. Their flashlights cut through the weeds like swords. The moon shone above, a spotlight for the fight. Storm clouds hid the stars; the smell of rain clung to the air, as did the undeniable stench of gunpowder.

Penny exhaled. This was it.

Right when the first man broke through the trees, she fired a shot over his head, being careful not to hit anyone. It went wild, yet he still dove to the ground.

Dozens of men emerged. Each of them wore dark camouflage, glowing green night vision goggles, and an array of weaponry at their waists. The man Penny almost shot climbed to his feet, saying, "Don't shoot! We can talk about this!"

"Talk about what?" She hated how unsteady her voice was. "How you're here to exterminate a bunch of kids?"

"That's not what we're doing." He took a step, so she fired again into the gravel, spraying rocks everywhere. He lifted his goggles to see her better. "You must be the healer."

"My *name* is Penny."

"Well, Penny, my name is Commander Arnold. I promise if you surrender, we'll take you peacefully. This doesn't have to end in death."

"Not tonight. But what will happen after you take us? It's going to be rainbows and sunshine?"

The man chuckled. "Take the deal, sweetheart. It's the only one you're going to get."

Penny glared at him. In the corner of her eye, she could see more guards creeping closer. Her grip tightened on the gun. "Tell them to back off," she ordered, nodding at the men mere feet from her. "Before I change my mind."

Commander Arnold waved a hand, excusing his team backward. As soon as they obeyed, she lowered her weapon. He lifted a walkie-talkie to his mouth. "Requesting backup. We've got a code yellow. Over."

He walked to stand in front of Penny, towering so tall he nearly blocked out the moon. Smiling, he reached out to take her gun. "That was easy, wasn't it? No battle necessary."

The second he touched her, she grabbed his wrist and flipped it behind him. Unfortunately, he was much bigger, stronger, and more trained than she was, so he broke away almost immediately. He snatched her gun and sent it flying twenty feet into the forest.

A bullet ripped through the air from the bushes and buried itself in the soldier closest to the front door. At the same time, Millie screamed, "Fire!"

The sudden onslaught of gunshots startled the commander. Penny kicked him hard in the stomach, sending him stumbling, and turned to Millie's troop in their hiding places along the bushes and walls of the cabin. Penny hoped they could hear her as she exclaimed, "Don't let them enter the ca—ack!"

Commander Arnold wrapped his arm around her throat in a choke-hold maneuver. Except he didn't squeeze hard enough to cut off her breathing. Yet. "Don't make this difficult," he hissed in her ear. "For every man of mine that dies, I'll kill two of your own."

While he was speaking, Penny worked her chin into the crook of his elbow. With one swift push, she sank out of his grasp. Her fists clenched, ready to attack him, but a terribly gut-wrenching sound cut her off.

"I've been hit!" Liam cried. The immense pain in his voice seemed to interrupt everyone.

Millie was the first to move. She broke out from her hiding place and sprinted to the opposite side of the house, dodging grabbing soldiers and flying bullets.

Purely out of instinct, Penny took a step to follow. Suddenly, her view of the cabin flipped sideways as her head hit the gravel rocks. Commander Arnold situated his position on top of her, pinning her arms above her and keeping his legs pressed tightly to her hips. Her squirms to escape did nothing but drain her strength.

"Healer is compromised," he announced proudly. "Take 'em out."

"What?" Penny strained to see what was happening as the shots and screams rose in volume. These soldiers had years of experience on their side. That, and they hated supers. This was probably like shooting fish in a barrel.

"Stop!" Penny writhed on the ground. "Let me go!"

Somehow, Millie's cursing was louder than anything else. Each shot she made hit its target, but it wouldn't be enough. In the distance, Penny heard Adam crying and begging for his life. Another singular shot echoed. His crying stopped.

"No!" Millie's footsteps crunched across the driveway, but she didn't even make it ten feet before she herself was shot. Based on her groaning, she was alive. Penny didn't know for how long, though.

"Why are you doing this?" Penny sobbed. "We're just kids!"

The commander altered his grip to hold her with one hand and stroked Penny's cheek with the other. "Don't cry, Angel. We've got special orders to keep you alive." He looked up and boomed, "Quit wasting ammo! Leave 'em and get inside that house!"

"Stop, please!" Penny's begging found no sympathy. The soldier's boots tramped on the porch. The front door splintered and broke. Penny didn't enjoy screaming, but she summoned her strength to yell, "Felix! They're c—"

Commander Arnold moved his free hand over her mouth, silencing her words. He pressed hard enough that she felt her jaw crack. "Shut up," he growled, "or I won't be so merciful to you."

She didn't need his mercy. In fact, he walked into the stupidest trap known to fighters.

In one sharp movement, she jerked her chin so that his thumb slipped into her mouth. She bit down as hard as humanly possible, determined to rip his thumb off.

Spewing swears, the commander yanked away. Penny scurried out from under his body and kicked him in the knee. A nice resounding crack echoed through the forest.

Yelling, he crumpled to the dirt, clutching the knee that wouldn't bend right. Penny swiped the gun from his holster and buried it in his head. "Tell them to leave!" she commanded. "Now, or I'll kill you!"

"Calm down, honey," the commander said, slightly strained. "They're only tranquilizer darts."

Could that be true? Perhaps this was a scare tactic, a bluff, and Principal Jones wanted them alive to serve as examples later.

But the screams sounded too painful. The shots were too loud.

Her eyesight blurred. What was going to happen in the cabin?

27

FELIX'S TIME TO SHINE

Man, I wish Theo was here, Felix thought as he dragged an armoire in front of the back door. It had only been twenty seconds since Penny left outside to distract the army, and already, Felix was beginning to worry.

There was no way of knowing where the soldiers would enter from, so he took it upon himself to block all entrances and exits, leaving the garage open for the kids. As far as he knew, most of them were already in the vans, ready to go.

With the back door successfully secured, he started for the front door, but a particular sound made him stop. Crying. More like sniffling, the kind someone does before they erupt into sobs.

He glanced behind the couch, finding one of the younger girls huddled there with her hands over her ears. For a fleeting moment, he saw his little sister hiding behind the couch instead, whimpering after she'd failed a math test. He comforted her in the best technique he knew how: by humiliating himself. Why not try it again now?

Felix bent down and crawled toward the girl, although the space between the couch and the wall didn't give him much room to move around. Carefully, he touched her knee. Her mouth flew open, and she was probably going to scream, but he raised a finger to his lips. "Shh, it's me. You remember me, right?"

The girl nodded.

Even if she remembered him, it didn't mean he remembered her. Theo was always so good at knowing the children's names. Felix wished he was too.

"I'm Felix," he said. "My friends are waiting for you in the garage. They're gonna take you somewhere safe, far away from here. But we gotta get there first, alright?"

The girl's tremors slowed. She nodded again.

He smiled. "Good. You should give me a head start. I bet you're faster than me."

Softly, she giggled and wiped her cheeks. He offered her his hand, and she squeezed it with her soaking wet one.

A flurry of gunshots rattled outside, alerting Felix to drop to the floor. His heart thudded against the carpet. He prayed the shots were coming from their side.

"Come on," he told the girl. "We don't have much time."

Without waiting for a response, he pulled her to her feet and ran from the living room, ducking whenever a shot echoed too close to the windows. They reached the door to the garage, and he nudged the girl into Natalie's arms. Giselle hurried to him and breathlessly explained, "We're missing three kids. I don't know where they are!"

"Doesn't matter," Carter countered. "Let's save the ones we have!"

"We can't leave children behind!"

"A few sacrifices are better than getting everyone killed!"

Amongst the chaos of their yelling, Felix knew one thing. Theo would return to save those three extra kids, even if it meant he died. Felix stepped into the hall, but Giselle grabbed his arm. As much as he enjoyed her touch, he tore away and said, "You can't stop me!"

"I'm not stopping you," she replied. "I'm helping you."

Despite this being the absolute worst moment ever—and not romantic in any way—he nearly confessed his feelings for her right then and there. She looked so hot with her messy braid and determined expression.

A thud came from the front door. Then another, and another. His love-stricken thoughts cut off, and the severity of the situation returned.

"The main floor is clear," Giselle said. "You take upstairs, I'll take the basement."

Before he could answer, she took off. The front door splintered. Felix dashed past it to the stairs and thought he caught a whiff of blood from the men's boots. They weren't shooting to capture. These were shots to kill.

On the last stair, Felix tripped and slammed his knee into the hard-wood floor. As he bit back his yelp of pain, he dragged his body into the nearest room, hiding himself right as the front door blasted into bits.

The harsh beams of flashlights cut across the walls. The soldiers' boots crunched on the floor of the foyer. Felix could hardly steady his breathing.

With a grimace, he forced himself to his feet and ransacked the first bedroom, tearing the beds bare and ripping every item out from under them. He found clothes, blankets, and coloring books, but no kids.

He crept into the hall toward the other bedrooms, listening intently for any signs of danger. As far as he could tell, most of the soldiers were on the main floor or in the basement.

He hobbled to the next room, stripping that one bare, too. Just as he started to lose hope, he heard the faintest, "Fewix?"

He whirled around to the owner of the voice. The youngest kid at the cabin, a boy only six, cowered in a closet. Felix and Peter referred to the boy as "Widdle Wobby," since the boy couldn't pronounce his R's or L's yet.

Felix swept the boy in a hug. "Robby! I can't believe you're alive!"

"What's goin' on?"

"Never mind. Is there anyone else up here?"

Robby shook his head. "Just me."

"Good. Let's get you to the vans."

Felix snatched the young boy's wrist and ushered them both into the hall. Robby pressed close and asked, "Are we gonna die?"

Felix neared the balcony and quickly scanned the foyer below. "Nope."

"Pwomise?"

"Sure. Stop talking."

Robby obeyed. Felix brought them both to the staircase, making their steps as slow and silent as possible. When they reached the top of the stairs, Robby stopped moving. Wordlessly, he pointed to the bathroom across from them. A flashlight beamed under the door. Then, the knob turned.

In this situation, Theo would do something heroic. He always seemed to make the right decisions at the right times. But right now, Felix wasn't Theo. He probably wouldn't ever be. Right now, Felix was Felix, and it had to be enough.

The door opened completely, exposing the soldier with his gun drawn. He hadn't noticed Felix or Robby; instead, he was occupied with switching his flashlight off. The one advantage Felix had over anyone else wasn't his powers. It was his impulse to act first and think later.

At home in California, Felix had the record for takedowns on his football team. He was used to tackling guys twice his size.

He slammed into the soldier's waist, catching him off guard. The two of them crashed into the bathroom, landing hard on the linoleum floor. Without hesitation, Felix wrestled the rifle out of the man's clutches, acting quickly while his opponent was dazed.

Felix tossed the weapon over his shoulder. Robby rushed to protect it, making Felix curse. Giving a gun to a six-year-old wasn't his best idea ever. He directed his attention to the man's belt, equipped with knives, extra magazines, and small orbs.

The soldier's fist collided with Felix's ear. Loud ringing burst in Felix's eardrum as he felt a trickle of blood drip down his neck. He staggered to stand, his injured left knee nearly giving out on him. The soldier also rose to his feet, much more confidently, too, and chuckled. "You're an idiot."

Felix blinked hard. Compared to past experiences, this pain was child's play. Using his good foot, he kicked the door shut.

"Thanks for trapping yourself in here with me," the soldier mocked. "You're making my job easier."

"Actually," Felix said, "you're stuck with *me*." He displayed the three silver balls he'd stolen from the soldier's belt. "And as an idiot, I think it's in my best interest to figure out what these do."

The soldier's eyes widened. He frantically searched for his gas mask, but it had flown off his head in the scuffle. In fact, it lay directly at Felix's feet.

He smashed the orbs on the ground, and a strange, white, wispy smoke filled the bathroom. Holding his breath, Felix fumbled for the mask and secured it on his face. As he sucked in choking gasps, he heard the soldier collapse.

Felix staggered to the door, but thanks to the thick haze, he tripped on the soldier's foot and smashed his head into the wall. Dizzy, disoriented, and likely concussed, Felix sprawled out on the cold floor. *I just need a minute,* he told himself. *Then, I'll get back in the game.*

But this was not a game. It was real—a matter of life and death. The longer Felix cowered in the bathroom, the less chance Robby had to survive.

Grunting, Felix rolled to his feet. Spots danced at the edges of his vision, yet the smoke had cleared slightly, allowing him to see a path to the door.

Luckily, it opened on its own. Robby stood at the threshold; his arm extended for the knob. Felix shoved them both aside and slammed the door shut, keeping the odd smoke inside the bathroom.

With a wheeze, Felix ripped the mask off and said, "Thank you, Robby."

"You're bweeding."

"Yeah, I know. Let's go." Felix swiped the rifle out of Robby's grasp and leveled it on his shoulder, just as he had done numerous times in practice. From the sounds of it, most of the soldiers had returned outside.

The pair passed the garage door, whereupon Felix knocked in their designated rhythm. Carter whisked the door open and yanked Robby inside, then reached for Felix next.

He resisted. "Is everyone accounted for?"

"Sure, get in!"

"Is Giselle inside?"

Carter huffed. "Just get in!"

"Not without her."

Carter locked the door once more while Felix continued to patrol the first floor. One soldier was poking around in the fridge and caught a glimpse of Felix, but he only managed a sharp, "Hey," before Felix whacked him on the head with the gun. As dangerous as this was, Felix couldn't pull the trigger to kill another man. He'd never be able to return home if he did.

Pounding echoed on the basement stairs, so he readied his weapon and aimed at the door. But instead of another soldier, Giselle burst through and slammed it shut behind her. Using her telekinesis, she shoved an armoire in front of the door, just in time to stop the other soldiers from pursuing her.

As she muttered in French, she dusted off her hands like she was saying, "Enough of that!" Her braid had evaporated entirely, letting her messy curls hang on her shoulders. She sported a cut on her forehead and another on her upper arm yet didn't seem to be in life-threatening condition. She glanced up and spotted Felix, who was still stupidly aiming the gun at her.

Giselle raised a brow. "You got the kids?"

"Huh? Oh, yeah!" He lowered the rifle. "Yep, I got them. They're safe."

"Good, let's head out." She moved to the garage door until Felix blurted, "Are you hurt?"

"What?"

"I-I mean, you look like you're hurt. I'm making sure you're not."

Giselle smiled. She actually smiled! "If anyone needs answers on safety, it's me. You look like you went through a wood-chipper."

Felix scoffed. "Me? Pfft, I'm fine."

"Well, let's meet up with Penny and get you better."

Felix almost wanted to explode from pure joy. At long last, he managed to hold a conversation with Giselle for more than ten seconds without saying something idiotic. While he followed her, he heard the worst sound imaginable.

"Felix?" Max whispered. "Is it safe?"

The third missing kid was Max. Both Felix and Giselle stopped, though he was tempted to continue walking. Max crawled out of one of the kitchen cupboards. The skinny rat must've squeezed himself inside to hide until the danger left.

"Yeah," Felix muttered. "It's safe. Let's go."

Max stumbled to his feet and shook his legs to wake them. When he was about five feet away, Felix noticed a stirring behind him.

The soldier at the fridge was waking. In less than a second, he drew a small pistol from his side holster and fired right at Max's back.

Time seemed to move in slow motion. And yet, Felix couldn't find the words to warn Max. This wretchedly annoying thirteen-year-old who harassed Penny, then Giselle, only stopped when he was intimidated by Theo and threatened at knifepoint by Felix. This dumb teenager, who shouldn't have been a super, was about to die.

And Felix wanted nothing more than to stop it.

He imagined himself freezing the bullet in midair. He saw himself saving Max—saving everyone—letting them go home to their loving families. They had so much to give and so much to live for.

But his powers didn't work. So, he stood there and watched as the bullet followed its trajectory right into the boy's chest.

Max was dead before he hit the floor.

The soldier aimed his pistol at Felix next, but it clicked uselessly. Jammed.

Felix lifted his rifle. In a voice too quiet to be heard, he said, "I'm sorry, Mama."

One shot was all it took. It killed Max, it killed the soldier, and it killed Felix.

Out of his friends, he had been the first to take a life. Deep down, he always knew it'd be him, but he thought he'd kill someone by accident or as a result of his temper. Now that he'd bridged that gap, he knew: If he had to kill for the sake of others, he'd do it. No hesitation next time either.

Giselle rushed to Felix and touched his face. Her lips moved with her words. Oddly, her mouth moved slower than normal, too. All he heard was ringing. She cradled his head against her shoulder. Her fingers delved into his hair.

Time resumed speed. He heard Giselle's soft assurances, felt them tickle his ear. With numb arms, he dropped the rifle and hugged her close.

"It wasn't your fault," she said, the sound rumbling against him. "We must bring you to Penny."

He didn't need it. Giselle's company was healing enough.

She pulled away a bit, allowing him to see her deep frown. Quickly, Felix wiped the blood off his forehead. "I'm good, trust me."

Without time to argue, she dragged him into the garage, leaving the carnage of the cabin behind. The children weren't screaming or crying, and sadly, Felix wished they were. He preferred chaos to silence.

"Penny's still out there," Giselle said to Carter. "There are more than a dozen soldiers outside with her—anticipating our escape."

"What are you suggesting?" Carter inquired.

"A diversion," Felix joined in. "Our main priority is getting these kids out of here alive. Those men will shoot at the vans the second they pull out."

"Maybe Giselle can use her telekinesis and block the bullets."

"It's charming you think I'm that talented."

Carter scowled. "Then, what other options do we have?"

"I can help!" another young girl suddenly blurted. She jumped out of the van, ripped her arm out of Natalie's grip, and walked directly to Felix. "I promise I can help!"

He stared at her, unable to remember her name. Thankfully, Giselle saved him with, "How would you do that, Rebecca?"

Rebecca distanced herself from everyone else and concentrated. A light pink bubble appeared around her, hazy and small, but it was the best forcefield Felix had ever seen. His face nearly split in half from his wide grin. Once the field vanished, he scooped Rebecca into a hug. "That's amazing, kid! You're exactly what we need!"

The little girl giggled. "Theo saved me and my friends. I should save his."

For the first time feeling ready, Felix looked at his friends. "I think we found our diversion."

28

WHO LIVES, WHO DIES

Thunder rumbled above the trees. The rainstorm had begun, soaking the gravel driveway and turning the ground into mud around Penny's feet. As she waited for the garage to open, she adjusted the wet hair sticking to her cheeks.

Beneath her, Commander Arnold shifted, so she dug the gun deeper into his neck and growled, "Move again and I'll shoot!"

Through his grimace, the man laughed. "You're not going to shoot me. You don't have the guts."

In response, she buried the gun in his unbroken leg and shot him.

Agony rippled through his screams, drowning Penny in guilt. Simultaneously, her instincts urged her to *heal him*. She tightened her grip on the gun and snapped, "Shut up. I can heal you, but only if you do as I say."

"Y-you're psychotic!"

"Tell your men over the radio that backup isn't necessary. Now, or the next bullet goes into your butt."

Commander Arnold was practically hysterical as he said, "I-I can't grab it!"

"Fine, I'll hold it for you." She settled her weight onto his back and unclipped the radio from his side holster, keeping her weapon trained on his head. She flicked the button and lowered it to his mouth so he could say, "Cancel the previous request. Repeat. Cancel the request. Backup is not needed."

The voice on the other end crackled. "Copy that. See you at base."

Message delivered, Penny flung the radio into the woods. Beneath her, Commander Arnold begged, "Heal me. I did as you said."

"No."

"What? But I—"

Penny pushed the barrel of the gun, so the momentum shoved his face into the mud. "If my friends walk out of that cabin alive, I'll spare your life. If they don't, I will make you suffer for every second you made them suffer. Do you understand?"

He didn't have the chance to answer. The remaining soldiers exited the cabin. Some were noticeably missing. The second they saw Penny, they drew their weapons and ordered her to drop hers. She didn't budge. At least if she died, she'd take this guy with her.

"What's going on?" Commander Arnold asked weakly.

"They're hiding in the garage, sir," one soldier answered. "What should our next move be?"

Penny paused for the commander to say, "Break the doors down," "Blow the garage up," or "Let's wait them out." But he didn't speak. Maybe he knew the second he responded, if it was violent in any way, Penny would've shot him dead.

He took in a shaky breath, yet the sound of old rumbling garage doors silenced everyone. Before they were open, the two vans barreled out, clipping the bottoms of the doors. No damage was done to the vans because they were encased in bright pink forcefields.

Penny laughed. She actually, genuinely laughed. She didn't know which child created the forcefields, but she admired them for their bravery all the same.

One of the van windows opened, and a boy hung halfway in and halfway out. His hand reached toward the woods. Rainwater rose from the dirt and flooded the army, sweeping them off their feet or swallowing them into the mud. Since Penny was standing on the rocks, the water didn't wash her away.

Natalie kept on the road as she sped off, but Lily chose a different path—barreling right through the soldiers. A few of them managed to dive out of the way, but some were clipped and thrown to the side. Penny swore she heard Rebecca yell, "Eat our dust, jerks!"

Penny smiled to herself as the pink-bubbled vans disappeared into the night, transporting the kids to a safer place. She slid her gun into her pocket and bent to heal Commander Arnold. "A promise is a promise," she said.

Tenderly, the man touched his leg, then locked eyes with Penny. Right when he dove for her, an invisible force flung him into his row of soldiers.

Penny glanced behind her, finding Giselle standing in the now-empty garage. With another tug, Giselle dragged Penny into the garage with her, Felix, and Carter. Each of them appeared exhausted, but Felix looked the worst, covered in blood and bruises.

"We did our job," he explained, shrugging off her reach. "It's time to finish this."

As he rushed into the rain, he shouldered his rifle, firing at anyone who dared get close to them. There was something different about him in the way he carried himself, in the heaviness of his walk.

Giselle followed him, leaving Penny in the garage with Carter. "Good idea, right?" she attempted weakly.

"It'd be better if you had an ending." Carter retrieved a revolver from his back pocket. Out of everyone in the cabin, he'd trained with weapons the least. But at least he was willing to fight.

She dropped her chin. This night wasn't going according to plan at all. Was it because of her? "I'm not as good a leader as Theo."

Carter snapped in her face. "Don't start feeling down on yourself. We have a chance of surviving, so buck up and let's do this."

For the first time, Carter was right. She couldn't waste a second, not when her friends' lives were on the line. Penny wiped her cheeks, steeled her determination, and retrieved her weapon before meeting with the others outside. Carter fought to the left of the yard, with Giselle and Felix on the right and Penny in the middle.

However, where was Daniel? Did he escape with the rest of the children, or had the soldiers caught him?

A bullet whizzed past Penny's ear. *Focus!* She told herself, ducking behind a trash can. *You have to stay alive.*

She crouched from her hiding spot and analyzed the yard. The one benefit Penny and her team had was that the vans' escape rattled the soldiers. Nevertheless, whatever happened inside the cabin clearly weighed on her friends' shoulders, particularly with Felix. If it weren't for Giselle fighting at his side, he likely would've lost his composure.

Penny glanced once more to Carter, finding him wrestling a soldier in the mud. The man grappled for Carter's gun, making Penny's heart skip a beat. Before she could rush to his aid, Carter yelled in rage and thrust his hands into the soldier's face. Immediately, the gun dropped to the dirt with a splatter. Then, the soldier's body tensed tighter than a taut rubber band. Scrambling to stand, he blurted, "What's going on? Where am I?" He caught sight of the bodies, the blood, the fighting, and took off into the woods screaming.

Uninjured and unbothered, Carter wiped his jaw and stood. His eyes glimmered, almost like he was excited. His prideful expression was the same Penny remembered seeing on Principal Jones.

Penny swallowed. Although it was necessary to survive, she couldn't help but be disturbed at how easy it was for Carter to steal memories.

Crackling resonated in the storm as Giselle uprooted an entire tree. She brought her fist down over and over, smashing the tree into the soldiers and forcing them to scatter. She broke off one of the branches and literally swept the men as she would with a broom.

Completely in awe of her crushing power, Felix, Carter, and Penny were basically immobilized. Until Penny noticed a soldier near the trees whipping out a small black ball. She almost screamed, "Bomb!" Except it wasn't a bomb.

A loud screeching filled the air. Everyone covered their ears, but Giselle did more than that. As her control of the tree faded, she dropped to her knees. Her screams made no sound.

The screeching rose in pitch, and she fainted. With her defeated, the remaining soldiers inched forward, guns drawn.

Felix slammed into the closest one, catching him off guard and allowing Felix to steal his gun. As he put himself in front of an unconscious Giselle, he downed a couple of soldiers, but his rage could only take him so far. A bullet ripped into his thigh. Another pierced his arm. He crumpled next to Giselle and held her hand.

Someone yanked on Penny's hair, throwing her into the trash can and spilling the contents. Commander Arnold grabbed the front of her shirt, no longer holding her with caution. Blood flowed from a gash on his head; another sliced his arm, right through his clothing.

"I was told to keep you alive," he growled, spit dripping off his lip. "This fight is reason enough to defy orders." His gun burrowed deep into Penny's stomach. The trigger neared the edge.

"Stop!" Daniel shouted. He stood on the muddy lawn, soaking wet and trembling. Based on his ragged appearance, he'd been hiding in the woods. He raised a pistol to his own head. "Let. Her. *Go.*"

Commander Arnold stiffened. "Easy, Daniel, you don't have to do this."

"Let her go or I'll shoot myself! Then, you can explain to Jones why I'm dead!"

"Alright, fine!" The commander shoved Penny to the gravel, letting her scramble to Daniel's side. "Come with us. This doesn't have to end badly."

Daniel pressed the muzzle harder to his head.

"There's no escape," Penny whispered. "Let's give in." There were at least five soldiers left. Felix and Giselle were hunched in the mud. Nearby, Carter clutched his ears, whimpering quietly. Millie and her team's groans had ended long ago. As far as Penny was concerned, the fight was finished.

Daniel's jaw set. Gently, he nudged her aside and approached Commander Arnold, still holding the pistol. Penny believed Daniel was turning himself in.

She couldn't have been more wrong.

In the blink of an eye, Daniel disarmed Commander Arnold and shot him dead. In a panic, the remaining soldiers fled. Wielding two weapons, Daniel fired at their fleeing forms. He knew exactly where to shoot—where their armor was the weakest. All the while, he remained cool and collected. It was like he'd been trained for this. Trained to *kill*.

Finally, the violence ended. Soldiers and supers lay scattered around the cabin. Daniel had saved Penny's life by ending theirs. He returned to her, yet the sight of him made her stomach roll—blood spattered and covered in gunshot residue.

"Don't touch me," she said, angling away from him.

Her small resistance seemed to startle him. He caught sight of himself and recoiled; his weapons clanked to the mud. "I'm sorry," he said. "I-I'm so sorry."

Penny stared at the dirt, willing herself not to feel guilty. This *was* his fault. No apology could've fixed the damage he caused.

Footsteps rattled across the gravel, accompanied by Carter's, "Is it over?"

Nodding, Penny accepted his arm to heal him. "Yeah, it's over. Find Millie and any survivors. I'm going to go heal Felix and Giselle."

Without speaking, Carter joined Daniel as they searched for living, breathing bodies. Penny rushed to Felix, and, not knowing where to start, pressed her palms flat against his chest. At first, he winced, then relaxed as her healing spread through his body. His bullet wounds sealed; his skin returned to its pristine, non-injured state.

"Thank you," he murmured.

"Thank you for being a hero," Penny answered.

Felix's jaw dropped. Once he recovered from his initial shock, he stammered, "W-wow. Sure thing."

Just as Penny directed her power to Giselle, Carter called, "Penny, I need you."

Felix lifted Giselle into his lap. "Go on," he said. "I've got her."

Penny didn't want to debate. She returned to Carter, finding his expression a mask of stone. Wordlessly, he led her to Millie's body, where Daniel was testing the pulse on her wrist. Expecting the worst, Penny's heart sank.

Suddenly, Millie gasped. In a flash, Penny dropped to her knees and healed her. Based on the numerous wounds, she should have died. Penny urged her power to move faster.

Millie's eyes were unfocused and blurry. She stretched a bloody finger at one of the boys nearby. Believing they were asleep, Penny reached for them, but stopped when she realized the horrifying reality.

There would be no healing tonight. Not for the dead.

Stomach acid crawled its way up Penny's throat. Quickly, she turned her face into a bush and vomited. At the same time, she began sobbing, all of her emotions spilling onto the forest floor.

"It's okay," Carter whispered as he patted her back. "Don't cry."

"How is this okay?" she managed to answer. "They-they're—"

"I know."

Penny tried to keep talking, but her words came out in broken cries. Carter enveloped her in his arms and held her, allowing her to drench him in her tears.

Her main job was to heal others. But she wasn't there when they needed her most. The sky echoed with thunder, and the clouds wept over the broken battlefield below.

"In accordance with the United Nations Agreement, every soldier applying for any branch of the military must engage in a series of tests and doctor visits to ensure they are not super. This is intended to protect the other soldiers from unfair treatment or unforeseen dangers. We strive to achieve equality in our troops. If you have questions or concerns, please get in touch with our HR department directly."

-Official Home Page of the U.S. Military Website

29

THE SACRIFICES OF WAR

As the sun rose and cast a golden glow over the muddy forest, Penny and Carter buried Millie's teammates, along with Max, who Felix couldn't look at without crying. Out of the thirty-one people in the cabin last night, six had died. Thanks to the wet ground, their graves were easy to dig.

Before they were buried, Millie gave each of them a smooth stone. "Since we don't have Purple Heart medals," she explained, "I'll use these. Just know that you deserve them."

While Carter settled the dirt evenly, Penny stood by Millie. Strong as ever, Millie cried silent tears. She saluted her friends until she could no longer see them. "They were the only family I cared about," she said. "I can't believe I let them die."

"We can't save everyone," Penny mourned. "Believe me, I wish we could."

Millie rolled the last stone in her palm. "My father used to say this life was picked for me because I was strong enough to endure it. Pain is not a weakness. It reminds me that I'm human. But there's a man out there who doesn't have an ounce of humanity in his entire body." Millie gripped the stone. "I'm going to kill him."

Carter rested the shovel against a tree. "Hold on, hotshot. We can't kill Principal Jones. We need to find Theo first."

"That'll waste time."

"I'm sorry, Millie," Penny interjected, "but Carter's right. We can't kill Jones without Theo's power."

"Well, what about Daniel? He can remove Jones's invincibility, and then we can shoot him!"

"It won't be that easy," Daniel called from his spot on the driveway. "He has a lot of allies, so he won't be alone. And I would need quite a bit of time to take his power. Either that, or he'd need to be weakened by Theo."

Millie grumbled. "How are we supposed to find Theo?"

They looked to Penny, expecting an answer. But she couldn't look away from the fresh mounds. Theo would never have allowed this to happen.

"We should head to New York," Daniel suggested. "I told Theo that's where I left Jones. He's likely still there, anticipating my return."

Millie flung her arms out. "Then, what are we standing around for? Let's get a move on!" She began to tramp down the path, but no one followed.

"We can't leave," Penny said numbly. "Giselle is knocked out cold."

"Then, Felix can carry her," Millie argued.

"He's tired."

"So?"

Penny tore her gaze from the graves. Her well of sadness had dried, leaving little energy to be squandered. "We need to make a plan."

Millie crossed her arms. "We're relying on another one of your genius ideas?"

If Millie's best friends hadn't died, Penny would've punched her.

Thankfully, Carter placed himself between the two of them and said, "Don't argue. We have to wait."

"I'm not wasting my time," Millie repeated.

"Fine," Carter relented. "You and I will head to Theo's old house to make sure the kids got there safely. Then, we can check around for Jones."

"You don't have any money," Penny pointed out. "We gave the rest to Natalie and Lily. And we don't have a vehicle."

"Unlike you," Millie said, "Carter and I are willing to do whatever is necessary to accomplish our goal. Even if that means stealing."

Though hesitant, Carter nodded, agreeing with her. There was no convincing Millie of anything after she set her goals.

"Okay," Penny said, "but if you run into Jones, don't get into a fight. I doubt you'll be able to hold him off by yourselves."

Millie scoffed. "That's what you think." She delved into her pockets and pulled out two radios, extending one to Penny. "When you find Jones, call us. We'll be there in a flash."

"Deal," Penny answered. "I'll take Felix, Daniel, and Giselle. Are you sure you don't want to wait for us?"

"I don't need you," Millie stated. She wandered to the pile of weapons they'd recovered from the woods and stuck the smaller guns into her cargo pants.

"What she meant was, 'we'll be good,'" Carter corrected.

Penny snickered quietly, but a deep sadness rooted inside her. Although she and Carter had never seen eye to eye, concern for his safety plagued her. "Good luck," she offered.

"Yeah," he responded, "you too."

Together, he and Millie walked out of the woods, hardly casting a backward glance.

Dawn was breaking through the trees, casting broken shards of sunlight across the dirt, so Penny ventured to the rest of her friends, her mind a never-ending whirlwind. The rain had cleaned the blood and dirt from their clothes, except it couldn't hide the trauma they'd endured. She was tempted to bring her friends inside to change, but Felix vehemently refused to go near the cabin.

Authorities hadn't reported to the gunshots yet. Maybe the distant neighbors thought it was a hunting party out late last night. Regardless, there was no point in lingering to find out.

Daniel stood guard by Felix and Giselle, avoiding eye contact when Penny approached. Felix cradled Giselle in his arms, holding her with the care he would with a newborn baby. Every few seconds, he'd reach up to test the pulse in her neck. His eyes housed a faraway look; he hardly blinked.

Penny bent over the two of them. "She's alive, you know."

Felix brushed the hair out of Giselle's face. "I know. I just have to be sure."

His gentle touches reminded Penny of Theo. It was a soft love—quiet yet powerful. "This crush means a lot to you," Penny mused.

"It's more than that," Felix said. "I think I can see myself being happy with her." He shook his head. "That was dumb. Forget I said that."

"Actually, I think it's sweet. And Giselle will too. Be yourself."

Although Felix wrinkled his nose, his tone remained playful. "Ugh, *that* was cheesy."

Penny rolled her eyes. Months ago, she'd never tell Felix to be himself. But lately, his behavior had changed from that of an immature boy to a hero.

"We should get moving," she said as she dusted the dirt off her pants. "Daniel might've chased some soldiers away, but they might return with reinforcements."

Felix stood, carrying Giselle bridal-style. "Hold on, what did Daniel do?"

"Nothing," Penny cut in, noting Daniel's uncomfortable shifting. "It all happened so fast."

The answer appeased Felix's curiosity. As they started down the wet, mossy path to town, Daniel threw Penny a grateful look. Though she'd been horrified during the fight, she understood why he did it. After all, she'd shot a man last night out of necessity. It wasn't bad; it was complicated.

Maybe that was why Theo lied.

Halfway into the forest, Giselle awoke. Felix sat her against a tree and asked, "You good?"

Wincing, she massaged her temples. "Je me sens comme la mort."

Felix beckoned Penny, but she was already on her way. She laid a hand on Giselle's head, instantly soothing the pain. Whispering a "thank you," Giselle relaxed against the tree. With her healing finished, Penny said, "We should start moving soon."

"We can go now," Giselle insisted as she climbed to her feet. "I feel fine."

Felix's face fell, but before Penny could speak, Daniel interrupted their conversation to say, "I think you should rest for a little while longer. You're already a liability to us. If you pass out again, we might have to leave you."

Giselle's jaw dropped. Equally shocked, Felix shouted, "How dare you! Giselle is the best among us!" He led her away to complain, yet when she wasn't looking, he threw Daniel a quick, thankful nod.

Having successfully bought Felix more time, Daniel sat cross-legged on a patch of grass. Warily, Penny knelt a few feet from him, watching him for any signs of last night's aggression. "That was nice of you," she said.

"I tried. Sadly, I can't give them privacy."

Penny glanced over her shoulder at the couple. "…catch up to Theo," Giselle was saying. "We can't leave him alone."

Her mention of Theo made Penny tense and Felix frown. Giselle had always been oddly obsessed with Theo. Clearly, Felix noticed it too.

"I hate what I did last night," Daniel said, redirecting Penny's focus. "I know it frightened you to see me like that."

Rather than confirming, she countered with a question of her own. "How did you know they weren't going to kill you?"

"My uncle might be evil, but we're family."

Penny picked at the grass. The next question she asked quietly. "Why didn't they kill me?"

"Jones has always liked you, Penny. He'd never willingly harm you."

Why? I've consistently ruined his plans. She let her pile of grass float in the breeze as she joked, "I'm not scared of you as long as you're not scared of me."

Daniel laughed. "It was surprising. Seeing you fight...you're remarkable."

"It always surprised Theo, too."

Birds chirped in the trees above them, robins and mourning doves competing for listeners. Daniel seemed at peace, but his forehead was wrinkled.

Penny scooted closer. "Where did you learn to do that shooting stuff?"

"Jones trained me. Initially, he envisioned us slaughtering supers together. Then, he decided he wanted to strip them of their power in silence to maintain his public image."

It didn't feel right to leave the conversation at that, so Penny added, "I'm sorry you had to deal with him."

Daniel shrugged. "He's the only family I have. How's yours?"

"The last time I talked to my parents was almost two years ago. I hope they're alright, but..." she blinked, and two teardrops dripped onto her jeans, "they probably don't even know I'm alive."

Daniel's fingers twitched like he wanted to reach out for her, yet ultimately, he didn't. "I'm sure if they could see you now, they would be very proud."

She wiped her cheeks. "Thanks."

"You, um, you never met Theo's mom, did you?"

"Not yet."

"How do you think that'll go?"

At this point in life, Penny doubted she'd ever meet Theo's family. But a girl could dream. "Probably pretty awkward. She's a celebrity model, and I'm a random girl from Ohio. That, and I just sent twenty kids to her house."

"I bet she'll mistake you for a model too."

Daniel sounded a bit reluctant saying that, but Penny giggled. "I'm more concerned about meeting his sister," she admitted. "I've heard Tara can be kind of intimidating."

"All girls can be."

Penny smiled so wide it made her face hurt. "I hope they think I'm good enough for him."

"They will." Daniel heaved a sigh. "I hope you're not mad at him. From what I know of Theo, he's extremely ambitious, loyal, and protective."

"And jealous," Penny tried to joke, but it was strained. With Theo gone, it felt like there was a string pulling on her heart, leading her in his direction. Regardless of how much space was put between them, they couldn't be separated. Her vision blurred. "I miss him," she whispered.

Daniel scratched his head. "You talk like you'd die for him."

Penny considered that. Her affection for Theo had always been automatic. It was a piece of her that could never be hidden. A person like him deserved to stay alive.

Felix interrupted her response as he announced, "Well, Giselle is ready to leave!"

Giselle fixed her glare on Daniel. "And I'm *not* a liability!"

He raised his hands in defense. "Sorry. Let's go find Theo."

30

THE GREAT (AND UNBEARABLE) ROAD TRIP

T he small town outside the forest consisted of a grocery store, a gas station, a post office, and a few other miscellaneous buildings and houses. A road stretched long and far to the left and right, both directions leading toward uncertainty.

Penny studied the street. She was sure there was a bus, yet didn't know its schedule, and the team didn't have any cash to buy tickets.

"We need wheels," Felix said, voicing Penny's exact thoughts. He shifted his gaze to Giselle and said, "We need you to steal that car." He pointed at the gas station, where a big, burly man was climbing out of his truck.

Her blue eyes widened. "What?"

"It's easy. Just use your feminine wiles."

"That's not all it takes," she pointed out, her cheeks turning pink.

"It would be for me." He raised his hand for a high five, adding, "Am I right, Daniel?"

Refusing to answer, Daniel shook his head. Left hanging, Felix said, "Does anyone *else* have any bright ideas?"

No one said a word. Until Giselle muttered, "Fine."

Felix pumped his fist in the air. "Let's do this!" Then, he accompanied Giselle across the street and into the gas station.

"Is it silly that I'm scared?" Penny asked, slightly humiliated to speak the words aloud.

"Believe it or not," Daniel said, "I'm scared too."

No kidding. She could sense his terror as plainly as if she were holding onto him. As they walked to the gas station parking lot, she joked, "So, feminine wiles really don't work on you?"

His ears burned red. "I'm not going to dignify that conversation with a response."

She laughed, and her fear slowly vanished. It couldn't have come a moment too soon. The gas station wasn't packed with people, but the man they were targeting hovered near the fridges of chilled beers and already looked like he'd had a few to drink. His mouth scrunched in a frown; his forehead crinkled in a permanent glare. He clutched his car keys in a fist, the chain adorned with a skull.

Penny caught Felix and Giselle whispering to each other, so she interjected, "We should think of another plan. If anything goes wrong—"

"Oh, it'll be awesome!" Felix cracked his knuckles. "Watch the master at work."

Felix and Giselle approached the man, pretending to be deeply engrossed in conversation with each other. Waving her off, Felix spat a final, "We'll talk about this later!" He turned to the man, saying, "My girlfriend and I are on a camping trip, and she doesn't like my drink of choice. What do you get?"

The man snorted. "Quit trying to fool me. You're not twenty-one."

"Thank you!" Felix swept his fingers through his hair. "If you want, I can give you some tips on how to stay so youthful."

No longer amused, the man's eyes narrowed into thin slits. Gruffly, he stuck his keys into his pocket and grabbed a case of beer, purposely bumping Felix in the process. Penny took a step forward to intervene, yet Daniel restrained her.

Luckily, Felix recovered the conversation with, "I noticed your truck outside. It's super cool. How much did it run you?"

"Ten thousand. I got a buddy who works at a dealership."

Felix shook his head. "Man, you're living the good life. I've always wanted a car like that. It's the kind of thing real men drive, am I right?"

The man straightened with pride, suddenly interested in the conversation. "Yeah…right."

"My girlfriend wants us to buy a Prius." Felix tossed a thumb over his shoulder, pointing to Giselle. "I wish she'd let me make the decisions—I'm gonna look like an idiot!"

This time, the man laughed heartily. "You know what, if I were you, I'd get the light beer. It's good for first-timers like you."

Felix smiled widely and shook the man's hand. Since he was carrying a case of drinks in the other, he didn't notice when Felix slipped the keys out of his coat pocket.

The man, unaware he'd been robbed, made his way to the cash register. Giselle rushed to Felix. "Do you actually like trucks?" she asked, her nose wrinkled.

Felix chuckled awkwardly. "Nah, I'm more of a Ferrari kind of guy. That's the car that'll really impress chicks."

Giselle cringed, but no one could ignore the tiny glimmer in her eye.

"I didn't know you were a pickpocket," Daniel said, somewhat teasingly.

Felix spun the keys on his finger. "I got sent to the villain academy for a reason. Now that my plan has been executed flawlessly, I think it's time we—"

"Hey! Are those my keys?"

They whirled around to see the man standing a few feet away. His free hand was in his pocket, probably to find his wallet, and he noticed he didn't have his keys. He stomped closer, each step adding more dread to Penny's already worried mind.

Giselle swiped the keys from Felix. "Apologies, sir. They dropped on the ground, and we weren't sure if they were yours. Here you go!" She extended her palm, but the keys fell to the floor before the man could accept them. Giselle blushed. "Oops, I got it." She bent to retrieve them, yet they always slid just out of her reach.

At one point, the keys skittered under a newsstand. The man nudged Giselle aside and yelled, "Let me do it!"

She obeyed and gave him space. He fished beneath the newsstand, and his keys scattered across the tile.

Felix burst into laughter. Penny grinned, too. Surely, this man had to know how ridiculous he looked!

As Giselle controlled the keys, she squinted a little, making sure the movements weren't too sharp or obvious. Penny couldn't help but feel a twinge of envy. Giselle's power was *way* more impressive than Penny's, not to mention useful.

The man slammed his case of beer onto the floor and dove to catch the keys, but right as his fingers grazed over them, they rolled underneath one of the aisles. He stood too abruptly, knocking his head against one of the shelves. While he cursed and rubbed his new bruise, he spotted Giselle tilt her head and slide the keys further. He couldn't say anything except, "Help!"

Immediately, Felix stepped in front of her, shielding her from the approaching cashier. "Is there a problem?" the cashier asked.

The man pointed a shaky finger at Giselle, who, like the others, did her best to look innocent. "That girl! She's using magic! I saw it!"

The cashier raised a brow. "Magic?"

"Yeah!" The man jabbed his fingers into his temples. "She's moving my keys with her mind."

The cashier rubbed her temples. "Sir, how much have you had to drink?"

Red engulfed the man's complexion. "I-I ain't drunk! I saw it with my own eyes—I swear it!"

"Sure, and I get paid a reasonable salary. We all have fantasies." She motioned to the teens, adding, "Come with me, kids. I'll have the cops handle this weirdo."

"I'm not drunk!" the man screamed. Unfortunately, the louder he spoke, the drunker he seemed.

While escorting the team behind the counter, the cashier flipped her phone out of her pocket and dialed 911. Another man, likely her manager, hurried from the back room to calm the man.

Truthfully, Penny wanted to explain the situation. The man, although he *was* drunk, truly saw Giselle use her powers. Now, he was being treated like a psycho. Honesty would cure her guilt, yet it would also worsen their journey. For once, she had to do the wrong thing and live with it.

The police's arrival intensified the man's anger. First, he attempted to fight the manager. Then, he tried to fight the cops. Needless to say, he was forcibly dragged into the police cruiser, given a breathalyzer test, and failed horrendously.

The team followed outside and waited on the sidewalk. Despite the car windows being secured, Penny could see the man screaming about "supers." She concealed her trembling hands in her pockets.

An officer nearby removed his hat, beads of sweat speckling his skin. "Sorry you had to see that," he said. "Did he hurt any of you?"

"We're unharmed," Giselle insisted. "Thank you."

"You kids get home safe."

Felix smirked. "We will."

The cruisers fled the parking lot, and once the cashier returned to work, Giselle pulled the truck keys from her pocket and announced, "I call shotgun."

Felix jumped into the driver's seat, silently admiring the leather seats and steering wheel. As he was buckling himself in, he spotted Penny's sorrowful expression. "Chin up, Pen! He's not gonna miss his truck in jail. Besides, it would've been towed anyway. We'll take good care of it for him."

"I feel bad," Penny defended. "We stole his car."

"We'll return it." Felix paused. "Hopefully."

Before anyone could protest, he started the car, revving the engine to a volume too loud for comfort. Despite that, they were able to drive undetected, the trees shrouding them from being seen.

Penny massaged her tired, sagging eyelids. It felt like it'd been an eternity since she'd slept last. She rested her head against the window, but the constant bumping of the truck nearly gave her a headache. She situated herself in a few positions, each one more uncomfortable than the last. And each time, she grew more desperate for slumber.

Daniel cleared his throat. "You can lie on my shoulder," he offered.

The temptation to refuse clutched Penny's brain, making her limbs stiff and immovable. Daniel was a traitor—he led Jones's soldiers to the cabin.

Warmth spread through Penny's body, encouraged by her healing power. *Daniel apologized. You can trust him again.*

Whether she could or couldn't, that was a debate for later. Ultimately, she scooted to rest against him and surrendered to her fatigue.

31

PUPPET MASTER

When Penny awoke, the views of her jade forest were replaced with a concrete jungle. Through blurry vision, she surveyed her surroundings: a nearly empty parking lot in front of an expansive mall. Felix and Giselle were absent from the vehicle, but Daniel stayed loyally by Penny's side. She rubbed her eyes. "How long have we been driving?"

"About two hours. The car's almost out of gas, so Felix and Giselle went to see if they could find a working ATM. I'm not sure what they're planning, though."

Penny yawned. "It's getting hard to care about the rules."

Daniel didn't respond, but she could feel him staring at her. Ever since she slept on his shoulder, the tension between them was as thick as molasses. The leather seats crackled as he scooted forward, saying, "Penny, I—"

Felix whipped the door open, startling both her and Daniel. "Look who's awake!" Felix teased. "We've got great news!"

Penny straightened in her seat. "You found Theo?"

"Okay, not *that* great. But we found money!"

"You found it or stole it?"

Felix shrugged. "As long as we got it, who cares?"

"We should go shopping!" Giselle jumped in, squishing Felix against the open door.

"We're not wasting money on clothes," Penny pointed out. "That would be stupid."

Giselle soured. "Have you seen us lately? We look like we climbed out of a gutter. I prefer not to attract negative attention, unlike you."

"It's your call, Penny," Felix cut in. "Whatever you say goes."

Penny glared at Giselle, but unfortunately, she made a good point. They could blend in better with cleaner clothes.

"Fine," she muttered, "let's make this quick."

Giselle whooped excitedly and skipped for the mall, with Felix trailing close behind.

"Should I stay in the car?" Daniel asked.

"Why would you do that?" Penny snapped, sounding harsher than intended.

"I-I don't know. You seem upset."

Penny's need to be a healer chased away her desire to be a leader. She wiped whatever expression she had off her face and insisted, "I'm fine! Come on, this will be a nice distraction."

Without waiting for him to answer, she took his hand and led him to Giselle and Felix inside the mall. Like her childhood mall, this one was deserted. Teenagers hung around in the food court, but the rest of the building was a ghost town.

Giselle pranced from one store window to the next, leading Daniel along, too. Neither of them had ever been in a mall before. Their shared enthusiasm was equal parts entertaining and heartwarming.

"Great idea, right?" Felix teased, falling into step beside Penny. "Go ahead, tell me how smart I am."

"I'm not going to do that."

"You're such a party pooper. Even if you won't tell me, I know you're thinking it." Playfully, he knocked into her shoulder. "Look how happy they are."

To Felix's credit, he was right. Daniel was close to smiling as Giselle gushed about the dresses in a store or swooned over the smell of perfume wafting from another.

"You know," Felix said, "I've been trying so hard to be a better person. Like Theo. Maybe then, she'll like me."

The floor might've been flat, but Penny almost tripped. "What?" she blurted. "Giselle likes Theo?"

"Who doesn't?" Felix's comment oozed with sarcasm. Too much, in fact. And it was all to conceal his hopeless crush on a girl who ignored him.

Penny had to slow to a stop. Her head jerked in Giselle's direction. The negative treatment she endured finally made sense. Giselle didn't hate Penny; she was *jealous* of her.

"Do you really want to be with her?" Penny asked, unable to keep the sharpness out of her tone.

Felix rubbed his neck. "I know you two don't get along, but I feel a connection with her. I can't explain it."

"Hmm." Penny dug the toe of her tennis shoe into the floor. To be fair to Giselle, she treated everyone in the cabin with care and kindness. Just because she was rude to Penny didn't mean she was a bad person. "You're a good guy," Penny said. "Any girl would be lucky to have you."

"And how do I know if it's real?"

"If what's real?"

Felix locked eye contact with Penny. "Love."

Instantly, the air deflated from her lungs. Ever since Theo left her, she did her best to avoid thinking about love. She didn't need to be disappointed. "Why are you asking me?" she asked, feeling faint.

Felix cleared his throat. "I don't know. What you and Theo had, I thought it was pretty close to love."

"What we had...I'm not sure what it was. I don't know if it's still there."

"What was it like, then?"

Bursts of memories and emotions flooded Penny, too discombobulated to make sense of them. *Butterflies. Valentine's Day. Kisses. Secrets. Betrayal.* She would need weeks to explain her relationship with Theo—to understand what it meant to her.

"I can tell you I cared about him more than words can say," she started. "I thought about him almost every single second. And even if I didn't see him, I saw things that reminded me of him." Penny smiled. "He made me frustrated, but he also made me proud. Love is very complicated, but you'll know if it's real."

"Did you feel it for him?"

Not quite sure how to answer, Penny hesitated.

"What are you two slacking for?" Giselle exclaimed, hands on her hips. "The store is almost closed!"

"Be right there!" Felix called after her. More privately, he added, "For the record, I think Theo liked you a lot. I'd hear him talking to Dion about you all the time. I think he's just scared you won't like him, especially after the school." Felix quickened his pace. "When we see him again, you should tell him how you feel. He might look confident, but deep down, he's more self-conscious than any of us."

The team walked into a clothing shop. Racks and shelves decorated the walls and floor, each one stacked or hung with dozens of colorful selections. Creepy blank-faced mannequins lurked at the ends of the aisles, posed to show off their new outfits.

A middle-aged man sat at the cash register in the middle of the shop. "Welcome," he greeted, "what can I help you with today?"

"Just looking," Felix answered with a wave.

"Well, if you need me, my name is Lennon."

Penny strolled by a full-length mirror, catching sight of her filthy clothes and ragged appearance. Regrettably, Giselle's insistence to shop had been correct. To fit in, they needed to look presentable.

Practically reading Penny's mind, Giselle snatched a shirt off a hanger and dove into the dressing room, fully prepared to play around.

"Stay with her," Penny suggested to Felix. "I'm up for getting new clothes, but nothing too expensive or flashy."

Winking, Felix spun to follow Giselle, leaving Penny with a leather jacket. Right when her fingers grazed the fabric, Daniel took her elbow and hissed, "We should leave. Now."

Her brows furrowed. "Why? We're safe here."

His grip tightened on her arm. "Penny, something is *wrong*. I can feel it."

In the corner of the shop, Giselle skipped out from the dressing room, eliciting a flurry of compliments from Felix. They sounded like they were having fun; what was the big deal?

But Penny couldn't look away from Daniel. Silently, he begged her to believe him, to trust him.

She stepped backward. She'd trusted him earlier, and he broke it by leaving a trail to the cabin. "I don't know what you're feeling," she said, "but I'm not leaving."

"Penny, please."

"If you're uncomfortable, go wait outside." She hated using a rough tone with him, but her annoyance got the better of her. "I'm not leaving my friends."

Daniel muttered to himself as he stomped away, the most frustrated she had ever seen him. She ignored the anxiety creeping in on her and perused the aisles. Unlike Giselle, who had found a white frilly shirt to wear, Penny decided to pick a practical outfit.

She grabbed a few articles of clothing and locked herself inside another tiny dressing room. The fluorescent lights highlighted the dark circles under her eyelids and her frizzy hair.

Penny hummed to the song blaring on the speakers and removed her ponytail, running her fingers through it to detangle it. Once she was satisfied, she pushed at her cheeks, wishing she didn't look so fatigued. She'd picked out a plain black T-shirt, new blue jeans, and an army green jacket. Unfortunately, the shirt was too big, so she removed it and put the coat over her regular white tank top.

She almost giggled at her reflection. She looked like a battle-worn soldier returning home from war. Penny bent down to tie her shoes, but a sound outside the room made her pause. Or rather, a lack of sound. The music was still playing, yet Felix and Giselle's playful banter had stopped.

Quietly, she nudged the door open, finding Lennon with his back to her at the cash register. "Find what you need?" he asked, as chipper as ever.

A hand slapped over Penny's mouth, filling her with panic. At the same time, an arm wrapped around her, trapping her limbs to her sides. She thrashed against the binding, alerting her attacker to hold her tighter.

"I wasn't sure about you kids," Lennon said. "Then, I realized who you were." The man swiveled in his chair, an inhuman smile on his white face. "And how much money I could get for your capture."

Felix and Giselle were nowhere to be seen, and Daniel had abandoned them outside. Alone again, Penny bit down on the hand covering her mouth, yet it was like biting on plastic. Proving her suspicion, more mannequins shifted from their places in the store and turned toward her. They moved like marionettes—sharp and jerking instead of smooth and controlled.

"Do you like my toys?" Lennon said. "I've got a few tricks up my sleeve too."

He snapped, and the one holding Penny squeezed the breath out of her. Her eyesight blurred; her lungs screamed for air. If the mannequin hadn't been holding her upright, her knees would've given out. Convinced she was dying, she thought through her last words, but a crash sounded from behind her, and she was released.

"I leave to the bathroom for two seconds, and you almost get killed?" Felix helped her to her feet. "Honestly, Pen, you're a mess."

She blinked hard, but there were three Felix's to choose from. As she reached for her head, she sank fully to the ground. The bell on the door dinged, the sound chiming in her ears.

Someone grabbed her arms. She tried to push them away until Daniel's panicky voice interrupted with, "Penny, stop! It's me!"

With her fight instinct subdued, he dragged her into a corner. Her focus returned just enough to see him awkwardly fix her jacket. "Nice outfit," he said.

In a different time and place, Penny would be blushing about the compliment. Theo was the only boy who really made mention of her appearance.

But this wasn't an appropriate moment. She stood, yet Daniel resisted. "Don't go," he pleaded. "I had a feeling this guy was a super, but he's too powerful for us. Let's run."

"We can't leave Felix and Giselle." Penny tried to force Daniel to his feet. "You can help us! You can take his powers!"

Daniel sucked in a short breath. The black in his pupils almost overwhelmed his irises. "I-I don't want to do that! Please don't make me!"

Inwardly, Penny kicked herself. During those lengthy hours of healing children, she'd learned how to avoid triggering trauma. And yet, she did that with Daniel. "Hey, you're okay," she murmured, holding his arm. "Taking his power doesn't make you bad."

"Yes, it does," Daniel insisted. "I've taken so much—I can't even remember it. Why can't I remember?"

Penny's healing felt stalled, similar to how it felt when she was unable to heal Theo. In both instances, the boys were spiraling too quickly for her power to take hold. Perhaps she couldn't heal everything.

"Stay here," she said, releasing Daniel. "I'll take care of this."

He blinked repeatedly. "Will you be safe?"

"Of course. I'll be back before you know it."

With one last look, Penny rushed into the fight. From what she could assess, Lennon sat in his desk chair. In fact, his only movements were flicking his hands to work the mannequins. After Giselle ripped them apart with her mind, they repaired themselves. Felix wielded a pair of belts like nunchucks, swinging the buckles wildly yet with a shocking amount of control. The whole situation was so surreal, Penny had to pinch her arm to be sure she wasn't dreaming.

Giselle threw a mannequin into one of the circular clothing racks by Penny's side, almost striking her in the process. Penny glared as Giselle announced, "Sorry!"

Despite the violence, Giselle's attempt wasn't all for nothing. The force of her power had destroyed the clothing rack, making the metal poles and posts break apart. Penny retrieved one and tested the weight. Her new weapon couldn't have come a moment too soon, because the mannequin on the ground reformed and reached for Penny's ankle. She yelped and, without thinking, drove the metal post into its head.

Although the mannequin wasn't real and couldn't feel pain, Penny felt a bit queasy.

With it incapacitated, she redirected her attention. Three mannequins surrounded Giselle. One of them yanked on her hair. At the sound of her cry, Felix darted in her direction, swinging the belt buckle over his head. "Don't worry, Giselle! I'll—"

A mannequin cut him off by slamming a shelf into his stomach. Groaning, he crumpled to the floor. Giselle and Penny shared a wince, sympathizing with his pain.

"He's annoying," Lennon said unapologetically.

"You aren't allowed to make fun of him," Giselle fired back.

Regardless of how annoying Felix was, the girls needed him. There were too many mannequins and only two of them. Desperately, Penny swung and stabbed her metal pipe, yet within seconds, the mannequins would return for more. She swiveled to Lennon and said, "Why are you doing this? You're a super like us!"

He snorted. "Yeah, but I'm not stupid enough to let people know that! Runaway supers like you are worth twenty grand each! I'm not going to let that kind of money walk out the door, even if we are the same."

His hand closed into a fist, and the mannequin Penny was fighting snatched the metal pipe and ripped it clean out of her grasp. She stumbled until it caught her neck.

Penny never asked for help, especially in a fight. This was her comfort zone; this was what she knew best. But her fear outweighed her pride. "Daniel!" she screamed. "Help!"

The mannequin raised the pipe to strike her. Then, it stopped. Its limbs quivered; the metal joints rattled. From his hiding place in the corner, Daniel stood, both hands outstretched to Lennon. Finally, Daniel was rushing into the fight.

Lennon clutched his throat and slumped in his chair, wheezing for oxygen. As his power was stolen from his body, the mannequins clanked to pieces—an arm here, a leg there. Behind Penny were similar noises, freeing Giselle from the attacks too.

Daniel quivered uncontrollably, but when he met Penny's eyes, he couldn't have looked more courageous. "I'll do anything to protect you," he proclaimed.

If Daniel hadn't been so far away, Penny would've hugged him right then and there. Instead, she helped Giselle pull Felix to his feet and healed him. He glanced at the dismantled mannequins and asked, "Did we win?"

Penny patted him on the shoulder. "Yes, we did."

The four of them approached the cash register, where Lennon had dropped to the floor. "What did you do to me?" he asked.

"Took your power," Daniel answered. "I'd remove it permanently, but I don't want to. It'll fully return in about a minute or two."

"Then, you can get your creepy friends to clean up for you," Felix remarked.

"I'll be taking the jacket too," Penny added. "I assume after the trouble we went through, it's free of charge."

Giselle tapped her chin. "In that case, I'm taking this shirt."

Felix held the door open for everyone, and as they passed, he called out, "Thank you, sir! We're sure to come again!"

Laughter abounded amongst the team. At the same time, Penny felt the tension lift off her shoulders. Sure, there were security cameras, but she doubted Lennon would release the footage. Doing so would mean outing himself as a super, a risk he couldn't handle.

Briefly, Penny squeezed Daniel's hand. "Thanks for saving me."

"Thanks for believing in me."

On the opposite side of her, she elbowed Felix. "Where were you and Giselle when I was attacked?"

Felix tugged at his collar. "The bathroom. I told you."

Daniel's brows lifted. "You were in there together?"

"It's not what it sounds like!" Felix and Giselle exclaimed in unison. She continued, "Penny was busy in the dressing room, so I asked Felix to help me button my shirt. It's no big deal."

"Yeah, no big deal," Felix repeated. In an attempt to hide his blush, he scratched his nose.

The team hurried outside, where most of the cars had disappeared. Giselle slowed her walk to be beside Penny, allowing the boys to continue ahead. Penny expected some backhanded compliment or blatant insult, but all Giselle said was, "I should apologize."

Penny gasped. She didn't bother to stop it. "Really?"

"Earlier, Felix asked why I treat you so horribly, and I didn't have an answer for him." Giselle couldn't bear to look up, almost like she was embarrassed. "Seeing how bravely you fought in there—how you defend us without a second thought—it made me realize he was right. I've been awful to you, and I don't really know why. Maybe it's because I'm jealous of you, or maybe it's because your kindness reminds me of my sister."

"You have a sister?"

"I used to." Giselle's tone was short. Final. Clearly, she would not speak any more about her "sister."

As shocked as Penny was at the honesty, she said, "You have no reason to be jealous."

Giselle shook her head sharply. "Are you kidding? You're the most valuable member of the team."

"I'm just the healer," Penny said, doing her best to be dismissive.

Giselle made eye contact with Penny, declaring, "That's the *best* thing to be. I'm sorry I made you feel otherwise."

A part of Penny naturally denied the compliment. Even if it were true, being known as the only healer was a daunting responsibility. It meant that if she weren't around, then her friends would be in danger of injury, or worse, death.

Luckily, her rationality kicked in and warmed her heart. She hugged Giselle, grateful for the praise. Upon releasing each other, Giselle added, "Besides, you're not just a healer. You've taken on quite the leadership role with us! Without you, Felix would've led us to death."

Penny flipped her hair over her shoulder. "I guess I learned a thing or two from Theo."

The two girls giggled as they neared the truck. Penny motioned for Felix to start the car and asked, "How's it going with Felix?"

Giselle's eyes widened. "What do you mean?"

"I know he can be intense, so I was checking if you lost your mind yet."

"Actually," Giselle cut in, smiling shyly, "I think he's sweet."

Penny almost leapt with excitement. Thankfully, she was able to mute her reaction and instead said, "Good. I'm glad we're working together."

"I am too," Giselle agreed.

Though Penny couldn't be sure what tomorrow would bring, she knew they could handle it as a team.

AMERICA 75 YEARS AGO VS. TODAY

"75 years ago: 1 in every 5 babies was born super. The 'nuclear family' remains intact, regardless of intermingling. Divorce rates are lower between supers and humans than they are for humans.

Today, 1 in every 25 babies is born super. Most of these children are abandoned at hospitals, fire stations, or orphanages. Divorce rates have skyrocketed.

Conclusion: Without stable foundations at home, supers are more likely to spiral."

-Birth study performed by Harvard University

32

PRESS IS FOR THE BIRDS

Theo studied his reflection in the hotel bathroom mirror, pulling at his eyelids and messing with his hair. After his friends had forced him to sleep by giving him Axel's special tranquilizers, Theo didn't know what it would do to him long-term.

His eyes appeared their usual blue, and his hair wasn't falling out. He didn't feel nauseous from withdrawals. Clearly, the one adverse side effect was losing his powers for hours at a time. However, he liked it better when they were gone.

During the quiet, Theo was allowed to ponder on what Dion advised—healing from the past. Theo's control over his powers worsened every time he lost someone close to him, namely Professor Beckham and Camilla. Rather than accept the loss, Theo threw himself into burying the dark emotions. And by burying what he was inherently feeling, the shadows grew stronger.

It would take a long time to accept their deaths. Time he didn't quite have.

He switched on the shower and removed his clothes. He could feel his powers slowly returning, but they wouldn't fully impact him for another hour or so. In the next room, he heard Peter turn on the TV.

Theo stepped into the shower and sighed with relief at the comforting warmth of the water. He hadn't had a warm shower in months, since he always gave that to Penny. Though it pleased him to see her comfortable, he regretted not using it for himself.

He almost smiled at the feeling of being clean. There wasn't much that made him happy lately, but this small act seemed to do it.

Once he finished washing his hair, he stepped out of the shower and dried himself with the scratchy motel towel. He made the mistake of glancing into the mirror, and in that instant, his happiness disappeared.

Earlier, when he stood a centimeter away from the mirror, he couldn't see the overall state of his appearance. In reality, his skin was as white as paper. His eyelids were dark and baggy. He was almost horrified at his reflection. Being the son of a model, she instilled in him a desire to always present himself as polished and professional. But he looked like a zombie.

Interrupting Theo's sorrow, Peter knocked on the door and announced, "We made the news. You should see it."

Quickly, Theo dressed and hurried from the bathroom to see the television playing security footage from their escape. One reporter nodded solemnly. "We have information that the man seen being thrown through the window is currently being hospitalized for his injuries. It's unknown if he will survive."

"Have you ever seen such a blatant disregard for human life?" the other reporter said. "It's absolutely despicable!"

"Are they forgetting we were kidnapped?" Dion exclaimed. "How is this fair?"

"They might not know we were kidnapped," Theo pointed out.

"Even if they did, I bet they'd blame it on us." Dion scoffed. "Apparently, defending ourselves is a crime now."

Peter turned off the TV. "It is when you're a super."

Theo drew the curtains on the windows, letting sunlight flood into the room. Still in bed, Yasmine groaned and covered her head with a pillow. He sat at the desk, reorganizing the papers scattered in front of him. Underneath the passenger seat in the van, he'd found a map of the United States with certain parts circled or highlighted. One of them was Florida. The others consisted of Texas, California, and New York. Peter believed they were somewhere in Norwalk, Ohio, only an eight-hour drive from New York. It was the last place Daniel saw Jones. A man who feared flying and hated travel would stay in a singular location to guarantee his safety.

"What are you planning?" Dion said, appearing behind Theo.

"Nothing," he answered. "I'm thinking."

"No, you're scheming." Upon studying the map, Dion added, "Are we going to Florida?"

"Never, I don't hate myself." Theo pointed to a different state, one higher up and more familiar. "We're going home."

Dion's amusement dropped in an instant. "New York? Why?"

"Jones is there."

"Wouldn't it be risky, then? We can't just walk in—he has spies everywhere."

"True, but he won't attack us in broad daylight. Too many people know my face, and they might come to our defense. Plus, he won't attack us at night, because it gives me a significant advantage. We'll be fine."

Dion let his smile break loose. "You're awfully confident, Nightwave."

"It's a blessing and a curse. Now, wake Yasmine. We've got to get going."

Adding in the hour it took to rouse Yasmine awake, the time to siphon a little bit of gas from another car in the lot, and all of Peter's essential bathroom stops, Theo estimated they would arrive in New York in two years. A trip that should've taken roughly eight hours was proving to be a much more difficult task. He wished Penny were here to reassure him.

Within a few hours, the team reached Akron. Upon catching Dion dozing in the driver's seat, Theo snapped to wake him. Dion jumped, exclaiming, "I'm awake!"

"Sure." Theo unbuckled his seatbelt. "Pull over. We need gas anyway."

Squinting, Dion turned into the nearest gas station. "Are we really going to waste our last seventy dollars on gas? We still have to eat and sleep, y'know."

"I have an idea," Peter said, stretching in the back. "We could rob them."

Theo frowned. "Then, we'll be no better than people think."

"Maybe Yasmine could sing and earn us some cash," Dion suggested. "Like a street performer!"

"We're in the middle of nowhere," she answered, fanning herself. "The best I could do is sing to the birds."

Theo chewed on his bottom lip. He had a portion of an idea, but if it didn't go exactly as planned, they could be in a lot of danger. "Stay here," he ordered as he exited the car.

He entered the store, and the bell chimed happily. The shop was much like the one Tara used to work at. Rows of refrigerators lined the walls, with aisles of chips and candy separating them. The singular difference was that this store was much darker. Only three of the lights were on, one in the front and two in the back. A security camera loomed in the corner, but judging by the exposed wires and absent red light, Theo assumed it was out of order.

A girl sat at the front counter. Her black pixie haircut had been streaked with bright pink and purple strands. A plethora of earrings adorned her ears; two pierced her nose, and one pierced her bottom lip. Her makeup was so dark that it made her already pale skin appear paper white. She barely noticed Theo's entrance and stayed engrossed in her magazine.

"Welcome to Super Stop," she said. "What can I help you with today?"

"Where do I start?" he responded sarcastically, hoping to match her personality.

She didn't respond.

Realizing his jokes weren't getting him anywhere, he cleared his throat. "This place doesn't look very busy."

The girl popped her gum. "Yep."

"You must've scared everyone away. You seem like a troublemaker." He leaned against the counter. "What are you doing in a place like this?"

"Just trying to make a living. It's not the most glamorous job, but it's all I got." She looked Theo up and down. "What are you doing this far out of town?"

"I'm on a road trip with my friends." He pointed at them out the window. "But since none of us plan very well, we ran out of gas."

A corner of the girl's mouth twitched. "So, you want me to give it to you for free?"

"We want to work for it."

She snorted. "Like, you'll do my job for me?"

Shrugging, Theo moved to the door. "It was just a suggestion."

"Wait!" The girl leapt to her feet and glanced at their surroundings; her hand outstretched to freeze Theo in place. "It's okay, um…let me find stuff for you to do. There's plenty, since I hate my job."

While she hurried to the closet, Theo waved the rest of his team inside. The bell jingled again as Yasmine said, "What's going on?"

Theo stood taller. "I found us some work! In exchange, we'll be able to get gas. Isn't that great?"

Dion high-fived Theo, almost the same level of excited. But Peter and Yasmine remained unsure. "How long are we going to be here?" she asked.

"Yeah," Peter added, "because if we're working based on their salary, then we realistically won't have a full tank unless we work for five hours." Suddenly, he drowned off and corrected, "I mean, great idea, Theo! It's better than stealing!"

Theo stared at his friends. Not even three days ago, they were running from bounty hunters intent on their demise. Why was he being treated like he was made of glass?

The girl returned from the storage closet, interrupting his curiosity. "Did you pack any other clothes?" she remarked as she shoved the broom into Peter's hold. "Seriously, you look like you've been through crap."

"Technically—" Peter began.

"I don't care. Go sweep." She pointed at Yasmine and Dion, saying, "You two can clean the windows and doors." She directed her attention to Theo. "And *you're* coming with me."

Dion wiggled his brows at Theo, a teasing gesture. Rolling his eyes, Theo followed the clerk into the back of the store. A large cardboard package sat on the floor, sealed with multiple layers of plastic.

The girl removed a pocketknife and sliced through the tape. "I need you to stock the shelves," she said. "I'm not paying you until this whole aisle is done."

"How much gas is this going to get us?" Theo inquired. "Because we're sort of in a rush."

"Then, you'd better hurry."

Theo did exactly that. He tore the box apart to access the supplies inside and threw them onto the shelves. ***This'll go by faster if you use*** *your powers*, the darkness tempted. ***If the girl sees, then rob her and run. What's she gonna do?***

A scream snapped Theo out of his daze. He sprinted to the end of the aisle, finding a pale and shaking Dion clutching onto Yasmine. Dion was unable to speak, so Yasmine casually explained, "We saw a rat."

Theo smiled yet furrowed his brows at the same time. "I thought someone was hurt!"

"We see rats here all the time," the girl chimed in from her place at the counter. "It's not a big deal."

"Not a big deal?" Dion was hysterical; Theo had never seen him like this. "The one we saw was ginormous!"

Yasmine tapped him on the head like a dog. "Sorry to break it to you, but it wasn't." She raised her fingers to show how big it was, no more than an inch or two. "It was an itty-bitty baby."

"Then, I don't want to see what the adults look like! Ever!"

The whole team laughed, and the clerk released a slight grin. They returned to work, though Dion did so with great reluctance. The store didn't have any customers, but the chance that it could happen filled Theo to the brim with anxiety. His hands shook so badly he could barely place the candy bags on the hooks.

After thirty minutes, the girl wandered to Theo's area. "How's it going?" she said.

"I think you should start counting how many rats you see in a day," he answered. "You might set a world record."

The girl snickered. "You're doing great. Keep it up, and I'll have to hire you for real."

Theo couldn't share in her amusement and shook his head. "That won't happen."

"Why not?"

"Because I'm—" Theo stopped himself. "My life is really complicated right now."

The girl crossed her arms. "If you have time to take a vacation, you have time to get a job." Her bossy tone faded. "Unless…you ran away?"

Theo flipped the bag in his hands. "I didn't have another choice."

Gently, she patted him on the shoulder. "Don't stress, I ran from home too. In case you ever need a place to crash, I've got an apartment in town. It's not the best, but kids like us gotta look out for each other, right?"

"Kids like us?"

"Yeah, you know, runaways. Freaks. Lone wolves. But it's better to be by ourselves." She dug into her pocket for a scrap of paper and scribbled on it. "Here's my number if you ever need anything. I'm Vanessa, by the way."

After Theo pocketed the paper, Vanessa knelt to stack the snacks. "Where are you guys heading?" she wondered.

"New York City."

"That's quite a drive."

"It'll be worth it. I've got some unfinished business to take care of."

"Once you're done, you should visit me. I'd love to hear how it went." Vanessa's lanyard swung back and forth, as if it were trying to hypnotize him. "Maybe then we could hang out."

His mind flooded with answers. *I have a complicated relationship with my girlfriend. I'm busy trying to kill my evil principal.* Aloud, he said, "Sure, that sounds fun."

A rush of color bloomed in her cheeks; the most expressive he'd seen her since he arrived. "Tell you what," she mused, stroking her chin, "I'll give you guys half a tank. You did my job, and you entertained me. That's a win in my book."

That's not enough to make it to New York. Steal the rest!

Theo pushed his dark thoughts down. A little was better than nothing.

While Peter, Yasmine, and Dion left to fill the van, Vanessa suggested, "You should stay. I'm off at five, and there's a really good Chinese place in town."

"I really have to go," Theo said. "Thanks for your help."

Vanessa stuck her lip out in a pout. "Well, if you *have* to leave, then take a few snacks for the road."

Theo felt rotten for taking advantage of her trust, but to avoid drawing suspicion, he begrudgingly returned to the candy aisle. As he was selecting a bag, Vanessa clicked on her television, jumping right to the news.

"Turn it off!" Theo accidentally blurted. In his rush to the counter, he dropped his candy. "You don't want to watch this!"

Vanessa threw him a confused look. "What's your damage? This is the only channel other than the Spanish one that always plays soap operas."

Theo braved a glance out the window. His friends hadn't found the gas cap yet. Desperately, he brainstormed ideas to escape, to distract Vanessa, to fix this! He could kiss her, but he felt squeamish thinking about it. Or, he could break the TV. Unfortunately, that'd get her in trouble.

Dion managed to pop open the gas tank and stick the hose in, so Theo let his shoulders fall. There were five minutes left until the news ended. There was no way they'd replay his escape in five minutes!

He returned his discarded bag of candy and said, "It was nice to meet you. Thanks again."

Vanessa didn't answer. The TV went silent. Cautiously, Theo turned around, unsure of what he'd find.

Vanessa had moved to a corner of the counter, where a wired phone was raised to her ear. The frozen TV had paused at the moment where Theo's team escaped in the van parked right outside. The quality of the picture was grainy, but there he was—on screen.

His gaze shifted to Vanessa, who jumped. "Don't move!" she screamed.

"I'm not going to hurt you," he said, his voice cracking. "That's not who I am."

From the other end of the phone, an operator said, "911, what's your emergency?"

Vanessa pressed herself deeper into the corner. "I'm at the Super Stop on Route 80 and there's a supervillain in my store."

"Do you know who it is?"

"The one on TV. I think his name is—"

Theo sprinted over and slammed his hand on the button, ending the call. Upon seeing Vanessa's terrified expression, he said, "I'm so sorry." Then, as an added precaution, he ripped the telephone cord from the wall and took off outside.

"Get in the car!" he yelled. "We have to go!"

His friends scrambled into the van; Dion barely had a chance to close the gas cap. "What happened?" he exclaimed.

"She saw the news," Theo said, climbing into the passenger seat. Through the windshield, he could see Vanessa using her cell phone to make another call. "She recognized me."

"The tank's not even a quarter full!" Dion exclaimed. He turned the key in the ignition, forcing the engine to sputter to life. "What are we going to do?"

Theo pulled his door shut. "We'll have to ditch the car. The police know we have it."

"After the work we just did?" Peter groaned dramatically. "This sucks!"

Dion pressed the gas pedal to the floor, sending them screeching out of the parking lot.

"I thought you were the charming one!" Yasmine said, climbing to the front and bracing herself between Dion and Theo's seats. "Couldn't you have convinced her not to rat us out?"

"I'm not going to play with someone's emotions!" Theo protested. "It's wrong!"

Peter squished into the group, too. "I'll remember that when we're having our brains cut up and inspected by scientists."

Dion's nose wrinkled. "Gross."

Theo was a split second away from going completely insane. Doing anything with this team was like herding cats. "Can we focus, please? Dion, at the next intersection, turn left."

He obeyed. "Do you know where we're going?"

"Uh, yep, sure do! Turn right!"

The car swerved so hard it threw Peter and Yasmine into the far wall. They whined amongst themselves, but there wasn't time to sympathize with them. Dion barreled down a few more streets.

"Okay," Theo said, "park here."

The car slowed, then rolled to a stop. They'd parked inside the lot of a hotel yet had no intention of staying. Theo stuffed the map, the first aid kit, and a few other essentials inside his backpack and slung it on.

Tip toes and hushed tones were all that escaped the van. It would only be a matter of time before someone found the car and reported it. They had to move fast.

The town was mostly empty. A few stragglers remained outside; older teens who were ready to hit the clubs. From across the street, a boy whistled at Yasmine. Thankfully, the boy's girlfriend shoved him, her glare as sharp as her nails.

The boy tried to weasel out of it, saying, "I was joking! Come on, babe, you know I love you!"

Their argument gave the team a chance to slip away unnoticed. "Quit drawing attention to us," Peter hissed. "Geez, Yasmine, I wish you were ugly."

"This isn't my fault," she snapped.

"How do you suggest we stay out of sight?"

An idea exploded to life in Theo's mind. He didn't bother thinking it through before blurting, "We could be invisible."

Peter squinted at the sky. As the early evening approached, the sun hung low, coloring the clouds with murky golds. "It's not dark enough for your shadow tricks."

Theo shook his head. "Not me. *You*."

"What?"

"How do you make your clothes invisible?" Theo asked patiently.

Peter's body flickered, an instinctual response to avoid conversation. "Um, they're touching me, so I extend my power's focus to them."

Theo shook Peter by the shoulders. "Exactly! If we're touching you, you can make us invisible too!"

"That won't work."

"How do you know?"

A siren wailed a few streets over, and although it was far from their current location, they tensed.

"Fine," Peter said, extending his arms. "But don't blame me when it fails."

The teens grabbed hold of him. His eyes closed and his nose scrunched, indicative of his efforts. The sirens grew louder.

Take matters into your own hands, the darkness urged. ***Peter isn't capable of being a hero. You can only rely on yourself.***

"You can do this," Theo urged Peter.

Practically in response, he disappeared. Theo lifted his free hand in front of him and confirmed that he, too, was invisible, as were Dion and Yasmine. And not a second too soon. A police cruiser sped past them, barreling in the direction of their abandoned van.

Once the cruiser couldn't be seen, Yasmine gushed, "You're amazing, Peter!"

"Whatever," he said, breathless, "it's just my job."

He moved to take a step forward yet stumbled. If it weren't for the others holding onto him, he would've collapsed to the sidewalk. "We have to get out of sight," he gasped. "It's hard enough focusing on my own invisibility, but expanding it to you guys…I-I won't be able to last."

Theo adjusted his grip to prop Peter up. It had only been a few seconds, but Peter was already trembling. Theo understood the exhaustion. At the academy, he'd used his powers to conceal Dion and Penny on two different occasions, and it always left him feeling more drained than usual.

Instead of dwelling on their shared distress, Theo glanced at their surroundings. On his left side, the road stretched out far and wide. On his right, an abundance of brick buildings shielded them from being seen—a couple of yellow lights burned above them.

"It's okay," he assured. "Let's get away from the road."

The further they walked into the city, the more densely packed it became. The sidewalks narrowed, allowing the roads to conquer the space. The light came in plentiful amounts, as did the people. Theo's heart slammed against his ribcage, convinced that at any moment, Peter's power would drop, and they'd be recognized and caught.

"I feel like I'm going to hurl," Yasmine whispered. "I've never been so stressed."

"Really?" Peter joked weakly. "I find this experience extremely relaxing."

"Just a little bit farther," Theo instructed, hoping that was true. The path to their right dipped down into a tree-filled park. Judging by the vacancy of the field, it was closed for the night. A perfect place to regroup. "This way," Theo said, pushing Peter in the direction of the park.

"Are you sure?" Dion asked. "It looks pretty dark down there."

By this time, the sun had set completely. And without the street-lights to guide them, they were essentially walking into the unknown.

"I'll lead us." Theo switched to stand in front of Peter. "Stay quiet."

The order was as empty as Theo's stomach. He could hear his friends' breaths hitch and catch, consumed with the anxiety they likely felt. Without the night vision that Theo possessed, they could only hear swings creaking or owls hooting. There was one broken lamppost, standing alone in the darkness, casting its pathetic white light across the basketball court.

"This is the kind of scene in horror movies," Peter said softly. "You know, right before the teens get brutally murdered."

Behind them, the bushes rustled. The source of the sound must've been relatively large, judging by the snapping twigs. However, any ounce of fear from Theo would inflict it on his friends tenfold. In order to make it out of town, they needed to be calm. So, Theo didn't risk a second glance. Instead, he led the group onto the basketball court. There was enough light that they could see each other, but not enough to see into the distance.

As soon as their feet touched the pavement, Peter's power faded. Upon reappearing, Dion and Yasmine supported Peter to stand. A faint moan escaped him. The life seemed drained from him, leaving his complexion colorless.

"Don't worry," Theo told them. "I think we're in the clear." He faced the shadows again, this time staring down the cold black chamber of a gun.

Theo didn't know whether to be relieved or terrified that it wasn't a cop. Instead, Simon came into view as he said, "Miss me?"

33

CHILDHOOD GAMES

Theo expected to be terrified, but all he felt was annoyance. Seriously? Another gun? Would he ever have a break from these wretched weapons?

"Simon," a buzzing voice cracked. "What's your status?"

He lifted his radio to his mouth. "I found the packages. Meet me in the park." After returning the radio to its secure place on his belt, he plucked the broken branches from his jacket. The odd sounds coming from the bush were due to Simon.

"You kids aren't very good at staying out of the spotlight," he said, almost joking. "Figuratively and literally."

A pale Peter made a motion to his hair. "You got a little…"

Simon swept a hand over his head, letting the last few leaves flutter to the pavement. "I forgot how polite you are," Simon said, laughing. Then, his demeanor shifted, and he demanded, "Stay like that and put your hands up. Let's not make this difficult."

Theo's team didn't have weapons to protect themselves. They had their powers, but any noise they made would attract attention. And attention would *not* help them.

Without warning, Dion leapt forward and slammed into Simon, taking both of them to the pavement. Theo almost screamed at Dion for his abruptness. Was his plan to get them killed?

Dion wrestled the gun from Simon. It skittered across the ground to rest at Theo's feet. Theo's knees nearly buckled at the sight of it.

Before Dion could escape, Simon wrapped an arm around his neck, yanked him to his feet, and pulled out another gun to press to his head. "That was a waste," Simon hissed. "You think I'm stupid enough to carry one weapon?" He straightened to his full height, forcing Dion to stand on his tiptoes. Desperate for air, he clawed at Simon's arm, but the man didn't give in.

With sweaty palms, Theo swiped the gun off the concrete and raised it to level with Simon. Darkness entwined around the barrel. ***Don't use the gun. Use your powers.***

Admittedly, Theo's stomach rolled at the feeling of holding such a foul weapon. But it was a greater guarantee than using his powers. "Let him go!" he demanded.

"Drop the gun," Simon fired back.

No one moved a muscle. After a beat, Simon relaxed to allow Dion to stand. "Since you're children," he said with a sneer, "let's play a game you'll understand. Simon says 'Drop the weapon.'"

"I'm seventeen," Theo retorted, "not five."

"Alright, I'll repeat myself in your language." Simon's grip tightened on Dion's neck; his revolver buried deeper into Dion's temple. "Drop the gun or I'll shoot your friend."

Theo didn't budge. It was like a Western stand-off until one of them fired.

A car squealed into the lot outside the park. Axel's voice carried through the night like a menacing warning.

In a flash, Peter swiped the gun from Theo. He didn't aim it at

Simon; instead, he lowered it to the ground. Everyone gawked. Simon even stammered, "What are you doing?"

"I'm sorry you were hurt by supers," Peter said, being the only one able to talk. "But humans hurt me, and I don't hate you for it. Please let us go."

"*Please*?" Simon spat. "You're pathetic. Why would I help you when I'm not getting anything in return?"

"That's not why you do good things," Peter insisted. "You do it because you understand what it's like to be afraid."

The word made Simon's eyes widen. He was frozen—petrified at what he heard. The yelling got closer.

"Is this how you want your granddaughter to know you?" Theo spoke. "By being a murderer?"

"Don't guilt me!" Simon said, growing more panicked by the second.

"Let us go," Peter repeated, more urgently this time.

Simon's breath came in quick gasps. "If I let you go, I'll have to fight an invincible man all by myself."

"What if he wasn't invincible anymore?" Theo said.

"You'd have to take more than just his superpower," Simon pointed out. "You'd have to take his status, his influence—everything."

"And we can. Why else would we be trying to stop him?"

Simon's darting, unsure gaze said he didn't want to listen. Quite frankly, Theo couldn't blame him. The man had to watch his closest friends be killed right in front of him. It was the same reason Theo hated Principal Jones.

But then, with sagging shoulders, Simon released Dion.

Someone broke through the trees lining the park, and Theo caught a glimpse of Roger. Thick gauze wrapped around his face, hiding his hideous appearance.

His bandages wrinkled with anger. "What are you doing, Simon?" he exclaimed. "Shoot them!"

Simon glanced at each of the teens in turn. "Don't look," he mouthed.

None of them obeyed. They watched as Roger drew nearer. The second he was close enough, Simon shot him square in the chest. Peter was quick to cover Yasmine's mouth. Her scream could be deadly.

"I'll drive them off your trail," Simon said, surprisingly casually. "I can't protect you forever, so stay hidden." He tossed a pair of keys to Theo. "Take my car. It's faster, and Axel won't report it missing."

Axel and his men sprinted at the first gunshot. They screamed for Roger and Simon.

Theo focused as much as he could. "You can come with us," he said.

"I'll meet you when the time is right. I've got to work to regain my family's trust." Then, as if the situation couldn't get any worse, Simon pressed his gun into his own leg and shot himself. Immediately, he dropped to the concrete.

"What are you doing?" Peter exclaimed. "Are you insane?"

Rather than answer, Simon yelled, "We're over here!" Then, to the teens, and with an expression ravaged in pain, he said, "Run."

Theo didn't have to be told twice. He took off to the street, hoping his friends were following him. Though trembling, he pressed the button on the key fob, hearing the car beep in response. It was a sleek black sports car, and in any other situation, Theo might've stopped to admire it.

Right now, they piled inside the vehicle, putting him in the driver's seat. He floored it away from the park, yet the engine was nothing more than a quiet hum.

"I can't believe he did that," Peter said breathlessly. "He actually shot himself!"

Dion burrowed into the passenger seat, holding his neck and shivering. "M-maybe he did it so he could claim we attacked him and killed Roger."

The explanation made sense, but it didn't ease Theo's mind. As amazing as the car was, he didn't know how to work it. He pushed random buttons, finding the heater and the radio. Warmth spread into him, almost calming him. Then, he glanced up, and his heart stopped.

Red and blue lights reflected in the mirror.

Theo looked down at the speedometer—fifteen miles above the speed limit.

"Maybe we can escape," Dion said, his head swinging from the police car to Theo.

"I can't run anymore," he answered, nearly breaking down at the admission. He drove the car onto the side of the street, and the others didn't object. Yasmine held her head in her hands; Peter leaned against the seat. They were done.

Both cars stopped. The officer walked alongside the team's vehicle, the gravel crunching underneath his boots. He knocked on the driver's side window, so Theo rolled it down. Their fate would be sealed in a matter of seconds.

The officer flipped through a notepad. "Do you know how fast you were going?"

"Yes, sir."

"You have to be more careful at night. License and regis..." The man peeked up, and his jaw fell to the ground.

"I don't have it," Theo whispered.

"You don't?" The officer switched from his notepad to his gun, then to his radio, and back again. He noticed the others in their seats. "And what about your friends?"

Theo just shook his head.

"I see." The officer clicked his pen a few times. "Where are you kids off to in such a rush?"

No one had the energy to lie.

The man answered for them. "Home to your parents, I bet."

Theo nodded once.

"And what have we been up to tonight? Trouble?"

"Technically, sir," Theo said, "I think trouble seems to find us."

"Ah. I hear that happens with supers." With a final click, the officer returned his pen to his shirt pocket. "This car obviously doesn't belong to you. Where'd you get it?"

"We didn't steal it," Theo explained. "A friend lent it to us. We're trying to get home."

The officer leaned close to the window. "Y'know, my sister is a super. I can't imagine living the life she has—the injustice she faces, all because of her power. She tried to become a police officer, but they rejected her. She's the bravest person you'll ever meet, too. It's a shame what our world has come to, huh?"

Theo could barely force a nod. He was absolutely paralyzed with terror.

"Well," the officer said, standing straight, "since this is your first offense, I'm gonna let you off with a warning. Try to be more cautious, alright? I can't guarantee my colleagues will be so generous."

Theo squeezed his eyes shut, yet it wasn't enough to stop his tears. "Yes, sir. Thank you."

The man patted Theo on the shoulder. "Get home safe. I'm sure your mother is very worried about you."

Theo couldn't have agreed more.

Once the police car pulled away, Peter said, "We can't afford another mistake. I'm driving."

That couldn't be argued. The two switched seats, allowing Peter to follow every rule of the road. "I'm going to start gambling," he joked. "We're clearly very lucky. It's time I put that luck to good use."

Theo settled into the backseat. It was true that they were lucky—once with the officer, and again with Simon giving them his car. But eventually, their luck would run out.

34

IN THE COMPANY OF RATS

Theo stared out of his window, admiring the passing scenery. Cool purple moonlight shone across yellow fields. Soft pop music played; Peter and Dion's voices were hushed as they discussed the car.

Despite not hearing them, Theo agreed with whatever they said. The car's tank was full; the leather seats and heated cushions were to be envied, and it could jump to speeds Theo only imagined. How many supers had to be captured so Simon could afford it?

Yasmine snored loudly in Theo's ear, interrupting his pondering. It had been less than an hour since fleeing Akron, but apparently, the quiet thrum of the car lulled her into slumber.

Similarly, he let his eyelids drift closed. Although it had come at a heavy cost, this was peace. He wished Penny were here to enjoy it.

If they mended their relationship and decided to take that next big step, he would've bought her a huge house. They could've lived in the country like she wanted. And every morning, they would sit outside together and watch the sunrise, enjoying their rare, fleeting moments of joy.

Theo rested his head against the cool window. *What a wonderful imagination I have,* he joked to himself. *Living in a fantasy I'll never get.*

"Welcome to Youngstown," Peter read off the sign. "Oh boy. Does it get any better than this?"

"Penny used to live here," Theo said, loud enough for him to hear. "I wonder if her parents are here."

"We don't have time to visit," Peter said. "Seeing them will put them in danger."

Peter and Dion continued to whisper, leaving Theo to zone out. *Penny loves her parents. She would've been ecstatic to keep in contact with them. Like I did with mine. I really was a jerk to her.*

What are you going to do? Apologize? That won't fix this. You failed. Again.

Theo glared at his reflection in the window. It was his best option, considering he couldn't find the source of this dark voice. Unfortunately, it was right. Theo couldn't apologize, not until he ensured Penny was safe from him.

Peter parked in a nearly empty motel lot. The three boys looked at Yasmine, then at each other. Whoever woke her would endure unspeakable consequences, so Theo whispered, "I think I'll take a walk." Cautiously, he scooted out from beneath Yasmine's weight.

"I'll go with you," Peter said, unbuckling his seat.

"What about me?" Dion asked.

"Go buy a room," Theo suggested, passing his backpack to Dion. "We'll be back in five minutes."

"I'm talking about Yasmine."

Peter smiled grimly. "I'll mourn you."

Huffing a chuckle, Theo cracked the car door open, shivering at the rush of chilly evening air. The motel was wedged between beautiful antique buildings, perfectly trimmed hedges, and colorful flowerbeds.

An invisible Peter elbowed Theo, saying, "Shall we?"

The two began their walk. Theo's legs ached from being stuck in the car for so long; exercise like this was very much needed.

"Never thought we'd live this long," Peter said. "I imagined we'd be dead by now."

"You could've stayed at the cabin," Theo replied.

"Please. Without me, you would've been caught five times over."

The darkness on Theo's arm prickled. *His ego precedes him. You don't need him.*

Aloud, Theo said, "I know. That's why I'm grateful we're friends."

Peter scoffed, yet his forced disgust couldn't conceal his apparent appreciation. "Whatever."

Suddenly, a mouse scurried across the sidewalk in front of them, shocking both boys into jumping. Once it burrowed into a gutter, Peter exhaled a shaky laugh. "Can you imagine how Dion would've reacted if he were here?"

"He'd scream louder than Yasmine," Theo teased.

"Such an odd thing to be afraid of," Peter said. "I fear much more realistic threats."

Theo chuckled. "Yeah? Like what?"

It was as if a vacuum sucked out the amusement from the conversation. Peter's light tone deepened. There was no longer a snicker behind his words. "Never mind," he said. "I don't know what I was trying to say."

Out of all of Theo's friends, Peter was probably the best at lying. He could pull a poker face like no one else, and it helped that he could turn invisible under pressure. However, Theo didn't need to see Peter to know that he was being deceitful. His abrupt shift in attitude was his tell.

Officers, the shadows hissed, alerting Theo to a stop. *Up ahead.*
Hide.

Without hesitation, he obeyed, fading into nothingness. Sure
enough, at the end of the opposite street, a group of men stood underneath a lamp post. Each of them wore military regalia or police badges.
Their heads were low as they talked, but there was only one possible
topic that they were discussing.

"I need to listen to what they're saying," Peter said quietly. "It
might be important."

Theo wrapped a shadow around Peter's leg, preventing his movement. It was Theo's way of saying, "It's too dangerous."

Grumbling, Peter shook the shadow off. "I can handle myself."

Theo gritted his teeth. Since he couldn't respond without reappearing and surrendering his disguise, he listened to Peter hurry across
the street. With nothing else to do, Theo stared at the dark blue sky and
the flickering silver stars. Perhaps Penny was looking at the sky
tonight, too.

His gaze lowered to the rows of flowers in front of a bookshop,
blossoming in bright magentas, reds, and yellows. He wondered if
Penny had ever stood in the same place he did now. Mostly, he
wondered how she was doing—if she missed him.

Who am I kidding? I did her a favor by leaving her.

"Hey," Peter said in a hushed tone. "We have to talk somewhere
else. Get out of the street."

Immediately, Theo listened. Peter might have been skilled at
concealing his emotions, but not even he could make light of this
situation.

They returned to the motel, finding their car abandoned. Dion and
Yasmine must've been inside their room, which was the only window
facing the parking lot that had a light on.

Both Theo and Peter reappeared, so Theo demanded, "What
happened? What did they say?"

Nonchalantly, Peter roamed to their room door and knocked. "The government sent agents and soldiers to all major cities in search of supers," he explained. "They're teaming up with the local police department."

"But why?"

"We've caused a bit of a rift between supers and humans. You know that, right?"

"Yes, but why are they looking for other supers?"

"I don't know. They just said they need them accounted for."

Theo picked at his nails. *What other reasoning can there be unless supers are about to be killed in a mass execution?*

As if Peter read Theo's mind, he said, "Murdering is off the table. Otherwise, it'd be considered genocide. They might be tightening a few laws. That's all."

Theo scoffed. "That's *all*? You make it sound so innocent."

The room door opened, revealing Dion on the other side. Ignoring Dion's concerned frown, Peter entered and said, "In any case, we should rest for the night."

His plan was too flimsy to reassure Theo. "What if they start searching the city?" he asked. "Wouldn't it be safer to leave?"

"I think they'll pull over a vehicle driving alone in the middle of the night faster than finding it in some trashy motel," Peter pointed out. He slapped Theo on the back, hard enough to make Theo cough. "We need sleep, anyway. If I have to spend one more minute cramped in a car, I'll turn myself in."

Theo crossed his arms. At least for a moment, he paused to think through his options. Disobeying Peter's request was Theo's preferred choice. While Peter wouldn't make good on his claim to turn himself in, he might cause a fight. In the long run, it would be much easier to take his advice and rest for the night.

Once Theo was in the room, Dion shut the door. Yasmine was asleep on the bed, forcing the boys to find places on the couch or floor. "Do I need to worry?" Dion said, nervously wringing his hands.

The less he knows, the better off he'll be.

"We're good," Theo insisted. "Get some sleep and we'll regroup in the morning."

The assurances smoothed Dion's forehead wrinkles, reflecting how worn out he was. Theo felt similarly, but as he watched his friends settle in for the night, he couldn't ignore the doubt burning inside him.

35

A LITTLE LESS SUPER

Growing up, Penny always fell asleep during car rides, regardless of how short they were. The constant rumbling lulled her into slumber, forcing her parents to carry her to her room. The memories were sweet dreams—recollections of a life she longed to have.

Her peaceful rest was suddenly interrupted when the truck rolled to a stop. She rubbed her heavy eyelids and yawned. So far, the group's plan for travel had remained relatively strict. Felix and Giselle were always in the front, with Daniel and Penny in the backseat. She was well accustomed to waking up on his shoulder.

However, this time, that wasn't the case. She bolted upright in her seat, her heart throbbing to match her terror. Before her vision could focus, he patted her arm and said, "I'm here. We have a bit of an issue."

Penny blinked hard. Lines of vehicles sat in front and behind them, so she assumed it was traffic, but a soldier approached Felix's window, making a motion for him to roll it down. Once it was, the soldier ordered, "Out of the car. Mandatory checkpoint."

"Checkpoint?" Giselle repeated. "For what?"

"Will this take long?" Felix added with a nervous chuckle.

Rather than answer, the soldier moved on to the next car. "Get out," Daniel said, already unbuckling himself. "It's easier to obey than fight about something we don't understand."

The others followed his lead and stood beside the truck. Felix chewed on his knuckle, undoubtedly worrying about their stolen vehicle.

Penny glanced at their surroundings, hoping it would provide some context for what was about to happen. There were at least fifteen cars lined up on the road. It appeared the original intention was to be a toll road, but instead, a barricade of metal detector-like objects prevented passage. A man from a few cars in front of Penny entered one of these detectors. After the light glowed green, he was permitted to return to his car and drive away.

Dozens of men and women in military regalia stood at attention, their eyes raking over the crowd. Daniel spoke to the nearest soldier—too far for Penny to hear—then returned to the group. "Apparently, Theo and his team have made quite an impact on the news," Daniel explained. "The president commissioned checkpoints at every state border. They said it's a safety precaution."

"What happens if they catch us?" Giselle bit her nails. "Did she speak about that?"

"No."

Felix tossed his hands in the air. "We're screwed."

"Not necessarily," Daniel said. "My power isn't always useful, but it is in this situation. I'm like a storage unit. I can keep powers for as long as needed and then give them to whoever." He exhaled shortly. "So, I can take your powers and—"

Felix's voice was a sliver from yelling. "Are you kidding? I'm not letting this guy take my power, even for a second!"

"Agreed," Giselle chimed in. "How do we know he won't take it for good?"

"What would I do with it?"

"I don't know," Felix fired back, "but you've already had a history of betraying us. Need I remind you about the cabin?"

Daniel stared at Penny, pleading, "You trust me, don't you?"

Did she? Or more importantly, should she? Everyone thought that Daniel was exactly like his uncle: power-hungry and evil. But all Penny had seen was a boy who had been caught in the wrong place at the wrong time. He had zero interest in stealing powers from supers; he was truly doing this out of necessity.

Though she trembled, she said, "Yes."

"*No*," Felix insisted, restraining Penny. "Won't the scanner read him, too?"

"My power negates other abilities," Daniel answered, his voice gaining an edge. "The scanner shouldn't be able to tell the difference."

"*Shouldn't*? So, you're not sure?"

"Not entirely, but we have to try!"

The line inched forward. Felix's clasp tightened on Penny's wrist as he whispered, "Theo wouldn't want us to do this. There has to be another way."

Penny had rarely seen Felix exude any emotion other than confidence. Yet right now, he couldn't have looked more distraught. "I'm not Theo," she said. "And there *is* no other way."

Before anyone could speak, she took Daniel's hand. The consequence was immediate. It felt like a giant mosquito was sucking every drop of blood from her body. As her power was drained, her instincts kicked in. She moved to run, but Daniel held onto her.

"I'm sorry," he choked out.

Felix reached for her, but she managed to shake her head. The absence of her power didn't hurt; it was more discomfort than pain. She squeezed her eyes shut, waiting for the sensation to end.

"Okay," Daniel said as he released her. "It's done."

Feeling naked, she wrapped her arms around herself. She'd never needed her power to fight or defend herself, but she never realized the comfort that came with it. She sensed the others watching her, so she mustered her strength. "Who's next? We've gotta get going if we want to find Theo."

Felix cast an uneasy glance at Daniel. "You promise to return it?"

"I have no desire to keep it."

Though hesitant, Felix gave a slight nod for permission. Daniel repeated his process, and once it was complete, Felix flexed his fingers and said, "Is it weird that I feel twenty times weaker?"

"That's normal." Daniel offered for Giselle, but she recoiled.

"Theo didn't trust you," she cried, tears dripping down her cheeks. "Why should I?"

Without Penny's power, she didn't feel the overwhelming urge to comfort Giselle. Instead, Felix intervened. He took her arms as he murmured, "Hey, I'm scared too. Which is weird, because I'm so amazing. But we don't have time to sit here and cry. Hero up and let's get going."

Surprisingly, Giselle's expression steeled. She let Daniel take her hand, thereby relinquishing her powers. When it finished, her knees wobbled until Felix wrapped her in a half-embrace. "Good job," he assured, rejoining the line. "It'll be over soon."

Beside Penny, Daniel frowned. "What's wrong?" she asked.

"I feel terrible for putting you in pain," he said. "I promised I'd never hurt you, but by taking your powers I did just that."

She wanted to remind him that it was her choice—their last option—but excuses wouldn't help. "Thank you," she said.

At long last, it was their turn. Penny stepped forward first, willing herself to stop shaking. The soldier operating the machine waved her forward and instructed, "Stand on the platform. Try not to move or we'll have to do it again."

She stood on the white-marked spot. The scanner cast its electric blue light over her, and she held her breath. If Daniel's idea didn't work, then this was all for nothing.

The light glowed green, and the soldier gruffly said, "Next."

Penny hesitated, her pulse skipping beats. "What?"

He jerked his head to the side. "Get out. You're good."

She bit her lip to hide her smile. One by one, her friends passed through the scanner, each time being tossed aside. Daniel was last, and the second he exited, she leaped into his arms.

"Thank you," she said, hugging him as tight as she could.

He held her, but not for long. "You're welcome. Let's get you back to normal."

After retrieving their vehicle, receiving their rightful powers, and speeding away, the team burst into relieved laughter. Giselle tested her telekinesis on a wrapper, floating it in front of Felix's nose. Teasingly, he swatted at her, making her giggle harder. Upbeat music thrummed between them.

Penny and Daniel sat close to each other in the backseat, much closer than in days past. "We can't thank you enough," she gushed. "We would've been caught if it weren't for you."

"It was nothing," he insisted. "I never thought of my powers as a blessing, but I guess in some situations, they can be."

"Ditto that, bro!" Felix called from the driver's seat. "I can't even use my power, but like you, I'm sure I'll be able to at the right moment."

"Time manipulation is incredibly complicated," Daniel pointed out. "Don't blame yourself if you can't do it."

Felix nodded. "Yeah, I know. I just wish I could contribute like everyone else."

"You do contribute," Giselle chimed in, leaning on his arm. "You're a great addition to the team, with or without powers."

Felix cleared his throat and switched the music louder. It didn't stop his blush.

Cloudy twilight fell sooner than expected, motivating the team to stop at a hotel. Penny volunteered to buy the room, and once the clerk handed her the key and left the front desk, the others rushed inside and escaped to their room. Upon opening the door, Giselle jumped onto the bed.

"I'm pretty sure I saw a pool out there," Felix announced. He extended his arms in an invitation and added, "Who'd like to join me?"

"We don't have swimsuits," Giselle pointed out, sitting cross-legged on the bed.

He smirked. "Who says we need them? Don't want to ruin your outfit, princess?"

Giselle rolled her eyes, yet her cheeks turned pink at the same time. As she raised the TV remote, she muttered, "You're so stupid."

Felix moved to block the screen. "You know you love me."

When she tried to push him, he grabbed her hand. "Stop being an idiot," she said with a laugh.

Daniel glanced at Penny and wrinkled his nose. Watching them made her cringe, but the hopeless romantic in her was overjoyed. To their credit, they seemed like a cute couple.

"I'll go to the pool," she offered. "I could use a bit of relaxation."

Giselle rose from the bed. "If Penny's going, I will too."

Felix beamed. "Well, what are we waiting for?"

The two of them rushed out of the room, but Penny paused to bid Daniel a proper goodbye. "Be back soon," she promised.

He returned with a timid wave and a quiet, "Have fun."

She closed the door to follow Giselle and Felix, yet for some reason, she couldn't stop thinking of Daniel.

The pool room reeked of chlorine. There was little else except for a pool that was no deeper than five feet, and a bubbling hot tub in the corner. White lawn chairs peppered the wall, two of which were already occupied by Giselle and Felix.

A small family of five played in the pool as Penny neared the hot tub, being careful in her movements so as not to slip on the wet tile floor. After removing her tennis shoes and rolling up her pants, she dipped her legs in the warm water. The heat instantly made her head drop to her chest. Without a doubt, this had been the longest week of her life. And it wasn't even over.

Originally, she'd come here to clear her brain, but instead, she watched the family. The father tossed his two young girls into the pool, their gleeful giggles echoing off the walls. The mother secured a barrage of floaters on their baby boy, so that only his chubby cheeks were visible. Finally, the two jumped in the water and were bombarded with happy greetings. The baby gurgled as his sisters spun him in circles and traded off silly faces for him to enjoy.

Penny shifted her glance to her lap. She remembered telling Theo she wanted to become a nurse, but really, all she wanted was a family of her own. She'd give anything to have one, even give up her powers. And after hearing Jade's prediction of the future, Penny assumed Theo would be a part of it.

She played with the water. It didn't seem that way anymore.

Instead of wallowing in self-pity, she forced herself to think optimistically. She would always have time to make a family. Right now, she had to make a better world for the people who already had one. Maybe the kids playing in the pool weren't super, but they deserved happiness.

Eventually, the young family packed and left. The two young girls waved to Penny, which she reciprocated. The second they were gone, Felix removed his shirt and dropped it on Giselle's head.

She kept it there, claiming, "Thanks! Now, I don't have to look at you!"

Felix walked to the edge of the pool. Right when he was close enough, Giselle flicked a hand toward him, telekinetically shoving him into the water. Hair dripping, he splashed to the surface and sputtered, "What was that for?"

"You know you love me," she taunted.

Fire sparked in Felix's eyes. Hardly a second passed before he was out of the pool and heading toward Giselle. She had the chance to stop him or defend herself, but Penny suspected she didn't want to.

As he scooped her up, Giselle shrieked and clung to his neck. Together, they jumped into the water, sending waves cascading over the wall and into the hot tub. Penny shook her head at them, soaked to the bone. She would've made a sarcastic remark about watching out for others, yet the words died in her mouth.

Giselle held onto Felix's neck, and he tucked away the curls sticking to her cheeks. Both of them wore smiles brighter than the fluorescent lights. It was like they were in love.

Penny's throat burned. Quickly, she stood, dried her legs off, and slipped her shoes back on. She didn't bother saying goodbye.

She pushed through the glass door to enter the hallway, and immediately the weight on her lifted. *It was the chlorine,* she told herself. *That's what made me so sick.*

To prevent her tears, Penny dug her nails into her arm. Once they subsided, she slid the key into their room lock and cracked open the door.

Daniel sat on one of the beds, jumping at Penny's entrance. "Oh, hi," he stammered. "Um, where are the others?"

Penny removed her shoes. "Still there. You should've gone with me. I was left to be the third wheel."

Daniel chuckled. "You know what they say: Three's a crowd. Four would be chaos."

"Four would be a party. At least I wouldn't have been alone." Penny sat beside him on the bed, pleased that it didn't make him pull away. She motioned to the paused television. "What are you watching?"

"I'm not sure," he admitted. "I couldn't figure out how to change the channel, so I'm stuck with the classic Hallmark stuff. The title of the movie doesn't matter much, since they're all the same."

This time, it was Penny who snickered. "Sounds good enough for me."

Daniel switched on the volume, and the pair watched the movie. Penny pulled the covers toward her. No one had been able to figure out how to work the air conditioning, so the room felt like the freezing Arctic. Now that she was bundled in the blanket, she had to sit closer to Daniel. Instead of scooting away, he leaned against her. His pain melted into her—an intense, agonizing mental stress.

"This has been quite an afternoon," he said.

"That's what happens when you're in the League of Heroes," she tried to joke. "Crazy is our normal."

"I see that." Suddenly solemn, Daniel's expression set in stone. "Listen, you should know how much I appreciate your company. I grew up alone, and I never imagined I'd be in a situation where I felt safe. You've helped me feel that." He squeezed her hand and grinned. "I know I don't deserve this, but thank you for being my friend."

As his pain morphed into acceptance, Penny felt her breathing slow. "I'm glad you're here," she said.

The movie continued playing, yet neither of them was paying attention to it. "At the academy," Daniel said, "Principal Jones couldn't understand why you treated the villains kindly. Is it the same reason why you're nice to me?"

Penny couldn't describe that desire. She'd always been propelled by an instinct to do good, and seeing the villains miserable made her feel similarly. Before Theo had arrived, she'd done her best to compliment, heal, and befriend them. The villains never trusted her, not for a second. One girl even told Penny that she "saw through her act."

"I guess I wasn't only healing them because it was the right thing to do," Penny explained slowly. "It was because…*I* needed to."

The admission wasn't easy to make. In fact, it left a lump in Penny's throat. She didn't see herself as a selfish person, but her powers constantly urged her to push others. She sought out problems so that she could remedy them, regardless of how closely she was involved in the situation. Healing meant more to her than accepting people where they were, than accepting the fact that she *couldn't* heal them and fix the problem so easily.

Perhaps this was what Lily meant; their powers predisposed them to certain emotions and instincts.

If that was the case, then no one, except for Penny, could be blamed for pigeonholing her into the role of "healer." A role that, while necessary and helpful, could be consuming. It was all about balance.

"Don't worry yourself too much with it," Daniel instructed. "Jones is ridiculous."

"Yeah," she said. *But he was also right.*

36

MEET THE PARENTS

Theo awoke to Penny's face hovering above him. Her blond hair surrounded her like a halo; her eyes glittered like the stars. In any other situation, there wouldn't have been a better way to wake up.

But she was crying.

"Theo, come on!" she screamed. "We need you!"

He leapt out of bed, catching a whiff of smoke in the air. He was in the cabin, so he assumed someone had set a blaze in the fireplace, but this smell was much more potent. Much hotter.

"What's going on?" he asked as she rushed out of the room. His question was immediately answered.

The entire back half of the cabin was on fire. The heat pushed against him, urging everyone to rush out the front door. But they didn't. They ran around in a panic, yelling louder than the gunshots outside. He froze at the sound.

The fire was to flush them out.

Penny tried to drag him down the stairs, but he was stuck. "What are you doing?" she said. "We need your help!"

He couldn't move—couldn't answer her. The roof above them creaked, and thankfully, she shoved them to the side before the beams could crush them.

"Use your powers!" she begged. "Save us!"

He managed to shake his head. No matter what he did, he couldn't save them. Not only was he too scared to use his powers, but he couldn't summon them anyway. The heat, combined with his lack of focus, ensured they were trapped.

The front door burst open, and the screams raised in frequency. One of Penny's tears dripped onto Theo's cheek. "You were supposed to save us."

He reached for her, but she was ripped from his arms. An army of guards stomped up the stairs; one of them already had a hand around her throat and a gun to her head.

"Penny!" Theo bolted upright on the couch, gasping for breath and covered in sweat.

His friends remained asleep, though Yasmine stirred at his voice. Whilst tugging at his shirt, Theo forced his breathing to slow. His dream had been so vivid it could've happened right in front of him.

He shut his eyes, then opened them when Penny flickered in his mind. He'd never been afraid of the dark, but right now, he couldn't have been more terrified.

It was a little after eight when Theo left the motel. He'd taken the time to brush his hair and fix his clothes, and also to replace the bandages on his arms. While his wrists had scabbed, he hoped to make a good appearance for Penny's parents.

He scribbled a note for the team, explaining he'd return soon, and placed it on the dresser. Then, he swiped the car keys. His deception made him queasy, but he didn't have another option. He needed to tell Penny's parents that she was safe.

Using the darkness to conceal himself, Theo crept into the motel lobby. A stack of yellow and white pages rested on the desk, which remained unoccupied. Tara used to talk about phone books and other outdated methods of finding people. She called it a "simpler, better time."

Of course, she only thought that when Mom used a tracking app to ensure Tara arrived home before curfew every night.

Still, if it had the information Theo desired, it was worth a shot to read. He hurried to the desk, grabbed the book, and slipped outside. As soon as he was safe in the car, Theo solidified and flipped through the pages. Youngstown was a reasonably large city. Finding Penny's home would be difficult. Hopefully, this antiquated booklet of information would give him a lead.

Then, Theo spotted her last name, accompanied by "Elizabeth and Charles." Along with their phone number, their address was printed in bold black ink.

"Bingo," Theo whispered to himself. There was no turning back now.

With a map in one hand and the other on the wheel, he spun onto the road. The streets remained almost empty, and if it weren't for Theo's nerves, it would've been a calm moment.

Theo analyzed every street sign he passed and every crease of the map. Before long, the quaint buildings and shops gave way to small homes. He almost became lost amongst the dozens of immaculate green yards and fields dotted along the sides of the road.

Until he came to a crossroads. Literally. He couldn't decipher the signs anymore and wasn't sure which direction would lead him to Penny's parents. A charming red house sat on his right, and through the lace curtains, he could see an older woman feeding her birds. She might know which way to go.

The shadows twisted on the steering wheel. ***Don't risk it. Stay in the car***.

He slammed the car into park and marched in the direction of the house. Asking for directions was his only idea. He knocked on the door and stuck his arms behind him, concealing his bandages. The sun had just barely begun to rise, pressing heat against him.

A few nail-biting seconds passed. Then, the woman cracked open her door. She fixed her glasses on her nose and croaked, "Hello, young man. May I help you?"

"Hopefully," he said, keeping a preppy tone. "My mom is old friends with Elizabeth Bradshaw, and I'm supposed to deliver a gift to her. Do you know where I can find her?"

"Oh, yes!" The woman stepped onto her porch and pointed down the road. "If you keep going straight for a few more miles, you'll find Lizzy's house. It's blue with a tire swing in the front yard. You can't miss it!"

Theo was already backing up. "Okay, thanks, bye!" Within moments of bidding farewell, he was buckled in his seat and speeding down the street.

Like the lady had promised, Theo found Penny's home a couple of miles later. The house had been painted a light bluish-gray, and a wreath comprised of brightly colored flowers rested against the front door. A white picket fence surrounded the equally small yard. A tree stood guard on one side with a tire swing hanging from one of the branches. He could almost imagine a younger Penny swinging on it, laughing without a care in the world.

Theo parked on the side of the road and walked across the stone path, his heart nearly beating out of his body. *This is a mistake*, he panicked. *What if her parents hate me? What if I have the wrong place?*

Heaving an exhale, Theo pressed the doorbell. He wasn't doing this for himself; he was doing it for Penny.

A man opened the door. He was dressed in his police uniform, probably on his way to work. His name tag bore his last name, "Bradshaw." Obviously confused, he squinted at Theo, yet greeted a very kind, "Good morning."

Theo shoved his hands into his pockets. "Good morning, sir. My name is Theodore Palmer. You don't know me, but I know your daughter Penny."

At the mention of her, Theo expected Penny's dad to be over the moon. But his forehead wrinkled. "Palmer...I've seen your mom on the news." His blue eyes dilated with recognition. "Oh no. You're *him*!"

Theo trembled so badly he could hardly speak. "Sir, I—"

"You're the boy who destroyed the school! My little girl must've been devastated!" Penny's dad stuck his finger into Theo's nose, pushing him down the front steps. "How dare you show your face here! You twisted, evil—!"

"Stop!" A burst of anger erupted from Theo, contorting the shadows on the sidewalk. He hadn't intended to lose his temper, but the darkness decided for him. "I came to tell you that Penny is safe and alive. Since I'm not welcome, I'll go!"

Equally furious and dismayed, he spun on his heel to stomp out of the gate. Behind him, he heard a rushed argument. One of the voices belonged to Penny's dad, but the other was female. Right as Theo made it to the gate, Penny's mother cut off his path. "Please don't go," she begged, tears already pouring forth. Her resemblance to Penny was uncanny; she had the same blond hair and green eyes.

Theo shook his head. "I shouldn't be here."

Elizabeth took his arm. "*Please*."

He cast a glance toward Charles, whose mouth was pressed into a thin line. He clearly disapproved of Theo's company, but wasn't about to interfere with his wife.

"Okay," Theo relented. "But only for a little bit."

Penny's mom swept him inside the home. She sat him in the dining room and said, "My name is Elizabeth, and that's my husband, Charles. I'll just be a second. Don't go anywhere."

As she hurried into the kitchen, which connected to the dining room, Theo let his gaze wander the home. Despite it being much smaller than his house, he could feel the love within. Penny's childhood had been etched into the scratches on the floor—marked in the notches on the doorframe. Vases of flowers stood on every surface imaginable, brightening the rooms in her absence. Theo almost smiled, but Charles entered next. He sat across from Theo; his glare searing holes into Theo's skull.

"So, your name is Theo?" Charles asked.

"Yes, sir, but you can call me Theodore if you'd prefer."

Charles gave a short nod. "I've heard a lot about you."

Worry racked Theo's pulse. "I hope it's all good things!"

Charles's unamused expression said it wasn't.

Relieving the tension, Elizabeth returned, carrying two glasses of orange juice. She extended one to Charles and Theo, each of them thanking her quietly. Finally, she placed a plate of blueberry muffins on the table and took her seat.

"Are you Penny's boyfriend?" she asked.

Theo couldn't help but blush. "We're close, but I don't know if we're that close."

Charles straightened at that. It was like he saw Theo in a whole new light. "Forgive me for saying, but she isn't usually into bad boys."

Bad boy? Theo shook that off. "Yeah, she's sweet."

The compliment made Elizabeth beam. "The few times she wrote to us, she talked *all* about you. She was head over heels for you."

Theo looked down. "I was too."

If they wanted to question his sudden change in mood, they didn't. "What happened to your arms?" Elizabeth inquired instead.

Instantly, Theo hid them under the table. "I got into an accident."

"You should have Penny heal you! She loves doing it."

If only they knew.

Elizabeth retrieved a picture album, rested it in Theo's lap, and motioned for him to flip through. In one picture, a six-year-old Penny beamed at the camera as an orange cat struggled in her embrace. In another picture taken a few years later, she had dressed as Dorothy from *The Wizard of Oz* for Halloween.

As Theo turned the pages, his heart ached. Until now, he hadn't realized how much he missed her, not just from his recent absence, but from their emotional distance.

His vision blurred. All at once, he remembered everything he said to her when he left—everything he'd done to make her hurt. It had been almost four days without her, and already, he longed to see her again.

He needed to make things right.

"Thank you for your hospitality," he said as he stood. "But I should get going."

Penny's parents stood too. "Wait," her mother ordered, grabbing Theo to prevent his escape. "She *is* safe, isn't she? And if so, could you tell her to come by?"

Theo nodded. "I won't let her be harmed."

As Elizabeth burst into sobs, she wrapped Theo in her embrace, holding him tightly. Theo met Charles's gaze and nearly pulled away, but the man merely said, "Be good to my daughter."

Theo blinked repeatedly. The shift in treatment was welcomed, yet surprising. "I-I will, sir."

Once they were finally outside, Elizabeth handed him a big bag of muffins. "Are you sure I can have these?" he asked.

She patted Theo's shoulder. "This is my small way of thanking you for coming into our lives."

If she knew the whole story, she might not be so thankful.

37

CATHEXIS

As the yellow sun lifted into the blue sky, Penny glanced out the window to see them drive past the "Welcome to New York" state sign. A long distance remained to reach the heart of the city, but none of them were in any rush.

Well, except her.

Her anxiety rushed at her in full force. She bounced her leg and incessantly tapped her fingers on her chin. She worried if Theo was already here, if he missed her, what would happen if he wasn't here, and what she'd say to him when he was.

"Are you okay?" Daniel asked, catching her attention.

Penny ceased her nervous ticking, but the sound of his voice added one more worry to her list. What would she do about Daniel? Their entire plan rested on his willingness to stop his uncle, the man who kidnapped and abused him for years. It would take insurmountable courage to act.

"I'm alright," she said, smiling. "It's just odd to be here."

"I'm excited!" Giselle gushed from the front seat. "I've never thought I'd visit New York!"

"We're not here to sightsee," Felix responded, for once sounding reasonable. "We've got a job to do, and the sooner it's done, the sooner we can return to a normal life."

Penny scoffed to herself, quietly enough that no one else heard. What did a normal life entail, anyway? And what made Felix think they could have one as supers?

Regardless of the truth behind it, it was a sweet statement. Given time, he could become a great leader.

Before Penny knew it, they had reached the heart of Manhattan, complete with its towering skyscrapers, terrible traffic, and hordes of strange yet eccentric citizens. Giselle soaked it up like a sponge, oohing at the buildings and gushing over the street art.

Her awe wasn't shared. Daniel remained silent through the drive, while Felix gave one-word answers. It seemed they were all unnerved to be back here—to be so close to something so scarring.

Penny retrieved her radio from under the seat and, upon switching it on, was pleased to find it worked. Now that they were in New York, Millie might reach out to them. "I'm hungry," Penny announced, hoping to lighten the mood. "Why don't we grab some food? Then, we can find a place to stay and make a plan."

"Great idea!" Giselle had already pointed out several restaurants she wanted to try.

"I don't know," Felix admitted as they rolled to a red light. "Being in public could be risky. What if someone recognizes us?"

Daniel unbuckled his seatbelt. "You guys eat, and I'll get the hotel room. There's one around the corner, so I'll pick you up in half an hour. You shouldn't be recognized in that short amount of time."

Felix gripped the steering wheel. His jaw was tight. "You sure?"

Giselle leaned onto his arm and batted her lashes at him. "*Please*?"

While Felix fought his shyness, Penny had to smile. Seeing

someone as strong as him crumble so easily under a girl's influence was exceptionally entertaining. "Fine," he said, "I'll pull off the road so Daniel can drive."

With a cheer, Giselle kissed Felix on the cheek. His satisfied, bashful grin finally slipped out, proving that even the most determined of men could be swayed by a girl's affections.

Everyone climbed out of the truck, and Daniel replaced Felix in the driver's seat. Penny lingered at the passenger side window. "Thirty minutes," he swore, crossing a finger over his heart. "Stay out of trouble."

"You too."

A car honked behind Daniel, annoyed that he was wasting a perfect parking space. He sped around the corner, allowing the newcomer access to the spot. Penny, too, scurried away, finding Giselle and Felix waiting in front of a pizza parlor. "So, you want authentic New York-style pizza?" Felix was saying.

While they debated, Penny stared at the blinking dot on the radio. "If anyone is listening," she said, holding down the button to speak, "we made it to the city. Let me know how you are." Just as she was about to slip it into her pocket, she heard it crackle.

"Penny," Carter whispered, his voice riddled with static. "Need— help."

Her pulse quickened. "Where are you? What's going on?"

"Jones trapped—barbecue restaurant—Tenth Avenue."

Then, the line cut. Despite knowing she wouldn't receive a response, Penny exclaimed, "Carter? Are you there?"

The walkie-talkie remained silent. For a moment, Penny couldn't do anything except breathe. Her worst nightmare was becoming a reality. The team didn't stick together, and Millie and Carter were at the mercy of Principal Jones. That was, if Millie was alive. There remained a chance to save Carter, but it meant throwing themselves into the belly of the beast.

Penny shoved the radio into her pocket and grabbed Felix's arm. He was smiling at Giselle, yet upon seeing Penny's big eyes, he frowned. "What is it?" he asked.

"Tenth Avenue," she explained. "We have to get to Tenth Avenue."

"What? Why?"

"Carter's in trouble."

Mimicking Penny, Felix blanched. With his free hand, he snatched hold of Giselle's sleeve and redirected her from the pizza. Over the sound of her confused complaints, he said, "Your call. Do we wait for Daniel?"

"No," Penny immediately answered, tugging on Felix. "He won't return for another thirty minutes, and I doubt Jones will let Carter live that long."

"And how do we stop Jones?"

"I might be able to restrain him," Giselle interjected. "I've never used my telekinesis on an invincible man, but it's worth a shot."

Finally, Penny managed to drag Felix to the crosswalk. They were about a few blocks from Carter's location, so if they hurried, they could get there within minutes. Once the light turned green, they darted across the street. Penny knew their plan was fragile, threatening to shatter at the slightest hiccup. However, hanging back for Daniel wouldn't guarantee success. Even if he returned early, he might not be able to take his uncle's invincibility.

Their only option to save Carter and Millie was to rely on Giselle. Hopefully, she'd be able to hold Jones down until they escaped.

After passing multiple streets, Felix pulled Penny to a stop and pointed at a dimly lit barbecue restaurant just adjacent to them. The exterior had been painted a deep maroon, and cartoonish cowboy hats and boots were plastered to the windows. It almost appeared closed or shut down; there was so little traffic nearby.

"That's it," she breathed. "That's where Carter told us to go."

322

The trio hurried to the door. The sign outside glowed with the red and blue letters of "OPEN," yet it seemed oddly abandoned.

"Penny," Felix whispered, "should we find another entrance?"

Tuning out his question, Penny pushed the door just enough so it cracked open. The interior was exquisitely decorated with antique bottles lining the walls, mahogany tables, and a quaint country vibe. Music played softly on the speakers, and she could hear clanging in the kitchen—normal sounds for a restaurant.

Penny opened the door all the way. Giselle and Felix remained close. "Maybe we have the wrong place," Giselle said.

"Actually," the person from the kitchen called, "you're exactly where you're supposed to be."

A splitting pain erupted in Penny's skull, sending her to the floor in a ball of cries. She heard a scuffle above her. Felix threw out a swear.

Another voice entered the conversation, one that was thick with honeyed sweetness. The owner placed a hand on her shoulder, a gut-wrenchingly familiar touch. "Hello, Ms. Bradshaw. It's wonderful to see you again."

That was all Penny heard before she blacked out.

The throbbing in Penny's head woke her. She tried to reach up to hold it, but her wrists had been bound behind her. Her ankles had also been tied together, leaving her to kneel in a very uncomfortable position.

Ten feet away, she blinked hard to see Felix and Giselle on either side of her. Both were bound too. Felix sported a bleeding nose and a cut above his left eye, while Giselle appeared unharmed. From what Penny could gather, they were in a storage room, based on the supply shelves around them and the cold concrete beneath her.

"It's okay," she called to her friends. "We'll get out of this."

Proving it, she felt the ropes along the seams, searching for the knot. The door opened, and her frantic scrambling ceased. A girl entered the room, stepping right out of Penny's memories. Except the girl's purple glasses weren't broken; rather, the lenses had been shined to a sheer finish. Her hair was tied down her back in a braid, and her smirk was the same as it was months prior.

However, a long, burned scar streaked across her nose and up toward one of her ears—clearly, a result of a fire.

Or an explosion.

It took every bit of strength for Penny to say, "Athena? You're alive?"

Athena brightened. "Shocking, right? You might have blown a building up on me, but I don't die easily." She grabbed Penny, her nails digging into the soft skin of Penny's cheeks. "Let's see if you will."

"How did you get here?" Penny asked, though it sounded a bit muffled thanks to her squished mouth.

"Firefighters saved me, and Principal Jones got me from the hospital. We're very alike, he and I, since we both can't wait to see your friends dead."

"Jones won't protect you," Penny insisted. "He's using you as a pawn. Once he gets what he wants, he'll discard you."

Athena's grip tightened. "You're so predictable, Angel. You're always trying to save others, even when they don't want it."

She slammed Penny's head into the pole. Metal jabbed into her skull, cutting her and sparking tears in her eyes.

"I hate you the most," Athena hissed. "You could ruin everything for him, and he'd still worship you. Why can't he see what I see?"

From the corner, Giselle snorted. "This is insufferable to listen to. First, the empty threats, and now the obsession? You must've been a bully in school."

Controlled by Giselle's telekinesis, Athena released Penny and was forced to sit on the floor. Felix laughed, making Athena blush in anger.

Her limbs quivered as she tried to fight, but the more Giselle focused, the more her power kept Athena pinned.

"You're a mind-powered super like me," Athena said, almost in awe. "I bet in different circumstances, we'd be best friends."

Giselle made a disgusted sound. "Doubtful."

"Geez, you're touchy." With a single glare from Athena, Giselle cried out, and her telekinetic control faded. She could move Athena's body, but she couldn't move her mind. While her whimpers continued, Athena pounced to her feet and glanced around the group. "Hey, where's Theo? I was looking forward to picking his brain! Metaphorically, of course, but I wouldn't mind doing it literally too."

Penny worked her hands against the ropes. Blood stuck to the back of her head, but seeing as she couldn't heal it, she'd have to distract herself. "He's somewhere you'll never find him."

"That's a shame. I really thought you'd live up to the Romeo and Juliet tale. Star-crossed lovers doomed to die."

"Stop it," Penny demanded weakly.

"You know he left because you're not good enough. You're just some pathetic girl who he feels sorry for."

"Don't talk about him!" Penny's voice cracked. "That's not what I believe!"

Athena yanked Penny's hair hard. "Denial is a river in Egypt. Not the weapon you use against me."

Penny almost burst into sobs. The pain, combined with her sorrow, dangled her on the edge of a breakdown.

"I knew you were a coward," Felix suddenly said. "But this is a new low. Without those ropes, Penny would put you on the floor in two seconds flat. Guess there's a reason Principal Jones likes her."

Athena's teeth ground together until they squeaked. "You heroes were always so prideful." She spun on her heel. "Speaking of heroes, let's see how Hourglass is doing!"

Felix smirked at her. "Go ahead. I'm not afraid of you."

"Sadly, you're telling the truth. But you're not honest about every-thing. Especially about…" Athena pointed at Giselle. "Her."

A flicker of panic crossed Felix's body, tightening his muscles. "You're lying—I don't keep secrets."

Athena laid a hand on her heart. "Me, the liar? You can't even admit your own feelings."

She snapped, and the mental agony ripping through Giselle seemed to dissipate, allowing her to relax. Yet the pain transferred to Felix. A strangled whimper escaped him, and he doubled over, resting his fore-head on the floor.

Athena cleared her throat. "So, Giselle! According to his timetable, he's had a crush on you for two—no, four weeks, on account of the time he first met you, and you spouted off French. From that moment on, he's thought you were the hottest girl ever."

Giselle's jaw dropped. As her stare darted to him, she whispered, "Felix? Is this true?"

He didn't look up. His silence was answer enough.

While Giselle pursed her lips, Athena giggled in delight. "This is so cute! Felix fell for a girl who doesn't like him!"

Slowly, Felix's head raised. "What?"

"Yep. Right now, she's thinking, 'Poor Felix, how am I supposed to tell you that I'm still more interested in Theo?'"

"That's a lie!" Giselle begged. She yanked weakly at her restraints. "Felix, I-I used to think that, but not anymore! I swear!"

Athena swiveled on her heels, taunting, "I can literally read minds, and you're twisting the narrative? How shallow."

Giselle's mouth remained open, yet nothing came out. No words, no sounds. She was truly stunned speechless.

On the other side of the room, Penny didn't care if it was true or not. All she saw was Felix's slackened shoulders and the frown clouding his expression. It was the same way Theo looked after Penny confronted him for lying.

Athena blew a raspberry with her lips. "Boy, Angel, could your brain calm down? You're constantly thinking about Theo and…" She tilted her head. The pressure on Penny's brain increased, stabbing like a thousand tiny pins. "Daniel? Isn't that the principal's nephew? Why are you obsessed with him?"

Penny stiffened. "I'm not. I was thinking how great it'll be when he arrives and drains your powers. Did you know he can do that?"

Athena's stance faltered slightly; her sarcastic cackling had a shake to it. "What does it matter? He's not here." The pain rose in intensity, making Penny outright scream. "And even if he were, it would be too late to save you."

The door suddenly clicked open again, and in an instant, the pain drained from Penny's head. Gasping, she glanced upward, wishing her blurry vision would focus. Despite her hazy view, she noticed a man enter. *No,* she thought, *it can't be him.*

Yet it was. Dressed in one of his fancy suits and ties, Principal Jones strolled in. "Athena," he warned, dangerously low, "we agreed you wouldn't hurt her."

"I forgot," she lied, "forgive me."

Once Athena stepped back, Jones took her place. Too close for comfort, he knelt in front of Penny. "It's good to see you awake," he said.

"Where's Carter?" Penny demanded.

"Here. Alive." Jones's fingertips ghosted her hair. "His little girl-friend is quite the firecracker, don't you think?"

Penny jerked her head away. "Don't touch me."

"Calm down, dear, I'm not going to hurt you. In fact, I'm relieved you're still in one piece after the cabin debacle. I regret letting any of those supers escape."

Penny glared. "I regret letting your men live."

"You can't kill anyone, Penny. Try as you may, it's not in your nature." Jones sighed. "It's a shame you've been living a life of exile.

Your power is incapable of hurting others. I never would've taken it from you."

"You hate supers."

"True, but I can't seem to hate you. You are one of the rare supers created purely to help. Which is why…" he leaned forward and untied the ropes around Penny's wrists and ankles, freeing her and helping her stand. "I want to offer you protection."

If the principal hadn't been holding onto her, she likely would've fainted. "What?"

"I know Theodore is close to finding me. I don't want to hurt you, Penelope, but I will if I must. If you abandon this pitiful team of dreamers and go on your way, I will let you live your life to the fullest. You may return to your family in Ohio. You will never have to worry about supers again, including me."

Through wide eyes, Penny studied her friends' surprised, sorrowful expressions.

At her hesitation, Jones pressed on. "I will guarantee your safety with the government. They are already considering stopping supers from procreating and eradicating you from existence won't be long after. Please take the offer."

Penny dropped her focus to the floor. Instead of risking her life, why *shouldn't* she go home to her family? According to Jade, Penny's future was limited. This may be her last chance at happiness.

A shadow on the floor shifted as an overhead light swung. But Penny could've sworn Theo was manipulating it. He never gave in, so she couldn't either.

Her head shot up as she exclaimed, "I'll never consider that! You're evil!"

Principal Jones's nostrils flared. "I've been nothing but kind to you."

"You tried to convince Theo to kill me."

"That was to show you that you've put your trust in the wrong person. He'll turn against you—against all of you, soon enough. And when he does, neither of us will be able to stop him."

Despite Penny's pounding heart, she said, "Theo's not who you think he is. And neither am I."

Jones's lip curled in a sneer. "Your defiance, while endearing, will get you killed." In a flash, he grabbed her wrist and dragged her to the door. "Finish them off," he ordered Athena. "I'll take care of the others."

"With pleasure," Athena responded as the door slammed shut.

Before Penny could even think about fighting from Jones's grasp, he threw her onto the floor. The wood paneling cut her palms, drawing thin lines of blood and making her wince. Based on the surrounding tables, they were in the main part of the restaurant, but the lights were off, and the shades were drawn.

In the middle of the room, a girl sat on the floor, bound and with a bag covering her head. Principal Jones ripped the bag off, and as soon as it was free, Millie spat on his coat. "This was your last mistake!" she yelled. "I should gut you like the animal you are!"

Principal Jones groaned. "She's so barbaric. Not like you, sweet Angel."

Seeing Millie battered, bloodied, and bruised unnerved Penny to the point of shaking. "W-where's Carter? You said he was alive."

"He is. And he's unharmed." Principal Jones made a grand gesture to the kitchen, saying, "Come on out!"

The door creaked open, every hinge squealing in protest. As promised, Carter emerged. He bore no injuries, but there was a distant look in his eyes that disturbed Penny almost as much as seeing Millie.

"There," Carter said. "I brought you Penny. Are we square?"

A sinking sensation claimed hold of Penny's body. The oxygen sucked out of her lungs. She dug her nails into the hardwood, trying to root herself to the ground. *This can't be real*, she thought. *Carter would never betray me.*

"What?" Millie exclaimed, sharing in Penny's confusion. "You sold her out?"

Principal Jones nodded. "Ah, yes. Carter and I made a deal. If he brought Angel here, then I agreed not to kill his parents."

Carter made eye contact with Penny. "I'm sorry," he said quietly. "I-I wanted to keep them safe."

"We're going to die because of you!" Millie yelled, kicking the floor in protest. "How could you be so selfish?"

"I'm not selfish," Carter insisted, sounding choked. "Jones promised he'd let you and me go."

Goosebumps prickled Penny's arms. Making a deal with the devil was the one act she'd never do. But it was too late for Carter.

Principal Jones chuckled. The singular, delighted laugh reverberated in the vacant room. It communicated everything he didn't say.

Devastation crumpled Carter's face. Trusting Jones had led him and the others right to their deaths. "At least let Millie go," Carter begged, breaking Penny's heart. "She had no part of this—not even from the beginning."

"Don't do this!" Millie growled, struggling in her bonds.

"Let her go," Carter repeated, ignoring her. "Please, I've done all that you've asked."

Principal Jones stroked his chin in mock consideration. "You always were an obedient sheep—tricking the herd to slaughter."

Tears gushed down Carter's cheeks. Incoherent pleadings and apologies mumbled from his mouth. He dropped to his knees, the picture of defeat. He had saved his parents, but at what cost?

As the weeping continued, Principal Jones grinned at Penny. "Once I've finished my job here, I'll make sure you're nice and comfortable. We have a long drive home."

"I'll do whatever you want," Penny blurted. "Just don't hurt them."

While considering the offer, Principal Jones chewed the inside of his cheek. Then, he lowered himself to Penny's level and said, "Too late."

Her despair didn't even get a chance to penetrate her fully. Suddenly, seemingly out of nowhere, Millie launched herself at Jones, brandishing a switchblade and slashing everywhere. The cut ropes dangled from her wrists, displaying the frayed ends from her feverish attempts to get free.

Through clenched teeth, she hissed, "You killed my boys! I won't let you win!"

Rather than fight, Jones stood there, laughing. That monster of a man laughed at a girl's attempts to protect herself and her friends.

"Millie, stop!" Carter pleaded. "You can't beat him!"

Except she didn't stop. She wasn't afraid of Jones. Not one bit.

Penny sat in awe, astonished that this girl, who knew she didn't have a chance of survival, fought tooth and nail to prove a point. It wasn't about winning; it was about looking death in the eye and challenging it.

Jones might've been invincible, but Millie was unbreakable.

The instant Jones noticed Penny's growing smile, his amusement faded. In that second, he grabbed the blade and twisted it out of Millie's grasp. Then, in one quick thrust, he jabbed it into her neck.

Penny had no voice to scream, yet saw the pain tear across Millie's body, stiffening her muscles, weakening her knees. It was so intense, Penny could feel it across the room.

Clutching her throat, Millie stumbled into a table and sank to the floor. Carter ran to her. As he held her and sobbed, Penny spotted Jones reach into his suit pocket. Knowing what he was doing, she reached for the gun first. The shot went awry, striking the wall near the front door. Jones kept a firm grip on his weapon, but as long as the muzzle was pointed in her direction, he wouldn't fire.

"Quit crying!" he demanded of Carter. "She was worthless!"

"*Worthless*?" Carter repeated. "You said that about every student!"

Jones sneered. "Every super is worthless. Especially you."

Abruptly, Carter's heavy weeping ceased. Instead, silent tears streaked down his cheeks as he propped Millie against a chair, adjusting her so she was comfortable in her last moments. Then, he stood. He moved with such apathy, such numbness, that it was almost disturbing to watch. Attempting to create space, Jones recoiled into the wall, inadvertently releasing his hold on the gun.

"You found use for my power," Carter said blankly. "You made my memories painful to remember. Let's take a trip down yours."

Without warning, he leapt at Principal Jones, blood-stained hands outstretched to the man's head. It looked like Carter was trying to attack Jones, but they both suddenly dropped to the floor like dead weight. As soon as Carter touched the principal, they were sucked into the memories.

Stunned and shaking, Penny threw the gun far from her and hurried to Millie's side. Her army green collar was stained with red. A gash sunk deep into her neck. An injury like this was too serious for Penny to heal.

"Oh, Millie," Penny said, her voice breaking. "Please forgive me! I-I wish I could—" In a desperate maneuver, Penny pressed her hands to Millie's neck, urging her power to heal her.

But it didn't work.

Yet again, Penny had failed to save her friends.

Millie scrambled for Penny's sleeve, her lips moving silently as she strained to speak. Penny studied closely, watching her mouth, "Help Carter."

Help Millie, Penny's healing instinct urged. *I have to heal her; I have to fix her; I have to make this better! If I don't, then who am I? What am I good for?*

But the rationality insisted, *She's too far gone. I have to keep Carter strong until Daniel gets here. He's the only one who can fix this.*

Penny forced herself to walk to Carter's side. There was no time to heal Millie, but Penny could save Carter. She held his arm and faded into the memories with him.

38

ONE LAST MEMORY

The world sparkled and clouded like fog filled with stars. It was as if Penny had been dropped into an outdated movie, surrounded by the monochromatic colors of black, gray, and beige. She was in a dining room; she knew that much, standing in front of a table occupied by two young boys.

"Penny?" Carter asked. "What are you doing here?"

Penny spun to see him standing beside the wall. Principal Jones was at the edge of the memory, hopelessly trying to open the front door and escape. "I couldn't leave you alone," she answered.

"If you're here..." his expression darkened. "Then, Millie must be gone."

Penny would've extended her hand to heal him, but it would have no effect in here. "Yes."

"Why would she attack him?"

"Millie doesn't give in easily." Then, knowing he needed the assurance, Penny added, "She used her last words to tell me to help you. She really cared about you."

Unfortunately, the words had the opposite effect on Carter. He pulled at his hair and took to pacing. "You don't get it—I shouldn't be saved!" He muttered to himself, then more coherently stammered, "It-it was an accident running into Jones. When we arrived in the city, we stopped at this restaurant for a meal. I think the owner is friends with Jones because they snatched us after closing. After that, I went into survival mode. Just like at the academy, I had to do whatever was necessary to keep myself alive. I knew he wanted you, and I knew you'd come to save me." Carter couldn't look at her. "Penny, I-I'm—"

This time, Penny did reach out for Carter. "I would've come for you regardless of the reason," she assured. "You were trying to save your parents."

"But they hate me. They told me never to return home—with good reason."

"I'm sure that's not true."

"It is! I was sent to the villain academy because I erased the memories of a few neighbor kids. You know what makes it worse? I *enjoyed* it." Carter laughed at himself. "Stealing the students' memories showed me how wrong I was to abuse my power, but there's still a part of me that likes to see people flounder and forget. Now, here I was, trying to redeem myself, and I ruined my chance." Carter dropped his head. His following words were barely audible. "I'm sorry."

"You can fix this," Penny insisted. "Daniel is on his way, and then we can escape!"

"The second I leave, Jones will wake up and attack you again. Daniel won't stand a chance."

As Penny pondered that, she darted a glance at Jones, who was preoccupied with trying to pry the window open. In every scenario where Daniel had the opportunity to fight, he chickened out. If he struggled to attack a crazy puppeteer super, then he'd be frozen at the sight of his uncle. Jones was terrible, but they were family.

Memory erasure wouldn't be an option either. Carter suspected it didn't affect Jones, and even if it did, he couldn't erase the memories while he was inside them. They were truly stuck.

"Not all of us are surviving," Carter said softly, "and I've accepted that. Ever since Millie died...I was done. I can distract Jones long enough for you to escape. You can be here to support me, but the second I say so, you and the others need to get far away from this place and find Theo. Got it?"

Penny couldn't respond before Carter pushed her behind a wall.

It couldn't have happened a second too soon. Principal Jones stomped over and yelled, "Where are we? What did you...?" He went quiet as the characters of his memory acted out their scene.

Two boys sat at a table. The younger of them resembled Jones, and the older must've been his brother, Aaron. A woman, Penny presumed to be their mother, swept the floor nearby, her hair stuck in a messy bun with dozens of loose strands.

She was probably beautiful. But right now, she resembled a disaster. Heavy bags hung under her lids. Her short, slender form hunched over the dustpan. A woman like her, being married to a powerful super, should've been wearing the finest clothes. Instead, she wore sweatpants and a sweatshirt.

"Gimme the last piece of pizza," a voice demanded, snapping Penny's attention to the kids.

"It's mine, you already had three," the younger boy whined.

Aaron's fists clenched. "I'm older, I make the rules!"

"B-but Mommy!"

"Just give it to him, Jason," the mother answered in exasperation. "It's a lot easier if you give them what they want. Trust me."

Young Jason begrudgingly surrendered the pizza slice, much to Aaron's smug pride.

"This is it?" Principal Jones scoffed at Carter. "You brought me here to watch me argue with my brother? How pathetic!"

"I didn't deliberately bring us here," Carter snapped. "Your brain subconsciously selected the memory. That means this moment stuck with you."

The front door clicked open. His mother dropped the broom.

Carter smirked. "And that's our moment."

Malcolm Jones, the founder of the superhero academy, walked into the kitchen. He wore a sharp black suit and a pristine blue tie. In an odd twist of fate, Principal Jones wound up looking almost exactly like his late father.

"Dad!" Aaron leapt off his chair and rushed to greet his father with a flurry of teasing punches.

Malcolm blocked each one with his hands. "Hey, kiddo! How was your day?"

Aaron made a face at his brother. "Jace broke my scooter today."

"No, I didn't! It was an accident!"

Malcolm raised a brow. "So, you didn't, or it was an accident?"

Tears bubbled in Jason's big eyes. Unwillingly, Penny's heart ached. "I-I didn't mean to break it," he said. "I said I was sorry!"

"Sorry doesn't cut it, Jason, you know that."

Malcolm stepped closer. The mom cut him off, one hand on his chest and the other protecting Jason. "Honey, he apologized."

"He deserves punishment! How else will he learn?"

"He's learned already! Surely his remorse is consequence enough?"

"If we don't teach our kids justice, then they will spend their whole lives believing mercy will save them! Move out of the way, Angela!"

Malcolm grabbed her to move her physically, but she didn't budge. She pushed against him, resulting in a tug-of-war fight. Both kids begged their parents to stop. Angela yanked at Malcolm's necktie, with barely enough force to move his head. Regardless, he reciprocated with a shove. She crashed to the floor, bruising her knees on the hardwood.

Penny covered her mouth to silence her scream.

Making matters worse, Malcolm didn't even apologize. His two boys stood there, watching in silent horror as their mother winced and cradled her scraped palms. Young Jason gathered his courage to exclaim, "Don't touch my mom!"

He took a step toward his father, but Angela restrained him with a hug and whispered, "It's easier this way. Remember?"

The memory dissipated into clouds as another formed. These were much quicker, simple flashes rather than prolonged moments. A teenage Jason moved out. In his college dorm room, he accepted a call and heard his mother had died.

And finally, he attended her funeral. Penny ensured to conceal herself behind people or objects as she watched the real Principal Jones. Even as he stared at his mother's dead body, he didn't react.

The memories shifted once more, this time reflecting the interior of the principal's office. Except it looked a little different, with Malcolm in the plushy chair and a young Jason on the other side of the desk. The two ate dinner together—Chinese noodles, chicken, and egg rolls.

Penny concealed herself behind a tall potted tree, watching the scene play out.

"It's a shame Aaron couldn't make it," past Jason remarked. "It's been, what, a year since we've been together as a family? Then again, we're not a *real* family. Not since Mom died."

The word 'family' moistened Malcolm's eyes. Being invincible, he never quite looked his age, but his hair glistened with speckles of gray. "I miss her every day," he said. "As I'm sure you do."

"Miss her?" Jason gritted out. "I didn't think you *loved* her."

"Don't say that," Malcolm said, gaining an edge. "I cared about her more than you'll ever understand."

"I'm just saying, you should've told me she was sick. I wanted to be there for her."

"You're starting this argument?" Malcolm sighed, easing his frustrated tone. "She couldn't be saved. Making you stall your college education on a lost cause would have severely impacted you. I didn't tell you because I was trying to help you."

Past Jason grinned. It didn't reach his cheeks. "Thanks, Dad. At least she can't be hurt anymore."

Malcolm nodded, clearly not picking up on the double meaning.

"Enough of the sad talk," Jason continued. "I'm not only here for dinner. I came to ask you an important question." He reached into the briefcase by his chair and removed a thick stack of papers. "I drafted this with a lawyer friend of mine. After your untimely demise, would you consider letting me run the school?"

Malcolm's jaw dropped. "*You?*"

Jason scratched his neck. Like a switch being turned on, his act began. "I shouldn't say this, but Aaron has already expressed his disinterest to me. He wants to focus on himself and start his own life. And since your friends want nothing to do with this place, I'd be willing to take over after you die."

"But you're a human," Malcolm protested.

"No one knows that. You kept quite the secret, because heaven forbid you have a son that isn't super." Jason's words came out biting. Harsh. Expressive of his years of abuse.

"I didn't mean to hide you. Not like that. But running a school of supers requires power."

"I'm already getting my teaching degree. And we could keep this in the family! Sort of like a tradition!"

When Malcolm didn't budge, Jason shrugged. "Sorry, I thought this would make Mom proud."

In that instant, Malcolm's hesitation disappeared. He accepted the packet and tapped a pen against it, contemplating. He merely scanned the papers, hardly read them with the care or attention he should've dedicated to them. Penny willed him to disagree. But she knew what would happen.

Malcolm signed the page, officially declaring that upon his death, Jason Jones would be the owner of the Academy for Young Superheroes. And his fate was sealed.

"Consider this my gesture of peace," Malcolm said. "I couldn't give you your mother's last day, but I can give you this."

"Thank you," Jason gushed, accepting the packet. "We have to celebrate!" After stashing his signed contract, he retrieved two fortune cookies and tossed one to his father. "I made sure these were cooked specially for you."

The two cracked open their cookies and read the fortunes to themselves.

Beside Jones, Carter snorted. "Let me guess," he said, "your fortune was, 'You'll obtain great power.'"

The real Jones remained solemn, a look so out of place for him. "I was told I'd 'Carry the weight of the world.'"

Suddenly, Malcolm choked. As he clutched his throat, bits of cookie flew from his mouth. Blue tinted his lips. He was only able to suck in thin, gasping breaths.

He's going through anaphylactic shock, Penny realized. She had seen it once before at the cabin; a boy had been stung by a bee, and his entire body had swelled. Since he didn't have an EpiPen, if Penny hadn't been there to heal him, he would've died.

She glanced at past Jason, whose smile turned a bit more real. "I had my suspicions," he said, crushing his own cookie in a fist. "Remember that time we went camping, and Mom accidentally gave you my peanut butter sandwich? You were lucky we were close to a hospital. She was lucky, too. No super on Earth is without weakness."

"Please," Malcolm wheezed. He clawed at his shirt. A few buttons popped. "Jason—"

"I told you these were made special," Jason taunted, throwing the cookie crumbs at his father. "Peanut oil really gets the job done. Although it is pathetic that your weakness is an allergy. But don't worry. I won't tell anyone. In fact, not a single soul will ever know how you truly died here today. The police can decipher that when they find your body."

"Why are you doing this?"

"I'm making Mom proud."

"Please," Malcolm begged, "help me!"

Jason's amusement soured into disdain. "If I don't teach you justice," he hissed, "you will always believe mercy will save you. Like you said—justice prevails."

The memory blurred. Penny swallowed, unaware of the burn in her throat. She doubted Principal Jones had such allergies, meaning their last resort was Daniel or Theo. She wondered which one of them would be able to kill Jones.

Principal Jones had remained eerily calm during each memory. Only now did he choose to speak. "The police did find his body," Jones explained. "But I'd bought the food with his card, receipt in the bag, and I had an airtight alibi confirmed by friends. As far as investigators were concerned, my father accidentally killed himself. Their story was helped by the fact that he always kept his EpiPen at home. Even if he wanted to save himself, he couldn't."

"Wow," Carter stated, "and not a single tear shed for your old man?"

"You might think I'm heartless, but he abused his powers. He deserved to die."

"And what about all those students? Did they deserve it?"

"At the beginning of owning the academy, I only got rid of dangerous or selfish hero students. I let the good ones go home. Until…"

"Until what?" Carter pressed. "What made you decide to build the Academy for Young Supervillains? What made you take their memories and powers, rather than their lives?"

Principal Jones met Carter's gaze. "I wanted to make them human."

When the memories cleared, they reflected a night, a burning apartment building, and a bright, raging fire. Penny could smell the stench of smoke, ash, and something much more sinister. A badly burned and blistered woman lay on the sidewalk a few feet from where Carter and Principal Jones were standing. A man wearing black hovered nearby, but disappeared into the shadows upon being seen.

Beside the woman, a group of people sat around a young boy. They squeezed his tiny fingers, not too tightly, but enough so that he wasn't tempted to touch his wounds. His coughs were too feeble—too frail.

Oddly enough, the woman on the concrete looked shockingly similar to Penny. Her blond hair splayed around her head, and her eyes glittered like hazel-colored gemstones.

Penny's intestines twisted. For years, she assumed Jones idolized her because of her ability. Was it possible he didn't just idolize her, but *obsess* over her?

Past Jason fell to his knees beside the woman and grasped her hand. "Samantha, please!" he begged. "Stay with me!"

Meanwhile, the real Principal Jones watched. He couldn't comfort his wife or son and stood there as she took her last, shuddering breath. Then, and only then, did he turn away from the scene. There was no crying—no tears shed from the memory.

"You started planning for the Academy for Young Supervillains not long after this." Carter glanced from the principal to his wife. "Was this why?"

"I couldn't let a single super escape from me again," Jones answered blankly. "The mere presence of supers threatens the safety of humans."

"And kidnapping Daniel? Killing your brother? Was it for power?"

"Once I became invincible, I was finally strong enough to stop them. *All* of them."

Carter shook his head in disbelief. "I get it now. This whole time, I thought you were a jerk because you wanted to be. But you lost someone."

Principal Jones whirled around. "I didn't just lose someone! I lost *everyone*! Every person who ever cared about me was gone in one fell swoop! If it weren't for supers, my family would be here! The world would be safe! My life would be *perfect*!"

Strangely, Penny could understand. The people in Jones's life had all been hurt or killed by supers. He was right to be afraid of them—to want them dead. He saw it as protecting those who were defenseless.

But his logic was twisted. Deep down, he didn't want to protect humans. The power meant more to him.

Carter gaped. "You're a—"

"Call me a monster," Jones snapped. "Make me the villain, the bad guy—I don't care. Everything I have done has been for the safety of humanity."

"I wish I could feel sorry for you," Carter said. "I really do. I wish I could apologize for your terrible upbringing and mean it. But I can't. You deserved *all of it*." Carter gained momentum. "I'm glad you lost your family! I'm glad you endured so much pain! It's just too bad your wife didn't live to see who you'd become." Carter grinned, wider than Penny had ever known possible. "She'd despise you."

Jones scowled. "You're a miserable child."

"And you're a miserable man. I guess we're not that different."

A disjointed tap on Penny's elbow alerted her that it was time to leave. Leaving meant solidifying Carter's fate. He shouldn't be alone.

The tap turned into a yank. Yet again, the feeling was odd, like it wasn't real. She couldn't leave without making one last statement.

She darted out of her hiding spot, allowing Principal Jones to see her. Before he could turn on the charm, she exclaimed, "I'm going to find Theo, and we're going to teach you a lesson for abusing your power! The only person who deserves to die is you!"

A disturbing mixture of confidence and mocking twisted in Jones's sneer. "Not if I kill him first."

"New studies show that over 62% of marriages between supers and humans end in divorce within the first five years. Of that 62%, more than 25% of couples report facing abuse from their super spouse. These claims have yet to be proved by investigators, but they certainly raise concerns.

If we can't trust the people we marry, who can we trust?"

-excerpt from Isabella Porsh's online article, "Something Borrowed, Something New, Something Black, Something Blue"

39

L'AMOUR ET LA PERTE

Penny opened her eyes, straining with the effort. The strength was drained from her body, as if someone had wrung her out like a sponge. She collapsed onto the cold wood floor, the temperature relieving some of the heat in her mind and body.

A hand touched her cheek, and, assuming it was Athena, she rolled away from them. That hand gripped her arm and hoisted her upright, their fingers digging into her skin. The person snapped in front of her nose. The sound echoed. Penny's head fell onto their muscly shoulder, and only then did she realize who it was.

"Felix?" she mumbled.

He held her to his body. "Yeah, I'm here. You're safe."

She wrapped her arms around his neck. Her limbs trembled, whether from the trauma or muscle weakness, she didn't know. "I think my brain is melting," she muttered, her voice slurred as if she were drunk.

Despite his own apparent exhaustion, Felix scooped her up. "Nah, you're good."

Penny blinked repeatedly to clear her hazy vision. She saw Millie's body wrapped in a tablecloth and Athena crouched on the floor, sobbing. Another figure, Daniel, stood over her.

"Daniel," Penny cried, "what took you so long?"

At her voice, Daniel turned. His eyes caught on Principal Jones on the floor, and he paled momentarily. "I'm sorry. I had a bad feeling at the hotel, and after I went around the block, I had to find you."

"Some pedestrian told Daniel where we went," Felix finished. "Guess not everyone here is heartless."

"Maybe not," Daniel agreed, turning to Athena. "But she is."

"Please," the girl wailed, crawling to Daniel's feet. "Give it back! Without my power, I'm no one!"

"You can still be someone, Athena. But you can't be trusted with powers anymore."

Her sobbing increased in volume, yet it reached deaf ears. Daniel, especially, appeared uninterested. Unlike his panic at Lennon's store, Daniel had finally come to terms with the weight of his power's responsibilities.

Felix released Penny to escort Athena into the room where they'd been captured, letting her crazed pleadings echo in the restaurant.

Penny tugged on Daniel's shirt sleeve and begged, "Take Jones's power, too. We can end this here."

Immediately, Daniel's breath caught. Despite his willingness to take Athena's powers, he wasn't as eager with Jones. "I-I would need a lot of concentration," Daniel excused. "And we have no idea when he'll wake up."

At the mention, Principal Jones stirred. Making matters worse, sirens whined down the street, undoubtedly reporting to the shots fired. Penny almost burst into sobs. This was what Carter meant when he said there wasn't an escape for him. He had to keep Jones occupied in his memories so the others could flee the scene. Once the police and investigators arrived, they'd naturally take Jones's side.

He'd conjure a lie of self-defense, reasoning away his murder of Millie.

At the very best, Carter would be arrested and taken to prison. But Penny doubted he'd be lucky enough to have that happen. Jones would interfere again. He couldn't have any living witnesses, and that included Athena. By any means necessary, he'd guarantee that they died.

Just then, Felix returned from the back room. He must've tied Athena to the shelf, considering she was suddenly quiet.

"We have to leave," Daniel announced solemnly. "We'll go through the alley door."

"What about Carter?" Felix asked. "We came here to save him."

Penny shook her head an inch, allowing the realization to settle in for Felix. "Daniel," Felix began, "you sure you can't stop this?"

"There's no time," Daniel said. "We have to go."

With gritted teeth and clenched fists, Felix shoved past Daniel to the alley door. Penny couldn't read minds, but she knew precisely what Felix was thinking.

Giselle held the door leading into the alley, and the team hurried through. The cool air brushed past, clearing the fog from Penny's mind. Some supers—like Athena or Lennon—used their abilities to make others suffer. That was why Jones started his tirade in the first place. Perhaps there was logic underneath Jones's madness.

And that scared Penny more than anything.

The group finally made it to their hotel room. Upon arrival, Penny rushed to the bathroom. Her stomach was near empty, but her nausea convinced her she was sick. She crouched over the toilet, shivering. She could feel her powers gradually healing her, yet not at the usual speed.

Felix brushed her hair onto her neck. "Hey," he said, "come with me."

She staggered alongside him, following him to the bed. Without being told, she flopped onto the mattress, allowing Felix to drape a cool washcloth across her forehead.

"Stay here and relax," he instructed.

I don't need to relax, Penny's instincts said. She needed to heal them, not be healed. Ultimately, *thankfully*, her fatigue won, and she fell into a deep sleep.

Two hours passed before Penny finally roused herself from slumber. Felix sat on the other bed, watching the TV on a soft level so as not to disturb her. He must've heard her wake, because he asked, "How're you feeling?"

She sat up. Her stomach didn't roll, and her head didn't throb, meaning her powers must have returned in full force. "Better," she said. "How are you?"

As if the question permitted him to rage, he gripped the remote. The fire in his eyes could've burned the hotel down. "Frustrated," he said. "Annoyed. We went to save Carter, and Daniel just quit!" Felix slammed his fist onto the bed. "Maybe there wasn't a chance to take Jones's powers. Maybe if we had stayed, we would've been caught by the police. But it bothers me that Daniel didn't even try!" Exasperated, Felix grunted and ran his fingers through his hair. "Sorry, Pen, I didn't mean to yell. It just sucks to fail so often."

Penny traced a frowning face on her own bedsheet. "I know what you mean."

Her mind threatened her with images of Millie, the boys at the cabin, Carter—the people she'd failed to save. Whilst digging her nails into her palms, she stood, ready to heal the friends she had left.

"We don't need to be healed," Felix interrupted.

Penny blinked. "A-are you sure?"

For once, he didn't look at her with sarcasm. Instead, his gaze was sympathetic as he repeated, "We don't need it. Keep it for yourself."

He's lying. He needs you to heal him.

Penny bit her tongue, resisting her instincts with all her might. The hotel door opened, the sound shocking her out of her internal dilemma.

Giselle walked in, arms wrapped around herself. "Hi," she greeted sheepishly. "Um, I hate to interrupt, but can I talk to Felix? Alone?"

Both girls looked at Felix, who shifted on the bed. "Sure, I guess."

Unable to endure the awkwardness, Penny scurried to the door.

There was the squeaking sound of Giselle sitting on the bed, and then, she said, "Athena was lying earlier. I mean, I liked Theo in the past, but not after what you and I have been through."

"It's okay," Felix said. "Talking about crushes is so juvenile."

"Right." Giselle paused, then whispered, "Athena didn't lie about all of it, did she?"

"I don't know about that."

"Yes, you do. Do you like me or not?"

Worry thickened Felix's voice. "What do you want me to say? Regardless of what comes out of my mouth, it'll ruin this little bubble we have. Our world might be ending soon, and I don't want to lose you."

The silence was agonizingly uncomfortable, and Penny almost reentered the room to spare Felix the humiliation. Finally, Giselle said, "Maybe we should start slow. Enjoy the time we have together, no matter how much it might be."

"I like that idea."

Thinking it best they be alone, Penny closed the door completely. In the hallway, Daniel sat against the wall. He didn't move upon her arrival and said, "Regardless of what Felix believes, I wanted to end it today. But I couldn't guarantee our escape, and I promised Theo your safety was my number one priority."

Penny stepped back in shock. It all made sense—Daniel's constant company, his overwhelming concern, his assurance of her safety. Although Theo wasn't here, he was still protecting her. It came at the expense of Carter's life, but Daniel had made a promise, and he'd kept it.

"Are you ever going to be able to take his invincibility?" Penny asked.

Daniel chewed on his cheek. "I'm working myself up to that." His tone changed and he added, "How are Felix and Giselle? Are they kissing yet?"

Slowly, Penny sat on the carpet with Daniel and dragged her knees to her chest. "No, but I'm sure it won't be long now."

"Guess we'll be stuck out here for a bit."

"As long as they're happy, I don't care."

"And you? Are you happy?"

Penny pondered to herself. The loss of Millie and Carter weighed heavily on her heart, as did the fright of seeing Principal Jones again. But they had escaped, and Theo would be here soon; she was sure of it. A pull in her heart connected them, stringing across time and space.

Penny nodded and smiled, pleasantly surprised at how easy it was. "I will be."

40

BLACK SHEEP, LONE WOLF

When Theo returned to his friends, they were waiting in the motel parking lot. Each of them wore glares, but Dion's dropped the second Theo gave him the bag of muffins. Without exchanging words, they climbed into the car with Peter in the driver's seat and Theo in the passenger seat.

"So," Peter began begrudgingly, "you met her parents?"

"Yep," Theo answered, keeping his stare out the window. "Her dad didn't like me."

"I don't know why you bothered them. You already burned your bridge with her."

Theo's jaw clenched, the only thing he could do without hitting Peter. "You just love to be a jerk, don't you?"

Peter's knuckles turned white on the steering wheel. "Get mad all you want, but this trip has been a disaster. We're lucky we didn't bring Penny. Danger follows you."

Usually, Theo would've yelled right back at Peter. But his tone remained calm. "I won't deny that, yet you stay by my side. Why can't she?"

"Because she means more than I do," Peter snapped. "You think I cared about my well-being if I came with you?"

"Careful, Peter," Theo advised. "Your humanity is showing."

That shut Peter up. For the next long, grueling hours of driving, getting gas, and scrounging for meals, he didn't say a word. Theo didn't mind. He just wanted to reach New York. The sooner he did that, the sooner he could see Penny again. Plus, the peace and quiet allowed him to complete his letter to her.

With only half an hour remaining until they arrived in New York, Yasmine leaned into the front and suggested, "I saw a campsite nearby. Why don't we rest before going into the city?"

Without speaking, Peter obeyed.

Once parked, the group found an empty site with forgotten lawn chairs surrounding a fire pit. Dion scurried to find sticks, bragging, "I had a lot of experience in Boy Scouts. I'll make the best fire you've ever seen!"

Yasmine plopped into one of the chairs and sighed. "I should've never come with you guys. I could be sitting at the cabin drinking a lemonade, but instead, here I am. Dirty, greasy, and tired."

"And alive!" Dion chimed in. He dropped a pile of twigs into the fire pit and built a pyramid-like structure. "Is the glass half full or half empty?"

"It's empty," she snipped. "We haven't had much to drink in days."

Dion neglected to answer and sparked two rocks together. His teepee creation burst into flames, the warmth instantly spreading around the circle. Yasmine visibly relaxed, and Theo felt his own bones turn to liquid. A sliver of his power shrank away from the fire, a weakness he hadn't realized until reading his dad's journal.

Peter snapped a branch into tiny pieces. His blue eyes glinted with the reflection of the fire. "They made me hate who I was when I used my powers."

Yasmine glanced at him. "Who? The school?"

"My family." The fire crackled as Peter tossed his wood pieces in it. "I learned that the best way to keep myself safe was to be invisible. Even though my parents hated it, they can't hit what they can't see."

Dion and Theo made eye contact, sharing the same uneasy look. Peter had never spoken about his family before, let alone this honestly.

He drew farther into his chair. "I forged a letter to get into the academy. Upon arrival, Jones hardly said five words to me. And I was visible then—I thought I didn't need to be alone. You wonder why I was at the school for so long? It's because he forgot about me."

The crackling embers almost hid Peter's sniffles. Almost.

"Jones said a lot to me, too," Yasmine admitted, resting her chin on her hand. "He said that my attitude was deplorable, and it would make people hate me. I guess he was right."

Dion stared at his palms. "He told me my powers were too remarkable to be stuck with a teenager. He called it, 'a waste.'"

Everyone turned to Theo, obviously anticipating him to confess his deep, dark depression. Without considering the consequences, he said, "I'm scared that everything Jones said about me is true. That I'm worthless, and a monster, and no one likes me."

The others didn't react.

"I know I'm not easy to get along with," Peter confessed. "Having friends is…hard. I'm glad I have you guys."

"Me too," Dion said, reaching to pat Peter's arm.

Yasmine flipped her hair over her shoulder. "I had friends way before I met you guys, but I guess you're my favorites."

Dion and Peter laughed, and the former looked to Theo, probably expecting him to laugh too. But he couldn't tear his gaze from the fire. A similar feeling burned inside him, calling him.

His friends had been tortured by one man: Principal Jones. None of them could regain their years from the school, but they could feel some comfort, knowing their abuser was rotting in the ground.

"I'll be right back," he said, standing from the log.

"Where are you going?" Dion interjected.

"A walk," Theo responded, already leaving. "Need to clear my head."

And my conscience.

On the journey to the campsite, Theo recalled seeing a small gas station three hundred yards away. It was the only place he could think of to catch a glimpse of the news and perhaps discover what Jones was planning.

Theo eased the door open. This gas station was the tiniest he had ever seen. It had little else, other than a single-stall bathroom in the back of the store, a few fridges for water and beer, and three shelves for food. Stranger still, the place was deserted. A TV played behind the register, but there was no cashier to accompany it—no clerk to serve the customers.

"Hello?" Theo called out. "Anyone here?"

Silence.

He glanced at the bathroom one last time, checking for the light underneath the door or the sound of a toilet flushing, yet once again, he came up empty. Quickly, he ran to the TV and flipped through the channels, searching for the news, a mention of his name, his family, anything. When he passed every channel and couldn't find a single piece of information, he wondered if that was a good or bad sign.

The front door creaked open, and out of instinct, Theo morphed a nearby shadow into a blade. Of all people to run into at the gas station, he never would've expected to see Jack, Axel's henchman, standing there.

Like earlier, his disheveled beanie was stuck on top of his greasy hair, almost like it had a permanent home there. Although he appeared messy previously, he had clearly sunk to a new low. Not to mention the smell emanating from him. The amount of dedication that Axel put into finding Theo was impressive. Maybe a little disturbing, but impressive.

Upon seeing Theo's weapon, Jack skidded to a stop. He raised his hands, palms out, to show he had no defense. "Hold on! I'm not here to fight!"

"How'd you know where I was?"

"Axel never really trusted Simon, so he put a tracker on his car. We've been trailing you since you shot him and put him in the hospital."

Theo gritted his teeth. He'd been stupid to accept any help from Simon. Theo pointed the dagger at Jack, saying, "I suggest you leave my friends alone, before I harm yours."

"Chill, bro! I came here alone—without Axel. I'm just here to deliver a message." Keeping one hand up, Jack reached into his pocket and removed a flip phone. He rested it on the counter and backed away, arms stretched high into the air.

Theo shifted his glare from Jack to the phone. It began to buzz, an annoying, repetitive sound. Theo flipped it open, and, predicting who was on the other line, he spat, "Hey, Jones. How's New York treating you?"

Theo could hear the man's evil smile in his voice. "It's wonderful, Mr. Palmer. Knowing I scourged this city of your sickness fills me with insurmountable pleasure. I heard you took your team and started camping out in the Pennsylvania forest. How was that?"

Theo stiffened. Even if he wanted to respond, he couldn't. He prayed Penny had left the cabin—hoped she saved the children before Jones could lay his disgusting hands on them.

Jones clicked his tongue. "I didn't scare you that easily, did I? Can't we carry on an adult conversation?" He paused, then added, "I saw your precious Angel today. She's looking nice, despite the trouble you put her through."

Was Penny in New York? No, that wasn't possible. Principal Jones must've been mentioning her to taunt Theo, to goad him into speaking.

"She's such a good girl," Jones continued, his words slick with honey. "So determined, so loyal, so…moldable."

The torture was too much to bear. "What did you do to her?" Theo exclaimed, composure breaking.

"It's a secret."

"I swear, if you so much as harmed a hair on her head, I'll rip your heart out!"

Jones laughed, a loud, carefree sound too innocent for such a terrible person. "There's the Nightwave I remember! You know, Penelope reminds me a lot of myself. We're both seeking the best for everyone."

Theo's fingers tightened around the phone; he almost felt like snapping it in half. "You're a murderer. That's it. There's nothing good about what you're doing."

"I started this because there is nothing good about your *kind*." A sliver of hatred returned to Jones's tone, making him shaky, so he cleared his throat. "The crimes I've committed are inconsequential. The lives I've sacrificed are meaningless. Face it: No one cares. If they did, they'd defend you, not attack you."

Theo couldn't dispute that. In his time on the road, he'd met a few humans who'd been kind enough to help him, but he doubted any of them would ever take their defense higher. They were trying to be generous, not show their support.

"What have you done to my family?" Theo asked.

"Nothing yet. Your father was smart to keep them in the dark. As far as I could tell, your mother had no idea about his history with me. Now, she's too involved. You understand I must take care of that."

"She doesn't have a part in this," Theo pleaded. "What will it take to leave her alone?"

"Isn't it obvious? I'd want all superhumans dead!" Jones guffawed heartily, the noise so loud that Theo had to pull the phone away. "Of course," he continued through amused sniffling, "that'll happen anyway. I don't need you to bargain with me."

Theo scowled. He hated that he'd begged for mercy, especially knowing there was none to be had. But where mercy failed, justice prevailed.

"Okay, Jones, you know what? I was trying to make a deal, but you don't deserve such kindness. When I find you, I'm going to make you suffer."

"You talk big game for a teenager."

"And you talk like you're not afraid of me. The truth is: You're *terrified* of me. You're sending lackeys and hunters to find me because you can't do it yourself. I'm the one person who stands between you and controlling the world, and you hate that. You hate that your hard work, your years of dedication, are going to go crumbling to dust because of some seventeen-year-old kid."

Theo's anger spiked. He felt his power make the lights flicker and spark. "You say I'm not human. I definitely won't be when I come to kill you. Mark my words. If I die, I'm taking you with me."

Theo slammed the phone on the ground, breaking it into pieces and shattering the screen. He fired a glare at Jack, who was frantically yanking the door handle. "I don't want trouble, man!"

"I'm not going to hurt you," Theo said, his voice low. A flurry of shadows swirled at his feet and around his hands. "I need you to deliver a message for me."

Jack's head bobbed up and down.

"Tell Axel that after I'm finished with Jones, I'm coming for him next."

"I will, I promise! Anything else?"

A razor-sharp shadow pierced the door, throwing it off its hinges and blowing it open. "Leave. Don't let me see you again."

Jack took off so fast that he could've beaten Aiden in a race.

Darkness perched on Theo's shoulder. ***Isn't this nice? Being feared is far preferable to being loved.***

The way he felt right now—confident, strong, capable—was such a welcoming difference to the depression he dealt with. Was it wrong to relish this?

Penny's voice popped into his head, telling him to calm down, take it easy, remember this wasn't who he was.

Theo shook his head. The darkness hissed, ***You can't rid us of forever. You'll need us to win.***

Despite feeling like he was two steps away from a panic attack, Theo managed to stumble into the campsite. When he staggered into their circle, his friends stood, their shared concern hitting him in waves. The last thing he wanted was a confrontation. His powers stirred within him, pumping his blood with chilly anticipation. He needed to use it again. He needed to let loose. But not here. He might hurt someone.

"What's wrong?" Dion asked, noticing Theo's discomfort right off the bat.

"Nothing."

"Something must've happened, or you wouldn't be acting like this." Dion frowned. "Just be honest."

"That's too much to ask of him," Peter stated, only sounding half-joking. "He's never been an honest kind of guy."

Peter is a hypocrite. He never knows when to stop talking.

Theo clenched his fists, hoping to curb his powers. "I'll be honest," he began, "as long as you guys are. I know you're hiding a secret from me, so what is it?"

Yasmine and Dion glanced at each other, giving Peter the freedom to say, "Why don't you tell the truth first? You've been a disaster since we got on the road. There's gotta be a reason for it."

Dion elbowed Peter.

"It's okay," Theo said, "he's right. Why wouldn't I be a disaster?

We've been kidnapped, we've been on the brink of death, and we're on our way to kill an invincible man. Just another week for me!"

Yasmine shook her head. "Let's relax."

But Theo was just getting started. After he caught his breath, he said, "You guys don't understand the pressure I'm under. Too many people better than me have died so I could be here. They made a mistake keeping me around!"

Yasmine and Dion shared a troubled look. Even Peter seemed unnerved by the words; he shuffled his feet and pulled at his collar.

Dion attempted to intervene. "Theo, you don't mean that."

"Maybe I do! What should it matter?"

It was then that Theo felt the creeping shadows clinging to his shirt and pants. When he tilted his head, he spotted them slithering up behind him. A few crawled across the grass in his friends' directions. Grim-faced, Dion angled in front of Yasmine, while Peter placed himself behind the fire. The slightest moves, yet they carried so much weight.

"You're afraid of me," Theo said. It horrified him to say that. "You said you weren't, but you are."

"Theo, wait," Dion blurted, "let me explain."

"You lied to me! You said you weren't scared of me—that I would never turn evil, so there was no point in planning. How could you lie?"

"I didn't lie," Dion pleaded.

"Sure, you were just protecting Yasmine for fun!"

Dion grimaced. "It was an accident. I wasn't thinking."

"You seem pretty aware!"

Yasmine crossed her arms, yet it appeared to be a comforting mechanism. "Theo, calm down! Can you really expect us *not* to fear you? You've been so unpredictable lately."

Hurt speared Theo's heart. However, his rage bubbled over, momentarily burying his pain. "It doesn't matter," he spat. "After we're done, I'm going home, and you'll never have to see me again."

The proclamation saddened Dion and confused Yasmine.

And it infuriated Peter. "Are you kidding?" he yelled. "You're going to quit? What kind of hero are you?"

"I'm just a kid!" Theo shouted. "We all are! Why not throw in the towel and let someone more experienced handle the big problems?"

"If anyone else cared, they would've!" Peter jabbed his finger at Theo. "We are the only ones that care about any of this. There are no heroes left in the world, so *we* have to save it."

When Peter got too close, Theo shoved him. "If you had a family that cared about you, you'd be ready to quit. But you don't. That's why you're trying to hold us back—so we don't leave you, too!"

Peter's eyes widened in a mix of despair and shock. Except Theo wasn't done. "My family is eager for me to return home. So is Yasmine's. I'm sure her little brother is heartbroken, wondering every night if she'll be alive the next day."

As Yasmine looked down, her lashes fluttered.

"Even Dion misses his mom," Theo continued. "None of us should have to stay out here. We deserve a normal life."

Peter's forehead wrinkled, creased by the emotions he didn't dare to express aloud. His fists were clenched, but there was an under-standing in his gaze.

Sensing the end of the argument, Theo moved to leave.

Until Peter fired one last parting shot. "Look who's hiding in the shadows again. Guess you didn't learn anything from your dear old dad's death."

Theo's composure didn't just snap. It evaporated. He felt himself shift into his shadow form, but it wasn't human. It was feral. Wild. Capable of ripping out Peter's throat so he'd never speak again.

It leapt at Peter, pinning him to the dirt with sharp claws. Everyone was screaming; Yasmine ordered Dion to grab Theo while Peter yelled for help. The shadowy wolf snarled. Its claws pierced Peter's upper arms, making him cry out in pain.

The beast spotted Peter's throat—the despicable thing that voiced such horrible insults, such insensitivities. The wolf bared its teeth, ready to sink in.

A sudden, searing pain burst into the beast's side. Yelping, it crashed to the ground, squirming to escape the fiery sensation. In a snap, the shadows disappeared, leaving Theo in their place, whole and burned. He gingerly touched his waist, which sported a bright red burn mark.

Dion held the weapon aloft: a short log with a burst of flame at the top. As he angled the branch down to Theo's chest, he could see Dion's tears glistening in the light.

At the scorch of heat, Theo scrambled backward. He almost yelled at Dion for his negligence, because what if the fire spread and killed Theo for good? The shadows couldn't exist in light or fire, so he very well could have died.

Yasmine dragged Peter to his feet, whispering assurances amidst his groans. Theo stretched forth to help but stopped. His hands were speckled with blood.

Not just any blood, though. *Peter's* blood.

Theo sucked in a shallow breath. Then another, and another. He glanced up at Dion, who gripped the torch with white knuckles. Before he could say a word, Theo found his feet. He bolted to the trees, letting the branches slap his face and whip his legs.

When he could no longer smell the fire, he sat on the muddy ground. He stared at his shaking palms, then rubbed them on his shirt. Despite the warm air, he shivered. He felt dirty. Guilty. His friends were terrified that he would turn evil, and he proved their fear tonight. He couldn't control his own powers; he didn't even understand them. Someone like that should stay far away from people at all costs.

Principal Jones was right. Theo *was* a monster.

You should've hurt Peter, the terrible darkness hissed. ***He made you hurt. He needs to learn that enough is enough.***

Then, the thoughts took a turn. *They're right to hate me. Mom was right to prevent me from going to school and making friends. I'm worthless.*

Theo covered his eyes. Silently, he begged the accusations to disappear. This was why he had to hide his sorrow. The second he broke, so did his friendships. He could only imagine the horror Penny would feel when she learned what he'd done. The realization as she finally understood why she couldn't be with him, not in any capacity. The words she'd say—it wasn't him, but her, and that she "wasn't in the right place to be dating." She would be so pitiful it'd kill him more than her honesty.

He released a short, choked breath. *I can't do this anymore. I'm done.*

As hard as it was, he climbed to his feet and began the walk into the city. Principal Jones wanted him dead. That was it. If they killed each other, this ridiculous battle would be complete. No matter how their fight ended—who lived, who died—it would be finished. And regardless of what Theo's friends said, it was better to work alone. Fewer casualties that way. Less regret, less rocky emotions.

So, here he was, a black sheep in more ways than one.

MISSING CHILD

"Please help me find my daughter!

Her name is Katie Williams. She never returned home from school. Last time I saw her, she was wearing a pink backpack, blue jeans, and a yellow t-shirt with flowers. She has dark brown hair and blue eyes.

And because I know people will ask: Yes, she is a super. Her DNA shouldn't dictate whether or not she's cared for. Please don't let her be another statistic."

-Social media post from Darla Williams

41

REUNION

As much as Theo hated using his power, he couldn't walk all the way to New York. So, he traveled through the shadows and arrived in downtown Manhattan. Though he regretted ditching his friends, he hoped they wouldn't follow him. This was a fight he needed to handle on his own.

Admittedly, he felt like a tourist in New York. The air still reeked of cigarette smoke and sewage; the streets were still littered with trash and people, but *he* had changed.

He stopped at a payphone. Whilst digging in his pockets for spare change, an older woman tapped his arm and passed him a couple of quarters. He hadn't bothered to draw his hood or conceal his identity, so she must've recognized him. Not a hint of emotion crossed her face.

"Thank you," he said, accepting the coins.

"Stay safe," she responded and shuffled away.

Theo stared at the silver in his palm, enough for one phone call. He slipped the quarters into their slot, punched in the numbers, and waited.

Two rings. Three.

The line clicked, and Theo's heart sank. Until Tara said, "Who is this?"

Despite his horrid week, he smiled. Everything might have changed around and within him, but Tara remained the same. Her tone was as sharp and commanding as ever.

"I'll give you one guess," he teased.

She sucked in a breath. Anticipating her shriek, Theo continued, "I can't talk for long. I need you to do me a favor."

"Where are you?" she hissed, ignoring his request. "Judging by the noise, you're in the city. I can pick you up!"

"You can't. Jones is here, and he wants a fight."

"I won't let that happen!" Tara's vigor suddenly cracked. "He might kill you."

Theo entwined the phone cord around his finger. "That's a possibility, but I'm not planning on dying today. I have a plan to stop him. For good."

Tara snorted. "And how are you going to do that? Mom has been trying to take him down for the last four months with zero success."

Theo did have a plan, though it was rough and comprised of moving pieces. Regardless, he knew it'd work. He'd wait until late at night to engage in a battle with Jones, allowing Theo the upper hand in the darkness. However, he needed one last assurance.

"Mom has been failing because she doesn't have any evidence," Theo said. "I can give it to her. All I need are cameras."

Unfazed by Theo's oozing confidence, Tara clarified, "You've thought this out, right? No impulse, no instinct, just logic?"

"I promise, Tara."

She sighed into the phone. "Fine. Tell me what you need me to do."

Theo described his plan in a hushed tone, cupping his hand over the mouthpiece to further limit the possibility of eavesdroppers. Once he was finished, Tara said, "If this guarantees you come home to us, then I'll follow your instructions exactly."

Theo grinned ruefully. "Thanks, Tara. You've always been there for me."

"It's what big sisters do." She hesitated, then quietly added, "I love you, Theo."

He had to jab his fingernail into his hip to prevent himself from bursting into sobs. A breakdown wasn't what Tara needed; she needed to hear his determination. "I love you too, Tara. I'll see you later."

After ending the call, he tried to flag down multiple taxis and buses, but not a single vehicle stopped for him. Although it bothered him, he let the experience roll off him like water. He'd set out to accomplish one goal, and that was to kill Principal Jones. Then, Theo would go home. End of story. He didn't want to spark an equality debate or cause a big commotion. He was just a kid born with powers, not some political hotshot.

He craned his neck to look at the sky. A few stars peeked out from the smog, but it wasn't dark enough yet. Luring Jones into a fight would be easier at night, so until then, Theo decided to visit every place he remembered going to with his family. Then, if his plan didn't work, he could rest easy knowing his last few memories were positive.

First, he walked to a high-end clothing store that Tara enjoyed dragging him to. At least, she liked it when she liked Mom. After the pair had their falling out, Tara didn't shop for expensive clothes. Theo hoped they'd get along again. They had their differences, but they needed each other.

The store had bright white lights and extravagant chandeliers hanging from the two-story ceiling. All kinds of expensively dressed men and women perused the aisles, murmuring about the quality and what they'd pair the outfit with.

Theo gulped. Compared to the customers, he looked severely out of place, almost like he'd gotten lost and stumbled in here for directions. Whereas his younger self would feel completely comfortable in this shop. Theo could practically visualize himself and Tara poking fun at the impractical clothes, their own form of bonding. He wasn't that boy anymore, and hadn't been for a while, but he'd give his soul to have one more day with Tara, laughing and joking like they used to. To the world, Theo would forever be a fugitive—a danger.

To her, he'd always be her little brother.

As Theo swiveled to leave the store, he caught sight of a magazine on the cashier's desk, decorated with the familiar letters *La Mode*. Despite the trials he'd put his mother through, she'd managed to balance her time between her business and her personal vendetta against Principal Jones. Growing up, Theo viewed his father as the strong one. Theo had been mistaken.

Mom raised two children alone while managing a business. She had her faults, yet she would defend Theo until her dying breath. More than any super or force on Earth, Mom was the most powerful person he knew.

Exiting the store was like abandoning a piece of himself. Returning home didn't mean returning to a normal life or the life he had before. In fact, he'd be lucky to have a portion of that. For better or worse, Theo had changed. It was his family's choice to love him once more.

Down the street, Theo stumbled across a restaurant he and his father used to enjoy. Theo didn't have a dollar to his name, yet the smells of baking bread and savory sauce sustained him. After many baseball games, Theo and Dad would share a pepperoni pizza.

"Wish you could see me now," Theo whispered to his reflection in the shop window. "Hope I'll make you proud tonight."

A shadowy tendril tickled Theo's cheek, wiping away his tear. The motion made him chuckle. His powers were intimidating, but they were the last part of Dad he had left.

Theo walked to Times Square, and while waiting for the streetlight to turn, a teenage girl bumped into his shoulder. Her gigantic iPhone rested in her monopod, where she was currently conducting a livestream. Based on the flurry of hearts and comments she was receiving, she must've been fairly famous.

She offered him a quick, "Excuse me," and in the second she spared to glance at him, her jaw dropped. Instantly, her dismissive expression shifted to excitement as she gushed, "Oh my gosh, it's you, that fugitive kid! Can I take a picture with you?"

Considering Theo was already in the frame, she'd gotten her picture. Hundreds of comments flooded the screen, flying too quickly for him to read. This would be exactly what he needed to lure Jones out of hiding.

"I'll do you one better," Theo said. He snatched the selfie stick out of her hand and declared, "I have a message for Jason Jones. I'll be waiting for you at the ruins of your greatest failure. Since this is a strictly super dispute, I encourage any and all humans to refrain from interfering. Other casualties won't be my fault." Theo looked to the girl. "Still want that picture?"

Her gaping jaw prevented her from responding, so Theo returned her phone and continued on his path. Jones might've been invincible, but his own weakness, other than Theo, was his own pride. Without a doubt, Jones would find Theo and initiate the fight, putting an end to their rivalry.

And maybe then, Theo would finally be happy.

Penny stared out of the hotel window, head on her arms and her eyelids heavy with exhaustion. It'd be wise to go to sleep, but she had to remain alert, just in case.

"Good evening," Daniel said, patting her on the arm. "Felix and Giselle went to get a late-night snack. They weren't sure if you were hungry, so I told them I would ask you—"

As Penny drowned out Daniel's voice, she zeroed in on the crowds below. Per his suggestion, the team would journey to Mrs. Palmer's house tomorrow morning and check that the children had arrived safely. But Penny hesitated. The pull in her chest to Theo felt tighter; what if he was here in the city? She opened the window and leaned out of it, hoping the night breeze would calm her.

Chattering directed her view down at the streets, where people were clamoring amongst each other. She almost dismissed it, but New Yorkers didn't stop for many things. Perhaps there was a car wreck or some other horrible accident. Maybe there was a celebrity walking amongst them.

And there was. But he wasn't a movie star.

"Theo!" Penny reeled into the room and pulled her jacket on, startling Daniel.

He grabbed her by the shoulders and said, "Whoa, hold on. What are you talking about?"

She pointed at the window. "Theo's here! I saw him!"

Daniel hurried to check for himself, but he didn't light up with excitement like Penny did. After a moment, he looked at her. "You sure you saw him?"

Penny dismissed that thought from her mind. "Of course I did! He was on the other side of the street!"

"What if it isn't him?"

"Are you hearing yourself? There's only one Theo in the entire world. And I have to talk to him."

"No!" Daniel leapt in front of her and blocked the door. "He told me to keep you safe. You're staying here."

Penny's fists clenched. "You can't make this decision for me! I'm fixing this!" She tried to shove past him, yet he didn't budge.

"You're not leaving! It's too dangerous to go on your own!"

"*He's* on his own out there! He needs me!"

"And what if he doesn't?" Daniel's loud, harsh tone made Penny jump. Seeing him burning with anger finally made her realize why Theo was so scared of him. Daniel softened his voice. "I-I'm sorry for yelling. But you need to face facts. Theo has changed."

Penny crossed her arms. "That doesn't matter. I wasn't there for him at the cabin, so I have to be there for him now."

This was what Jade was referring to. Penny pressured her healing power on Theo, and it drove them apart. Because he didn't need to be healed by her, he needed to be *accepted* by her.

Regardless of how much she tried, she couldn't heal the emotional damage he'd endured. It was too intense, too deep for her capabilities.

The words weren't easy to admit. Being unable to help gutted Penny to her core. For years, she wondered if healing was the only part of her identity.

Luckily, Theo saw more than that. He saw every piece of her, the good and the bad. She had to do the same for him.

Daniel's dark brown eyes narrowed. His jaw clenched, as did his fists. Penny mentally prepped herself for a fight, but Daniel released his tension, huffed, and crept out of her path. "Good luck," he offered. "I'm sure there'll be quite a ruckus, so I'll get Felix and Giselle ready."

Penny didn't want to spend the time to thank him. She rushed out of the room, practically flying down the hall, praying she'd be able to catch up to Theo before it was too late.

42

THE MONSTER

If Theo thought being in New York was weird, it was nothing compared to being back at the ruins of the academy.

The rubble was almost completely removed, the premises surrounded by construction vehicles and equipment. The foundations remained, as did a few exterior walls, but the rest had been destroyed. There were no flags, statues, or evidence that this school was special. It had fallen to dust.

Theo released a breath he didn't know he was holding. Any normal person would feel elated or relieved to see it gone. But this school didn't abuse Theo. It didn't make him question his identity, strip him of his happiness, and rip apart every belief he had about the world. That was all thanks to Principal Jones.

Theo shifted his weight on the sidewalk. Very few people were in this side of town, yet the stragglers ran from him immediately.

Except for one.

Just across the street from where Theo stood, he noticed a short, blond girl hustle into the glass doors of an in-progress office building complex. A sign posted outside claimed it belonged to the Jones Business Association. Revenue for Jones's next project? A cover-up for another school? Regardless of what it was or how stupid it would be to go inside, Theo sprinted through the glass doors, following right behind the girl.

The first floor was stocked like a typical office space—a front desk in the center, an elevator in the corner, and stairs leading off to the left. Plastic hung over the windows, the paint wasn't finished, and the carpet wasn't fully applied yet. But in the midst of it was…

"Penny?"

The sound of her name made her jump, but when she turned around, she relaxed. "There you are! I've been looking for you."

Theo didn't want to believe it, yet here she was. Her short hair had been tamed into a tiny ponytail, and she wore her faded blue jeans and white T-shirt. The one accessory she was missing was her ring. Without thinking, he walked toward her. "What are you doing here?"

She threw him a teasing look. "You really think I would let you go off on your own? You need all the help you can get."

"I know, it's just…it's been dangerous. I don't want you here."

Pain flickered across her face, contorting her sweet features.

"Not like that!" Theo quickly explained. "I don't want you here because you might get hurt. I can't take that chance."

She looked down. "Does this mean you don't hate me anymore?"

He reached out to take her hands yet stopped himself. As much as she shouldn't be here, she shouldn't be around him more. What if he accidentally attacked her like he did with Peter? "I never hated you, Penny," Theo said. "I know there's been some distance between us, but it's not your fault."

As her gaze drifted up to meet his, a small smile spread on her lips. "No, it's not." That smile turned into a sneer. "It's yours."

She whipped out a knife from her pocket, but thankfully, Theo was already pulling away due to her harsh words. At the sight of the weapon, he gaped. Was she really *this* mad at him?

She slashed it in his direction, her movements so rapid he could hardly dodge them. He'd never seen her fight with a knife before, let alone this skillfully. The blade barely caught his arm, yet it was so sharp it cut him instantly. Wincing, he cradled his wound and exclaimed, "I'm sorry, is that what you want to hear? Do you really have to kill me over it?"

Penny didn't even look remorseful for injuring him. In fact, she appeared pleased. "Why aren't you fighting me?" she asked, pausing to catch her breath. "I was expecting a bigger challenge."

"I'm not going to hurt you," he insisted. "Not for any reason."

As if she were offended by his sincerity, she scoffed. With a shove, she pinned him to the wall. "Jones was right about you," Penny spat. "You're not a hero. You're just a little boy. At this rate, you'll never—"

Suddenly, Penny's head whipped back as if someone had yanked on her hair. With a shriek, she released Theo and whirled around, revealing yet *another* Penny.

It was like seeing a ghost. This Penny was disheveled and dirty. She wore a green jacket over her white tank top and ripped jeans. Shadows darkened her complexion; her arms hung heavily at her sides. He remembered her as soft and kind, not the hardened warrior before him.

But she was wearing his ring. The green gem glinted, the one spark of light against her dark aura. And he knew. This was *his* Penny.

Fake Penny swung and stabbed her knife, but the real Penny was far too fast. Amidst her evasions, she delivered numerous, hard-hitting punches into her clone. The last punch slammed into her nose, making her scream and drop her knife. The real Penny didn't waste a second and knocked her faker to the floor.

Blood poured from her changing nose. Her blond hair faded into brown; her features morphed to those of a stranger—a shapeshifter.

Theo scrambled away. In all honesty, he would've thrown up given the chance.

"I should've known you'd come to his rescue," the shapeshifter taunted. "You're so predict—"

Penny threw a final kick to the woman's head, striking her in the temple. Immediately, the woman dropped in an unconscious heap. "You're a terrible fake," Penny growled. "Learn how to take a hit." Upon catching sight of Theo, she visibly softened. "Did she hurt you?"

Questions spilled from his mouth instead of answers. "What are you doing here?"

Penny frowned. "I'm here to save you. Isn't that obvious?"

Theo felt the darkness move. *She's here. She came for us.* One shadow attached itself to Theo's leg. He shook it off. "How did you find me?"

"Despite being able to control shadows, you don't blend in well." Penny checked the shapeshifter woman for a pulse, verifying she was alive. "We've been in the city for a while. I caught a glimpse of you earlier. Then, I saw me, or I guess fake me, and knew you'd fall for it, so I followed her here."

Theo scanned Penny for injuries. "Are you okay? Jones said he…"

The name made her swallow. "He didn't hurt me. I'll tell you more later."

"Cool." If it weren't for Theo's anxiety swarming his mind, he would've continued talking. But between the darkness focusing on Penny and his own self-doubt telling him to leave her, he could do little more than stand there.

Penny glimpsed at Theo's arm. To her, he probably looked like a mess. His wrists were wrapped in dirty bandages that lifted at the edges. He hadn't slept in a day. Worst of all, a deadly, blistered burn tore across his waist. Carefully, Penny removed his bandages. Healing flooded into him.

"I met your parents," he blurted. "They said that they miss you and love you a lot."

Her brows furrowed. "You talked to my parents?"

"Well, we were passing by and I—"

"What did they tell you? Did my mom show you any picture albums?"

Theo felt himself blush, which was the only answer needed. "They were really nice," he added. "Your dad did accuse me of being a 'bad boy,' though."

A tiny smirk perked Penny's lips. "A bad boy, huh?"

"Am I?"

She wiped away a streak of dirt on his jaw. "Nope. Keep it like that."

The gentle, loving way she looked at him was almost more than he could handle. He relished the feel of her touch, the sight of her smile, the sound of her voice. Now was the perfect time to tell her everything he had been feeling since he left the cabin.

Ready to admit it, he opened his mouth, but the terrible wail of sirens filled the air outside the building.

Instinctively, Theo grabbed Penny. Through the cloudy windows, he could see police cars surrounding them, boxing them in and preventing their escape. He ushered her to the stairs, thinking there had to be a place to hide.

"Were you followed?" he asked.

"I-I don't think so." She paused. "I think they were following *you*."

Theo cursed himself for his sloppiness. He'd been so consumed with finding Jones that he'd forgotten about the dangers of his other enemies. He spun to find the stairwell and rushed Penny up flight after flight. Regardless of what happened to him, she would survive. He'd make sure of it.

Penny held tight to Theo's hand as he encouraged her to move faster. Her foot caught once or twice on the rough concrete stairs, yet he was always there to stabilize her. Each time he helped her regain her balance, her heart warmed. She missed many things with him, but knowing he had her back was one of them.

When they reached the seventh floor, she stopped him at a door. "Let's take a break," she said in between her gasps. "We'll be safe, I promise."

Based on his furtive, darting glances at their surroundings, he didn't want to stay. To ease his stress, Penny caught his gaze and said, "I missed you. You don't know how wonderful it is to see you."

The shadows behind him warped. His grip on the railing slackened. "We need to focus," he said, distancing himself from her. "We'll be safe if we can find a good hiding place." He tested the door beside them, then eased it open wide for Penny to pass by.

Like he guessed, the hall was abandoned. The lights were switched off, limiting her vision, so she stuck close to Theo as he led her to another office.

Despite this being a terrible time for personal talk, she whispered, "I feel like you don't trust me."

He stopped dead in his tracks. "What?"

She toyed with the zipper on her jacket. "You hid a lot from me. It's how I felt."

"But I do trust you!"

"So, why weren't you honest with me?"

Theo's blue eyes burned with fiery intensity. "Penny, I trust you more than anyone. My problem was that I couldn't trust myself. My powers have been overwhelming lately, and I couldn't guarantee your safety. Not even you could guarantee that. If you died, I—" he couldn't finish the sentence.

There remained a million questions he had to answer. But this was a start. Penny moved to embrace him, but he resisted. "We need to go," he said as he hurriedly blinked away his tears. "Talking will increase our chances of trouble."

He swept them both into another office, this one adjacent to the hall. Thanks to his previous admission and the yellow lamplight, the vibe felt slightly romantic.

Unfortunately, the fighter side of Penny analyzed the room. One entry and exit point. Windows on the far wall; the drop would kill them. As for possible weapons, there were scissors on one of the desks, and she supposed she could snatch a letter opener off another if needed. She grabbed the scissors and slipped them into her pocket.

Theo was studying the room, but kept his attention fixed on the windows that separated the office from the hall. She inched toward him. "I have to tell you I'm sorry," she said. "What I said before you left was—"

"Shh," he demanded, insistent but quiet. He nervously scanned the room.

Penny glared at him yet kept silent. He glanced once more at their surroundings, then stuffed them both underneath a desk—a tight, compact space that made them sit pressed against each other.

Within minutes, voices passed the windows of the office. They didn't sound like police officers, as their footsteps were too heavy. It might've been members of S.W.A.T., called in to handle a dangerous super like Theo. He extended his arm in front of Penny, shielding her from sight.

The motion consumed Penny with pride. Pride for him, for his efforts, and for every second he thought of someone other than himself. Amid his lies, he still cared about her; he still trusted her. Now, *she* needed to confirm her trust in him.

As he strained to hear the voices again, he leaned out from the desk. Then, he returned to their corner and whispered, "I think we're in the clear."

Penny kissed him on the cheek, not knowing how much it would surprise him. He yanked away so fast he slammed against the opposite side of the desk. A loud bang echoed as he winced and held his head.

"Why did you—?" he began, until she cut him off with a kiss. He wriggled in her grasp, unable to escape when trapped beneath the desk. "This isn't the right time," he managed to say.

"I know why you lied," she explained. "It was because you were worried I wouldn't accept you, right? You were scared of my reaction, weren't you?"

Theo's left hand gripped the corner of the desk while his right pressed against one of hers on his knee. It was like he simultaneously wanted to move and stay. His grip fell from the desk as he touched her cheek. "Penny, I—" An explosion boomed outside the building, one that made Theo shudder.

"Don't worry," she murmured, smoothing his hair. "It's not for us."

"Get up," he answered, cautiously crawling out from beneath the desk.

The building remained quiet, except for the honking cars outside. It was like the explosion hadn't happened, simply a hallucination or false alarm.

Then, the building groaned. It creaked down to its iron supports and concrete floors. Penny felt the tilting in her stomach way before she felt it in her legs. She stared at the carpet, expecting it to break like ice at any second.

Was Principal Jones behind this? If so, he no longer cared about keeping her alive.

Interrupting her pondering, Theo pulled her into a run. Stealth was no longer on his mind as he flung the office open and bolted to the stairway. He released her to yank on the door handle, which refused to budge. Cursing, Theo kicked at the door, apparently resolving to rip it off its hinges.

Searching for another exit, Penny hurried to the nearest window. Police officers had barricaded the building and cleared the roads and sidewalks; it was the emptiest she had ever seen New York. Black-clad men and women in S.W.A.T. uniforms also littered the road, speaking into radios and staring at the smoking building. Whether by fire or gunfire, Nightwave would be killed today.

"Penny!" Theo shouted. "Move!"

She turned around to see an all-too-familiar black ball roll between them. As the high pitch started, she covered her ears. Through blurry vision, she saw a soldier rush at her, and she tried to grab the scissors in her pocket, but her limbs didn't budge.

The soldier forced her to the ground, bound her arms behind her, and smashed her face into the floor. The ringing ceased, allowing her to hear him say, "I got the healer. Bringing her down."

If his job was to keep her alive, then he was failing. His entire weight settled on her back, and he nearly dislocated her shoulders from holding her arms too high. Blood dribbled from her nose.

From somewhere behind her, she heard Theo, weakened and panicked, beg, "Don't hurt her!"

The soldier snorted. He pushed her harder against the carpet, squishing her nose and limiting her oxygen. Desperate for air, she squirmed. The soldier forced her arms higher so he could cuff her, but the shooting pain made her scream.

All of a sudden, the pressure on her body disappeared. It was like the soldier had jumped off her altogether. Immediately, her arms went to her sides as she pushed herself onto her back, wheezing for oxygen.

After her eyesight cleared, she stabilized her head and sat up. The soldier cowered against the opposite wall, cornered by a horrifyingly huge black beast. The soldier fired a dozen shots into the being, but to no avail. The bullets passed right through and buried into the wooden stairwell door.

The creature roared and sank its claws into the soldier. Penny didn't know whether to cover her eyes or her ears.

For all her uncertainty, she sat there in disbelief, watching the whole thing. Crimson speckled the beige walls. The soldier's radio crackled and shorted out. When it was clear he was dead, she directed her attention to the monster itself.

The beast had the same qualities of Theo's creations—being made from the shadows—but she had never seen him make an entity as heinous as this. Penny crawled to get a closer look. And then she froze.

It wasn't a creation. It was *Theo*.

His hands had morphed into long, defined claws, sharpened to a knife's point. Spikes arched out of his back, directly where his spine would be. Though he remained hunched over the soldier's body, Penny could tell he was at least three sizes larger than normal. Yes, he looked like a monster, but not an evil one. She could see past the facade to the boy she loved. The darkness she'd been so afraid of was now protecting her.

"I said not to hurt her," he growled. His voice was unrecognizable, a deep guttural replacement of who he usually was.

Anxiously twisting her ring, Penny wobbled to her feet. "Theo?"

He whirled to face her, a monstrosity of shadows and sharpness. She expected to be afraid—to be absolutely consumed with fear—but she wasn't. Instead, she smiled. "Hey, it's alright. I'm safe, see?"

His eyes narrowed then widened suddenly. Roughly, he shook his arms, forcing the darkness to disappear. As he shrank to his original size, he exclaimed, "Go away! Don't look at me!"

He sank into the far corner from the soldier, becoming nothing more than a trembling, huddled form. His hands plunged into his hair. His shoulders heaved with desperate gasps.

Penny neared him and repeated, "Theo?"

He pressed himself harder against the wall. "Don't come any closer!" Under his breath, he added, "I can't believe this is happening! First Peter, now this? What's wrong with me?"

Although Penny wanted to know what had happened to Peter, she knelt in front of Theo. His whole body shook. "L-leave me alone, Penny! I'm a monster, I-I can't help it!"

"Shh," she assured, touching his cheek. He tried to flee, so she said, "Stop and take a deep breath."

He swallowed. "I-I can't!"

"You can." She placed his hand on her heart. "Feel this? Match my breathing."

Slowly, she inhaled and exhaled, and he copied her pattern. As much as she wanted to heal him, there was a barrier fighting against her. His panic was too intense, too extreme for her to heal easily. She'd have to stick with words and actions.

Theo's breaths fell into a rhythm yet continued to hitch at the end.

"Good job," she murmured. "What makes you think you're a monster?"

Tears sparkled on his lashes. "I just killed a guy, Penny!"

"Were you doing it to save me?"

"I mean, yes."

"What else makes you a monster?"

He averted his gaze. "I can't control my powers."

"I can't control mine either. I wish I could decide on my own when to heal others, but I don't get that luxury yet. Still think you're a monster?"

He leaned forward, hesitated, then bridged the space between them and rested his forehead against hers. Finally, his breathing evened out. "I feel dark inside."

"I've felt that, too," she admitted. "But you wanna know what made it better?"

"What?"

"You."

Like she hoped, he grinned. It was the kind of lazy, lopsided grin he usually wore when he was at ease. She'd seen it on rare occasions, but it was one of her favorites. "See that?" she said. "A monster wouldn't smile like that. He wouldn't hold me like this. And he certainly wouldn't risk his life to save mine." She left a small, careful kiss on his lips.

"I missed you, Penny. Thank you for finding me." His grin slipped. "But I can't do this."

"Do what?"

"Use my power. Stop Jones." Theo's eyes glistened. "What if everyone sees me as the bad guy?"

The building rocked again, but Penny's expression didn't change. Indulging in their private moment, she settled onto his lap and draped her arms around his neck. The darkness separated from the wall and brushed along her arm, a chilly feeling similar to a gust of wind.

"I have a confession," she said. "When we returned to the school to find Camilla's sketchbooks, I found a supervillain patch. I wanted to give it to you, but I was worried you'd misread the offer."

Theo chuckled ruefully. "Because I was a villain?"

"Not because you're a villain, but because even when you had that stupid label, you were the greatest hero I've ever seen." Penny caught his wandering eye. "I'll admit it—I used to be afraid of your darkness. I didn't understand it—I thought it was evil. So, I promised I would fix you. But I was wrong to think you needed fixing or changing. All I care about is that you're safe."

From his attempts to prevent his crying, his bottom lip trembled. "You mean it?"

"Absolutely. You shouldn't worry about being yourself around me because I'll care about you no matter what. I accept you for who you are, Theo, darkness and all."

She embraced him, and for the first time in forever, he sank into her arms. It was like holding water; he couldn't sit upright. But she loved every second. She relished the heat of his skin and the smell of his hair: smoky, with a hint of the cabin's familiar pine. The darkness on her arms melted around her waist, holding her closer to him. Any fear or frustration she harbored toward him crumbled to pieces.

He loved her too much to hurt her. And she loved him too much to let him go.

As she withdrew, she wiped his tears. "If you don't want to fight, then we can leave. We can run away and never return."

"You would be okay with that?"

"I would," she said. "I'm sorry you've felt alone these past months. I wish I could've done something then, but I *can* do something now. I won't leave you alone anymore."

He nodded. "So, we can leave. Or?"

"Or we can stay and fight and probably die."

He smiled a little. "It'll be a heroic death, right?"

Penny laughed, yet it lacked some of her usual brightness. "The most heroic death in the world."

"What a way to bookmark history. Two supers, fighting the good fight, and dying in each other's arms."

Penny brushed the hair off his forehead and murmured, "As long as I'm with you."

"As long as I'm with you," he echoed.

Together, they stood and forced the stairwell door open. Seven flights of stairs lurked downward. Seven flights, and that was it, until their time together would end.

Despite the building threatening to crumble, Penny forced Theo to a brisk walk instead of a run, wanting to enjoy every second she could with him. There was no predicting what would happen when they reached the ground, but whatever it was, it wouldn't be easy.

It took every morsel of Theo's self-restraint not to kiss Penny. This was quite possibly the worst moment as they hurried to escape a falling building, but the structure had been oddly silent. It was almost as if time had stopped around them, giving them an extra opportunity to flee.

Unfortunately, she looked too cute not to kiss. That, and the barriers between them had fallen, a glimmer of trust returned.

However, he couldn't deny his other feelings. His heart ached with the weight of his crimes; his stomach churned to remember what he'd done to that poor soldier. But what would've happened to Penny if he hadn't interfered?

If killing that man meant she lived, Theo would do it again.

Knowing she cared about him, even if he was a monster, was better than anything he could've ever imagined. She accepted him *and* the darkness, the part he wished to be loved the most. After months of fighting himself, he could finally be free.

She must've felt him staring, because she paused briefly at the fifth-floor stairway. "What's wrong?" she asked, her cheeks flushed from the exercise.

"Nothing," he answered. "I couldn't ask for more."

Penny threw him a half-grin. "Getting out of here alive would be good."

"That would help."

"Or killing Jones, that would make it perfect."

He groaned. "You always have to prove me wrong."

Her giggle echoed in the stairwell. "I try."

As she attempted to pull him further down, he blurted, "Hang on, I have to say something."

Penny stared up at him. "Yes?"

He couldn't say it. He couldn't find the courage to say, "Do you love me?" It felt so juvenile; what did he know about love? He was just a teenager!

But he'd lived more lives than a typical teenager. He'd asked her multiple times to leave with him—at the beach, at the cabin, and *she'd* asked *him* hardly five minutes ago! Certainly, that was love!

The building rocked again. Clearly, it was done waiting for them to leave. Penny didn't budge, most likely resolving to stay until Theo spat out whatever he needed to say.

"I didn't just miss you when I left the cabin," he said. "I missed you before that. I missed having fun with you. I missed having your trust. I'm glad I can earn it back."

She kissed him on the cheek, a light, gentle touch that eased the worry in his mind. "You already have it."

And somehow, knowing that was better than knowing she loved him.

43

---

120 SECONDS

Dion never liked New York City. As a kid, he'd visit with his mom for business, and each time, he hated it more than the last. There were too many people—too much noise.

This trip was no different. Well, except for the fact that he was chasing his best friend before he could get himself killed.

"This is stupid," Peter lamented from the backseat. "We're never gonna find him."

"Yes, we are," Yasmine snapped. "All we have to do is follow the sound of trouble."

Dion pointed at the barrage of police cars and F.B.I. vehicles speeding past them, sirens and lights blaring. "Guess we know where they're going."

Yasmine sat up straighter. "Wherever Theo is, Jones will be there too. This might finally be over."

Dion smiled at her. "It will be."

Then, Peter groaned, ruining the moment. "Can we please stop the sappy stuff? I'm in agony here."

"Your wounds were shallow!"

"I'm talking emotionally! Your flirting makes me want to die on the inside."

Dion gripped the steering wheel. Usually, Peter's teasing could destress any situation. Right now, it was simply annoying.

"Park here," Yasmine commanded, her arm extended to the side of the road. "The school's only a block away, and if it's what I suspect, they've got the street restricted."

Dion obeyed and turned the car off. "Smart. So, you're thinking of a stealth approach."

She smirked at Peter. "Precisely."

The invisible trio hurried through crowds of people and honking traffic to reach the street leading to the school. Much like Yasmine predicted, it had been blocked off with barricades and uniformed officers. Cameras were everywhere; news reporters were live at the scene, and random pedestrians filmed the chaos as if it were a historical occasion.

People crowded in front of the barricades, asking questions or demanding that they be allowed to pass through to get home. One boy amongst them was particularly enraged. "Let me in, you muscle-headed jerk!" he said. "My best friend is in there and he needs my help!"

Fury like that could only belong to a single person. Dion released his hold on Peter and crept forward, whispering, "No way."

By some stroke of luck or coincidence, Felix glanced behind him, locking eyes right with Dion. Before Dion could sputter a greeting, Felix tackled him in a bear hug.

"You're alive?" Felix exclaimed, squeezing Dion harder. "I can't believe this! How are you alive?"

"I won't be for long," Dion gasped.

Felix laughed yet didn't release him. "Where are the others?" he asked. "They're here, right?"

Both Peter and Yasmine reappeared, startling the people standing closest to them. Immediately, Felix snatched Peter into the hug. "I missed you punks so much! You don't know what it's like being stuck with a bunch of weirdos!"

Giselle cleared her throat behind him, and he released Dion and Peter. "I was talking about Daniel!" Felix explained. "You're perfect, dear."

Shaking his head, Daniel approached the group and said, "Penny claimed she saw Theo and ran off. I'm guessing they're together."

"That makes this easy!" Felix announced. "Where's Theo at?"

"We got into a fight," Peter said, subconsciously grabbing his arm. "Haven't seen him since."

Cursing, Felix rubbed his forehead. "Now, where are we supposed to find them?"

Suddenly, an explosion cracked and boomed. Smoke billowed into the sky from a building on the blocked street, eliciting the horde of people to start screaming and running.

"Never mind," Felix quipped to himself.

Without a doubt, Dion could bet that Theo and Penny were in that building. "It takes roughly two minutes for burning effects to take place on the human body," he shouted. "One hundred and twenty seconds until they're either charred to death or passed out from the smoke."

The bully-turned-friend cracked his knuckles. "Sounds like we need to buy them more time. Get me close to the building."

"Are you sure?" Giselle asked. "What if your power doesn't work?"

Felix gave a short, grim nod. "Then, I'll die trying. But it's time to be a hero."

Peter ran directly to the barricades, where officers were trying to calm New Yorkers. "Hey," he exclaimed, "you gotta let us pass!"

"You'll have to wait, sir," one of the female officers said. "It's too dangerous for civilians."

"But I'm not a civilian. Look!" Peter disappeared from view, and the woman gasped.

"It-it's a super!" Shaking, she unclipped her taser. "O-on the ground!"

In one swift whoosh, her weapon flew far out of her reach. Giselle stood beside Peter. "Apologies," she said, "but we're not in the position to be taking orders."

By now, the remaining police officers and pedestrians had noticed the team. A middle-aged man gruffly pushed Dion, saying, "Dirty supers! They caused the explosion!"

"We didn't!" Daniel pleaded. "Please, we must get through. Something terrible is happening down the block!"

"Yeah, and it's your fault!"

The accusation was generalized, but based on Daniel's hurt expression, he took it personally. He looked between the supers, then at the gathering smoke.

More bystanders joined in, insulting the teens and grabbing at them. The cops had their guns drawn, shouting orders. Dion rolled his eyes. His friend was trapped in an exploding building. This was a waste of time.

He extended a hand toward a stranger, dropping a spell of possession over him. When Dion blinked, he found himself in the stranger's body. He kept his movements abrupt to spook the crowd, which worked wondrously. "Where are you going?" he asked, following a woman for a few steps. "Come on, guys, I'm not that scary!"

The crowd quickly dissipated, allowing the cops to see the supers. Immediately, Giselle lifted the guns from their reach and pushed them to the ground.

Dion shot a glare at any stragglers and dropped his possession, bracing his head as dizziness struck him. The man he had possessed jumped to his feet and took off, yelling for help. If they decided to think Dion was evil, so be it. It wouldn't stop him from doing the right thing.

"You're getting good at that," Yasmine remarked, flicking Dion's ear.

He felt his heroic courage diminish. "You think so?"

Ruining the moment yet again, Peter called, "Guys, you can kiss later! Theo's about to die, remember?"

While Felix and Giselle were already sprinting for the building, Peter pocketed a few weapons from the cops, and Daniel was nowhere to be seen. Dion paused to analyze their surroundings, hoping to find Daniel amidst the thundering panic, but Yasmine grabbed Dion's hand and yanked him into a run.

The street in front of the building was nothing short of a war zone.

Giselle was busy fending off the S.W.A.T. and simultaneously defending Felix by shielding them with a car door. A glow of cloudy energy wrapped around the bottom half of the complex, encompassing the exploded area. The effects of the explosion—the smoking, burning, and collapsing—slowed but didn't stop. Dion spotted Felix standing with his arms outstretched toward it, a similar energy emanating from his palms.

Despite being bullied by him at one point, Dion couldn't help but feel a surge of pride. It was no secret that Felix had struggled with his powers, for reasons unknown to Dion. Not that the reasons mattered. After all this time, Felix could finally control his powers.

"Felix!" Dion exclaimed. "You're—"

"You're using your power!" Peter finished with a cheer. "Guess the stress of losing Theo was enough to snap you into focusing for once!"

Felix risked a glance over his shoulder to look at them. Based on his colorless skin and tight grimace, it almost appeared like he was in pain. "Help Giselle!" he ordered. "I'll be fine!"

"I can handle this!" Giselle argued. "Get in that building and find Theo!"

Both Yasmine and Peter looked to Dion, and he finally knew what it felt like to be the leader. Whatever Dion decided would determine their fates.

"Cover Felix!" he proclaimed. "If he goes down, the building falls and everyone dies!"

Felix grunted out a laugh. "Nothing like a little pressure."

Giselle lost her strength and dropped the sign, leaving the team vulnerable. But the gunfire ceased. Through squinted vision, Dion spotted a man standing between the supers and the soldiers, his arms raised high in the air. A cast covered his right leg, and his buzzed hair was eerily familiar.

"Simon?" Peter said.

At the sound of his name, Simon jerked his head to the side. He had donned his military attire, complete with the dog tags and medals he'd earned. "Hey, freaks," he said, grinning. "Need some help?"

"What are you doing here?" Dion asked.

"Agreed," a soldier said. "Civilians are not supposed to be on the street. We must eliminate any possible threats."

Simon didn't budge. "Why don't I qualify as a possible threat?"

That gave the S.W.A.T. pause. A woman in the front lines said, "Sir, we appreciate your service to this country, but we have orders."

"Stupid orders, no doubt. If you kill these supers, the building falls and we're all buried in rubble." Simon pointed to the hazy windows. "Sooner or later, you will see what kind of man Jones is. Shoot them if you must, but you'll have to shoot me too."

Amidst the standoff, Giselle crawled to Dion's feet and inquired, "Do you know this guy?"

"He's a bounty hunter," Dion said. "He wanted us dead."

"Guess he had a change of heart."

It couldn't have come a moment too soon. Seeing the soldiers' hesitation, Yasmine screamed, "Put your weapons down!"

Her high, shrill voice was more than enough to disorient the soldiers. One by one, they either covered their ears or lowered their guns. Peace had been achieved for now, but at the drop of a hat, it could've changed. Dion looked once more at the smoking building. *We'll buy you as much time as possible, Theo. But you'd better get out of there soon.*

44

THE END

T heo and Penny rushed down flight after flight of stairs, stumbling in their haste. He squeezed her hand as he led her, repeating the same comforts. "Keep going, we're almost there."

When they reached the second floor, the shadows prickled on the stairs. *Someone's coming*, they said. *Run*.

The warnings arrived a second too late. The door behind Penny burst open, making her yelp. Behind it, a soldier waited, gun already raised. The trigger pulled.

And Theo's heart stopped.

It was a direct hit in Penny's chest. Within seconds, her eyes rolled back into her head, and she collapsed. Theo dove to catch her, skinning his knees on the concrete but protecting her from further harm.

"She's out," the soldier said into his radio.

Theo couldn't hear the rest of it. With trembling fingers, he pressed everywhere on Penny's body to find her heartbeat. He could hardly see through his tears.

*If **she's dead**, I'll **kill everyone** on this block.*

Finally, he found a pulse on her throat, thrumming as soft and slow as a butterfly's wing beats. A tiny dart with a red feather stuck out from her shirt. Relieved it wasn't a real bullet, Theo plucked the dart out and tossed it far away. For a length unknown to him, she would be asleep.

He'd have to finish this on his own.

Gently, he laid Penny onto the concrete and stood to face the soldier. He had an array of weapons, bombs, and concussion grenades at his waist, and all Theo had was the will to survive.

The soldier noticed Theo and whipped out a small black remote, but he didn't switch it on. "Why aren't you attacking me?" the soldier asked.

"I will when you're ready. I want this to be a fair fight." Theo flexed his fingers and adjusted his stance, preparing for a brawl.

The soldier scoffed. "You're not using your powers?"

"I can beat you without them."

The man's amusement faded into spite. As Theo predicted, the soldier dropped his gun and whipped out a knife instead. "Jones told me to keep you alive. I'll have to disobey that order."

Theo lifted his fists. "You can try."

On a scale of one to ten, Theo's fighting skills were probably a four. Maybe a seven if he was really invested in winning, but he didn't usually try. Instead, he spent his time listening to Penny. Although she didn't have time to spar at the cabin herself, she instructed the team.

Flashes of her movements burst in Theo's memory. He'd *have* to win this fight. And what better way to win than to fight like her?

He narrowly dodged the slashes of the knife, growing more panicked with each miss. Penny's peaceful voice entered his mind, erasing his fear. *If the opponent has a weapon, you're going to have to work around it. Move fast, move light, and don't get caught.*

The blade nicked his pant leg, slicing it open and drawing a thin cut across his skin. Air brushed over the new wound, making Theo wince.

Wait for the perfect moment to disarm them. When you do, don't get too close. Just enough to take the weapon.

Theo ducked again. The soldier had thrown too much of his weight into the jab, evident by his rocking balance. Theo kicked him hard in the back of the knee, making him buckle. The soldier used his free hand to brace himself on the concrete, allowing Theo to snatch the knife and throw it across the room.

Panting, Theo taunted, "There. Now, we're evenly matched."

The soldier growled in frustration. He punched at Theo, but Theo was ready. He evaded and swerved and dodged. The soldier's attacks grew slower and farther apart. His armor would be tough to get through, but it was certainly weighing him down.

Wear them out. Utilize your strengths. Don't be cocky; be cautious. The jaw is the knockout button. Worst-case scenario, go for the groin. There's no shame in playing dirty to save your life.

The soldier paused to remove his helmet, staggering as he did so. It allowed him greater access to oxygen, yet it also left him vulnerable.

Theo feinted a jab to the left, and when the soldier jerked his head to the right, Theo met him there with his other fist. The man cursed and cupped his ear.

Don't hesitate. A few seconds can mean the difference between life and death.

Theo sent a flurry of blows aimed at the soldier's nose, cheeks, and jaw. The last hit sent the man to the ground. Blood trickled from his cut lip. One of his eyes had swollen shut. Without pausing to feel remorseful, Theo grabbed the man by the throat, using both hands to squeeze tight. His anger threatened to boil over. This man had tried to kill him, and do who knew what with Penny?

"Please," the man rasped, "I have a family."

Theo's grip weakened the tiniest fraction of a measure. Until he heard the shadows whisper, ***Let him go and you die instead.***

Theo didn't want to believe it. Surely, releasing this man would also result in mercy for Theo. But that wouldn't be the case. This man had made an oath to kill Theo.

There was only so much mercy could do. And where mercy failed, justice prevailed.

"So do I," Theo said.

Rather than kill the soldier, Theo retrieved the tranquilizer gun from the man's waist and shot him once in the neck. This man would not die a slow, agonizing death. He had the chance to survive, so long as he awoke before the building crashed. And, as long as he slept, it would allow Theo and Penny to escape.

Call it whatever. But to Theo, it was a mixture of both mercy and justice.

He returned to Penny, lifted her into his arms, and said, "Don't worry. I'm going to get us out of here." Limping, he carried her down the last flight of stairs. When he reached the bottom floor, his heart sank.

Fiery debris had broken from the weak ceiling and covered the windows and doors. Smoke thickened the air.

Before hurrying to the windows, Theo rested Penny against the stairs, the only place that was somewhat remotely safe. Thinking he could break the glass, he tried prying a large wooden beam out of the way, but the beam was much too heavy to move. He alternated to a different window, this one with a smaller barricade in front of it. Upon touching it, he cried out and recoiled in horror. Though the wood wasn't presently on fire, it carried heat as if it had been recently.

While backing away, Theo cradled his burned palms. As much as he hated to admit it, he was stuck here.

He returned to Penny's side and held her on his lap. Despite his aching hands and throbbing leg, he held her as carefully as he could, protecting her from the reaching flames and creaking ceiling.

"I'm sorry," he whispered, brushing the hair out of her face. "I promised I'd save us, but I can't. I'll add that to the list of promises I broke." He ran his thumb along her soft cheek, which was tinted slightly red. The hint of a smile teased her full, pink lips.

He loved her. But he'd never felt so sick.

"You should've had someone brave," he choked out, "not someone who was scared of his own shadow. The truth is, I never told you what I was going through because I didn't want to lose you. I know you care about me, but what about my dark side? Seeing you afraid made me realize that we shouldn't be together, because the shadows will always be a part of me. I thought if I took care of myself—if I rid myself of the darkness altogether, we could both be at peace. But I think I made things worse."

As much as he hated crying, he felt hot tears trickle down his cheeks. "I pushed you away because I hated who I was. I thought I was protecting you, but really, I was protecting myself."

You're pathetic, the shadows growled. *She can't hear you. Stop this, now.*

It didn't matter if Penny heard him. After all this, Theo needed to be honest with himself. "I regret so much," he continued. "I regret not bringing you with me. I regret lying, fighting, and arguing. I regret not telling you how I felt. Maybe if I'd admitted it sooner, we could've been closer. I robbed us both of that opportunity."

A beam crashed in front of them, startling Theo into squeezing Penny tighter. He felt her breathing on his neck. It was much too shallow. "I've never really known what loving someone feels like," he said to her. "Not including my family. But I do now."

He looked down at her. "I love you, Penny," he confessed, wishing she were awake to hear him. "With every part of me, from now until forever, I love you. If we survive, I-I'll be brave for you. Just stay with me."

With those last words, he finally broke down. He held her so close he could feel her heartbeat against his chest, though slow it was. The one fact Principal Jones got right about Penny was her name. She truly was an angel. She saved Theo from his own worst enemy.

Himself.

His crying was interrupted by the sound of wood cracking and glass breaking. Heart pounding against his ribs, he focused on the side wall. The tip of an ax cut through the debris and hacked away the remainder, clearing a path to the outside. Theo scrubbed his face, thankful to whatever deity had answered his silent prayer.

Through the thick, heavy smoke, Theo thought he could spot the outline of a person entering the building, flanked by two extra people. Were they firefighters? Police officers? More soldiers, perhaps? The flickering light of the flames accentuated the newcomer's black suit.

And Theo's stomach plummeted.

Principal Jones leered as he came into view. "Welcome home, Nightwave."

45

MERCIFUL JUSTICE

"Don't come any closer," Theo warned.

Principal Jones extended his arms open wide.

"I'll give you one free shot. Kill me."

Theo clenched his jaw. The heat engulfed him, making it nearly impossible to summon his powers. The only way he'd be able to use them was if they controlled him. And he wasn't about to let that happen—not without Penny to calm him.

"How noble of you to continuously protect others," Principal Jones mourned. "Even when you're in no position to do so."

The pair of hunters grabbed Penny, forcing her to stand. After her legs gave out and her head rolled to the side, one of them opted to carry her instead.

Theo reached for her, ignoring the shocks of pain shooting through him. "Leave her alone!"

Principal Jones blocked Theo's view of her. "Where's your fight, Nightwave? I expected a challenge."

"You have me. What are you waiting for? Just kill me already!"

"I'd love to. Unfortunately, you've caused quite a commotion and damaged my reputation." Principal Jones scowled. "So, I think I'll take my time. I'm going to tear you apart piece by piece until there's nothing left for your pitiful family to mourn."

Sweat beaded on Theo's forehead from fighting the urge to scream. His eyes flickered to Penny. "What are you going to do with her?"

"Great question." Principal Jones motioned, and the hunter standing beside Penny flipped a knife out of his pocket, one so small and defined it would make the agony of dying last. "Originally, I wanted to keep her alive. Her healing services would help humanity long after other supers are dead and gone."

Theo tried not to show the horror he felt. He could only imagine Penny—poor, sweet Penny—being worked to death healing every single person in the world. Jones would force her to do the one thing she didn't want to be known for. "You're going to use her as a slave?" Theo accused.

"That's such an ugly term. Not a slave, but a…helper. Meaningless words aside, after what she's done to ruin me, I no longer wish to spare her life."

"You can't," Theo demanded, struggling to stand. "You won't!"

Jones shoved Theo onto the stairs and dug his foot into Theo's chest, keeping him pinned. "I *can* and *will* do whatever I want. I already killed two of your teammates. What's stopping me from killing her?"

Theo bit his tongue hard enough to bleed. He wondered who those teammates were; what if it had been Dion?

"Penny knows where Daniel is," Theo managed, breathless from the pressure of Jones's foot. "He's the only family you have left. Don't you want him?"

Jones's expression froze, plastering his surprise in place. The fire crackled; orange burning ashes floated through the air. Finally, the man chuckled. "I don't have a family left. Your father made sure of that."

Jones snapped, and the hunter angled his knife inward, touching Penny's neck. Theo thrashed to escape until Jones stomped harder into Theo's chest, cracking his ribs.

"He didn't kill your wife and son!" Theo wheezed. "He was trying to protect them!"

"Then, he failed!" Jones's voice broke, the slightest shred of humanity in an otherwise emotionless man. "He used to be a friend. He made me believe that not all supers were harmful. That maybe, I could trust them." The gentleness sharpened. "Well, he proved me wrong!"

Jones picked Theo up by the collar of his shirt and threw him into a low-burning table. The flames touched his skin, but only a second passed before he was tossed against a chair.

Jones's words echoed in the building, broken by the sounds of wood creaking or fire flaring. "Superhumans are treated like gods because everyone fears them! My mother and I weren't worth the dirt on the ground to my father. That school meant more to him than a family.

"*Real* power is control. Not those flimsy abilities. That's an intimidation tactic. And once I've rid the world of supers, people will thank me! There will be no more threat to their otherwise meaningless lives."

Jones was now close enough that Theo could see his own reflection in his finely polished shoes. He crawled to brace himself on his knees; his bones popped with every move. "You don't care about that," Theo hissed. "You just want revenge!"

"Yes, that is an added plus. But that's the thing—" The principal wrapped his hand around Theo's throat and shoved him against the wall. "Real heroes are the ones who are daring enough to elicit change. Your dear father told me that once."

Theo strained against the grip, feeling his lungs burning. "You're... psychotic."

Jones smiled a cruel, unfeeling smile. "I'm a visionary. There's a difference." He grappled Theo into a chokehold, turning them both around so they could see Penny. "For months, I've been pondering how to punish you. Killing your girlfriend in front of you seems effective, hmm?"

The hunter lowered the knifepoint directly over her heart.

"Stop it!" Theo begged, using every drop of strength to struggle. "She doesn't deserve this!"

"A dying man's desperation comes from a lifetime of wasted potential." Jones patted Theo on the head, feigning sympathy. "You've been a thorn in my side since, well, probably since you were born."

The knife pressed in, piercing a hole in Penny's shirt.

Every time Theo had watched a loved one die, it had been by a gunshot. His father, Professor Beckham, and Camilla each had quick, rapid-fire deaths. Penny wouldn't be so lucky. Jones wanted to make Theo suffer. And what better way than by making Penny suffer?

Kill him, the thoughts persisted. *This is my last chance.* The monster begged to be let loose, but without Penny to calm Theo down, he might hurt more than just Jones.

Theo clenched a fist, trying to force the shadows to obey, but they didn't move. "Let her go," he cried. "Please…I love her."

Jones adjusted his grip tighter. Stars erupted in Theo's vision from the lack of oxygen. "Too bad she'll never know."

The knife twisted. A drop of blood stained Penny's white tank top, and even in sleep, her brows creased in pain. Her lips formed the smallest word, whispering a silent, "Theo."

Every shred of self-restraint dissolved. The few bits of darkness overwhelmed him, separating him from Jones. Like last time, Theo felt himself morph into the beast—felt his fingers lengthen into razor-sharp claws. Unlike last time, he was aware of everything.

He would save Penny by *any means necessary.*

Despite the heat, Theo maintained his bond with the shadows. He refused to be afraid, not when Penny was involved. He whirled on the two bounty hunters, both of whom were trembling. Without being told, they set Penny on the ground and backed away. But it wasn't enough.

Two shadows shot forward and pierced each man in the torso, pinning them to the far wall. The fire continued to rage. Ceiling beams weakened and crashed to the floor. With every second that passed, Theo felt his humanity slipping further out of his grasp.

A burst of pain struck his back. As he turned, he found Principal Jones standing there, holding a fiery plank of wood.

"There's the monster," Jones said, sounding somewhat awestruck.

"You're not a monster," Theo remembered Penny saying. He could practically feel her palms on his face and hear her voice in his ear. *"A monster wouldn't hold me like this. He wouldn't risk his life to save mine."*

Except, Theo *was* a monster. He was the very definition of the Boogeyman—the creature he never wanted to be.

But if being the Boogeyman kept Penny safe from harm, he would do it. He would become the nightmares, so she'd never have to endure them herself.

Theo grabbed Jones by the throat. Claws dug into skin, puncturing the soft tissue and drawing blood. Little by little, the pressure increased. Theo was determined to prolong Jones's agony as long as possible, squeezing until the man turned blue.

Not an ounce of fear crossed the principal's expression. He was practically prepared to meet his end. Jones's blank eyes flickered to the exit, and a breathless chuckle slipped past his mouth. "They made it."

Theo threw a glance over his shoulder, prepared to kill anyone who had set foot in the building. Until he noticed Dion. He staggered through the debris, propping a hand on the broken frame of the wall. Peter trailed close behind, rushed to Penny's side, and scooped her off the floor.

He's going to hurt her!

Theo released Jones, letting the man groan and crumple to the ground. The haze in the room, combined with the shadows twisting Theo's vision, made it appear like Peter was holding Penny too tightly, choking her.

"Stop!" Theo yelled, his voice contorted. "Put her down, now!"

"Theo, it's okay," Dion insisted. "We're your friends."

Lies! You have no friends!

The darkness urged Theo to walk. But his conscience told him to *stop*. Slowly, Peter continued to the exit. A shadow pierced the space two feet in front of him—a warning.

"It was never me that anyone needed to be afraid of," Principal Jones said. "It was you, Theo."

"Stop it!" Theo repeated to himself. "G-get out of my head!"

Only we can protect Penny. Stop them.

Theo reached for his friends. They jumped, probably thinking he was attacking them. But really, he wanted to beg for their help.

Peter shifted Penny's weight, almost dropping her. The remaining overhead lights exploded. "Leave!" Theo roared, unsure if he was saying it to himself or his friends.

They're hurting her, like they did to you. Hurt them back.

In the corner of Theo's eye, he spotted an open flame. He plunged his arm into it, sending searing pain throughout his entire body. The darkness shrieked and dissipated, leaving him with a burned arm.

Simultaneously relieved and horrified, Theo half gasped, half sobbed. Under no circumstances could he ever become the monster again.

He lifted his head to see Penny being escorted outside. Nearby, Dion maneuvered around burned wood. "I'm so sorry, Theo," he said. "Let's get you out of here."

Theo struggled to stand and followed Dion. "Quit saving me."

"Just keep walking."

In the cleared wreckage, Theo could spot Yasmine and Giselle surrounding Penny. Peter stood nearby, speaking to a familiar soldier.

Theo couldn't bear to meet their eyes. Yet again, he'd lost control and threatened them. He didn't trust himself to stop Jones, not without Daniel.

You can't do this! We make you who you are!

Dion passed the exit first, then extended his arm to help Theo.

A boom echoed. A sharp pain struck Theo in the stomach. Adrenaline numbed the area almost immediately, but it couldn't stop the reality from sinking into his mind.

I've been shot.

Theo clutched his abdomen, trying to contain the blood seeping past his fingers. Behind him, Jones huffed a laugh—a terrible, evil sound. "Watch out, Achilles. I found your heel."

"No!" someone screamed. Or maybe it was a few someone's.

Reeling from the rush of pain, Theo glanced at Dion, who had a hand over his gaping mouth.

And Penny. She lay on the concrete, asleep, ignorant of the panic around her. With red fingertips, Theo fell to his knees and disappeared into the darkness.

7-Year-Old Boy with Powers Saves His Sister from Dog Attack

"Early Thursday morning, in Salt Lake City, Utah, young Ryan Roberts was playing with his two-year-old sister out in their front yard. According to Ryan's mother, who was watching her children nearby, she saw her neighbor taking his pit bull on a walk. She'd expressed concern about the dog before, explaining it had rushed her and her family multiple times. Sure enough, the dog broke from the leash and leaped to attack the kids. Ryan, like his late grandmother Annabelle Maryweather, wields the ability of teleportation, so he was able to portal himself and his sister to safety. However, the children weren't found until five hours later. Officers are currently in the process of convincing Ryan's mother to place him in a safer institution, one where he cannot use his powers on anyone else.

'It's wrong,' she stated. 'He should not be punished for protecting the people he loves.'"

-Article by AllThingsSuper

46

EVERYTHING I NEVER WANTED

"How long until she wakes up?"

"The darts can incapacitate a human for three hours. Supers? I'm not sure."

The muffled conversation above Penny roused her from slumber. She shook the fatigue out of her head, her mind and body aching as though she'd been asleep for 100 years. Slowly, her powers worked to heal her, yet she was too weak to push herself into a sitting position. Instead, she blinked hard and analyzed what little surroundings she could.

She felt a jacket beneath her on the filthy concrete. Buzzing pounded in her ears. An ache in her chest drew her attention. A wound punctured her shirt and skin, directly over her heart. While it wasn't currently bleeding, the stains on her shirt told a darker story.

With as much energy as she could summon, she rolled onto her stomach. The building continued to burn, but the process seemed slowed, almost as if it had stalled.

She glanced at the street in front of her. A dozen soldiers pried at the building's front doors, and a few had ventured to the side, seeking alternative entrances. Yasmine spoke to a woman soldier a couple of feet away—the two who had been talking about Penny. Felix knelt on the sidewalk; his shaking arms stretched toward the building. Giselle sat with him, her lips moving in indecipherable words. A distraught Dion paced the street, while Peter conversed with a man wearing a leg cast.

But Theo was nowhere to be found.

Penny's hearing cleared the tiniest bit, allowing her to hear the front doors collapse open in a crumbling whoosh. At the same time, Felix dropped to the ground, and the fire reignited with renewed vigor. A shadowy figure exited the building, and Penny's hope lifted.

That was until Principal Jones stepped further onto the street. He hobbled; puncture wounds penetrated his neck and shoulders. Theo had clearly inflicted them. So, where was he?

Jones pointed to a nearby soldier, saying, "These supers have destroyed another one of my buildings, and they've attacked me. Shoot them! Stop their destruction!"

The woman soldier holstered her gun. "I don't think we're going to do that, sir."

A muscle in Jones's jaw twitched. "Excuse me?"

"We were called to apprehend Nightwave. These other supers have not proven to be an immediate threat to themselves or others. Therefore, we don't have the jurisdiction—"

"*Jurisdiction*? This is a joke!" Jones shoved the soldier beside him and stomped to the woman. "Do you know what I've done? I kept you safe!"

The woman's eyes narrowed. "You ordered the destruction of your own building, knowing it might injure civilians. Without the help of these supers, it would've collapsed, possibly claiming all of our lives. You're the real threat here."

Principal Jones's balance faltered. "Nightwave attacked me!" he tried to say. "I-I had to—this was the only way to stop him!"

Penny's brows furrowed. *Stop him? If Theo isn't here, then that means he must have…no. He's alive.*

Watching Jones spiral was almost like watching a trapped lion gnawing at the bars of its iron cage. The pure hopelessness was animalistic.

"I think we've seen enough," the man in the cast said. He approached Jones, adding, "Give up the fight, Jason, it's over."

"You're going to let them go?" Jones screamed, practically foaming at the mouth. "Nightwave killed your men! Where are his consequences?"

"Where is Nightwave?" the woman retorted. "If he were here, we could punish him accordingly. It seems you're the only one who'd know what—"

Jones whipped out a gun from his pocket and fired once. The shot echoed in the street, accompanied by the sound of the woman dropping to the pavement. Yasmine jerked to the side and vomited. Every soldier raised their weapons, but they would be useless against Jones. Nothing could stop him.

Panting, Jones turned his gun on the cast-wearing man. "I have sacrificed too much to let you try to be the hero! Arrest these supers, kill them, I don't care! I want them gone!"

Hesitantly, the soldiers shifted their guns to the supers. All except for Penny; she suspected no one had noticed she'd awoken yet. Peter attempted to turn invisible, but at the mere glimpse of his fading form, an agent yelled, "Stay still!"

"Seriously?" Dion exclaimed, waving his arms out. "Jones murdered one of your own right in front of you, and you're gonna take orders from him?"

Smiling, Jones tilted the gun in Dion's direction. "You can't refuse an invincible man."

The cast-wearing man tackled Jones, making the shot go awry. During the chaos, Giselle flung a stop sign at the line of soldiers, knocking over four of them.

She had fought back. The battle officially began.

Gunfire rained above Penny's head. Jones had continuously insisted that she be kept alive, but not even he could keep her safe from a shootout. Nearby, Yasmine retrieved the revolver from the dead woman's belt and slid it to Penny. Then, Yasmine stood and screamed.

The sound shattered windows. It rumbled the ground. Penny covered her ears, muffling a bit of the noise. At the same time, her healing pulsed through her, easing the ache.

Disoriented and groaning, more soldiers crumpled. The few that remained standing fired. Except the bullets stopped in midair, as if frozen in time. Using one hand, Felix continued to slow the deterioration of the building, and with the other, he made a dropping motion, letting the bullets plink to the concrete.

One of the soldiers swiveled to his comrades. Through his helmet, Penny could see his irises glow a bright, unnatural green. "Fall back!" he declared, sounding a bit like Dion. "We need reinforcements!"

"No!" Principal Jones growled, finally wrenching free of the cast man's grasp. As the soldiers scrambled down the street, assisting anyone too weak to walk, Penny saw Dion's eyes shift into their normal brown, fading from possession.

"No, no, no!" Jones emptied every shot in his pistol chamber, all aimed at Felix. Giselle slid a garbage can in front of them, deflecting the rounds. "You can't hide forever!" Jones boomed. "Nightwave's gone. Who will save you now?"

Penny climbed to her feet, though it felt like the world had dropped out from under her. "What?"

The sound of her voice drew everyone's attention, most notably, Principal Jones.

"Where's my boyfriend?" Penny shouted.

"You mean that self-righteous, cocky—"

"Where. Is. My. *Boyfriend?*"

Principal Jones's mouth split apart in a wide grin. "Gone. You're stuck with me."

A shiver traveled down Penny's spine. *This isn't possible,* she insisted to herself, feeling her breathing spiral. *He's not dead.*

And yet, the evidence stacked against her.

With trembling hands, she lifted her revolver. She wasn't sure what she'd do; she couldn't kill Jones, not without Theo or Daniel. And neither of them was here.

"It's alright, Angel," Jones continued, creeping closer. "My associates are going to take you someplace safe. Someplace far away from Nightwave."

Penny's healing power had usually drowned her other emotions. It smothered her anger and dried her anguish. Unfortunately, the pain she felt was too intense. She bit into her bottom lip, drawing blood. Her entire body weakened. The revolver dropped from her grip.

"Penny, run!" Peter called. "Theo will be back s—" A strangled scream suddenly cut him off. Hardly twenty feet from her, Peter flickered in and out of existence repeatedly and without rhyme or reason. Even through the invisibility, she could see dark red blood dripping onto the gray concrete.

And a long, serrated dagger sticking out of his stomach.

A horrifically scarred man yanked his knife out of Peter, wiping it clean on his shirt. From the alley and behind buildings, more hunters appeared, all out of breath and pale. They must've run to reach Jones. "Hope I'm not too late to collect my payment," the scarred man said, waving to Jones.

The cast-wearing man coughed. "Get out of here, Axel."

Axel's scars contorted. "I'm disappointed in you, Simon. Siding with supers is so unlike you."

"Enough of the small talk!" Jones snapped. "Kill the supers!" He pointed at Penny. "Except her."

A terrible rumbling rippled through the ground, stopping everyone in their tracks. It was a sensation Penny had felt once before. *Explosion.* She glanced at Felix, who, though depleted of energy, grinned smugly. He was no longer using his powers.

"Oops," he said, and the building caved in.

The supers moved faster. Giselle grabbed those closest to her— Felix, Peter, and Dion— and lowered the large garbage bin on top of them, sealing them on all sides. Penny retrieved the revolver, snatched Yasmine's arm, and rushed the pair for cover behind another brick wall. The older man, Simon, limped his way to them, too.

The hunters were not so lucky. Overrun by panic, they clambered over each other, pushing comrades down in their haste. As the roar of screeching metal and shattering glass deafened them, a cloud of dust billowed out from the debris. Ashes rained from the sky and swallowed the street whole.

Unlike the academy explosions, this one was much more violent. Jones *really* wanted Theo dead.

After a final, booming crash, the dust settled. Penny and Yasmine were speckled with it, yet nowhere near as covered as Principal Jones. He was gray from head to toe. With an annoyed grumble, he brushed off his suit and skin. Almost all of the hunters had fled, including Axel, yet a few remained, wheezing.

Giselle lifted the garbage can above her head, showing the others unscathed.

But Jones wasn't paying attention to them. He noticed Penny and sprinted to her. Out of instinct, she pulled the trigger on her gun. The smoking shot bounced harmlessly off his chin. "That almost hurt," he said, rubbing it.

"Get away from her!" Yasmine screamed, swiping a mangled piece of metal to slash at Jones.

Deftly, he seized the pole, yanked it from her grasp, and kicked her to the curb.

Felix also ran in their direction, yelling Penny's name. He swung at Jones, but the man caught Felix's punch and broke his fingers like they were pencils. The pain etching across Felix's entire body didn't stop him. He punched again, commanding Penny to, "Go!"

She staggered. Dion and Giselle were holding off the hunters, leaving Peter to shiver on the pavement alone.

Penny's heart ached with every beat. She could feel their hope waning, their exhaustion growing. At this point, it'd be a matter of seconds before they lost, or their powers ceased to work. None of their injuries were as serious as Peter's, but she felt the overwhelming need to *heal everyone*.

Principal Jones cracked his jaw as he stepped over a groaning Felix and a whimpering Yasmine. "Do you accept my deal now?" Jones taunted, extending a hand to Penny.

Without answering, she bolted to heal Peter. Jones reached for her, but Simon kicked at his legs, knocking them both to the dusty ground. With Penny freed, she scurried to Peter's side. He didn't utter a sound as she pressed her palms to his wound.

Simon and Jones scuffled for Penny's abandoned revolver. Although she admired Simon for his bravery, he seemed much older than Jones. Not to mention the cast on his leg, which limited his movements. Jones closed his fist on the gun and bashed it into Simon's nose.

Unable to witness the bloody affair, Penny diverted her attention to Peter. She forced more healing energy into his body, quietly begging him to wake up, to stay alive, to come back.

Abruptly, he sucked in a deep breath and choked on the air, launching into a coughing fit. The noise startled Jones into glancing to the side. Penny grabbed Peter and scooted them against the wall.

"Penny," Peter cried, "what's going on?"

She couldn't answer. Maybe if she stayed completely still, Jones wouldn't see her. She shut her eyes and hugged Peter to her, waiting for their inevitable demise.

47

NIGHTWAVE

Theo landed hard on a patch of concrete. Grimacing, he spat gravel out of his mouth and propped himself onto his knees. His arms trembled with weakness; the stench of blood coated his clothes and skin.

He was dying.

He'd heard that his life would flash before him, or that he'd hallucinate, but right now, he only saw his red knuckles against black stone. His head lifted a little, and he spotted his father lying dead in the corner.

Okay, maybe he *was* hallucinating.

Theo blinked hard, and the image of his dad dissipated. Instead, Daniel sat there, trembling harder than a leaf in a hurricane. He noticed Theo, and his cloudy eyes cleared. "Theo? W-what are you doing here?" Daniel's gaze dropped. "What *happened* to you?"

In Theo's rush to flee, he'd inadvertently traveled to the exact place where Dad died—only a few blocks away from the academy. He forced himself to his knees, the effort making him gasp for breath.

Tears pooled on his bottom lashes, both from pain and disappointment. After his hard work, he would die the same way his father did. Like Professor Beckham did. Like Camilla did. Theo was too slow to disappear, just like Camilla was too slow to form her crystal armor. Those simple mistakes cost them their lives. How terribly poetic.

"Jones found my weakness," Theo joked quietly. "I always wanted to be like my dad, and I guess, tonight, I got what I wished for." As the throbbing in his abdomen grew, he settled onto his butt.

The alley was dark and vacant, much like it had been during that terrible night. His fingers brushed against the brick wall, the same one that had supported him in his anguish. Being in this place should've unnerved him, yet oddly, it comforted him.

Theo choked out a sigh. "Why are you here?"

"Because I ruin everything. I failed to act here years ago, just like I'm doing now." Daniel scrubbed at his cheeks. "I'm sorry, I-I can't beat Jones. All I can think about is what he did to me—what he made me do."

A shadow curled around Theo's fingers. "I was stupid to think I could beat him, too. He's invincible and I'm just a little kid playing make-believe." Theo rested his forehead on his arms and let his tears fall into his lap.

I've lost, he thought, unable to admit it aloud. *Jones is going to kill everyone soon, so what does it matter if I die?*

Of course it matters, his heart responded. *Mom wants to see you again. Tara wants to hug you again. You can't leave them without a goodbye. Not like Dad did.*

Theo scrubbed his eyes on his shirt sleeve and stared at the corner. Dad's death was unavoidable. Maybe Theo's was too. But his friends were counting on him to save them. Their deaths could be avoided.

The shadows on the ground covered Theo's hands. Every time there was a disconnect with his powers, it was because he worked too hard to fight himself. Out of fear, he never embraced who he truly was.

Perhaps his powers had never intended to kill him; rather, they had wanted to protect him. Monster or not, he had a chance to rescue his friends.

"I can't fight this anymore," Theo said. "I tried to distance myself from my powers, but they're who I am. I have to accept them."

Theo managed to stand, but he swayed and had to hold his head to stop his spinning vision. Daniel stood, too, only to stabilize Theo's balance.

Jones was better at fighting, always had been, always would be. Theo could hope to injure him at best, but he couldn't defeat an invincible man.

Unless Theo was invincible, too.

Retaining his shadow form allowed him to escape battles basically unscathed. It would give him the upper hand he needed. And it would slow, if not erase, the effects of being shot. Without a physical body, he wouldn't bleed. He wouldn't die.

But holding it for too long, especially at nighttime, could prove deadly. If he did this, and truly did this, there might be no way to return to his physical body. Not that he'd have a body to return to. In order to prevent himself from dying, he would have to do the one thing he never tried—the one thing he hoped he'd never have to do.

He'd have to let the darkness take over.

"What are you planning?" Daniel asked.

Theo stared at his hands. This power terrified him. It was uncontrollable, intimidating, and demanding. But it was a part of him. His friends needed him, now more than ever. He'd made many mistakes, but he wouldn't let this be one of them.

"I'm taking Jones's power," Theo answered. "It's up to you if you're going to help me."

The shadows collided with his ankles, swarming upward. Rather than slow or stall the process, Theo thought of Dion—his best friend, his closest confidante, his *brother*. He'd be devastated by Theo's decision, but more than anyone, he'd understand. Dion always understood.

The darkness claimed hold of Theo's legs.

And Felix, the bully who made Theo's life miserable in school, had become a surprisingly vulnerable and supportive friend. How would he react? With denial and anger, or mute acceptance?

Theo's torso faded, surrendered to the night.

He never got to apologize to Peter for their fight. But Theo wished he could. He'd say, "I didn't mean to hurt you, Peter, as I'm sure you didn't mean to hurt me. I hope we can be friends again someday." Theo would never know Peter's response. Forgiveness might not have been an option.

Theo took one last look at his arms, solid, before they darkened. Giselle and Yasmine might've been the least affected. Or perhaps they cared about Theo more than they portrayed. He hoped so. He'd miss them, too.

The shadows engulfed his neck.

And Penny. There was too much to say to her and not enough time. Theo hoped she'd move on, though he doubted she would. Her loyalty was crippling; she and Dion were alike in that way. Regardless of how much time would pass, she would always be waiting for Theo to find the nerve to say, "I love you." Yet those words would never be spoken by him again.

As the last bits of his body dissipated, he thought of Mom. Tara. Dad. Hopefully, after this, Theo would make them proud. That was all he really wanted, anyway. In life and in death, he could be the hero his family deserved.

Finally, Theo closed his eyes and let the darkness consume him.

48

THE DARK NIGHT

Penny never told Theo, or anyone, how much that last day at the academy scarred her. Every night, she'd have nightmares of never escaping, watching her friends die, or being killed in the dark. The odds were fighting her that day. She should have died. But she'd been lucky.

Once again, the cards were stacked against her. Although all of the hunters had been subdued, Principal Jones remained. Penny's luck had run out.

"Don't cry," Jones said, two feet away from her. "I hate seeing you sad." His blood-stained hand stretched out for her.

Unable to witness another second, Penny buried her face into Peter's shoulder.

"I know how you feel!" Dion blurted. There was a skidding sound as he slipped on the asphalt. "My family never accepted me. I was the odd man out, too."

Penny peeked to see Dion standing in front of Principal Jones. The man grabbed Dion by the shirt and growled, "What are you blabbering about?"

"You chose to become a villain. You allowed your experiences to shape you into a bad person."

"If you're trying to convert me, it isn't going to work."

"I know." Dion grinned. "Which is why I was only trying to distract you."

A rustling from the end of the street caught everyone's attention. Penny straightened to see what it was and covered her mouth when she realized.

"Theo!" Felix exclaimed, sounding more excited than she'd ever heard him.

Jones scoffed, but then a shadowy form of Theo walked forward, gathering more darkness with each step he took. He was the night itself.

Cursing, Jones pushed Dion into the ground and yelled, "You're annoying me an awful lot, Nightwave! What'll it take to get rid of you?"

Though Penny couldn't see Theo's face, she could tell he was smiling. His voice came from nowhere and everywhere all at once as he mocked, "I guess you'll have to kill me."

Jones whipped out his gun, but every shot passed through Theo's form. Before Jones could recover, a shadow wrapped around him, locking his limbs to his torso.

"We're taking this fight elsewhere," Theo said. "There's something I want to show you."

Jones thrashed against the bonds. "No, let me go!"

As darkness began to envelop the two, Penny couldn't contain herself. She rushed forward and begged, "Theo, wait!"

He paused just enough to say, "Goodbye, Penny. I'll be back soon."

Nodding, she allowed him to disappear and take Jones with him. "Please," she whispered, "don't break this promise."

Being one with the darkness was utterly consuming. As Theo made the duo reappear in the alley, he shook his head. This was drastically different from his simple shadow form. Normally, he couldn't talk in the shadows. This time, perhaps due to becoming fully connected to the darkness, he could.

Making matters worse, the voices were multiplied by thousands, filling him with the whispers of the city, the secrets spoken in dark corners. He no longer felt like himself. Instead, he was *everything*.

Jones collapsed to the ground with an "oomph," startling Daniel into standing. "You brought him here?" Daniel asked, almost screaming.

Huffing a laugh, Jones pushed to his knees. "There you are, Daniel! I never got to thank you for leading me to the cabin. I can always count on you to fail." Directing his taunting to Theo, Jones added, "This is your grand plan? Bring me to your father's grave to make me feel guilty?"

Darkness twitched at Theo's feet. "I brought you here to remind you of what you took from me."

"You think I care? Don't be so naïve, Nightwave."

"You don't care," Theo said, ignoring Jones, "but I do. For the past seven years, I've been reliving my father's death, punishing myself for what I couldn't prevent. You're doing the same with your family. When I was at the academy, you told me your son was in school. But he's not. He's dead. After you lost him, you chose to freeze that moment and live in it, even if it's not real."

Jones scowled. "You know nothing."

"I know everything. Because I'm you." Theo paused, watching Jones's fury change to recognition. "When you killed my dad, I reveled in my grief for a long time. Seeking revenge and holding onto my anger has only made the pain worse. You have to let it go."

Principal Jones gritted his teeth, a stark contrast to the tears in his eyes. "Let it go? My family was ripped away from me!"

"I'm giving you the chance to move on. Cruel men still deserve to die with closure."

The shadows dissipated from Jones's body. "You think this will make you a hero?" he spat. "You think it'll redeem you from the crimes you've committed, the people you've hurt?"

During these last few moments of Theo's life, he wanted to be human. "I'm just trying to show you mercy," he said. "There's too little left in the world."

Somberness contorted Jones's forehead. A flicker of regret softened his gaze, almost like he realized what he had done.

Then, that short second of emotion disappeared, and he withdrew a tiny flashlight from his coat pocket. The light flicked on and burned a hole right through Theo's arm.

Literally. A chunk of his arm completely disappeared, leaving an empty gap in its place. Much like when Dion attacked him with the fire, Theo felt the burning spread up the remains of his arm and down his torso. He was half tempted to revert to his normal body yet resisted the pain. With significant focus, he rebuilt his arm, somewhat repairing the damage done.

Jones grinned. "Hurts, doesn't it? You're not indestructible either."

Theo's focus wavered. In his shadow form, he couldn't feel emotion, but he felt his pain as clear as day. It hurt worse than being shot.

"Leave him alone!" Daniel shouted, tackling his uncle. The two tussled and wrestled, rolling over the concrete and crashing into a trash can. The flashlight flew out of Jones's grasp, but it remained on, spearing a bright beam of light to the space right next to Theo. The sheer heat emanating from it scalded him.

Attack them both. The voices slithered around him. ***You've never liked Daniel anyway. If you don't take this chance, Jones might escape.***

Kill them to save the others. Kill them to save Penny.

For months, Theo had dreamed of this moment. By killing Jones, Theo would avenge his father and all those whom the academy had hurt. Jones's reign of terror would finally end. But Theo paused.

In the near distance, he heard a patter of footsteps, combined with the confused whisperings of a group. Jones, however, was too occupied with strangling the life out of Daniel.

Theo couldn't win, but Jones could lose.

Jones slammed Daniel against the brick wall, eliciting a loud, pain-filled cry. "I told you," the man hissed, "you don't have friends. As soon as I'm done with you, I'll rid of Nightwave and every other super."

"We're family," Daniel choked out, "the only family we have. You wouldn't kill me…right?"

"I don't have a family. Not anymore." Jones moved both of his hands to Daniel's throat and squeezed.

The darkness prickled along Theo's arms and legs, a feeling both ominous and welcoming. In a matter of seconds, Daniel would die. If Theo acted, he could save Daniel.

But he didn't move.

Daniel's skin turned purple. Uselessly, he kicked and clawed at Jones's grasp. Jones glowed with delight.

And a camera clicked.

Still holding Daniel, Jones whirled around, finding a group of horrified reporters standing at the alley's entrance. Thanks to Jones's fearmongering and manipulation, the media believed every word he said. But if they saw who he really was, then his control over them would die. At long last, he was powerless.

Practically sick with relief, Theo sank into the shadows. Earlier, he'd asked Tara to round up every reporter she knew and give them this exact location. He claimed there would be a groundbreaking story, which was technically true. Theo always knew he'd somehow lead Jones here. After all, it was the best way to correct Dad's mistake. He'd never collected evidence on Jones's crimes, so Theo did. Evidence was always essential, especially as a super.

"Mr. Jones?" a woman inquired. "What is going on here?"

Every speck of color drained from Jones's complexion. He didn't release Daniel, but he did loosen his grip. "Th-this super attacked me! I'm trying to defend myself!"

"That's not what I saw," a cameraman retorted.

Theo snickered silently. The shadows shook with him. The cameraman had run ahead of his group—probably heard the commotion—and had been silently recording the entire encounter, from the moment Jones began strangling Daniel.

"Please," Daniel wheezed, "help…me."

Whether he knew it or not, his sorrowful display made the reporters visibly soften. "We've seen enough," the woman said. "Put the boy down."

Jones kept one hand on Daniel's neck and waved the other at the dark alley. "If I do that, Nightwave will kill me! He'll kill all of you!" Jones pivoted his gaze from left to right, yet never landed on Theo.

A male reporter stepped forward. "Mr. Jones, let the kid go. We can discuss this with the police."

"I'm not the villain here! They are! These reckless supers have—"

"We won't ask again! Let him go!"

Jones reached for his pockets, but he didn't have any weapons left except for his flashlight, which illuminated the backdrop of the fight. His ragged appearance, combined with his vehement desperation, evaporated every drop of charm he had. "After all I've done to help the world, you think you can get rid of me?"

Despite almost suffocating, Daniel mustered his remaining vigor and grabbed both of Jones's wrists. "I can."

The power drained from Jones's body. First, his knees wobbled. Then, he staggered. It seemed he was split between pulling away and continuing to choke Daniel, leaving him in a state of frozen indecisiveness.

"Stop!" he ordered, finally releasing Daniel. "Y-you can't take this from me!"

Daniel held tighter until his knuckles whitened. "It was never yours to begin with."

The reporters murmured among themselves, asking questions like, "Is he taking his power?" "Should we interfere?" And, "How quickly can we release this footage?"

With a final yell, Jones pried himself free from Daniel. His posture was hunched, his hair looked grayer than usual, and his skin appeared shockingly human-like. Coughing, he held his ribs. The wounds Theo had inflicted on him were setting in; his power would no longer protect him from the damage to his mortal body.

Jones touched his neck, drawing away with bloody fingers. "How could you do this to me?" he whined. "We're family!"

"You said it yourself," Daniel stated, "you don't have a family."

Theo had seen men on the verge of death before, but it never made the image any easier to witness. To see Principal Jones, a once invincible man, be reduced to a blubbering, bleeding mess, unnerved Theo.

One of the male reporters offered his arm to Jones. "Let's get to the hospital and sort this out."

Jones slapped the man's arm. "You don't know what you've done! Without me...they'll come again! They'll tear the world apart!"

"Who will? What are you talking about?"

"The ones who came first!" Jones blabbered. "They're going to kill everyone!" Judging by the whiteness in his pupils and the vagueness of his words, he was close to death. Dying men do desperate actions.

He's reaching into his shoe, Theo heard the darkness say. *A weapon is concealed there.*

Sure enough, Jones dug into his shoe, disturbing the shadows underneath him. As expected, he whipped out a small switchblade. Right when he raised it over Daniel's head, Theo directed a single tendril of darkness to spear Jones in the stomach.

Theo could never kill Principal Jones. But Nightwave could.

A spurt of blood dripped from Jones's mouth. He dropped to his knees, then sank fully onto his back. His knife clattered to the ground. Shrieking, the reporters ran, scattering in opposite directions. The cameraman whipped his camera from side to side, searching the darkness for Theo.

"Sawyer!" the female reporter exclaimed. "The police are on their way. Let them handle this!"

Sawyer didn't need another invitation. He took off down the street.

Daniel knelt as Jones sputtered and grimaced. "You'll...wish you had me," he rasped. "I was just...trying to save..." His words trailed into mumbles. Then, his eyes glazed, and his limbs went limp.

The fight had ended. Jones was dead.

It almost didn't feel real. Theo half expected the man to cough back to life; roaches tended to do that. But at long last, Jones was gone. Theo should've been jumping into the air with elation, celebrating that his father's killer was brought to justice.

Unfortunately, Theo was still made of shadow.

He appeared at Daniel's side. "Jones had to die," Theo said, suddenly feeling breathless. "You know that."

"I do." Daniel brushed his hand over Jones's eyelids, closing them. "How were you sure people would come?"

As an unexplainable wave of emptiness washed over him, Theo sat on the ground. He felt weightless, both on the inside and out. "I didn't," he answered. "I just had to trust them. And I had to trust you, too. I know it wasn't easy standing up to him."

"I should've done it years ago. But you gave me courage."

The sun bloomed into the sky, tainting the indigo clouds with orange and yellow. Theo hoped he wouldn't disappear with the night, though there was no telling what was about to happen.

Daniel sighed. "Well, let's find the others and announce the news." He stood, yet hesitated. "Aren't you coming?"

Theo tried to force the shadows from him, but they refused to budge. *You'll die without your power,* they reminded him. *You aren't escaping your fate.*

Dad's warnings were correct. Theo had let the shadows take over, and they took everything they could—including his dying body. In a twist of fate, his powers *were* keeping him alive. Unfortunately, he would be condemned to the darkness, likely forever.

"I can't," Theo managed. "I'm stuck."

Confusion twisted Daniel's expression. He scanned Theo up and down before gasping in surprise. "I can take your power! That might help!"

Taking Theo's power might've killed him. Despite being honored by the offer, he forced out, "I don't…need to try that."

"Theodore, please! I can save you!"

"Can't."

"But—"

"Penny. Need to tell…Penny."

"Yes, she can heal you! I'll find her, don't move!"

The statement was as poorly timed as it was ironic. Although they were only a few blocks from Penny, Daniel wouldn't be able to reach her in time.

Theo twitched the sleeve of Daniel's shirt, prompting the boy to pause. "Tell her," Theo said, "I did this for her."

Daniel nodded. "Yes, absolutely. What else?"

That I love her.

Theo shook his head. Those words were supposed to come out of his mouth, not stay in his brain. He tried again.

Nothing.

He reached for his mouth, but it was gone. The features of his face had also disappeared, fading into the shadows that now consumed his body.

Daniel tried to put a hand on Theo's shoulders, but it passed right through. "Theo? Are you okay? Can you hear me?"

Hoping Daniel could see the slight movement, Theo shook his head once more.

Daniel's posture straightened. "I'm not letting you die! I'll be back —I swear it!"

He ran out of the alley, leaving Theo to sit alone. The last shreds of his humanity slowly waned. Now that his voice was gone, he couldn't admit how scared he was. Then again, he didn't really know what being scared was like anymore.

All he had were his thoughts. If he could cry, he would. If he had a voice, he'd tell Penny how much he loved her. He loved her more than anything, enough to stay away and keep her safe—enough to die for her. Knowing she'd be alive, he didn't regret a single decision. He hated that he couldn't return to her, but she'd be okay without him.

He couldn't be with her—couldn't love her as she deserved. At least in another time, he would have. They'd be there in that place, where they didn't have to be supers. They would watch every sunrise and sunset together, relishing the light for chasing away the darkness.

No matter what happens, he thought to himself, *I will always love Penny.*

I will always...

Love...

...

49

DAWN AND DUSK

A warm dawn lifted over the horizon, enveloping the city in dusty oranges and foggy blues. The windows glittered with morning sunlight, sparkling like amber and diamonds. The sun had risen. The darkness was gone.

So, where was Theo?

Penny staggered to her feet, and when she swayed, Dion was there to support her. Felix moaned and cradled his broken hand. The sound triggered Penny's instincts, but Giselle cut her off. She tackled Felix and immediately began covering him in kisses. Forgetting his injuries, he enveloped her in his arms.

Dion gaped. "When did that happen?"

Penny couldn't help but smile. "It's a long story."

Yasmine rushed over next, hair tangled, and clothes ripped, truly a result of her efforts. Instead of wrapping Penny in a hug, she embraced Dion. His eyes widened bigger than the sun, and he kept his arms locked to his sides, resulting in an awkward pose.

"I can't believe you're alive!" Yasmine exclaimed, squeezing him tighter. "I was certain the principal would kill you after you said all that stupid, sappy junk. Don't ever do that again."

She was turned away, allowing Penny to mouth, *"When did this happen?"*

Dion answered, *"Longer story."*

Penny giggled until Peter shuffled behind her. She dove to the concrete and scooped his head off the ground. "Hey, it's okay," she murmured, "I'm here, you're safe."

Tears streaked through the dirt caked on his cheeks. "Why would you save me?"

Penny wiped his face clean. "Because I care about you, Peter. We're family."

As if the words scalded him, he recoiled. "D-don't touch me," he said shakily. He scooted into a corner, covering his ears.

Rushed footsteps echoed down the street. A bloody Daniel skidded into the alley. Gasping, Penny shot to her feet. "Daniel! You're hurt!"

"Where's Theo?" Dion added, shooting his gaze all around.

Daniel paused to inhale, yet when he spoke, he still sounded breathless. "He-he's gone."

The word shocked everyone into freezing. "Gone?" Dion repeated. "Gone like he's...?"

Daniel nodded. He couldn't look at anyone.

Felix, with his arm around Giselle, chuckled. "Hilarious, Daniel! Seriously, where's Theo?"

"I-I don't know what happened, but—"

"But what?" Felix demanded, no longer entertained. "What did you do to him? *Where* is he?"

"Take me to him," Penny ordered. "I can heal him—I can fix this."

Daniel shook his head, the smallest motion. "I thought you could, too. But he's dead."

The ground engulfed Penny, trapping her in its void. She felt her legs numb. Slowly, she sank to the cold pavement. Vaguely, she heard

Felix scream a swear. Judging by the scraping, pounding noises, he'd chosen to take his emotions out on the nearest brick wall.

At the same time, a ghostly pale Dion insisted, "No, he's not, he's alive! Where is he, Daniel? Where's Theo! Tell me *now*!"

"I knew you were a liability!" Yasmine joined in. "Did you even try to help Theo?"

Their continued argument sounded like monotone blurbs to Penny. Jones got exactly what he wanted. Theo was dead. And she wasn't there to save him.

Daniel sat beside Penny. Quietly, he said, "Before Theo disappeared, he told me to give you a message."

Hoping Theo's last words were sweet, heartfelt, maybe romantic, Penny looked up.

"He did this for you."

Tears welled in her eyes. "Did what?" she cried. "Died for me? Why would that make me feel better?"

"He's not dead, not really. He just…I don't know, he disappeared."

"That doesn't take away the fact that he's gone, Daniel! Why couldn't you have stolen Jones's power? Why did we have to be so dependent on Theo? If you dared to act, maybe he'd be alive!"

Daniel flinched, but it didn't deter Penny's anger. He had made too many mistakes too often. He couldn't be relied on. Not anymore.

"Leave me alone," she grunted, swiveling away from him. "I don't want to see you."

There were the hesitant, slow sounds of Daniel's tennis shoes crunching on the ground as he backed away. Someone replaced him and hugged her.

"Let go," she demanded, struggling out of Dion's embrace. "Don't touch me!"

"Penny, I know you're upset—"

She whirled on him. "Upset doesn't even *begin* to describe what I'm feeling!"

"We all lost him, Penny, remember that! You're not the only one who cared about him!"

She gritted her teeth hard enough to make them squeak. She wasn't trying to discredit Dion and Theo's friendship, but the least Dion could do was give her some space. As she folded her arms, she challenged, "If you know so much about him, then why did he do this? Why couldn't he stay?"

"There was nothing else to be done," Dion said, his tone heavy. "While you were unconscious, Theo was shot. You weren't awake to heal him, and he was already dying. He was trying to delay the inevitable."

She didn't answer. Refused to, actually, because she didn't want to believe what she'd heard. Perhaps if she'd been awake, she could've saved him.

"Leave her alone," Yasmine instructed, physically redirecting Dion. "She needs a minute."

In the absence of conversation, Penny touched the green gem on her ring. The last shred she had of Theo wasn't *him* either. "You promised," she whispered. "You said you'd come back for me. You said you'd take me to a place where we could be together. If you don't keep this promise, I'm going to be very mad at you." Her voice cracked; she felt her throat thicken. "I didn't even get the chance to tell you…how much I…"

She dropped her face onto her knees and wept with every drop she had. The future she'd imagined, the life she longed for, would never happen. All because she was a super.

A brush of wind suddenly tickled her hair, almost like someone had placed their hand there. Ready to lash out at her friends, she spun around to see Theo's shadow form standing behind her.

Penny inhaled sharply and dove to hug him, but her arms wrapped around nothing. While horror froze her blood, the realization dawned on her.

He was gone. Truly gone.

Her legs gave out from beneath her. She knew what he'd done—what his last option was. To protect himself from dying, he sacrificed his body. Perhaps he wasn't dead, but he also wasn't alive.

Instead, he was consumed by darkness, never to be heard from again.

50

FORGET ME NOT

The sun shone on the day of Theo's memorial. Penny thought it was inappropriate for the sky to be happy on such a dreadful occasion, especially considering that not a single person in attendance smiled.

The Palmer's mansion was the only place big enough and private enough to host. In any other situation, Penny would be gushing about the fancy home and sprawling yard. But this was not a day for celebration and excitement.

While she watched the people milling about, she stood on the back porch, shrouded in the shade. She spent much of her time there, constantly searching for Theo. Since losing him a week ago, she hadn't found him, nor had any of her friends. If he was around, then he didn't want to be seen.

The phone in her pocket vibrated. It had been lent to her by Teresa. She'd offered to allow the rest of the team a chance to communicate with their families, yet no one accepted. Peter and Felix explained their situations were "complicated," and Dion had been too distraught to even think about calling his mom. Giselle, on the other hand, claimed she "had no family left." And with Yasmine's aunt and uncle on a flight to take her home later that day, Penny was the last super remaining.

She lifted the screen to her face and read the message from her mom.

> Hope you're doing alright. Can't wait to see you tomorrow.

Penny typed a response yet hovered above the "send" button. She'd invited them to the memorial, but Dad resisted. He didn't think it was smart to "get involved until all the details came out." His focus on his career made Penny wonder if he'd ever accept the super side of her. Instead, they decided they'd pick her up after the chaos ended.

So, without a second thought, she deleted her response.

While returning the phone to her pocket, she shivered. Ever since losing Theo, her powers seemed to cease working. She couldn't heal herself, let alone her friends.

Dion's wet misery had depleted, thanks to his crying for days on repeat. Right now, he looked like he did at school: pale, ghostly, and unfocused. He sat underneath the tree in the yard, back against the trunk, and head buried in his knees. Earlier, Penny had heard his sobs, his mumbled begging for Theo to "Stop leaving me. I can't be alone again."

Felix had tried to coax Dion from his spot, but he refused to budge. Not even Yasmine could convince Dion to move. Unlike the others, Felix was more furious than upset. Angry at Theo for losing a fight. Angry at Jones for killing his friends. Penny knew, above all, that he was angry at himself for not being able to help. Giselle consoled him as much as she could. It was only a matter of time before his rage shifted into sorrow.

Daniel could hardly bring himself to attend the memorial. Like usual, he fled into the house, away from everyone else. His guilt must've been eating him whole.

Footsteps echoed behind Penny, pricking her senses. The person touched her elbow, a hesitant brush given by a stranger. As she turned, she saw Teresa, Theo's mom, standing there.

"Staying out of the sun?" Teresa asked, managing a tiny smile.

"It's a bit too warm for my taste," Penny answered.

"Sounds like something Theo would say."

The pair gazed across the lawn, watching the parents and kids converse. After Natalie and Lily had brought the children to Teresa's house, she had instantly welcomed them in, contacted their parents, and helped them get home. Almost every single one of them had a family to return to, but the few who didn't were placed in foster care, overseen by Teresa and other supportive individuals. Today, those children had returned with their families to pay their respects.

"It was nice to keep them here," Teresa said. "Before they arrived, I wondered if Theo was actually saving this many children, or if he just wanted extra money every week. Now, I understand what he had to endure." Teresa moved her hand to Penny's shoulder. "And what you had to endure, too."

Without realizing, Penny leaned out of Teresa's grasp. Her soft, sympathetic tone was almost physically painful to listen to. Penny didn't need anyone to feel sorry for her. "You lost him because of me," Penny said. "Why don't you hate me?"

Teresa wrapped Penny in her arms, squeezing with unbelievable strength. In that moment, Penny felt Teresa's immense misery from losing her son, her Teddy Bear, and the last reminder of her husband.

Teresa would never be healed, but she knew that. She wasn't hugging Penny to feel healed. She was doing it so Penny could feel loved. "Because you lost him, too."

And finally, Penny's own sadness broke through her wall of forced apathy. Crying would not fix anything. But it certainly helped.

"Mrs. Palmer?" a new voice interjected. "I hate to interrupt."

Teresa released Penny, allowing them both to see a young girl and her mother. Immediately, the girl—Rebecca—rushed to Penny.

"Let's talk," Teresa said, guiding the woman a few feet away.

Judging by Rebecca's swollen cheeks, she had been crying. But Penny couldn't heal her. "Hi, Becca," Penny said, kneeling on the porch. "Good to see you."

Rebecca sniffed. "My mom put bows in my hair for Theo. Do you like them?"

Gently, Penny touched the silky black ribbons, admiring their sheen. "I love them. And he would too."

"I miss him. Why didn't you save him?"

I should have, Penny thought, feeling her heart twist. *I should have been there for him more. I should've told him I loved him when I had the chance.* Penny's instincts urged her to comfort Rebecca, but Penny denied them. Rather than healing the young girl, Penny said, "I'm sorry."

With a wail, Rebecca flopped into Penny's lap. Sweet, innocent Rebecca was right. Penny's entire purpose was to protect others. And she had failed the one person she truly wished to die for.

She looked up to Teresa and Rebecca's mom, two mothers brought together by loss. One child had to be sacrificed to save the other. Based on their grim expressions, the sacrifice wouldn't be easy to bear.

After Rebecca and her mother chose to leave, more people took their place. Out on the grass, rows of supers gathered to give their condolences to Teresa. Even Simon, the man who'd assisted them that day, arrived. A young girl and a couple accompanied him. Rife with pity, he offered a half-wave to Penny.

She distanced herself further onto the porch. Regardless of what anyone said, part of this *was* her fault. Theo abandoned his family and his home for her.

Why? What was so important about her?

A woman bustled about, asking every attendee about her missing son, Max. The police hadn't been able to give her answers, so she hoped to find them here.

Near the tree, Felix and Giselle abandoned Dion to take the woman aside. Given the distance, Penny didn't know what they were saying, but the conversation ended with all three of them weeping.

Today wasn't just about losing Theo. It was about *everyone* who had been lost: the boys who defended the cabin during the attack; Millie and Carter's sacrifice in the restaurant. To people outside of the cabin, those supers would be blotted out from history.

Penny wasn't sure what had become of Carter. Considering the fact she hadn't heard from him or heard about him, he was gone. However, she could imagine what became of him. After forcing Jones to relive his darkest memories, Carter had likely been caught by the police. Jones must have fabricated a self-defense lie, explaining why he shot Millie and why Athena was captured in the storage room. Jones would've convinced the officers to get rid of Carter and Athena to keep the world safe.

Rather than dwell on fantasies, Penny chose to remember the reality—the selfish jerk who gave his life to save her. He might never be found, but he'd never be forgotten either.

Unable to bear the cloud of pain, Penny entered the house. Pictures of Theo's childhood lined the walls. A grand piano lurked in the middle of the living room, obviously the instrument that he used to play. To be so close to his past should've remedied some of Penny's grief. It only made her feel worse.

"He was always better than me," a woman suddenly said.

Pulse racing, Penny spun around to Tara. She looked exactly like her mom—flawless skin and caramel-colored hair. And even now, when she was destroyed by grief, she still looked stunning.

"Not just with music," Tara continued. "He was a better person than me, too."

Penny tucked her chin to her chest. "He never believed that."

"I know." Tara straightened a photo of him hanging on the wall. "He called me before it happened. He needed people to see who Jones really was, even if it meant..." Quickly, Tara dabbed at the corners of her eyes. "He knew what it would cost to win."

That was the smallest consolation. In Theo's sacrifice, he had exposed Jones's true nature. The reporters who'd witnessed his attempted murder of Daniel released the footage, and every news outlet repeated the story. Members of the S.W.A.T. troop admitted they'd seen Jones kill their commander, but because he was invincible, they feared for the safety of their own lives.

For every supporter who renounced their beliefs, there was a protester to combat them. They claimed that the supers were responsible for every tragedy on that day. Penny and her friends had yet to be arrested or questioned, after Teresa used her costly attorney to protect them.

However, now that Jones was dead for good, humanity couldn't be manipulated by his lies any longer. The world was healing, but Penny stayed hurt.

"It's my fault," she whispered, her vision going blurry. "I should've stopped him."

"I doubt you could've," Tara said. "According to Dion, Theo had no choice but to disappear." The slightest edge sharpened her voice. If she was bitter, then rightfully so. While she started off, she called over her shoulder to say, "It's nice to meet you. Although it isn't the best of circumstances."

Penny managed a nod. Admittedly, she pictured meeting his family in a happier atmosphere. A little tense, a little awkward, sure, but at least they would've had each other.

Once Tara left, Penny sat on the piano bench and lightly pressed on one of the keys. A low humming tone echoed from the instrument. She sensed someone approaching, so she said, "I'm not in the mood to talk."

"Can I be silent company?" Peter teased weakly. Without waiting for her answer, he sat next to her. "I'd kill to be healed."

Penny's shoulders drooped. "I don't do that anymore."

"I'm kidding. You're supposed to laugh." He elbowed her in the ribs yet couldn't entice a reaction from her.

Penny stared at the empty spot beside her. "Don't you miss him? You don't look like you care."

"I'm invisible, Penny. You don't know what I look like." Peter cleared his throat. "Not that it matters. I said some pretty awful things to him before he left. I'm sure he doesn't care about me."

"He did. But you won't admit that to yourself."

"Forgive me for my ignorance. After so long of being unloved, you can't believe anyone would treat you differently."

Despite wanting peace, Penny leaned into Peter. "How are the others?" she asked.

"Dion's talking to himself outside. Yasmine is helping Giselle calm Felix down—the mention of Max really set him off. And Daniel is doing what he does best. Hiding."

Since Penny didn't laugh, Peter released a heavy breath. "Theo wouldn't want you to beat yourself up about this."

"I could've saved him," she insisted. "If I had been more careful, I could've healed him."

"Even if you were awake, you wouldn't have been able to fix it. Jones made sure that Theo wouldn't..." Peter deftly changed the subject. "You can't ruminate over the loss. It'll hurt more."

Penny crossed her arms, both to stay warm and to comfort herself. "Maybe I deserve to hurt."

With a muttered curse, Peter stood from the bench. "Fine. Clearly, I can't help you, so I'll leave you to suffer."

Except he wasn't leaving Penny empty-handed. In the place of his seat, he left a tattered, worn, green notebook, one that was identical to Theo's old red one.

Immediately, Penny snatched it and flipped through the pages. It was almost empty, except for a few pages of scribbled, half-completed letters. All of which were addressed to her.

Dear Penny, you mean so much to me. That's why I pushed you away.

Penny- you've been one of my closest friends for such a long time.

Finally, on the third page, a much longer and more cohesive letter awaited.

Penny- I love you! Please don't ask me how I know because I actually have no idea. Maybe this isn't love, and I'm an idiot. Maybe I just really, really like you. How should I know?

Through the tears in her eyes, Penny laughed. Theo's voice was prominent in his words; she could practically envision him writing this message. He wasn't lost to her after all. She continued reading.

This is stupid. I wish I could say this aloud, but every time I look at you, I'm reminded how amazing you are. Sometimes I feel like I don't deserve you, and that if I'm with you, I'll bring you down to a lower level. Other times, I'm overwhelmed with my feelings, so I can't speak. I hope you never notice my awkwardness.

I do love you. Regardless of what happens to me, I hope

you will continue to be happy. I hope you continue helping people, because you can make a greater difference than I can.

I don't regret going to the academy. Everything I wanted out of attending school was fulfilled there. I learned more about my powers, I made friends, and I met you. My life has been filled with a lot of bad, but you are the good. The great. The phenomenal. Every positive word in the dictionary describes how I feel.

If this fight ends like I think it will, I'm going to die. But I'll gladly die a million times over if it means you live. So, LIVE.

I don't want to say goodbye, because I can't help but feel like this isn't the end. I'll see you again someday, and when that day comes, we'll be together, the way we want. Then, I'll finally be able to keep the promise I made to you.

Don't forget me. Yours forever, Theo

EPILOGUE

A SECOND CHANCE

In a home nestled amongst the Rocky Mountains, an older woman paced in front of a television. The news pumped out tragic revelations of death and loss. Although she harbored no sympathy for one of the victims, the mention of a young boy caught her attention. He'd first gained fans with his escape from that awful school, a failed dream of her deceased friend. Now, with the news of his demise, humanity would crumble to pieces.

Unable to listen any longer, the woman turned the TV off. She whirled on the man sitting at the desk behind her, her fists so tight her nails made imprints in her palms. "Nightwave is dead," she proclaimed.

Her partner remained calm. "He's gone, not dead."

"Our plan revolved around him being *here* and *alive*. What are we supposed to do?"

"Not to worry. We have backups for occasions such as this."

The woman glared. "What are you talking about?"

The man stood and patted her on the shoulder, but not in a

comforting way. In fact, it felt rather demeaning. "If my suspicions are correct, then we have the tools to bring Nightwave back to solid form. In time, we will find him. And we will coax him onto our side."

The man started out of the room, but not before the woman could challenge, "You think this'll work, Stirling?"

The man shot her a charming grin. "Have you ever known me to fail, Maya?"

ABOUT THE AUTHOR

Taylor A. Jenkins has been writing for over twelve years. What started as simple school assignments quickly blossomed into a lifelong passion after a teacher's encouragement set her on this path. From that moment on, she devoured every book she could get her hands on until, eventually, she wrote her own.

After earning a degree in English and Creative Writing from Weber State University, she dedicated herself to crafting the worlds she longs to escape into. She now lives in Utah with her wonderful family and a lively assortment of noisy animals.

For updates on future books, extra content, and sneak peeks, follow her on social media or check out her website!

Find me on:

www.ingramcontent.com/pod-product-compliance
Lightning Source LLC
Chambersburg PA
CBHW020539120726
47903CB00001B/44

9798993639505